Borderline

The Agency

Volume Three

Borderline

K.P. Merriweather

Majestik Multimedia · St. Louis

Borderline
The Agency: Volume 3
Published by Majestik Multimedia
A subsidiary of Create Space Independent Publishing Platform

First Edition

This book is set in Georgia Type Text, with some portions in Imperial BT, Andre SF and Consolas.

Printed in the United States of America
First Edition: June 2015
First Printing: June 2015

ISBN-13: 978-0615881362

ISBN-10: 061588136X

For more awesomeness, visit *Majestik Multimedia*!

www.majestikmultimedia.com

ONE

If eliminating monsters became common practice, its right to existence is not merely questioned but energetically denied. There is only one step from suppression - anything that is found to be an impediment is a shameful thing...

***

"Are you awake?" a voice called from afar. "Wake up. I don't have all day."

Erik Hart's eyes fluttered open and he tried to get up, instead finding his arms bound to the back of a chair. He rocked rearwards, trying to break the legs, only to fall and face the ceiling.

Craning his head, Erik faced a middle-aged man with short blond hair and dark green eyes behind wire-framed glasses sitting in a bright red beanbag chair. He wore starched stonewashed jeans, white canvas shoes and a tan dress shirt underneath a dark brown blazer. Behind him rest a bookshelf filled with medical and psychology books and a television faintly played in the background in another room, spouting news and other current events.

"Who are you?" Erik demanded. "What am I doing here?"

"I'm your caretaker, Doctor Markensel."

"Untie me, Markensel!"

"That's not a fond hello," Markensel said, smiling.

"Do I have to hurt you to get you to do it?" Erik yelled.

"I hesitate to see that, but you've been given a special serum so you won't be compelled to do any of the sort."

"Once it wears off–!"

Markensel chortled. "I seriously doubt that as well," he said cheerfully. "You can't see it from this position, but you've got a constant drip to keep you in this state."

"I don't believe you!"

"Well, you're getting another batch made this instant if you keep acting up." Markensel smirked. "Don't worry; your veins won't be in danger of collapsing. There are many ways to put in an intravenous."

"You're a sick man!"

"No, you're the sick one!" Markensel toed Erik in the face with his shoe, rubbing his nose into the sole. "That's why you're here - to get well!"

Erik pulled his head away. "Why are you doing this to me?" he shrilled. "I never asked for this!"

"You were never meant to ponder your existence," said Markensel. "The suits thought you'd be stable enough for field testing, but it seems that you're sicker than we've assumed."

"What are you talking about, 'field testing'?"

Markensel extracted a titanium case from his suit coat pocket and opened it, withdrawing tinted half-lenses.

"Do you want any fresh air?" he asked instead, ignoring Erik's question as he clipped the tint to his glasses and pocketed the case.

"What good will it do me?" Erik retorted.

"I'm sure you want to stretch a bit."

Erik grunted once kicked upright. Markensel stood and grabbed the chair before it fell back, making Erik face a desk that had folders and papers scattered across its surface. A large overstuffed leather chair rest against the rear wall, its surface reflecting the afternoon sun from the window nearby that filtered through the blinds.

"If I try to run away again," said Erik as Markensel untied his binds, "will you shoot me this time?"

"Would you rather we did?" replied Markensel as he withdrew the intravenous needles in Erik's arms. He then approached his desk and opened a drawer, withdrawing gauze packets and tape.

"To put me out of my misery, yes," Erik said sourly.

Markensel tossed Erik the gauze and tape and he caught them. Erik glared back at the doctor standing near the door as he fixed his injuries. Markensel gestured toward the exit, waiting for Erik to follow. "After you," he said gently.

Erik blew a disgruntled sigh and rose to his feet. "I don't like you," he grumbled, rubbing his wrists.

"While we still have time, please?" Erik continued to glare. "Aren't you coming out?"

"What if I don't?" Erik snapped sullenly.

"I can have you shot on sight."

"That doesn't scare me." Erik grinned. "Maybe I really want

you to."

Markensel frowned. "You're lucky this time." He stormed up to Erik and threw a heavy punch, knocking him onto the floor. "Now I can personally beat you, but that won't make much difference to you, now will it?"

"I've been through it before." Erik groaned, holding his head. "You aren't the first to smack me around!"

"Now there are other means to force you to do what we wish," Markensel growled.

Erik scoffed and spat at him. "You guys aren't that originative," he retorted. "I can take a few hits to the chin."

"We can always humiliate you by violation." Erik paled and rose reluctantly to his feet. Markensel chuckled in response. "I see that's happened before."

"Shut up!" Erik shouted. "You don't know anything!"

"Come along now." Erik fell into his stride as they left the office and headed down a corridor filled with other doors. "Let's sit outside and enjoy the fresh air."

"How long did you animals keep me tied back there?" Erik grumbled.

"Why do you care? The information won't matter to you."

Exiting the hall, Markensel pushed Erik forward, then pointed ahead. Erik followed the doctor's lead toward the elevator. Glancing out the glass corridor, he watched people in suits walk below in an office park.

Markensel approached the cable car and pressed the floor direction button. The chime rang moments later then the doors opened. Stepping on, the doctor held out a hand, keeping the doors open.

"Are you getting on?" asked Markensel.

"I'm thinking not," Erik spat.

"If you try to run off, the guards will subdue you and you'll end up drooling in my office again, sedated heavily." Markensel smiled crookedly. "So I suggest you follow my orders."

Erik sighed and stepped on, watching the doors close before him. The cable car began moving downwards.

"Why are you trying to destroy me?" Erik grumbled. "I'm not telling you anything."

"No one is," insisted Markensel. "We're trying to get you well."

"Liar!" Erik turned and hurled a punch, knocking the doctor against the wall. Markensel grasped his side and Erik clenched his hands, heaving for breath. "Why are you so intent on destroying me? Just answer the damn question with a straight answer!"

The elevator bell pinged and the doors opened, revealing a spacious lobby.

"You'll get your answers soon enough," Markensel hissed and grabbed Erik roughly by the arm. He dragged Erik along another corridor with steel doors armed with electronic locks and keypads.

They approached a single door at the end of the corridor that had a red card next to the number plate, labeled 'CO-192-A.' The door had a bin that held a medical chart with a sticker of the same name plastered on the front. Erik yanked his arm out of Markensel's grip and pushed him away, then put his hands up on the defensive.

"I'm not going in there!" Erik said in defiance.

"It's not meant for you." Markensel reached into his coat pocket and withdrew a key card, then swiped it through the reader. A loud buzz filled the hall as the door unlocked. "He's a bit of a troublemaker," Markensel warned, "and we've had a hard time trying to find a way to make him stop doing that."

"Stop him from doing what?"

"After a battery of tests," Markensel continued, ignoring Erik's question, "when he requested you, we figured maybe you might be the key to help him get well."

"What are you talking about?"

"Go in there and see for yourself."

Erik pushed open the door and peered into the darkened room. Markensel pressed a button on the keypad, flickering the overhead lighting to life. Erik gasped when he spotted a young man huddled in the corner of the padded cell in a blue scrub suit, bound by a straightjacket with heavy buckles in the back. His long red hair graced his shoulders as a frizzy tangled mess and numerous heavy scars crossed his bare feet.

"Hello?" Erik called softly, stepping into the room. "Do you hear me?" The young man stirred slightly. Erik approached and knelt toward him. "Hey..." The young man looked up and Erik sucked in a shallow breath, noticing the scars across his freckled face when he glared back with dull violet eyes.

"What do you want with me?" the young man grumbled.

"The doctor brought me here," Erik replied nervously, "thinking I might be able to help you." The young man shut his eyes and dropped his head, muttering inaudible words. "What?" Erik leaned in to hear him better, only to hear nothing. "What are you trying to say?"

"That's too bad," Markensel called. "I thought for sure you might be useful, but there's nothing he can tell you, nothing at all. Isn't that right?"

"Why are you wasting my time?" Erik snapped, glaring back at the doctor standing at the door.

Markensel waved at him. "Come now, I don't have all day."

Erik blew a heavy sigh and rose to his feet. "I'm sorry I disturbed you," he murmured. "I have to go."

The young man slumped forward, murmuring muddled phrasing Erik could barely hear.

"Don't waste your breath on him," Markensel said in annoyance. "He's too far gone."

Erik clenched his hands. "Don't tell me what to do!" he hollered. "I'll go when I'm ready to go!"

"Now, Number Three," Markensel said in an exasperated tone. "Don't make me wait!"

"You said he requested me by name!" Erik shouted. "What game are you playing?"

"No games, Number Three."

"Hey," the young man mewed, "Justin..."

"What?" Erik cried. He dropped to his knees and grasped the young man's shoulders. "Talk to me! What are you saying?" He leaned in closer, straining to hear. "Please tell me!"

"Keep..." the young man murmured. "Keep..."

"Keep what?"

"Yourself..."

Erik let out a weak gasp as the voices in his head started again.

Keep yourself alive...

Until we meet...

The young man suddenly laughed and Erik slapped him across the face, instantly silencing him. "Stop that!" he barked and took in a shallow breath as the young man glared at Erik in return.

"You have to destroy..." he growled. "You have to kill..."

"You know that I don't--!" Erik seethed as his vision flashed in red and the pain quickly struck him hard in his head. He clamored to his feet and stumbled back as his hands twitched in response. The young man fell slack against the wall in the corner, becoming unresponsive.

Destroy... Kill... We must do this...

Erik panted weakly for breath and gripped at his head, shuddering from the pain that pulsed with each beat of his heart. "No!" he moaned. "Not again..." He slipped to his knees and hunched forward, grinding his teeth. "No, no, no..."

Punish him, destroy him, kill him...!

"No!" Erik screamed once the worsening pain settled sharply and he felt the skin on his left hand split open from the creases.

You need to focus, Ferdian...

Focus on me, not the pain!

We have to destroy them...

"*What do you know?*" Erik thought as he held his left wrist limply in his free hand, watching blood run from between his fingers onto the floor.

You know nothing about pain, nothing!

"*I know!*" Erik ground his teeth as the invisible forces clamped around his head, threatening to force him blind. "*You* want me to show you how much I know?" He jerked back when blood seeped from his nose.

I don't believe you!

"*I'll show you!*" Erik gnashed his teeth as the agony worsened.

Do you wish to truly know what pain is?

Do you wish to see what I am truly capable of?

"*Let go of me!*"

I'll make you see! Never forget!

"*I don't want to see anymore!*"

We have to destroy... we have to kill...

Erik tensed when he heard Markensel approach from behind. Markensel withdrew a hypodermic needle filled with a clear serum from his blazer pocket and used his teeth to pull off the cap. The doctor plunged the exposed needle into the back of Erik's neck, draining its contents. Erik jerked and shoved the doctor away.

"Don't touch me!" Erik shrilled. "I'll destroy you!"

"I don't believe a word you say," Markensel huffed.

Get up!

The pain in his head immediately subsided as the hold broke and Erik staggered to his feet. He clenched his intensely burning hands, glaring at Markensel who stared back with a grim expression.

"This seems to be too much for you," the doctor said, dropping the syringe. "If you cut up, you'll be put in solitary again." Erik bared his teeth and Markensel paled, taking a hesitant step away at the sudden change in demeanor. "Your eyes...!"

"What about them?" Erik snarled. "I see just fine."

"Please calm down," Markensel said faintly. Erik crossed the floor with long strides and Markensel hurried for the door. Erik yanked him by the arm and slammed the doctor against the wall. Markensel grasped Erik's wrist when grabbed by the throat. "Let me go," the doctor demanded, shaking against Erik's strength.

"I should punish you..."

"Try anything and your ass will be even more sedated than before!"

"Then maybe I should get rid of you before you have that chance!"

Markensel reversed Erik and flipped him over onto the floor. Erik rolled to his feet and paused when the doctor withdrew a small two-shot revolver from inside his blazer.

"You hurt me, so I hurt you back," Markensel snarled. "You don't like that, do you?"

"Go ahead," Erik retorted. "You already think of me as some monster to be poked on, some machine to be worked to death or some stupid plaything to be discarded at will!" He beckoned to the doctor. "Shoot me, and when you run out of bullets, I'll make sure to send you straight to Hell!"

"I'll blast off that smirk on your face, you beast!"

"Right here!" Erik shrilled and pointed at his forehead. "Come on!"

He ducked under Markensel's guard and grabbed his wrist, struggling for the gun. Biting the doctor's arm, the man yowled and dropped the weapon. Erik quickly grabbed for the revolver and pointed it at Markensel.

"You don't have the guts!" hissed the doctor vehemently.

"Say nothing," Erik said through gritted teeth and pulled back the hammer. "You think I won't shoot you?" Erik squeezed the trigger and Markensel let out a scream once struck. He staggered back from the blast and slumped against the wall, gripping his blown shoulder. "I got another bullet in this thing that's marked for your head!" Erik thundered and pulled back the hammer once again.

"What do you think it'll help by killing me?" Markensel groaned.

"We can see," Erik seethed. "Let's give it a try!" His hands shook as he aimed at Markensel. The doctor let out a weak laugh.

"What makes you think you could kill me?" Markensel crowed. "You can't do it!"

"Shut up!" Erik roared. "I can!"

"Pull the trigger again, boy," the doctor taunted. "Come on, you can do it." Erik gripped his trembling wrist as he heaved for breath. "You have one more in the damn thing. Do it!"

"Shut up!"

"You can't!" Markensel vaunted. "If you could, I'd be a dead man now!"

"That's enough!" Erik whacked the doctor across the face with the revolver and Markensel spiraled out onto the floor in a daze. "Bleed out already!" Erik shot the remaining bullet, blasting a large borehole near the doctor's head. Tossing the gun aside, Erik then kicked the doctor's face when he struggled to rise.

The door suddenly slammed open, revealing two guardsmen in black uniforms and armed with pistols.

"We've got a live one," one called over his two-way radio as the other advanced. Erik drew back and struck out with his fist, only to miss as the guard quickly sidestepped him. The guard swiftly took his arm and twisted them behind his back, forcing Erik to the floor.

"Take him down," Markensel ordered.

The guard kicked Erik in the back of his knees and hoisted him up then dragged him out of the room. Erik struggled to get free and yelped when thrown on the floor in the hall. He turned onto his back, ready to get up and fight, only to pause when the other guard withdrew an automatic pistol and jammed it into his head.

Erik tried to stand and the drug's power pulled him down, causing his world slipping beneath him into darkness.

TWO

Loud harsh buzzing brought Erik out the dark world of dreaming. He groaned and reached over, striking the alarm clock with a firm hand.

A sense of general unease, something ultimately *wrong* pulled at Erik once he sat up and planted his feet on the floor, rubbing at his face. He just *knew* as he took stock of his room around him, noting the dark brown curtains on his windows, the mid-sized chest of walnut drawers across the pale beige carpeted bedroom. Everything *seemed* fine, as they were unchanged, but the nagging sensation never left Erik's guts. It was something *else*, something Erik always knew about before but never took note of until *now*.

A crash of thunder rattled his windows as hard rain pelted from outside. Reaching across his nightstand, he scooped his cigarette pack and lighter once he got out of bed then shuffled toward his bedroom window. Pushing the curtain aside, he peered out onto the wanly-lit streets, watching the torrential storm rip into the city below, striking the cars and buildings with its fierce aqueous output.

Turning away, he shook out a cigarette and lit it as he approached his workstation where heaps of hand tools, nuts, bolts, screws and wires lay, surrounding a metal box that had a mass of wires dangling from the sides. He glanced at the various scattered papers showing hand-drawn diagrams and exploded views of a mysterious machine, matching the one he had.

Picking it up, Erik examined it and satisfied with his work, set it aside then padded down the corridor into his kitchen, casually tossing his pack and lighter on the table. While preparing a cup of coffee, his phone rang and he reached over to the partition, picking up the nearby receiver.

"What is it?" Erik grumbled into the line as he held it against his shoulder and ear while he rummaged through the cabinet drawer, finding a half-pint bottle of vodka wedged in the back and a small white bottle of sedatives.

"It's time," a cold male voice said in response. "The plan starts today. Come down to the disco at noon. You'll get your instructions."

"I'll be there," Erik replied and poured the liquor into his mug. "Do I need to bring anything special?"

"Just your tools. We have some bugs that need exterminating."

"Why not hire an exterminator?"

"That's what we hired you for."

The line cut off with a click and Erik cursed under his breath when his cigarette fell into his coffee. He fished out the logged stick and threw it on counter then took the receiver and placed it on the cradle, only to have the ringer sound immediately.

"What you forget now?" Erik grumbled as he picked up once again. "I want to drink in peace."

"Did you take your medicines yet?" inquired a familiar female voice.

Erik frowned, trying to match the voice with someone he knew. "I'm about to. Why?"

"I know the rain bothers you."

"Anything else?" Erik opened the bottle of pills and shook out two yellow capsules into his palm. He then broke them open and poured the powder into his mug. "I'm about to go to the disco later."

"Don't let illusions distract you from what's important... Once that sleeping monster wakes up, you'll disappear forever."

"What are you warning me about?" Erik demanded as he grabbed a spoon from the drawer and stirred his coffee. "Who are you?"

"I don't blame you forgetting who I am too... It's heartbreaking, but I understand."

"Forget who you are...?" Erik leaned against the counter and sipped his coffee, ignoring the ashes floating in it. "Look lady, I'm a functioning addict. You're lucky I still remember how to fight."

"I understand your lack of motivation."

"There's no lack. I just rather stay fucked up."

"Is it because you're trying to forget something? Does it really hurt that much?"

Erik winced when his left shoulder ached slightly. "Yeah, it hurts, always," he murmured. "That's why I don't think about it."

"What do you have planned today?"

"A bug-squashing mission. I'm waiting for the rain to pass."

"It might not for a while... Heard it's going to be nasty all day."

Erik blew a heavy sigh. "I have to walk in this mess. I don't drive."

"Do you want me to pick you up?"

"Don't waste your time."

"What time you have to leave?"

"I have to be at the disco at noon. He wants me to bring the box."

"I want to look at it before you go - I'll be there in a few. It's really bad out there."

"I'll have the door unlocked."

The line cut off and Erik let the receiver hang off the hook. After finishing his coffee, Erik returned to his bathroom where he showered and later dressed in dark blue jeans and a black zippered hooded sweatshirt.

Entering his parlor, Erik unlocked the front door and approached his couch, rummaging through the cushions. He paused when he heard a high whine and looked around, wondering where the noise came from. Shrugging his shoulders, Erik resumed his search and found a small amber bottle containing silvery white powder and unscrewed its cap. Snorting its contents, he grunted when hit with a blast of dull numbness emanating from his head and throughout his body.

Erik staggered into the kitchen, dumping the bottle into the nearby wastebasket along the way. Retrieving his cigarettes left on the table, Erik fumbled with the lighter, trying to light one.

Hearing another high-pitched whine, Erik paused,

listening intently.

What a wasted life...

Erik turned around, gazing at the young man with his looks wearing the navy Defense Forces Mariner Division uniform standing across from him, armed with a crimson saber. "Go away," he snapped. "You're not real. I'm just high and you're my hallucination."

How stubborn... The counterpart grinned. *I can help you if you just let me.*

"I'm not letting you control me."

Do I frighten you that much?

Erik turned out of swift drawing slash and kicked the mirror image in the back, sending him crashing to the floor. "You're really pissing me off," Erik growled. "Disappear!"

I'm not finished with you yet!

"If you're going to kill me, forget it. I'd rather do it myself."

What a joke...

Erik dashed for his bedroom and skid to a stop when he faced another variant wearing a dark olive Defensive Forces Infantry Division uniform. The other copy, armed with a bullet belt around his slender waist, held a coral-handled revolver at the ready. *So you rather fight me then? You really don't want to see me get serious.*

Erik turned as the duplicate in navy entered the room, pointing his sword in Erik's direction. *I'm erasing you completely. I'm tired of waiting.*

"Forget it!" Erik shouted. "I still have a lot to do!"

The copy scoffed. *You really think so? You never listen...*

"I'm killing you for real," Erik snarled as dropped what he

held and raised his hands in guard once the duplicate in navy approached, aiming his blade's edge at Erik's neck. "With my bare hands, I'm ending your life."

So close... You've got no choice now.

"Bring it!"

Who do you think is more dangerous? The counterpart in olive thumbed back the hammer and Erik quickly sidestepped the attack as he fired a shot. The swordsman in navy dashed in and Erik whirled out of his rush, grasping his wrist with his free hand.

"If I'm dead, you're gone too," Erik growled as he struggled against the swordsman while the olive gunman aimed again.

What if this is only a dream and you won't really die?

"I'm not listening to you."

But then again, what if this is real? The fighter in olive pushed down the hammer. *Go on, give it a try. See if it's really real.*

Erik yowled when struck in the upper arm as he forcibly turned the navy swordfighter around and threw him into the gunfighter, knocking them both down.

"This can't be real!" Erik thought in horror as he gripped his bleeding shoulder and raced out the room.

That's the spirit! Erik came to a dead stop in the corridor as he faced another copy in a tan Defense Forces Aeronaut Division uniform, armed with a high-powered rifle and dark glasses. *Draw your power and come at me with everything you have!*

"Damn it," Erik moaned as he backed away, "I'm tripping for real..."

Realize the position you're in. You can never defeat us, because we're always here. In your mind, your heart... We're tied to your pain.

"You want me gone, then go ahead!" Erik screeched and rushed forward, throwing a swinging uppercut. The rifleman in tan jammed his stock into Erik's guts, instantly dropping him to the floor. Erik's world tilted when he slipped to all fours, struggling for breath.

Stay down, the rifleman snapped and kicked Erik in the side. *Stay gone.* He stepped over Erik's fallen form and entered the bedroom.

Erik's eyes widened when he heard the three rummaging through his belongings. *"I'm losing my damn mind!"* he thought, terrified. *"They can't be real... They were never real..."*

THREE

Erik fought his drugged stupor as he rose upright and staggered to the door, watching the three combing through his articles. He clenched his teeth when he spotted the tan rifleman at his workstation, examining the box of wires.

"What you think this is?" he asked while the navy swordfighter used a small handheld drill into the bed's headboard, cutting a thin hole into the worn wood. The man then withdrew a small black node no bigger than a matchstick from his pocket and dropped it into the tiny gap.

The olive pistoler took out a small palm-sized computer device and tapped the miniature screen.

"Could be a bomb for all we know," he answered.

"You think someone warned him?"

Erik winced when he heard the high whine again and backed away, then made his escape outdoors.

Barreling into icy showers, Erik dashed out the lot and raced down the street, ignoring the pavement cutting his feet and the frigid waters pelting his skin. Spotting a taxi idle at a street corner, Erik flagged the driver down and hurriedly approached the car.

"Downtown disco," Erik said as he opened the door. "Fast as you can if you're able."

"From the way you look and out wandering in the rain," snapped the driver as Erik stepped inside, "I doubt you have the change."

"Please, I don't want to argue," Erik pleaded. "I got a job up there. I'll pay you then."

"I'll hold you to it."

Erik slumped in his seat and gazed listlessly out the window. The driver slowly and methodically wound through the city streets as the rain continued its relentless downpour, flooding the streets with surging water.

Suddenly the driver slammed on the brakes and Erik fell forward from the force, striking the seat before him.

"What's going on?" Erik cried as rounds of gunfire cut into the air.

"Shit," the driver yelped and Erik peered out the window, watching two armed men in black face down another group in navy uniforms. One black-clad fighter, dressed in a wide-brimmed outback hat, trenchcoat and glasses held a rifle, while the other, in a raincoat and broad-brimmed hat, had a pair of pistols.

"*More Agents!*" Erik thought in horror as the two in black shot at the navy-uniformed officers, quickly cutting them down. "Hey," he cried. "Get out of here before we die for nothing!"

"Not now," the driver growled when the engine sputtered and died unexpectedly. He quickly turned the key, grinding the starter as he pumped the accelerator. "Fuck!" he mewed when the rifleman in black approached the driver's side.

Erik let out a terrified cry as the pistoler also approached the rear passenger side and the driver tried to lock the doors when the gunmen yanked on the handles. The pistoler yanked open the door and jammed his gun to Erik's head.

"Get out if you want to live," he snarled.

The driver reached to his side and Erik yelped, ducking his head as the rifleman fired, shattering the window, immediately ending the coachman's life.

"Please don't kill me," Erik pleaded as the rifleman reached in, opening the door. Erik grunted when pushed and scoot over as the pistoler shoved his way inside while the rifleman pulled out the body, dumping it on the ground.

The rifleman then slipped into the driver's seat, slamming shut the door and tossed his gun on the front passenger side before speeding off.

"What about him?" the pistoler asked.

"Look at his eyes," the rifleman replied. "He's high as hell."

Erik faced the pistoler who leaned in close, gazing intently. He leaned back and immediately put up his hands. "Look, I won't remember shit once I come down," Erik admitted when the gunman poked his chest with his pistol. "So your killing me won't matter. I'm dying anyway."

"Blood disease?"

"What?" Erik shrugged. "My ears are ringing."

"Are you sick?" the pistoler called loudly.

"No," Erik answered, shaking his head. "I'm just waiting for the right time to kill myself."

"Why's that?"

Erik waved the man away. "Can't you just drop me off at the downtown disco, please?"

The pistoler smirked and tapped the gun against Erik's cheek. "You know what, that sounds like fun." He sat back, continuing to point his weapon at Erik. "Let's go for a dance, shall we?"

"What makes you think he'll be useful to us?" inquired the rifleman.

"I think he's a few hundred thousand or so the last time, right? And if we can blame him for that mess back there, a few hundred thousand more."

The rifleman adjusted his rearview mirror and glanced at Erik. "You know, he does look like that guy Public Security's been after," he noted.

"*Damn it,*" Erik thought, running his hands through his hair as he hunched forward in despair. "*I can't shake these guys.*"

"You're going to be our ticket out of town, little lamb," said the pistoler and the rifleman guffawed.

Erik clutched his searing shoulder as he shuddered from the cold.

"Drink more water," the pistoler murmured when Erik sneezed.

"A great fortunate occurrence," replied the rifleman when Erik sneezed again.

"Take care of your health!" the pistoler said after Erik's third sneeze.

"You think somebody's talking about him?" The two laughed and Erik groaned.

"I need to get out of these wet clothes," he complained. "Definitely it must be Death deciding what to do with me."

"We'll pick up something," the pistoler assured.

"What?"

The pistoler repeated what he said and Erik cringed.

The rifleman entered the Downtown Warehouse district, later pulling into an alley surrounded by refuse bins and several dark cars.

"I'm gonna ditch this," the rifleman said. "Keep him entertained until the boss calls us."

"Sure, right," said the pistoler as he opened the door. "You want anything?"

"I want a Tom Collins in a tall glass."

"Alright, out you go." When Erik failed to respond, the pistoler poked Erik's sore shoulder with the muzzle, making him wince, then waved at Erik to come out. Erik reluctantly followed the young man out the car and stiffened when he felt the pistol at his back. "Now be cool, Lambchop and no funny business," the pistoler snarled in Erik's ear. "You've thought about staying alive, haven't you?"

"On my terms, yes," Erik grumbled.

"Then you know what to do."

The club's rear door opened, revealing a young woman with bobbed dark blond hair, wearing a striped black and blue dress. In her hand she held a small black cigarette case.

"Ooh," she murmured as she stepped under the awning. "It's still nasty out here." She withdrew a hand-rolled cigarette from her case and nodded toward Erik. "I wasn't expecting you until noon."

"Yeah, er, hard night," Erik responded. "I wanted to make

sure I found the right place."

"Lose your shoes?"

"Logged, so I ditched them."

"And who's he?"

"My ride. I don't drive."

"Stop being a hipster and get a car. They've got electric ones now, you know."

"I don't trust them."

"Well, go on up. He won't be in for another hour or so. I'll see if one of the guys have a spare."

"Sure, thanks."

"Mind if I wait with?" replied the pistoler. "I'm not driving in that shit and draining my battery."

"Yeah, those bitches take ages to charge."

Erik entered through the door with the gunman following close behind. They walked down a dark hallway and Erik stiffened when the pistoler tapped between his shoulder blades with the muzzle.

"Good job, Lambchop. You really know how to jaw."

"One of my skills," Erik said weakly.

"Keep it up, but remember, if you do something stupid, bad things will happen."

"I won't be a problem, promise."

A small chime cut into the air and Erik stopped when the cold steel jammed into his spine. The gunman withdrew his phone with his free hand and thumbed open the hinged screen.

"We're waiting at the disco, Boss," he answered. "Picked up a real special package along the way too. I'll tell you the amount and exchange method later." He held his phone away when a strident voice squawked expletives over the line.

"I don't think your boss liked that," Erik said softly as the gunman flipped his phone close.

"What do you care, Lambchop? You're just my moneyaker." He tapped at Erik's back. "Keep it moving."

They continued to the end of the corridor, coming across a large wooden door. Opening it, Erik revealed a staircase, with one part brightly lit going upwards and the other ensconced in shadows going down. Pain thudded behind Erik's eyes as he took the descending stairs.

"Hey, Lambchop, where you think you goin'?" the pistoler snapped. "Discos's upstairs."

"What?" Erik stopped and whirled around.

"Ain't nothin' down there but waterworks. Let's go."

Erik looked back at the shadowy corridor below then hurriedly made his way to where the faint music and voices emanated from.

Entering the rear staff lounge area, Erik spotted several men and women in black uniforms and caps sitting at small tables. Some were playing cards, others chat to one another. One older man was stationed near the door leading to the disco's interior, reading a paperback book.

"What's that you got there, Toritino?" called one of the workers.

"Spare change," answered the pistoler, grinning. He jabbed at Erik's back. "Take a seat, Lambchop. You're hanging with us for a while."

"Does Boss know about this?"

"Sure, he does."

Erik unwillingly took a seat at the table, facing an older woman with short silver-streaked brown hair. "If I'm going to freeze to death," he quipped, "at least let me get in one last drink and a smoke."

The woman frowned as she studied Erik. "What you do," she demanded, glaring at Toritino as he pulled out of his raincoat and sat next to Erik, "get a drop on him?"

"He was already blazed when we found him," Toritino replied. "We lucked out."

"What do you want to drink?" she asked as she stood.

"Vodka," Erik answered. "Tall and go easy on the rocks."

"Hey, get me a Collins for Bortelli," Toritino interjected. "He should be on his way back."

"Soaking wet too! If we're using him for money, he needs to be alive, moron."

"So be a gal and find something."

The woman slapped Toritino upside the head, knocking off his hat and revealing his short curly brown hair, then left the table.

"So tell me something, Lambchop," said Toritino as he picked up his fallen headgear and replaced it on his head. "Who sends you to whack those guys?"

"What is it?" Erik replied.

"You heard me," Toritino snarled and leaned in toward Erik. "How you get your kill orders?"

"You're mistaken," Erik muttered. "I don't do anything."

"Don't be a liar, Lambchop. You're a Cleaner, ain't you? They call you and you pick up assignments, yeah?"

"I'm a stupid junkie," Erik said in a flat tone. "My memory's shit."

Toritino growled and grabbed Erik's collar, pulling him in nearly nose to nose. "Don't you lie to me," he snarled. "You're worth a lot of money, see? It's a wonder you was even out and about with that much cash on your head!"

Erik grinned. "Maybe I'm not real? Maybe I'm just a artificial construct and this is a bad dream?"

Toritino shoved Erik away as the young man broke out laughing.

"Stupid shit," Toritino grumbled.

A young woman sitting behind him snorted. "What a horrid comedy," she drawled. "He actually thinks he's some kind of Synthoid?"

"I'd be careful with that," said her companion across from her. "Next we'll have those Feds dropping in snooping on us..."

"Last we need is a matchstick scan," Toritino groused. "They sweep us and that's it."

"Did I hear you right?" Erik inquired, raising an eyebrow. "Matchstick?"

"Yeah, tiny cameras that look like matches," Toritino explained. "They're powerful as fuck and have real sensitive pickups. You can blast a radio and cover them, but their eggs can filter whatever noise you make and the cams have three sight levels."

"Is that even legal?" Erik smiled when the woman returned with two glasses of clear drinks, handing him one and setting the other aside. "Hey, where are the smokes?"

"Bum one off somebody," she answered. "I don't smoke."

"Here," said a nearby worker, tossing Erik his pack of cigarettes. "They're menthol."

"Don't care," Erik retorted and opened the pack, finding several cigarettes and a lighter nestled inside.

"Matchsticks are kinda murky," Toritino continued as Erik shook out a cigarette and withdrew the lighter, lighting one. "They were developed by Gateway and the Feds contracted it out once they saw potential for their spooks. If you destroy it and it's Federal property, you're looking at an instant twenty years."

"So it's not exclusive?"

"Nah, 'cause it was never Federal property to begin with," Toritino clarified. "Hell, if someone dropped one in your shit, the best you can do is get 'em charged on an illegal tap, but them computer lawyers ain't no better than live ambulance chasers."

Erik picked up his drink and gulped it down. "Then what's the point in going to court if you can only afford shitty lawyers?" he muttered.

Toritino grinned and nudged Erik with his elbow. "I got a good slant on the inside who always gets my angles dropped."

Erik smirked and swirled his ice. "What they look like anyway?"

"Like black matchsticks. Fit in a standard box too. Drop one in some unsuspecting place and the poor bastard would never know."

"Yeah," said the woman sitting behind Toritino. "You get one of those puppies dropped on you and it's game over."

Erik gasped when he recalled the apparition in navy using

one in his bedroom. He dropped his glass and immediately rose to his feet.

"What's your issue, Lambchop?" Toritino snapped.

"*Once I crashed and came down,*" Erik realized as he made a break for the exit, "*I wouldn't have remembered seeing them there!*"

"Hey!" Toritino roared after him. "Get back here!"

FOUR

Erik burst through the door, swamped by the swirling lights and driving music in the densely packed club. His heart pound in his chest as his fears ran circles in his mind while pushing through the crowded floor full of men and women in brightly patterned outfits dancing energetically to the beat.

Who authorized the tap?

Why was he being scanned?

What were they looking for?

Erik ran through his safety checklist, making sure he didn't violate anything. He usually stayed in extended stay hotels so he wouldn't be bothered with mail. He never owned a cellular as it had location tracking. He always kept his conversations short on the landline since it might be bugged. He owned no personal vehicle as it could be hacked. He paid in cash as charge cards created a paper trail and he always had phony VitaStat cards. Someone *wanted* him badly, even going to the extreme of surveying his activities.

Erik came to a stop once he reached the front exit when hit with a sudden revelation. Someone *close* had to be monitoring him, since they *knew* he took mind-altering substances that made him hallucinate and forget. They *knew* he took them, especially before sent on a mission, so by the time he slept that night in some random hotel after completing the job, he'd have no memory of what he had done.

"*Someone sent me on a fake run to set up those matchsticks!*" Erik realized, turning around, catching sight of Toritino emerging from the crowd. Erik immediately wound up for a swift jab then plowed his fist across Toritino's jaw when reached for, quickly dropping him cold.

Erik hissed in pain and shook out his hand, wincing from the crushing agony radiating through his fingers. He crouched down and sifted through the young man's pockets, recovering the flip phone that abruptly rang.

"What?" Erik answered once he yanked apart the lid.

"It looks like you figured it out," said the cold male voice.

"Who are you?" Erik snapped. "Why are you masking your voice?"

"We're going to play a little game, my friend," said the mysterious voice. "It's called 'Tick, Tick, Boom'. You do as I say and no one gets hurt. Simple idea, no?"

"I don't believe you."

"I figured you would say that. Here, let me demonstrate."

Moments later, the lights and sound system shut off, leaving the partiers and the staff confused and frightened, wondering of the cause.

"The storm got worse!" someone cried in the darkness.

"There's no tornado siren though," said another.

"That's child's play," Erik spat into the line amidst the tense murmurs. "You could easily tamper with the box downstairs."

"Maybe..." A single spotlight turned on, shining on Erik.

"Or I could be somewhere far away where you can't find me and control everything remotely. You try shutting down the Central Network and the Feds will be up your ass so fast before you could pull a hair out of it."

"Fine, I'm in," Erik growled and the lights and music returned as quickly as it stopped before anyone could inquire about the strange occurrence.

"Go to where ghosts tend to dwell and you'll get your next clue. You have twenty minutes."

"What if I don't arrive on time?"

"You'll see. Get there one second late and you'll know." The call clicked off and Erik was about to close the clamshell case when the phone rang once more, showing an unlisted number. Erik answered the call.

"The pickup is in the usual location," snapped a harsh voice. "Get it in an hour."

Before Erik could inquire where, the phone bipped and went dead. Looking around the club, he spotted Bortelli advancing in his direction and made his escape out the front door, returning into the rain.

Erik raced down the alley, clutching his shoulder steadily drumming in fiery pain.

"*I need to keep awake,*" Erik considered, panting hard for breath as the numbness increased down his arm and the fog in his head intensified. "*If I pass out now, I'm done. I have to go where ghosts dwell - is there a cemetery somewhere?*" Entering the street, he looked up and down the road, trying to decide where next to go.

The flickering neon lights coming from a small diner drew Erik and he approached the windows, peering inside. He caught sight of a slender dark-haired waitress who happened to look up, startled and Erik turned away, embarrassed. He walked several paces down the sidewalk before hearing the door swing open.

"Hey," a voice called moments later. "You want anything?"

Erik turned around, facing the waitress standing in the doorway under the awning.

"Coffee," he called back.

"Come in, it's on me."

Erik shook his head. "Got no shoes."

"Come around back."

Erik puffed a sigh and went around the block, passing a bank, eyewear fittings store, a clothing boutique, and a bowling alley. Reaching the side street, he happened upon a gate dividing the lot from the narrow alley.

"Over here," the young woman called, waving from the building's rear on the other side. "You can't cut across. Just go around and come in from the back."

Erik growled under his breath as he made his way to the connecting street proper and walked across the large parking lot, reaching the woman who stood at the door holding a pair of black thong sandals.

"Why are you doing this for me?" Erik grumbled when handed the footwear.

"They're size thirteen," she said instead as Erik slipped them on his feet. "I couldn't tell how tall you really are."

"I wear tens, but I'm not complaining."

"Come inside."

Erik ducked indoors and the waitress led him into the kitchen where several young men in white uniforms cooked on gas ranges, while two others manned the sinks, washing dishes and one chopped vegetables.

"Is that your latest boyfriend, Natalie?" hooted the prep chef, an olive-skinned wiry bald young man and the others jeered good-naturedly. The young woman's face flushed red in response as she led Erik toward a small card table with four chairs tucked in the rear.

"Here," said Natalie, "have a seat and I'll get that coffee for you."

"Thanks," Erik murmured and pulled out a chair. "I can't stay long though. I have to be somewhere."

"Somewhere like what?" asked one of the dishwashers, a skinny young man with shaggy blond hair.

"Looking for your next fix?" vaunted a large, beefy cook with cropped hair and guffawed.

"Naw, prolly diving in trash bins for his next meal," said the prep chef. "You got the wrong joint, man. We save our scraps for the soup kitchen down the street."

"I'm not homeless," Erik spat. "But whatever. I just need to find a hangout for ghosts."

"Ooh, it's a crazy one!" crowed a short stout cook. "Pay up, bitches!"

"Man," griped the other dishwasher, a slightly overweight middle-aged man as he wiped his hands on his apron and dug into his rear pocket. "Fourth time this week!"

The workers laughed and Erik ground his teeth, glaring at

them. Natalie returned with a mug and a carafe, setting them before Erik.

"Anything else?" she asked. "Cream? Sugar?"

"Black's fine," Erik murmured. "I need to stay awake anyway." He poured his first mug of coffee and tasted it, finding it slightly warm. "Can you tell me something?"

"Like what?"

Erik swallowed its contents and poured himself another cup. "Where can I find a place where ghosts hang out?"

"The cemetery's at the edge of town," Natalie explained. "If you're walking from here, it'll take you about five hours."

Erik groaned. "I need to get there in twenty minutes..."

"Why? What's the rush?"

"Holy shit!" another female voice squawked from the diner near the counter. "Guys!" A busty brunette with the nametag 'Rosalin' burst through the kitchen's doors, her face pale. "Some clown's jammed up all the stations! You can't get anything!"

Natalie gasped. "What?" she cried.

"Turn on the telly and the radio and look!"

"The telly and the radio?"

"There's the old test mode color bars and weird text and a robot voice saying 'calling all stations'." Rosalin trundled in and grabbed Natalie's arm. "Come on!"

Erik took his mug of coffee and followed the women into the main dining area, watching the overhead televisions displaying multicolored bars across the screen with a message in white LCD characters superimposed across.

ELECTROMEDIA IS YOU KNOW WRONG

NOW ALL YOUR BASE

ARE BELONGS TO US

HACK THE PERCEPTION OF DOORS

COMING A BIG BANG IS

"What does this mean?" Natalie wondered aloud. "You said the radio's off too?"

"It just has the same robot saying 'calling all stations' with this beeping going on in the background," Rosalin explained and withdrew her small brick-shaped phone from her blouse. "I was listening to my radio app it and it suddenly happened."

Turning it on, she poked at the cracked screen and moments later, tuned into the station where the same robotic voice echoed the call from the television. In the background played a melodic tone. Erik tensed, grasping harder to his mug.

"Is that Signal Code or something?" asked a diner patron at the counter with a plate of toast and eggs.

"No," answered another behind his cup of coffee, "it's too long to be. I used to be a Mariner and that's not it."

Erik heaved for breath and backed away. "I have to go," he said hurriedly once the others turned toward him.

"Wait," Natalie called after Erik once he turned on his heel. "What's wrong?"

When the tone abruptly changed, a surge of prickling agony struck the back of his head, making his ears thud strongly from the pressure change. Erik dropped his mug with a crash and clamped his hands over his ears, yowling in pain.

"Turn it off!" he wailed, collapsing to his knees. "Please!"

"I'm sorry!" Rosalin cried and fumbled with the cellular,

37

jamming her finger frustratingly into the screen.

"Why does it only affect you?" Natalie asked as she crouched at Erik's side, touching his arm. Erik whimpered, shying away from her touch and Natalie gasped when she found blood on her hand. "Hey, guys, he's hurt!"

"Got it!" Rosalin cried triumphantly as she successfully shut off her phone. "Since I dropped it, it's been fussy..."

"I can't go to sleep," Erik mewed once he lowered his hands. "I'll forget..."

"Forget what?" Natalie inquired and helped Erik as he rose unsteadily to his feet.

"The bugs..."

"Bugs...?"

"Back to your regular scheduled programming," declared the robotic voice from the television in the next room.

"Oh no!" Natalie yelped when Erik moaned as his eyes rolled to the back of his head.

"Hey, stay awake!" Rosalin cried and the stout line cook hurried over, grasping for Erik before he collapsed.

The prep chef ran over, helping the stout cook pull Erik over to a nearby stool at the counter and Erik slumped in it. The chef slapped Erik and Erik's eyes fluttered open, unfocused.

"Get the smelling salts and first aid kit," the prep chef shouted. "It's in the drawer!"

The dishwashers took off for the rear office.

"Hey, man, talk to us," protested one of the line cooks, a tall thin young man with big hair under a hairnet.

"What's going on here?" asked the middle-aged dishwasher as he returned with a small amber bottle and white kit. He tossed the bottle to the prep chef and the chef opened the vial, waving the opening under Erik's nose. Erik snorted and his eyes widened when he scented the hartshorn, immediately pulling away from the bitters. Erik glanced around, startled at the number of faces over him.

"Are you in some kind of trouble?" demanded the prep chef as the dishwasher opened the kit, taking out a gauze bandage and iodine pads.

"What do you want with me?" Erik snapped, narrowing his eyes.

"You're hurt, man," answered the middle-aged dishwasher. "Just let us help."

"Eh, got a plate order for table twelve," called an older waitress as she approached the line counter and tapped the bell. "Shortstack and a quarter link."

"Damn," grumbled the beefy cook, stomping back into the kitchen. "Don't worry, I got this..."

Erik debated leaving, but then realized he could hardly feel his left arm. "My arm..." he murmured and pushed back his hood then unzipped his soaked sweatshirt, peeling out of it.

Rosalin gasped and pulled Natalie away toward the other line cooks who looked on silently. "He's that wanted criminal!" she squeaked as the dishwasher knelt at Erik's side, inspecting the stippled bruises.

"A gunshot wound!" he yelped, surprised. "How were you running around like that for so long?"

"Is the bullet still in there?" Rosalin asked as the dishwasher cleaned and wrapped Erik's wound.

"Went straight through..."

"He doesn't look like that guy for real," Natalie murmured. "At least, not this close... Wasn't he blond...?"

"He kinda does," murmured the other skinny dishwasher as he returned. "I already called the cops. He's worth big money."

"The fuck, dude!" the prep chef squawked, glaring back at his co-worker. "He dint do nothing to us!"

"Look, I wanna go to culinary school!" the skinny dishwasher snapped. "I can't make it washing nothing but dishes!"

"You work your way up - that's what Raheem did!" the prep chef snapped, pushing the skinny dishwasher back by the chest. "He mopped floors and now he's the top cook in this joint!"

"Right," interjected the stout cook. "You pay your damn dues, like the rest of us!"

"Fuck you and your dues! I'm getting paid."

Erik grabbed his wet sweatshirt and pulled into it. "I have other things to do than get arrested," he growled. "I need to get those bugs out of my room..." He staggered for the door and frowned when he noticed the heavy rains continued falling in sheets.

"And you clowns are just gonna let him go?" the skinny dishwasher squawked. "He's a fucking *wanted criminal*!"

"Nobody knows what he really looks like," Natalie protested as Erik opened the door. "But unless they get a DNA match..."

Erik stopped dead in his tracks and his eyes widened at the mention of DNA. He whirled around and the diner workers looked back at him, equally stunned.

"Fuck!" the skinny dishwasher howled and jumped the middle-aged man holding the bloodied prep cloth, knocking him to the floor.

Erik hurried over into the fray as the two men fought, trading blows. He grasped the skinny dishwasher and hauled him off, throwing him to the floor.

"You want me?" Erik shouted as the young man rolled with the fall and bound to his feet. "Come on!"

"I'm gonna gut you good," the skinny dishwasher snarled, reaching into his rear pocket. "I'll get all the DNA I need to prove you're the one and your evil ass will make my life easy." He withdrew a switchblade and sprung the blade with a snap.

"Like hell!" Erik thundered and peeled out of his waterlogged sweatshirt. "Nobody controls me, not even you!"

The young man dashed in and Erik dodged several furious swipes, snapping back with his wet shirt, stunning him. Several patrons quickly moved out the way as Erik rounded the diner floor, keeping distance between himself and the blade.

Rosalin ran for the nearby coffee machines and picked up a glass carafe then hurried after her coworker, smashing the glass into the back of his head. He turned, swiping at her. The girl screamed and Erik pounced, taking the knife-wielding dishwasher down to the floor.

"You piece of shit!" Erik snarled in his ear, wrapping his shirt around the young man's neck and twisted the fabric.

Rosalin scrambled rearwards as the young man gasped for breath when Erik pulled back. He swung his blade wildly, jamming the knife into Erik's thigh. Rosalin hurried over to Natalie and the woman held her protectively in her arms, watching Erik struggle with the skinny dishwasher.

He ignored the pain and continued to squeeze, eventually

bringing the squirming young man down the floor, choking out his life. When his body stopped moving, Erik staggered to his feet, then stumbled when the fiery signal of pain flared up his thigh.

The middle-aged dishwasher raced up to Erik, taking him by the arm. "We'll tell them it was self-defense," he said, easing Erik into a nearby booth. "We'll all tell them," he promised. "You just came in for coffee..."

"I need this out of me," Erik seethed. "I can't go to the hospital... They'll get me."

"Quentin, take his shirt!"

The stout cook snapped to attention and hustled over, taking the sweatshirt off the dead young man's neck. He knelt at Erik's side and snatched out the knife in his thigh, handing it to the prep chef. The prep chef swiped the blade, snapping it close as he watched his coworker briskly tie the shirt around Erik's thigh, twisting the fabric as he did so.

At once, a siren blared down the street, steadily approaching.

"Shit, they're here!" Quentin squawked. "We gotta get!"

"You gotta go somewhere," the prep chef said worriedly as he grasped Erik's good arm and draped it over his shoulder. "Look, me and Lynne got break, so we'll drop you off wherever you want."

"Why are you helping me?" Erik grumbled as he limped with the prep chef toward the diner's rear.

"We were all stray dogs once," the prep chef replied and pushed open the door. "Hey, Lynne," he called, "start up the wagon!"

"Yeah," said the tall thin cook as he left his station and

rushed out the rear door.

"Come on, just hold up a little 'til we get to the car," the prep chef urged, leading Erik out the back.

"I was supposed to pick up something," Erik huffed as they exited outdoors, finding a dark navy station wagon sedan with wood paneling on the sides idling near the exit. "They want the box I made…"

"What are you talking about?"

The prep chef handed Erik the weapon in his good hand then opened the rear door. Erik clutched the switchblade as he fell in, too exhausted to move. The prep chef pushed in Erik's legs and slammed shut the door, then hurried into the front passenger as Lynne pulled away from the lot.

"He called," Erik said, "but my phone died…"

"What?" Lynne replied. "Hey, Palmer, your charger's in here?"

"Yeah," Palmer answered. "Check the console."

"What kind of phone you got?" Lynne called.

Erik pocketed the switchblade and withdrew the small flip phone. Palmer reached around, taking it from Erik's outstretched hand and frowned when he noticed the model.

"Shit," he groused, "this sucker's ancient as hell!"

"I need to pick up that package in an hour," Erik insisted. "I have to get it, or more bad stuff happens…"

"What kind of bad stuff?" Lynne asked cautiously. "Like some kind of 'big bang' 'cause of that 'box' you made?"

When Erik said nothing, Lynne paled and gripped tighter to the steering wheel.

FIVE

Erik groaned in pain and cringed as he turned onto his back. He looked up at his hand and gasped in horror when he noticed his pale skin appeared almost translucent.

"I'm fading," Erik thought in dismay. *"I can't die, not yet. I want to die on my terms..."*

The pain in your heart is deep and vast... Erik glanced over, facing the counterpart sitting next to him, grinning maliciously. *Let it consume you. Give in to it. Embrace it and you'll get stronger.*

"I refuse..." Erik rasped as he struggled to sit up. "I won't become a slave to your demands..."

I keep coming to you because you won't let the pain in! Erik grunted when slapped across the face and he crumpled against the door. *Give up your body to me. Your weak heart can't handle the pain anymore.*

"What are you saying back there?" Palmer called.

"I don't need you anymore," Erik growled as he struggled to get up. "Disappear!"

Then you're finished. The duplicate kicked Erik onto his back and sat on his chest, wrapping his hands around Erik's throat. *You can never escape me!*

"Wait," Palmer said, "Why are you changing your mind?"

Erik grasped the duplicate's wrist. "Then you know what to do," he hissed, glaring back.

"I think the poor bastard's delirious," Lynne said, alarmed.

"Shit, he probably lost a lot of blood too..." Palmer looked over the seat, watching Erik's pinched sallow face and his weak breathing as he twitched slumped against the door. "Whatever package he had to pick up's gonna have to wait. Drop him at County Health Control."

"Public Security might pinch him!" Lynne protested.

Palmer shook his head. "We can't stick around..."

Erik's shallow breathing slowed as the double continued to squeeze until he saw darkness.

The shrill electronic beep startled Erik and his eyes snapped open as he sat up with a start, gasping for breath. Once the shock of being awake faded, intense agony abruptly swamped his being. Erik cried out, clutching his head that fiercely pound in pain.

He shut his eyes, trying to recall where he had been and what happened to cause the searing pain throughout his body, especially on the side of his neck. Only blankness - and a queer sense of something *dangerously wrong* - appeared in his mind, aside from the hammering thud behind his eyes.

Erik groaned and wiped at his sweaty face, realizing he had no idea where he was. Looking around the darkened room, he noticed a space heater near the door with its golden coils dimly glowing.

Hearing a muffled sound behind him, Erik suddenly became aware he wasn't in his apartment when he sensed a warm body next to him since he usually slept alone. Erik sucked in a shallow breath once a slender hand pressed against his chest. He reached down, taking the foreign hand in his and clenched his teeth when he noticed he wore a band on his left hand.

"When did I get married?" Erik wondered.

"You up?" a woman's voice muttered behind him.

"Unfortunately," Erik answered. He grunted when pushed down into the mattress and felt the soft toned body clamber over him.

The woman swat at the clock, killing the screech with a chirp. She stepped out of bed, taking the sheeting with her and yawned loudly, running a hand through her hair. She then padded over to the door, toeing the heater and switched it off then stepped out the room, bringing in a cold draft.

Erik moaned as he sat up, rubbing at his continually throbbing temples. Swinging his feet over to the mildly warmed floor, he squinted at the digital readout, its glowing electric green numbers stating it was a quarter to five. Realizing he was naked, Erik left the bed and approached the door, peering out into the hall.

"Down on your right," the woman called.

"Thanks," Erik called back and headed in that direction, finding a soft amber glow at the corridor's end.

Opening the door, he noticed the shaded nightlight and flipped the switch, revealing a warm yellow and tan tiled bathroom with a lacquered beige claw-foot tub and simple white shower curtain on hooks hanging off a rounded rod.

Turning on the tap, Erik ran the water and splashed his face, then looked up, facing a tired young man with shaggy oily red hair, sunken violet eyes and freckled crooked nose. He noticed the scars on his face, with three prominent ones across his nose, down his right jaw and over his left eye.

Opening the cabinet, Erik found a half-empty tube of toothpaste, quarter half-pint of antiseptic mouthwash, a pair of toothbrushes, several packets of gauze, a roll of surgical tape and one white bottle and several amber bottles of prescriptions.

Turning the bottles around, he saw the white bottle labeled 'Sinnesloschen' and one amber bottle labeled 'Laudanum' filled for Ferdian Smith. The others were vitamins, anti-anxiety medication and hormones filled for Francisca Gallagher.

Erik grabbed the painkillers, quickly unscrewing the top and shook out a carmine capsule. He swallowed the pill with a handful of water, then shut the cabinet door. Searching for the bathroom closet, he found instead a single window leading to the fire escape and alley below.

"You all right back there?" Francisca's voice said suddenly outside the door.

"I'm fine," Erik answered, growing tense.

"Here are some towels." The bathroom door opened partway, revealing Francisca's tanned arm. She set several terry cloths on the sink's edge. "Put the towels on the rod when you're done."

"Sure."

Erik shut off the tap and entered the shower. Turning on the hot water, he hissed in pain when the scalding droplets struck raw skin on his left thigh, feet, right shoulder, left side and down his back. He quickly lathered and rinsed off and washed his hair, then dried off and carefully taped his injuries.

Wrapping the towel about his waist, Erik left the bathroom and entered the kitchen, finding Francisca sitting at a blue card table with a mug of coffee in her hands. On the table across from her was a tall empty white mug, shallow ceramic bowl, a tea spoon, a bottle of liquid sweet creamer, a jar of instant coffee, two packs of cigarettes - one menthol and the other plain - and a matchbook.

"Hotpot's behind me," Francisca filled in.

"Good to know."

Erik took the cup along the way as he passed her, eyeing her carefully. She had short sandy hair, narrow hazel eyes, high cheekbones, long thin nose and slender lips. He noticed the sheeting draped over her as a toga-like garment as she sat back with her legs crossed at her knee, revealing her athletic arms and shapely legs.

"Stop drooling, Doofus," Francisca muttered and sipped her coffee.

Erik's cheeks warmed and he approached the counter where the electric kettle rest. "How long has it been?" he asked faintly as he gripped the counter. "Ten years? Twenty?"

Francisca snorted. "What kind of question is that?" she retorted. "It's been a long time."

"Then why are you being salty towards me?"

"Who said I was being salty towards you?" Francisca spat. "You're the one treating me like a stranger!"

Erik puffed a short sigh. "You're right," he murmured and poured steaming water into his cup. He turned around, leaning against the counter. "I don't remember who you are..."

"That's terrible..."

"So, was this some pickup sort of thing?" Francisca suddenly burst out laughing. Erik frowned and set down his mug with a firm bang. "Why is that funny?" He approached the table, glaring at Francisca who covered her mouth as giggles came out.

"It's not," Francisca said between gasps of breath and leaned forward, hiding her face.

"Then what the hell is it?" Erik snatched up a pack of cigarettes and plopped into his chair, ripping off the cellophane.

"Now you're being weird," Francisca murmured after calming.

"How am I being weird?" Erik tapped the box against the table's edge, bringing up several filtered tips. "You act like you know me!"

"Well I do, obviously!" Francisca rolled her eyes. "I wouldn't take you home if I didn't!"

Erik narrowed his eyes as he withdrew a cigarette and tossed the pack on the table. "I don't see a ring on your finger," he spat. "I don't know you from a can of paint, other than your name."

Francisca sat up, quirking an eyebrow at Erik. "What's with that ugly look for?" she spat. "I didn't put it on because I didn't want you having ideas!"

Erik scooped up the matchbook and thumbed it open. "What makes you think I'd have that kind of idea?"

"We wouldn't be sitting here arguing about it, would we?" Erik sat back, slightly embarrassed from her chastising. "Do you know who you are?"

Erik tore off a match and folded the book, drawing the

head across the striking strip to ignite. "Apparently Ferdian Smith," he answered, lighting his cigarette. Taking a long drag, Erik expelled smoke over his head and shook out his match.

"Oh..." Francisca looked down into her coffee. "I thought..."

"So by that, I'm guessing we're not married or anything." Erik dropped his tapering match into the bowl and glared at Francisca when she snorted. "What's with that?"

"I've been married to someone else for the last ten years," Francisca said softly. "Not that I was waiting around or anything..."

Erik's eyes softened and his cheeks warmed. "Please don't say weird things like that," he murmured. "You're creeping me out."

"It probably would've been better if I did marry you instead."

"So we were something once before?"

"No. You drooled from afar, but you had eyes for someone else." Francisca glanced up and Erik's reddened face brightened as he met her gaze. She leaned toward him, tracing the scars across his bare chest with her finger. "You got some new ones."

"I-I guess so..."

"All this from Infantry?"

"I wish I could tell you." Erik shrugged his shoulders. "So, where's Mister Gallagher?"

"He's somewhere in the field gathering information, protecting someone, or doing security detail, I assume." Francisca leaned back into her seat. "He does a lot for someone who's just a SatCom specialist."

"What do you do?"

"I'm a TechCom Universal Specialist, contracted out to those idiots at Midco/Sanato."

"Never thought you were that smart," Erik quipped and tapped his ashes into the nearby bowl.

"Coming from the number one slacker I know, I shouldn't be surprised." Francisca gave a wry smile. "Who would've thought of me as some dumb jock, huh?"

Erik smiled and Francisca grinned, resuming her coffee. "Shouldn't you be getting to work then?" he asked moments later.

"I can take a day off." Francisca waved at Erik. "I washed your clothes and hung them up in the closets, so you can get dressed whenever you're ready."

"You're too nice." After several moments of silence between them, Erik finished his cigarette then left the table, taking up his mug he left behind on the counter. "Got something else for the coffee?"

"Sugar's above you."

"Something stronger, like vodka."

"I don't drink. Bad genes, you know."

"Oh, sorry..."

"When did it start?" Francisca suddenly asked as Erik returned and prepared his coffee.

"What?" When Francisca said nothing else, Erik continued. "The drinking or the memory loss?" He shrugged his shoulders. "I wouldn't know what to tell you."

"What about the nightmares?"

Erik paled. "Is it really bad?"

"I can handle myself fine."

Erik frowned and pushed away from the table. "I should get going then."

"And go where? I thought you wanted me to help you disappear."

"I asked you to...?"

"That's why I'm here. I promised you and I always keep my promises."

Erik gave a strained smile. "I'm sorry," he said sadly. "I really can't..."

Francisca's face became shadowed with worry. "I thought I would never see you again," she said softly. "Then suddenly after all these years I run into you..." She blew a disgruntled sigh. "Why did I even get my hopes up?"

Erik said nothing as he left the table and returned to the bedroom. Switching on the light at the door, he revealed a small room with a full-sized bed, covered by cream-colored turquoise spotted sheets and several turquoise and cream-striped pillows. On the floor near the foot of the bed rest the crumpled comforter matching the pillowcases.

Erik opened the closets, finding several button-down shirts and starched jeans hanging inside. Pushing through the rack, he withdrew a pair of dark indigo jeans and a tan shirt.

Draping the shirt over his shoulder, Erik dropped his towel and stepped into the jeans, hitching them about his waist. He grumbled under his breath when he found the pants difficult to fasten. After buttoning it closed, he kicked up the towel and tossed it on the bed.

"Aren't you going anywhere?" Erik called as he slipped on

the shirt. Padding out into the parlor, Francisca suddenly snorted and hid her face behind her hand. "What is it now?"

"Why the hell are you wearing my clothes?" Francisca shot back.

Erik's face reddened and he jutted a thumb behind him. "It was all men's clothes in there!" he protested. "It was either this or the suits - how could I tell the difference?"

"I don't wear men's clothes, Doofus," Francisca drawled and chortled. "Because I don't wear dresses makes me some kind of beard, huh?"

"I'm not saying that!"

Francisca laughed at Erik who stood in the room, confused and unsettled.

"Look, sit down," Francisca said, "and I'll take you somewhere for breakfast."

"Why not eat here?" Erik inquired.

"Stove's broken."

"Good call then."

SIX

Pulling into a diner lot, Francisca grumbled curses when the engine knocked.

"What's the matter?" Erik asked.

"It's been acting up lately," Francisca replied, pulling the hood release. "I don't know if it's the gas from the other station, just too cold or what."

"Want me to do anything?"

"Go on inside. I'll join you in a minute."

Erik stepped out the pickup and made his way indoors. He frowned when he passed an older man in dark brown, wearing a wool cap, bomber jacket, heavy jeans and steel-toed boots sitting at the counter.

"Thompson?" Erik suddenly blurted.

The man glanced up, surprised. "Yeah?" he answered, turning toward Erik. "Do I know you?"

Before Erik could come up with an answer, Francisca entered moments later and he immediately followed her to the diner's rear, taking seats at a corner booth.

"Order whatever you want," Francisca said as a waitress approached and handed them menus.

"Whatever's cheap," Erik replied and pulled out of his overcoat.

"Please, get whatever you like," Francisca insisted as she unbuttoned her padded jacket. "I'm getting waffles."

Erik blew an annoyed sigh and withdrew his cigarettes from his coat pocket. "Fine, same as you're getting."

"I told you, I can afford it."

"They pay you well, huh?" Erik cracked.

"They have to if they want to keep me."

"Are you still deciding?" the waitress asked in annoyance.

"Give me the special and keep the coffee coming, please," Erik answered.

"Why the hell are you such a cheap ass?" Francisca asked as Erik set his menu aside. The waitress collected the booklets and left.

"Why the hell are you giving me a hard time?" Erik retorted and withdrew a cigarette. "I don't want to owe you anything."

"I don't care. So stop worrying."

"So how are you going to help me disappear?" Erik asked instead.

"I've got a few calls to make - but let's not worry about that right now. Let me enjoy your company."

"You miss me that much?" Erik drawled, smirking.

Francisca snorted and the waitress returned moments later with a carafe, two mugs, and a bowl of creamer packets, setting them on the table.

"Why shouldn't I?" Francisca replied and poured in coffee into an empty mug.

"Why am I so important to you?" Erik pressed. He held up three fingers when Francisca picked up the creamer.

"How many times do I have to keep telling you?" Francisca

put in three packets and stirred the coffee then passed Erik his mug.

The older man in the bomber jacket appeared from offside and slipped Erik a white business card while Francisca prepared her coffee.

Erik looked at the man as he picked up the card. "What do you want?" he asked. "Thompson, right?"

"Yeah," Thompson answered. "What are you working on?"

"Business," Erik answered vaguely and took a drag from his cigarette.

Thompson narrowed his eyes at Erik. "I don't like you this way," he snapped.

Erik blew smoke toward him. "Savvy."

Thompson grunted and stormed out for the rear exit.

"What's that all about?" Francisca murmured as Erik glanced at the card's face. The text had a stylized 'K' over a large beaker. Beneath the logo read the label 'Kanbal Industries'. Erik turned it over, finding a phone number scrawled on the back.

"Know anyone with the number Central eighty-seven fifty-four?" Erik queried.

"We can call it and see."

"I'll do that after I eat something first."

"Why not get it out the way? I want you to enjoy your breakfast."

"Gimmie a quarter."

Francisca quirked an eyebrow. "For what?" she spat.

"Payphone, obviously!"

"There aren't any here, Doofus," Francisca shot back. "Here, just use my cell." She dug through her pocket and withdrew a mid-sized smartphone. Erik appeared lost when Francisca passed the phone toward him. "Don't you know how to use one?"

"Not anything that fancy," Erik murmured. "I'm afraid I'll break it."

Francisca rolled her eyes and dialed the number for him. Handing it over to Erik, he set down the card and picked up the phone, listening. After several rings, the line cut off and Erik shrugged.

"I guess the number's bad," he said and handed the phone back to Francisca.

"Let's enjoy our meals," Francisca murmured and set the phone aside. Erik set his tapering cigarette into a small glass ashtray near the condiments and downed his coffee.

The waitress returned with two plates, one with two large waffles with peaches, strawberries, and blueberries on the side and the other that had fried shredded potatoes and biscuits with sausage gravy.

"Enjoy," the server said as she set the plates on the table.

Erik frowned as he picked up the pepper, dousing it on his meal.

"Don't like it?" Francisca asked as Erik picked up his fork.

"It's food," he muttered.

"You're not going to say grace?"

Erik raised an eyebrow as he looked up at Francisca. "I'm not religious," he said.

"At least give thanks to the damn plants that's giving you energy, Doofus," Francisca spat.

"You can't be serious."

Francisca pointed her fork in Erik's direction. "If you don't," she threatened, "I'll stab you."

Erik smirked and looked down at his plate. "Thanks wheat, thanks potatoes, and thank you too, pig cut into giblets," he said. "Thanks for giving me energy to survive today." Francisca rapped Erik upside the head and Erik winced. "The hell!" he whined. "I was serious!"

Francisca's phone chimed and she picked it up, glimpsing at the screen. "I have to take this," she murmured, setting aside her fork.

"I'll wait on you."

"No, go eat."

Francisca took the phone with her as she rose from her seat and headed for the restrooms. Erik took a bite from his meal and frowned at the bland taste. Setting his fork aside, he left the booth and approached the rear toilets.

Sneaking toward the women's room, he took a quick look around and pushed open the door slightly, listening in.

"What do you mean by that, terminated?" Francisca's voice cried. "Please, I can do better; just allow me more time!" Erik opened the door wider and stepped inside. "But I thought everything was going along fine!" Francisca protested. "Our last evaluation was good enough!" Erik silently approached the stall Francisca stood in and waited outside the door. "Reprogramming?" Francisca shrilled. "What does this have to do with me? You saw my portfolio!"

Francisca let out a frustrated scream and hurled the phone to the floor, shattering it. The door slammed open and she stepped out, her face wet with tears. Francisca looked up and gasped, startled to see Erik standing there. She swiftly booted him in the groin and he crumpled to the floor on his knees.

"Damn it!" Erik yelped as he doubled over.

"You perv!" Francisca shouted. "Why are you here? What the fuck is wrong with you?"

"I was concerned..." Erik moaned.

"Get the hell out before I skin you alive!"

"I'm sorry!"

Erik put out a hand against the wall and staggered to his feet. Reaching out toward Francisca, she jerked away in response.

"Don't touch me!" Francisca snapped.

"Please," Erik pleaded, "tell me what's wrong."

"There's nothing to tell you!"

"Maybe I can help."

"I don't need it."

"I don't believe you."

Francisca clutched her hands at her sides, heaving for breath as she fought for control. Erik blew a hard sigh and left the restrooms, returning for the booth. He paused when he saw the receipt on the table with a label 'void' scrawled across the face.

Turning it over, Erik found a note in the same shaky handwriting: 'Skycatcher 172 - Operation delayed'. He grew ill to the pit of his stomach in response and crumpled the paper then pocketed it.

Erik sank into the booth, waiting for Francisca's return. After several moments when Francisca didn't come out, Erik lit another cigarette and poured himself more coffee. He wondered what the note could be about, and who else might know him.

Erik scoped the diner, unable to find anyone he recognized. He blew a sigh and held a finger to his throbbing temple, growing tense when the unease he felt stirred once again.

SEVEN

A half hour later, Francisca approached the table, her face shadowed in concentration.

"I'm all right," she murmured before Erik could ask. "Don't worry about me."

"I can't help it," Erik said softly as he lit another cigarette.

"That's for me to worry about. You're my main concern right now."

"You got a lot on your mind."

"I know."

"Let me help."

Francisca shook her head and picked up her fork, murmuring grace before cutting into her waffles. She raised an eyebrow when Erik poured himself another cup of coffee. "So you're not eating?"

"Don't like it."

"Have mine."

"I'm sick."

"Don't lie."

"Why would I?"

Francisca slammed down her fork and glared at Erik. "I told you," she snapped, "stop worrying about me!"

"I can't help it."

"You can't fix it."

"How can I if you won't tell me?"

"I don't need your help!"

"Why can't I help you?" Erik leaned back in his seat and picked up his mug of coffee. "You're helping me disappear, aren't you? So let me repay you back in kind."

Francisca narrowed her eyes. "What's going through that tiny brain of yours?" she grumbled.

"It sounds like you lost your job over me," Erik responded. "I want to help you get it back."

"I can't."

"Then let me help you get another."

"Don't be so nice to me."

"You need nice people in your life."

"Whatever." Francisca resumed her meal and Erik grinned.

Once Francisca finished, she withdrew her wallet and Erik reached over, grabbing her hand.

"Don't bother," he said. "Someone already paid for it."

"Don't tell me you did," Francisca said sourly.

"I didn't, honest." Erik smiled brightly. "I stay broke, but with this pretty face, I can get anything done."

Francisca laughed and rose to her feet. "You can't be serious!" She waved at Erik to follow. "Come on, we're getting you something different to wear. I'm not letting you wear my clothes."

Erik stood. "You don't think I look good in them?" he teased as they left the table, returning outdoors.

"I don't want to know what goes on in that pervy mind of yours."

"Yet you won't let me pick yours."

"There's nothing to pick. I'm a dumb jock, remember?"

Erik burst out laughing at the sheer hilarity of the idea.

Erik's afternoon was carefree as he enjoyed Francisca's company when she drove him around to different stores, soaking in the attention when he tried on various clothing and other accessories in the changing rooms and she critiqued his looks. As the afternoon wore on and they exited yet another store, Erik complained about his hunger.

"Of course you're starving," Francisca chastised. "You had nothing but coffee."

"Take me somewhere nice," Erik needled. "I know you can afford it." He entered the truck and stuck his shopping bags in the rear seat.

"Feel like steak?" Francisca inquired as she got into the driver's side and started the engine.

"I'm not much of a meat eater."

"There's this nice vegan place I know of. I think you might like it."

"Really now?"

Francisca left the lot and Erik looked out the window, watching the passing scenery.

"Hey," Francisca called to him, "don't go to sleep,"

"I had twelve cups in me," Erik replied. "I won't sleep." He directed his gaze toward Francisca. "Why are you afraid of my going to sleep?"

"I know that's when you forget," Francisca said softly. "I don't want you to forget about me."

"I won't."

Francisca later pulled in front of another restaurant and motioned Erik out. "I'll find a place to park. Go on in and order whatever you like."

"Will you be all right?" Erik asked.

Francisca snorted. "Sure."

Erik stepped out the truck and entered the eating establishment. The host directed him to a booth with orange cushions and a server approached with the menu. Erik took the seat provided and nodded his thanks once he received the laminated booklet.

While scanning his choices, suddenly soft hands covered his eyes and Erik stiffened when he smelled flowery perfume from behind.

"Guess who?" a voice purred in his ear.

"I'm bad at guessing," Erik replied, setting down his menu. "You'll have to tell me."

"No, keep your eyes closed."

Erik's cheeks warmed when he sensed the woman press against him. "Fine, I promise. Now what do you want?"

"I want you to see me later tonight."

"Really?" Erik smirked and reached for the woman's wrists. "Who am I seeing?"

"You'll see. Now keep them closed."

The hands let go and Erik felt a soft hand take his, placing something in his palm. He clutched it firmly, hearing the mysterious person walk away.

Opening his eyes, Erik turned around and watched a short young woman with dark bobbed hair heading for the front door, wearing a blue and white flowered dress that clung to her curves. After she stepped outdoors, Erik looked down at what he held, noticing he had a clip-on earring with the same flowered design.

Francisca entered moments later, pulling out of her coat. "Order anything yet?" she asked and joined Erik at the table. "What's that you got there?"

"I was waiting on you," Erik replied, pocketing the earring. "Some cute girl left it for me - she wants to see me later tonight."

"Did she give a name?"

"I didn't see her face," Erik murmured, "but she seems to know me somehow."

Francisca smirked. "Then how'd you know it was a chick?" she ragged.

"With a body like that?" Erik scoffed. "You can just tell."

"Doofus, these days you can buy a body like that, remember?"

Erik pouted. "You're saying that because you're jealous."

Francisca gave a slight smile. "Tea to start?" Erik nodded and pulled out of his coat. "What did you decide on?"

"Soba with all the veggies."

"Sounds good."

Hearing a small chime, Erik raised an eyebrow and searched his coat pockets, finding his cell phone. He withdrew it and pressed the talk button without looking at the caller ID.

"What is it?" he greeted.

"Are you going home tonight?" said a male voice over the line.

Erik furrowed his brows. "Who is this?" he demanded. "Why

do you want to know?"

"Just answer the question."

"Sure, I'm headed home," Erik spat. "Why, planning to throw a party for me?"

"I see."

The line cut off suddenly and Erik glared at his cellular in disbelief. He noticed the call came from an unavailable number.

"What's that about," Francisca snapped, "and why the hell didn't you call that number with your phone?"

"I forgot I had it," Erik retorted and pocketed the device. "Look, let's enjoy our lunch, okay?"

Francisca flagged a server and told him what they wanted. Later their tea came and Erik picked up his mug, blowing its contents. He glanced at Francisca, noticing she still stewed in annoyance.

"I'm sorry," Erik murmured. "Look, I'll make it up to you, is that okay?"

"I don't want to hear it," Francisca snapped.

"Look, since they now got an opening, let me take it, yeah?"

"The hell you know about computers?" She nodded in his direction. "You acted like you never saw a smartphone in your life, and that one was only six months old!"

Erik shrugged his shoulders. "I'm a quick learner."

"Fine, I'll see about pulling some strings." Francisca pointed at Erik. "You owe me, big time!"

"I promise to make it up to you."

Their meals came and Erik took a bite from the dish. He screwed up his face.

"What's the matter?" Francisca murmured.

"It's a bit salty."

"I'm surprised you can tell, given how heavy a smoker you are!"

Erik shrugged his shoulders and continued his meal. He later broke out in cold sweat and pushed away from the table.

"I'm not feeling so hot," Erik moaned.

"Restrooms are behind us," Francisca noted.

Erik staggered to his feet and hurried for the rear rooms. Before he could grasp the door handle, he gasped when his body turned numb and his word dissolved unexpectedly.

Erik slowly came to and found himself bound to a stiff chair in a darkened room.

"Where am I?" he demanded. "Get me out of here!"

"You must understand," called a familiar voice, "that there are nonhuman beings that prevail in this world, those that exist in the light and in the darkness…"

"What are you going on about?" Erik struggled in the chair, trying to get out of his binds. "Why are you here? Let me out!"

"I can't let you out right now… They think you're being punished and I needed a few moments to speak to you."

"Punishing me? For what? Why can't I see you?"

"You mustn't know who I am just yet."

Erik tried to rock the chair back, only to find he was against a wall. "Then what do you want with me?"

"Know that these monsters you will eventually fight were once human, robbed of their power of existence, a fundamental energy needed to live in this world."

"So you're saying they have no soul?" Erik scoffed. "That's

a little out there!"

"Without that power, they no longer think, nor do they feel and they can no longer care. They only follow orders and fight, then die."

"Then why do they live now, as 'monsters' as you say?"

"They live anew, created to move freely in our world and control terrible powers to perform as their power-hungry masters command. They act as they please as long as their power allows, until their final moments."

"What do you want me to do about this?"

"You are capable of destroying these monsters. You can stop them from extending their master's reach, from connecting with others like them and keep this darkness from spreading. You need to eliminate them."

"But you know I can't kill!"

"They're causing an enormous distortion in this world. Their irresponsible rampage must be stopped before it accelerates at an unprecedented pace, making them hard to put down."

"So you say I have some kind of power within me to put a stop to them?" Erik laughed bitterly. "I'm only one person - I don't have the resources and you're not making any sense!"

"There are others out there fighting for our cause. These monsters fear us, for they have been reprogrammed to hunt down their own kind."

"Why are you telling me this?"

"Because, with your help, we can emerge victorious in this battle and save the only world we have. You must now swear vengeance against these destroyers. Otherwise, this world will end and humanity as a whole will suffer."

"I don't have that kind of skill!"

"You will become a soldier, a living weapon, given abilities to cause mass destruction. You will hunt, you will strike them down, you will kill…"

"Is this any relation to Divinity…?"

"We'll see…" Erik seethed once struck in the back of the neck with a needle and injected with a serum. "I'm sorry, but I have to rough you up a bit. Hopefully this numbing agent is enough."

"Why…?"

"It's my job…" Erik grunted when he felt a heavy strike to his face, whipping back his head. He looked up through cloudy vision, spotting a man in a three-piece suit standing before him, shaking out his right hand. "Damn it…!" he hissed.

The man delivered a backhand, striking Erik so hard his vision darkened. Another heavy whack knocked him out of his world.

I want you to remember…

Erik woke up gasping in a darkened room, drenched in cold sweat. He choked for breath, coughing and wheezing while holding his head in his hands.

"Are you in pain?" a voice called to Erik.

"It's nothing," Erik called back as he sat up.

"Are you sick?"

"Leave me alone, please."

Erik held a hand to his mouth when a strained sob escaped him. The door opened slightly, letting in bright light.

"Are you crying?" said the concerned voice.

Erik clenched his hands, growing annoyed. "Leave me alone!" he shouted and drew up his knees to his chest as he fought the queasiness in his guts.

Moments later, Erik heard footsteps pad inside the room and he felt a cool towel on the back of his neck. He looked up, squinting at the shadowy outline sitting next to him on the bed.

"A lot of people told me about you," said the cautious visitor. "They told me a lot of things. But I know there are as many truths as there are people telling them and everything can be both right and wrong."

"W-what are you trying to say?" Erik stammered.

"I'm saying I don't know if you're a good person, or a bad person, or if I can trust you."

"So, why am I here?"

"Your friends said you needed a safe place to stay. So I told them you could stay here."

"I feel sick," Erik mewed and leaned forward, resting his head on the shoulder of the other person. He noticed the shoulder was small and smelled a faint trace of flowery perfume. "I'm still feeling a bit off," Erik murmured. "Please stay a minute longer..."

"Sure..."

Erik moaned and slipped back into darkness.

EIGHT

You have to destroy them all...

Until nothing remains...

The sound of rumbling thunder roused Erik, stirring him to consciousness. Unsure of where he was, he noticed movement and turned, falling on his back. He spotted a mocha-skinned young woman with big frizzy magenta hair in a white uniform sitting across from him, writing into a notepad.

She later looked up and gasped, astounded and jerked to her feet as she dropped the pad, knocking the chair over with a clatter.

"Where are you going?" Erik murmured as he sat up, watching her flee the room. His world tilted violently and he grunted, holding his head, then pursed his lips when he spotted his left arm wrapped in a bandage.

Moments later, the woman returned with a pale man slightly older than Erik with shaggy bleached hair and narrow dark gray eyes, wearing a dark brown suit underneath a white consulting jacket.

"You finally return, *mi amigo*," the doctor said brightly. "*¡Enhorabuena!*"

"Who are you?" Erik spat. "Where am I?"

"You're at my private clinic."

Erik's hands grew clammy as his heart suddenly thud in his chest. "I can't!" he yelped and pushed away the sheeting. "If I stay in County–!"

The doctor laughed. "This isn't County Health Control," he said brightly. "Far, far from it. If I reported you to Public Security, they'd shut me down for illegal operations."

Erik gave the doctor a wary glance. "Illegal...?"

The man nodded. "That's right. I specialize in transplants."

"Transplants?" Erik put a hand to his chest, wincing. "I can't stay..."

"You almost died from blood loss!" the doctor reprimanded. "You need to rest longer."

"Your name then?"

"Albero Hansen."

Erik took in a shallow breath, startled. "Albero...?"

"I'm sure you're still in a lot of pain." The doctor withdrew a pen syringe from his pocket filled with a red serum, flipping off the cap with his thumb. "This should help a bit." He took Erik's uninjured arm, jabbing the needle into his flesh. Erik grunted as the medication coursed through his veins. "Please rest."

Erik frowned when the doctor withdrew his syringe and left the room. He rubbed at his sore arm, furrowing his brow as he wondered about the doctor's familiarity with him.

The nurse blew a disconcerted sigh as she bent over, picking up the fallen notepad. Erik's eyes followed the length of the nurse's toned leg up her strong thighs, where the dress ended barely covering her wide hips and hefty rounded bottom.

"I don't know why the doctor chose to save you," she

murmured, blushing when she noticed Erik staring. "If the others find out about you..."

"What others?" Erik inquired. "What about me?"

"Public Security's really drumming up coverage about the terrorist attack this afternoon. Everyone in the Network's nervous with good reason."

"I'll be gone by morning," Erik promised.

"It's raining," the nurse said helplessly. "You came in soaking wet and close to death. It's a wonder you were able to warm up at all."

Erik gave a wan smile. "You really want me to stay a little while? There's no real reason for me to be here."

"Where would you go then?"

Erik shrugged. "I have to be somewhere."

"You don't believe me?"

"You could be lying to keep me trapped here."

The nurse huffed and stalked out the room.

Erik groaned and ran his hands through his hair. Hearing a faint high whine, he paused, breaking out sweating as his breath caught in his throat. His left arm seared in response and Erik dashed out of bed, only to lose his footing and strike the floor when a flash of fiery agony flared down his right leg, starting from his thigh.

He growled and gnashed his teeth, clutching his thigh. After the wave of discomfort passed, Erik staggered to his feet and ripped off the sheeting on the bed then wrapped it around his waist. After tying the sheet in place, he approached the door, perking up when he heard a voice outside.

"Did you think they sent him here?" a man's voice said.

73

"He didn't come with instructions," said a woman's voice. "How did he get here anyway?"

"Palmer dropped him here."

"How is that going, that deal?"

Hearing the voices grow fainter, Erik pushed open the door and peered out, finding a small complex of men and women in tan uniforms bustling about on their individual missions. Only few wore white uniforms and overcoats, while at the end of the corridor standing on ladders were two men in green uniforms, attending to fixtures in the ceiling.

The big-haired nurse entered the hall with a newspaper and a black cigarette case, nodding toward the maintenance workers who greeted her. She rolled her eyes as she approached Erik and jammed the newspaper into his chest.

"You shouldn't be out of bed," she said sternly.

"You shouldn't be smoking," Erik retorted, taking the paper. "If you give me one, I promise to be good."

"I'll take you to the patio then." The nurse continued down the hall and turned, finding Erik still at the door. "I'm not going to carry you," she snapped.

Erik puffed a hard sigh and hurriedly padded after her.

Entering a screened porch, Erik approached the chair next to a small ashtray stand near the door and plopped into it. He gazed out into a garden, watching the steady rain shower the wildflowers and medicinal plants.

"You know you're quite lucky," the nurse said.

"Oh?" Erik murmured as he sat back and shook open the damp paper, finding a sketch of his likeness and the headline

'DOMESTIC TERRORIST SUSPECT WANTED' above it. "What's this supposed to mean?"

"How could you not know about that?" the nurse retorted. "Lately someone's been systematically bumping off folks regarding the old CENTRA Project."

"I watch the morning news when I can," Erik replied while scanning the article, noting the names of the dead. "According to the paper, the ones they caught in the snooping sweeps turned out to be Synthoids..."

"Right, but they claimed to have found a partial print somewhere during one of their sweeps. Some claimed it was on one of the bodies dumped in a bin behind the Downtown Complex. The people interviewed gave the same description - pale, tall, thin, light hair, light eyes..."

Erik looked up at the nurse as she withdrew a cigarette from her case. "That could be just about anyone," he protested, taking it from her.

"The doctors here don't really trust you and want no trouble. If Public Security gets a whiff of our existence, it'll destroy everything we worked so hard for."

"Why would you care if some old CENTRA Project techs get killed?"

The nurse handed Erik her lighter, appearing distant. "Some of those technicians are hiding out here with us fighting the latest iteration of the program. As far as the Establishment's concerned, we're terrorists too."

Erik lit his cigarette, nodding as he took in the information. "The Synthoids are a government program, part of the Public Defense Works. They were built to replace live soldiers in the field. So I don't see why anyone would want to fight that."

"We oppose the mandatory implementation of Neuron Chips into soldiers when they volunteer for various engineering and defense jobs," the nurse explained. "Those tickers are unsafe..."

"What are you," Erik jibed, "hardcore Conscientious Objectors?"

The nurse nodded. "Well, I have to get back to work now. We'll talk later." She left his side and Erik continued paging through the paper.

"*Qué estás haiendo aqui?*" Albero's voice called. Erik glanced up at the doctor who stepped outside on the screened porch. "Enjoying the weather, eh?"

"I'm going to leave," Erik murmured, jamming his burned cigarette into the ashtray. "I'll need my things and be out of your hair."

"I can't let you leave like that," Albero protested. "It's a wonder you can still move about being seriously wounded and I'd like to run more tests."

"I'm tough, obviously," Erik quipped and set the paper aside. "Don't worry about me, Doctor Hansen. I'll disappear and you won't have to worry about anything." Rising to his feet, Erik froze when Albero blocked his path, wielding a scalpel.

"This really can cut, you know," Albero warned, waving it at Erik. "I'm asking you nicely to stay here a while longer."

"I'm not letting anyone test on me anymore," Erik growled, narrowing his eyes. "I don't like hospitals and I don't like being controlled."

"You rampage in doing whatever you like has only tightened

the noose about your neck. So I'd think very carefully about my next course of action, *mi amigo*."

"So are you really going to kill me, Doctor?" Erik spat. "I don't believe you."

"I have no reason to hesitate. I can slice you up and patch you together again and with my team's skilled handiwork, no one could ever tell."

Erik paled. "Y-you really are a bad guy," he stammered. "The nurse said you wanted me for something…"

"I do, and I need you well enough to do it."

"If it's something nefarious, count me out. Don't weigh my life against the group here." Erik pushed past Albero and leaned out of a swing, stumbling across the worn planks as he retreated.

"You're full of empty idealism, *mi amigo*," Albero said as he crossed the floor. "It's impracticable to leave no victims. Sometimes you have to be evil to realize the impossible."

Erik ducked when the doctor slashed again, cutting into the screen. Shouldering the man in the chest, Erik sent him tumbling to the floor and the scalpel clattered out of his hand.

"I'm not a puppet to be jerked around!" he shouted over Albero. "I don't want to hurt anyone anymore, don't you get it?" Erik picked up the fallen weapon before Albero reached for it and aimed it at his neck. "Don't force me to go there with you."

"What about those desires you have stirring in you?" Albero pressed. "Those urges to kill and destroy…" Erik tightened his grip, overwhelmed and nonplussed as the doctor continued. "You're still being controlled, even indirectly. Aren't you tired of losing someone important to you?"

"That feeling…" Erik's hand shook as he took a step away.

"Sometimes you have to sacrifice something to save and protect someone important..."

"Do you honestly believe that, or is that more of that empty idealism you were told?"

"Aren't you worth protecting?"

"Are you?"

Erik clenched his teeth when the maintenance workers in green uniforms appeared at the door.

"Doctor," one said, "this man has to go."

"He's a dangerous criminal," said the other, "and we can't afford to keep him safe anyway."

"Right, and besides, living under someone else's protection is still being controlled," Erik spat. "Being told where to go, what to do, who to speak with, who to avoid, checking in... I'm not up for that." He lowered the scalpel. "Look, I'll be good and leave on my own. I just want my stuff back."

"Let him go," Albero said as he rose to his feet. "It's best that way." Erik huffed and stormed past the workers who immediately stepped aside. "Don't think I'd let you go that easily," Albero called at Erik's back. "That serum I gave you was a live virus that'll shut down your organs. You'll die in seventy-two hours if I don't give you the antidote."

Erik froze, clenching his hands. "You're full of it," he called back.

"Think about it. If it were a painkiller, you'd be having a bad trip right now."

Erik broke out sweating when he quickly churned the possibilities in his mind. *"He's right,"* he realized in terror. *"I usually hallucinate when I take painkillers and sedatives..."*

"I bet you're wondering how much I really know about your medical history." Erik whirled around, facing the doctor across from him who had his arms folded across his chest, smiling smugly. "Now if you want to live, you'll have to listen to me."

"You really are evil," Erik snarled.

"Well, if I am evil, then I figure we all were too at one time. But unlike you, I learned to control my tendencies." Erik scowled and Albero held out his hand. "Give me the weapon and return to your room until you get further orders."

Erik held fast to the scalpel. "Forget it," he sneered. "Take it from me and I'll slice you into ribbons."

"I've got the others to think about here, *mi amigo*. Your disease will undo all the good work I've done so far if you don't get it under control. All that matters now is that you get some rest. You're tired and aren't thinking clearly."

Erik turned on his heel and stormed back for his room. The murmuring conversational voices from the others hollowed in his head, replaced by the dull thud pounding in his ears. He shut the door behind him and leaned against the panel, his legs shaking as if he suffered from severe fever while the world spun on an extreme wobble.

Erik shut his eyes and blew a heavy sigh. He wondered about the doctor, who seemingly took delight in administering his warning after he stepped out of line. His words knocked about in Erik's head, repeating the same echo again.

Putting a free hand to his forehead, Erik noticed his skin cold and clammy, slicked with sweat. The doctor thoroughly freaked him out, though he hoped the man was a liar and only told the tale as a means of control.

Erik groaned. "I'm still being controlled," he mewed, sinking to the floor. "Three days... I'm really going to die in three days." Erik rapped his head against the door in anguish, running through possible outcomes in his situation. He finally settled on figuring a plan with a clam clear head to get back at the doctor would be his first priority while using the man to his advantage in accomplishing his goals would be his second.

Taking a deep breath, Erik opened his eyes once the world stopped spinning and rose unsteadily to his feet. He set aside the scalpel on the nightstand and searched the room for his clothing, eventually finding a bin under his bed with several dark blue jumpsuits folded inside.

Taking one that he could fit, Erik pulled into it and moments later the door opened behind him, revealing the nurse.

"Where do you think you're going?" she asked. "You're ordered only bed rest."

"I'm going out drinking," Erik said sourly. "I'm dying soon, so it won't matter much what I do."

"You can't fight in your condition anyway." Erik stiffened when she approached and wrapped an arm about his slender waist, giving a squeeze. "How about this," she cooed. "You be a good boy and I'll take you out for steaks and all the wine you want." Erik gaped at her as his cheeks warmed and she grinned. "I saw the way you were checking me out."

Erik grinned. "I can't help it," he murmured. "You're pretty."

"So lie down and rest."

Erik puffed an annoyed sigh as she let go and he plopped on the edge of the bed. "Doctor Hansen didn't send you up to boss me, did he?" he protested.

"No, I did it on my own."

"At least tell me your name?"

"Tell me yours first." Erik gave a faint smile and the nurse chortled. "I'm Monica."

"Nice to meet you Monica."

"Dinner will be sent up soon."

"I'm not that hungry."

"You need your strength."

Monica swiped the scalpel off the nightstand as she left the room and Erik groaned, falling back on the bed. Placing his uninjured arm behind his head, Erik thought about his remaining time if he failed going against the doctor's orders.

"He knows my weakness and thinks I have some skills useful to his cause," he thought. *"If he's using me for something, I might as well stick around and see where this leads..."*

Finally able to relax, Erik gave in to exhaustion.

NINE

Erik groaned and rubbed at his eyes with his knuckles as he sat up, finding himself in an unfamiliar darkened room. He held his thudding head, tensing when he heard the voices.

You're on borrowed time...

If you don't fight them soon while you still have the strength, everything you've worked so hard for will vanish...

You have to keep fighting to stay in this world...

Erik moaned and clamped his hands over his ears. "Shut up!" he cried.

Stop playing around and show them your true strength!

Remember that you are no longer in control of your life...

Someone else has played god with your mind, your body, your soul...

You're just a soulless machine, a fighting apparatus, a monster, a beast...

"Stop it!" Erik screeched.

The overhead light switched on and Erik hissed in pain, shutting his eyes.

"It's okay," a soft voice said to him. "You're in a safe place."

Erik dropped his hands in his lap and looked up, facing Francisca standing over him wearing a yellow quilted bathrobe. He looked around, realizing he was on her couch in her apartment.

"How'd I get back here?" Erik demanded. "I'm still dressed..."

"You were passed out in the bathroom," Francisca explained. "When you didn't come back after twenty minutes, I asked someone to check on you." She sat next to Erik. "I'm guessing you hit your face pretty hard when you fell. It's nasty looking."

"I'm not hurting too bad, aside from the usual aches and pains," Erik quipped. "So, why no hospital?"

"I was afraid of losing you again," Francisca said softly. Erik's cheeks warmed in response. "I tried to undress you but you were combative again." Francisca shrugged. "It's pretty cold in here anyway."

"I'm sorry," Erik murmured.

"I had someone pull some strings to get you as my replacement at Midco/Sanato," Francisca said instead. "You start tomorrow."

"What about you? You got canned for some reason..."

"I can get another job." Francisca snorted. "Federal's always hurting for new zombies to man their idiot machines."

"But you were terminated..." Erik paled. "This is my fault..."

"Don't worry about it." Francisca smiled and pat Erik's knee. "I did some digging around and heard you have a decent memory."

"Long term's not so hot," Erik grumbled.

"But you can hang on to whatever you read, right?" Erik nodded. "So if you want, you can go over my reports and whatever else you want from my department." Francisca left the couch and headed into the kitchen, preparing the electric percolator.

Erik noticed a stack of folders on the small coffee table and picked up one set, scanning the label marked 'deliverables'. Opening it, he found documentation pertaining to data sheets concerning production of Synthoids.

Erik reached into his coat pockets for his cigarettes and his fingers brushed across the flowered clip-on earring there.

"That's right," he murmured, withdrawing it. "I was supposed to meet her..."

Francisca later returned with a mug of coffee and set it across from Erik. "She told me she'd see you later since you were too sick," she said.

"Oh?" Erik set the earring on the table. "Then how am I supposed to meet her again when I have no idea who she is?"

"Yeah." Francisca smirked. "She said she'll find you. You're not that hard of a guy to miss." She stifled a yawn and gestured toward her room. "I'm off to sleep. If you want more coffee, I left the fixings on the table."

"Sure."

Erik picked up his coffee and sipped it while he flipped through pages of thesis, dissertations, and technical reports concerning Synthoids. Once dawn came, he finished the last of the folders and yawned.

Erik left the couch and headed into the bedroom. He pushed open the door, noticing the space heater humming on the other side and Francisca wrapped in sheeting, snoring softly. Looking longingly at her for several moments, Erik then pulled out of his coat and left the doorway, dropping it on the couch along the way. He then turned out the other lights in the apartment and returned to the bathroom, opening the cabinet. Erik withdrew the pill bottles bearing his name and took the drugs with a handful of water. Leaving the containers on the counter, he splashed water on his face and looked into the mirror, facing his tired reflection.

"Why are you here?" Erik asked.

Why are you expecting an answer?

Erik gasped and turned around, finding no one else in the room. Slapping the nearby switch, the bathroom fell into the dim glow of the nightlight and he left the bath, making his way back for the warm bedroom. Erik peeled out of his remaining clothing and slipped nude in bed, only to freeze when Francisca turned over, draping an arm across his waist.

"Hey," he murmured, squeezing her hand.

"Yeah?" Francisca muttered.

Before Erik could say more, more snores escaped Francisca. Erik blew a hard sigh and stared up at the ceiling, holding Francisca's hand. He later dozed off.

Erik's eyes snapped open when he sensed a presence near him and looked up, facing the nurse Monica standing over him as she placed a manila folder on the nearby nightstand.

"What is it?" Erik asked, sitting up.

"Someone came in looking for you," she replied. "Well, they knew your general description, as we didn't have a name."

"What did they say my name was?"

"They didn't give a name, just this folder to give you."

Erik reached over, taking the folder and noting its heft, he opened it, finding a VitaStat card and National Identity Number card clipped to a Birth Certificate that shared his personal data. "Ferdian Ucal, huh?" Erik murmured as he found a hundred note folded beneath the cards and a thin leather holder holding a white key card with 'Ulvaeus Hostel' stamped on the front. "Anything else?"

"The doctor says you can return home and he wanted me to give you a set of instructions."

"What that might be?"

Monica chortled, waving at Erik while he put the paperwork and cards in the wallet. "Some weird message, something about spirit prevalence or something like that."

Erik shrugged his shoulders. "Right, that is weird." Pocketing the wallet, Erik rose to his feet. "So, let's find my shoes and get some food. We're going to the steakhouse, right?"

"Sure. I'm about to clock out anyway."

"I'll wait for you."

"Come with." Erik followed her out the room and down the corridor toward the nurse's station. "Wait here while I change." Erik nodded and watched Monica enter the rear office. He leaned against the desk, grinning at a senior nurse who scowled at him from his terminal.

"What's with that ugly face?" Erik cooed. "You act like I did something to you."

"You're too much trouble," the nurse snapped. "If you weren't an important member of INTERTEC, we'd long cash out."

"INTERTEC?"

Monica exited the rear office, wearing a short dark green

and yellow patterned shift dress and black peeptoe heels, revealing light green lacquer on her nails. In her hands, she held a large black golf umbrella, a small black clutch purse with a long silver chain and a pair of tan canvas slip-on shoes.

"Catch," Monica called and tossed Erik the shoes. He caught one and the other fumbled to the floor. "Not much of a baller, are you?" she teased.

"Not the right shape," Erik quipped and slipped on the footwear.

"Let's go," Monica said cheerfully.

Erik waved off the nurse, joining her side. "Why are you entertaining me?" he asked while they made their way down the corridor. "Did someone ask you to?"

"What if I just want to?" Monica retorted.

"No one ever gets close to me without a good reason."

"Maybe because I just want to?"

Puffing a sigh when he realized his questions were going unanswered, Erik took the umbrella from her and opened it as she pushed against the glass doors.

Exiting onto the walkway leading to a large parking lot, Erik followed her toward a white and chrome older model stretched sedan with tinted windows and a curved U-shaped antenna on the back.

"What a nice ride," Erik murmured as the driver's side door opened and a pale young man in a dark navy suit and cap stepped out. He nodded at them both and approached the rear doors, opening it for them. "Just for a nurse...?"

"It's the company car," Monica explained. "They drive us wherever we need to go for safety."

"Your umbrella, Sir," the driver murmured.

"Oh, right," Erik responded and handed it to him. The driver held it over the door as he clambered inside, followed by Monica. Erik pushed against the plush cream-colored leather seats once Monica sat across from him. "This is really nice," he marveled. "Is the work really that dangerous?"

"When you have haters trying to kill you over the critical work you do," Monica replied.

"What is it you do, exactly?"

"We help people," she said vaguely.

"Where to?" asked the driver.

"That really nice steakhouse Downtown. I'll call you when we're done."

"I might have a bite to eat there too," the driver said. "The steaks there nearly melt in your mouth."

Monica giggled as he shut the door and returned to the driver's seat.

"I wouldn't know much about that," Erik murmured. "I'm not a meat eater."

"Then why take me up on my offer?" Monica protested.

"I'm having a liquid dinner." Erik grinned. "You said all the wine I could get my hands on, right?"

"Don't tell me you're the type who can only remember where you live when you're drunk."

"You bet."

"I hope you're not a violent drunk."

"I'm not, promise." Erik reached across and pat her knee. "I might get grabby though." Monica's cheeks flushed and Erik guffawed.

At the steakhouse, Monica and Erik took a booth in the restaurant's rear.

"What are you ordering instead?" Monica inquired as Erik looked around.

"I want to hang at the bar and get some vodka in ice," Erik complained.

"Only wine here. What kind of red do you want?"

"Nothing too sweet then."

"I'm getting the largest leanest slab of beef I can get my hands on."

"I'm sorry I'm not enough," Erik quipped and Monica giggled.

"You're just a dirty little jokester," Monica responded.

"Where's a waiter when you need one?"

"Ooh, there's one!" Monica waved her hand and a wiry olive-skinned bald young man approached, wearing orange tinted glasses and a black dress shirt over matching slacks underneath a red apron.

"What'll be?" he chirped as he withdrew a notepad and pencil.

"Your best steak," Monica answered.

"You, Sir?" the waiter responded as he scribbled into his notepad.

"Palmer!" Erik gasped and the young man's eyes widened at the sight of Erik.

"What are you doing here?" Palmer cried, gaping back in shock.

"I could say the same for you," Erik retorted.

"Second hustle," Palmer replied. "You?"

"On a date."

Palmer glanced back at Monica and raised his lenses, giving her a long look. "Damn, she's fine," he murmured.

"Apparently she has a thing for dorks," Erik said and Palmer grinned as he released his glasses.

"Good taste," he murmured and waved his notepad at Erik. "What you want, man?"

"Three bottles of wine to start."

"Don't shit me."

Erik reached into his pocket and withdrew his wallet, taking out the bill. "Straight serious," he declared, slapping it on the table.

"Well!" Palmer smirked. "Does Sir have a preference?" he said smarmily.

"Nothing sweet, thanks."

"Never thought a garbage collector would carry that kind of bank," Palmer jibed and left their table.

Monica raised an eyebrow at Erik. "You know him?" she inquired.

"We've met," Erik admitted. "Now, let's chat." He leaned against the table and held his chin in his hand. "So, what is it you find so fascinating about me?"

"I just find you cute," Monica answered. "Like you said, I have a thing for dorks. Is that a bad thing?"

"Maybe, because not a lot of people do."

"Get used to it."

TEN

Once the food and alcohol came, Erik focused on downing as much red wine he could in succession, while Monica silently dined across from him. Her glass of Shiraz rest next to her untouched.

"You're pretty quiet this evening," Monica noted, gazing at Erik. "How is it you're still upright?"

"Oh, I'm hammered," Erik slurred. "You'd be too with three bottles in you."

"What is it you're trying to forget?"

"It's what I'm trying to remember." Erik staggered to his feet and wavered. "I'll be right back. Order two more for me, please?"

"Would Sir like anything else?" Palmer's voice called as he approached. "Are you enjoying yourselves?"

"Toilets," Erik grumbled.

"To the rear beyond the plants," Palmer directed. "Please, don't piss in them."

Erik chortled and clamped a heavy hand on his shoulder. Palmer stiffened when Erik leaned in to his ear. "Let's have a talk later," he muttered and pushed away, tottering off in the direction Palmer indicated. He threaded himself around the other tables then entered the dimly lit corridor leading to the washrooms.

Nearing the men's rooms, Erik pushed aside the tall potted ferns blocking his view. Before he could reach the handle, the door unexpectedly opened, smacking him in the face.

"Fuck," the patron on the other side yelped when Erik let out a yip in pain, sagging against the wall as he cupped his nose. "Sorry about that."

Erik looked up with bleary eyes, squinting at a lean tanned young man wearing a brightly patterned chartreuse shirt and brown slacks. His dark wavy hair lay slicked back on his head, ending as curls on the nape of his neck.

"I know you from somewhere?" Erik murmured and the young man grinned.

"No, but do you want to?"

"Never mind then."

"Hey," the young man said as Erik pushed past him. He grabbed Erik's arm, whirling Erik around and slammed him into the wall. "Why proposition me then blow me off?"

"I don't blow dudes," Erik said and giggled. "Where'd you get that idea?"

"You're roaring drunk."

"And you're in between me and the toilet. Lay off." Erik shoved him away and pitched forward, collapsing against the door. He immediately turned away, barely missing a punch aimed for his head and the young man jammed his fist into the door frame. "That's what you get," Erik spat, kicking the young man in the back down to the floor who doubled over in agony. "I've had it with you. Leave me alone."

Stepping over the man's downed form, Erik swung open

the door and stumbled into the restroom, making his way drunkenly for a urinal. He leaned an arm against the wall for support as he unzipped his fly and relieved himself, trying to figure why he reacted to the stranger the way he did. The harder he tried to piece together faces with names, the more blanks in his memory produced.

"I'm trashed and nothing comes to mind," Erik muttered. "Nothing, not a damn thing... Maybe I'm not drunk enough..."

Pulling the handle, Erik zipped his fly and stumbled to the sinks, washing his hands under the automatic faucets. Hearing a faint high-pitched tone once the water shut off, he tensed as he sucked in a shallow breath, listening intently. Erik backed away from the sinks, clenching his hands in anticipation as his eyes focused on the door.

When no one else came through, he puffed a resigned sigh and pushed the swinging door open, meeting up with Monica who stood in the corridor.

"Oh," she said, slightly startled. "I was wondering what took so long..."

"Big input," Erik said, ginning. "Lots of output."

Monica laughed and waved him away. "I already paid for the bill and you have two waiting. So you want to finish here?"

"Let's take it with us," Erik declared. "Drop me off at the Hostel."

"Which one?"

"Ulvaeus."

"Sure, I'll call the driver."

Erik returned to the table, collecting the two bottles of wine.

"Hold up," Palmer called and Erik turned around as the young man approached with a small navy case. "Here, somebody said to drop this off somewhere."

"What's that?" Erik inquired. "Nothing illegal, is it?"

"Hell if I know," Palmer grumbled. "Just take the damn thing."

"Stick it in my pocket. I don't want to drop these." Palmer rolled his eyes and dropped the case into Erik's jumpsuit's pocket. "Hey, what's a good way to remember something when you can't remember no matter how hard you try?"

Palmer screwed up his face and broke out laughing. "You serious?" he crowed and laughed harder when Erik glared at him. "It's Sinnesloschen but that shit's controlled as fuck and only if you're in the Defense Forces."

"I really need to remember something," Erik growled. "It's driving me nuts - like it's *right there* and it won't come to me."

"Is that what you wanted to talk to me about?" Palmer asked. "What makes you think I'd know?"

"The place where you dumped me has some people there who apparently know who you are." Palmer paled behind his glasses. "So I'm thinking you're involved in that sort of thing, if you catch my drift."

"What else you want from me?"

"I'm at the Ulvaeus and ask for Ferdian Ucal, okay?"

"Sure."

Erik left Palmer's side, meeting with Monica at the phone booths near the entrance. "I'm ready to party," he announced. "Is our ride here yet?"

"They're sending one now," Monica answered. "Should be

here any minute."

"And there he is," Erik exclaimed when the white limousine pulled up to the curb. He shouldered open the glass door and staggered into the rain as the driver exited.

"Sorry about that," the driver said as he hurried for the rear passenger and opened the door.

Erik ducked in and rest the wine bottles on the floor. He stretched out, lying on his back and Monica joined him on the other seat.

"What are you thinking about?" Monica asked as she pulled shut the door.

"Room's starting to spin," Erik said and hiccupped.

"You're not going to get sick, are you?"

"I can handle myself fine." Erik glanced to Monica who appeared concerned. "What's with that look?"

"I can't worry about you?"

"You can if you want, but then you're wasting your time."

Monica switched sides and pushed Erik sitting upright. He fell over and leaned against her, sensing her tense underneath him.

"You're not going to sleep, are you?" she asked.

"No, I need to keep awake."

"Maybe you want some coffee?"

"Sure, I'll take you up on that."

The limousine pulled onto a large lot before a tall building with many windows. A large white signboard gave the name in blue script near the entrance.

"What a fancy place," Erik said, peering out the window. "I

thought hostels were little run-down places."

"Not all international hostels are like that," Monica admitted. "It's an industrial town and we get a lot of international contracts; we we have to look good."

Erik snorted. "I got a room and everything," he said, taking up the bottles of wine. "Let's have some fun together."

"What kind of fun?" Monica asked.

The driver opened the door and Erik stepped out.

"Dancing," Erik called over his shoulder. "What kind of fun were you thinking?" He staggered up the walkway and a uniformed doorman appeared at the entrance, pushing the glass doors for him. "Thanks," Erik said brightly. "Ask my lady friend for a tip."

The doorman grinned and walked up to Monica.

Entering a large navy carpeted lobby with cream-colored walls, Erik lumbered over to the front desk where a young woman sat before a terminal, placing his bottles nearby. "Hey," he said to the clerk, "would you tell me what room I'm in?"

"I'll need a name," she replied nonchalantly.

"I don't have one."

The clerk snorted. "What are you," she replied dryly, "some secret special agent?"

"I work for INTERTEC, what do you think?" Erik dug through his pockets and withdrew his wallet. "This key card's unmarked," he said, handing it to her. "Find out for me, please?"

The young woman paled as she took the key card and slid it through the reader. The machine bipped and data appeared on her computer screen.

"Your room is seventy-three, in the rear. Take the left

hallway. ”

Erik took his wine bottles as Monica entered behind him. "Take the key," he told her. "I'm in suite seventy-three."

"Want me to go ahead and set up?" Monica asked as the clerk handed her the key card.

"Sure, take these too." Erik shoved the bottles into her arms. "I need to do something."

Monica grabbed the bottles from him and left down the corridor.

"What is it?" the clerk grumbled as Erik leaned against the desk.

"Who made the reservation?" Erik demanded.

"What do you mean, 'who'?" the clerk snapped. "You have the key, so obviously…"

"Some guy? Some girl? How long ago?"

"The room was reserved yesterday morning and paid for two weeks. Any other questions?"

"If some bald guy asks for Ferdian, send him up. If it's anyone else, don't bother."

"Anything else?"

Erik waved her off and stumbled down the carpeted corridor.

ELEVEN

Staggering toward room 73, Erik knocked on the plain door and it opened, revealing a plush suite, with navy carpeting, a large bed with starched sheets to his left, a kitchenette on the other side and a flat screen television to his right before a small table and pair of cushioned chairs.

"You put some coffee on?" Erik asked as he entered the room and plopped on the bed, grabbing the cigarette case and lighter left there near a beige touch-tone phone. "Hand me an ashtray, will you please?"

"I thought we were going dancing," Monica protested as she shut the door.

"Sure, in a bit." Erik lit a cigarette, watching Monica take the ashtray from the table and approach, handing it to him. "Hey, let's get some food."

"Oh, *now* you're starving?" Monica snapped.

"Grab some vodka, please?"

"Can't we just talk?"

"No." The phone on the nightstand suddenly rang and Erik picked up the receiver. "What is it?" he greeted.

"There is someone here for you," said the clerk. "Should I send them up?"

"Go ahead." Erik put the receiver back on the cradle and

looked at Monica who stood over him with her arms folded across her chest. "Do you want to sleep with me?" Erik asked and Monica's eyes widened.

"No, why?" she blustered.

"I don't mind cuddling," Erik insisted. "I get lonely too."

"Wait, what?"

"Just sleep. What did you think I was talking about?" He laughed when Monica's face burned red. "Please get some vodka. I'm serious. I think I'll remember when I have the right booze in my system."

Monica blew an annoyed sigh. "Fine," she grumbled.

"Get the big one. I'm making some mixers."

"I'll see you in a bit."

"Leave the door open. I had some stuff sent up."

Monica grabbed her purse and stormed out the room. Erik laid back in bed, smoking in silence and tapped his ashes into the glass tray he held against his chest.

"Hey," Palmer's voice called moments later. "It's cracked open."

"Come in," Erik called. Palmer entered the room and crossed the floor. He dropped a paper sack near Erik's head and Erik glanced up at the young man frowning at him. "What's your issue?"

"Man, my issue's gettin' mixed up with you," Palmer snapped. "You were supposed to be some homeless drunk."

"Maybe I am."

"Naw, that chick said you're a fuckin' INTERTEC agent. I din't do shit to have your boys investigating me!"

"You're not being investigated," Erik said calmly and sat

up. "You get the Sinnesloschen for me?"

"Synthetic, man. Where the hell you think I'm gonna find the real deal?" Palmer scoffed. "If I go asking, it'll flag me. That shit's a Schedule One."

"You can go now."

"Pay me for my time," Palmer growled. "I'll forget it then."

"I just wasted my last hundred at the steakhouse. You'll have to get it off Monica." Erik calmly put out his stub into the ashtray and put it aside on the nightstand. He raised an eyebrow at Palmer who continued standing there, steaming. "Why aren't you gone yet?"

"I'm waiting to get paid," Palmer snarled.

"Wanna party with me?" Erik grinned. "I got that wine and soon have some more booze sent up."

"I don't do that shit. I want money."

"You might as well wait. I don't get paid until the job's done."

Erik reached over and shook out the brown bag on the bed, revealing two small amber bottles. He took up one and unscrewed the cap, pouring pale green powder into his palm.

"What job that supposed to be?" Palmer demanded.

"Hence me taking this to remember," Erik answered. He sniffed the powder into his palm, then pinched his nostril, snorting more from the bottle. Erik's skin immediately flushed and he broke out sweating. Taking the rest into the other nostril, all sound suddenly dropped into a low wash of static while his heart pound hard and fast in his chest. A prickly burning sensation raced across his skin, traveling from fingers through his arms and Erik clenched his hands.

100

"Hey, man…" Palmer started.

"What a rush," Erik said, standing. "You don't know how alive I feel right now." He giggled as Palmer appeared worried when he dropped the bottle aside on the bed. "You said you wanted money from me, right?" Erik dug through his pockets and withdrew the case. "This thing here, what's it worth to you?" Opening the case, Erik revealed a translucent violet pen with blue nib. "Check this out." Taking the pen, a flash of white light surrounded his hand and a blue steel saber appeared in its place with a violet handle. Erik turned the blade with flourish and pointed the edge toward Palmer who quaked slightly. "Want to check out my moves? I'm a pretty decent fencer, I have you know."

"Shit!" Palmer cried. "I don't wanna die, man. I din't mean it."

"Oh no, you don't!" Erik growled when Palmer took off for the door. Erik gave chase and grabbed his sleeve before he met the exit, hurling him back into the room. Palmer let out a stunned cry as he crashed into the table and tumbled over onto the floor. Erik threw the door shut and turned around, keeping his blade trained on Palmer.

"I'm sorry," Palmer yelped as he crawled away. "Just let me go, man. I din't see shit and I don't know shit, all right?"

"You're going to stay and play with me," Erik said, grinning. "You're going to watch me dance." He dashed forward with a lunge and Palmer scrambled to his feet, leaning out of his furious attacks.

"Shit, you're crazy!" Palmer screamed as Erik continued his frontal assault, swiping and stabbing at him, though missing his target entirely. Erik kicked Palmer in the guts and shoved him into the wall, then jammed the blade between his legs with an underhanded throw, leaving the blade nearly cutting into his crotch.

"If you're not careful," Erik teased, "you just might lose something important."

A sudden pounding erupted on the door as Erik grabbed Palmer by his face. "Don't look at me like that," Erik cooed and took Palmer's glasses. Placing them on, he grinned and pinched the other man's cheeks. "Don't I look good in them?"

"Answer the door, man," Palmer pleaded when the hard knocks continued.

"Fine," Erik grumbled and yanked the sword embedded in the partition. Leaving the frightened young man behind, Erik sauntered over to the door and opened it, smiling. "What's up?" he greeted.

A shattering blow plowed into his side, knocking Erik off his feet. He dropped to his knees and immediately vomited on the floor. Another combination of punches to his head and face jarred his head around, sending his world reeling.

Erik received a hard kick into his chest that forced him rearward onto the floor. He hit the carpet and looked up through his haze at a pair of men in all black - with caps, turtlenecks, jeans and dark glasses. The only difference between the two were that one was pale and the other dark-skinned.

Erik booted the pale aggressor in the crotch and yowled when his foot smashed into solid metal. He slashed at the other with his blade, driving him away then scrambled to his feet as he backed into the nearby table, holding up his sword in guard.

"You got the drop on me," Erik heaved, "I'll give you that..."

The pale fighter reached into his jacket and flicked his wrist, unleashing a telescoping steel baton. He dove after Erik with the baton held high and Erik immediately blocked, only to gain another powerful blow into his side from the darker fighter. Erik countered the baton wielder's swift swings, grunting as he absorbed the fast furious punches from the other. Before Erik could swing again, the two redoubled their efforts, with the pale fighter banging his weapon across Erik's knees while the darker fighter closed in with hard elbow smash into the back of his head once he faltered, bringing him down.

"You're not gonna kill him, are you?" Palmer called as the darker fighter kicked aside Erik's sword from his limp hand.

"Pick him up," the pale fighter snapped over Erik's semiconscious form.

Palmer approached and supported Erik under his armpits, dragging him toward the bed. He hurled him onto the mattress and Erik tried to get up, only to gain a swift blow into the stomach, sending him crashing on his side in a daze.

"What are you doing with him?" Palmer demanded.

"What do you think we should do?" the pale fighter asked. "We're just paid to beat him up."

"I don't think he gets the message, *hombre*," said the darker fighter. "We're supposed to give him *una paliza* he'd never forget."

"What do you think?" the pale fighter directed at Palmer. "I don't think this shithead's getting it."

"What are you gonna do," Palmer asked quietly, "torture

the poor bastard?"

"Good idea!" The pale fighter snapped at Palmer. "Take his clothes off. Chayo, gimmie the cuffs. Let's string his ass up in the bathroom."

Erik grunted when pulled off the bed and dragged into the nearby bathroom by his ankles. Thrown down onto the tiled floor, Palmer kicked Erik onto his back and crouched at his side, unzipping the jumpsuit.

The dark-skinned fighter named Chayo entered and gabbed Erik's hair, pulling him upright as Palmer undressed him, taking his arms out the sleeves. Chayo then withdrew a pair of silver handcuffs from his pocket and took a firm hold of Erik's wrist, latching one brace around it.

Palmer hoisted Erik upright and Chayo raised Erik's arm, throwing the cuff over the brass shower curtain bar. He grabbed Erik's free wrist and clamped the remaining brace on it, leaving him hanging listlessly with his arms above his head.

The pale fighter entered the bathroom, holding a small red container. "Strip him," he ordered. "Gag him too."

Palmer yanked the jumpsuit down off Erik's waist, pooling the fabric around his ankles. Chayo grabbed a nearby towel off the rack, bunching it into a ball and shoved the cloth into Erik's mouth.

"Look at you," the young man snarled and kicked at Erik's side. Erik grunted and looked up from his hazy stupor, meeting his gaze. "You piece of shit - I'm gonna have a good time torturing you slowly." He set aside the red container on the sink counter and unbuckled his belt, sliding it out from the loops of his jeans. Looping the leather, he ran the cool band down Erik's back, making him shudder. "You're gonna like what I'm about to do to you, Punk," the man snarled. "You're gonna feel my hate on every part of you."

The young man drew back and slammed the belt across Erik's back with a swift crack, cutting into his skin. Erik grunted when struck repeatedly, breathing heavily through the pain as the man slashed into his back.

"*Eso no es suficiente,*" Chayo murmured from his place at the door when his partner grew steadily enraged by Erik's lack of reaction.

The pale fighter growled, shaking and pointed his bloodied belt at Palmer. "Look at that stupid fuck!" he screeched. "That son of a bitch hadn't made a goddamn peep! Not a motherfucking peep!"

"Obviously he's tough," Palmer said quietly from his place on the toilet seat. "Or he could just be high from the Emerald Dust... Can't feel shit on it, you know."

"Oh, you knew we were coming, huh?" the pale fighter sneered and wrapped the slack end of the belt around his hand, letting the buckle dangle. "What about this?" He hurled the belt forward with renewed strength and Erik jerked when the metal cut deep into his skin. "You like that, you sick fuck? Huh?" Erik violently shook his head as the buckle hit at random places on his back, slamming his kidneys and bruising his spine.

Erik sweat profusely, nauseated and blinded by the severe agony radiating off his back. He jolted and screamed when slapped with the buckle across his penis. His eyes snapped open and the young man grabbed his face, peering into his unfocused eyes.

"You're a sick, sick, fuck, you know that?" the man sneered. Erik whimpered, looking back at his muted reflection from the smoky lenses. "I can't believe how turned on you are by this. You like it when I beat you, huh?" Erik shook his head and the young man grinned. "You're right, it could be just an aftereffect of the Emerald Dust too..." Erik cringed when the young man grabbed his erect member and gave a firm squeeze. "Are you going to get off for me?" Erik shook his head again. "Show me how much you like it and I'll let you go." Erik shook his head once more. "I warned you, Punk."

The young man yanked down with a firm pull, forcing a loud pop and Erik seized in pain, screaming. His torturer laughed cruelly and shoved Erik aside, then picked up the small red bottle off the sink.

"You have enough yet?" he roared and slipped his belt over his shoulder, then unscrewed the cap. "You two, get back," he warned.

Palmer hurried away from the toilet seat and Chayo backed out the door. His partner took several paces away and hurled the liquid on Erik's back, splashing his skin that immediately puckered and burned in response.

Erik jerked as the chemical seared through his open wounds, charring his skin at the edges. He thrashed wildly when struck across his burning skin with the belt buckle, sending another flash of intense agony through him.

After the third strike, Erik sagged limply as his eyes rolled to the back of his head, succumbing to extreme pain no drug could ever dull.

TWELVE

Erik sat up with a start as a digital ring pierced the air. Falling back, he shut his eyes and exhaled a long breath as he gathered his bearings, trying to focus on the moment. Concentrating on where he was, the phone continued ringing and Erik reached over, picking up the receiver. He felt around, pushing a button with his thumb. Killing the sound, he then put the device to his ear.

"Yeah?" he muttered.

"Hey!" a female voice chirped. "What are you doing over there?"

"Sleep," Erik grumbled, "what else?"

The woman over the line giggled. "Ooh, naughty."

"What do you want?"

"I got you assigned over at Kanbal Industries. They need a new body to warm the seat in data processing."

"Sure. What time?"

"Today, Mister. Get up!"

"What happened to Midco/Sanato?"

"Don't worry about it." The line cut off and Erik glanced over at the clock, squinting at the digital numbers.

"Eight-thirty?" he muttered and looked at the cordless he held buzzing off the hook. Erik turned it off and set it back in the base, then sat up, rubbing his face.

Looking around the room, he noticed a navy suit with light blue dress shirt left for him on the bed. Erik picked it up and shuffled out the room.

"Morning," Erik muttered to Francisca dressed in jeans and sweatshirt sitting on the couch upon passing. She glanced up from her newspaper, looking at Erik.

"What's up?" Francisca asked.

"Coffee. Cigarettes. Tell you in a minute."

Erik drifted into the bathroom, hanging his suit on the back of the door. He struggled to figure out where he was while he showered, trying to piece together his memory, only to draw a blank. Erik looked at the gold band he wore and frowned, unsure if he was really married to Francisca.

Erik later taped his injuries and dressed then returned to the kitchen, grabbing for the coffee left for him cooling on the table. He plopped into the chair and sipped his hot beverage, then moaned in distress.

"What's the matter?" Francisca asked.

"I'm not sure anymore." Erik looked up at Francisca who entered the kitchen and stood at the doorway. "You sure we're not married?"

"Does it bother you that we're not?"

"A little."

"So if I say we were, would that make you feel better?"

"Maybe."

"Just so you know, I wear the pants around here."

"Yes, Ma'am," Erik replied and grinned when Francisca tossed him his pack of cigarettes and book of matches, landing them on the table.

"Where are you going today?"

"Got assigned to Kanbal Industries. I'm jockeying a desk again."

"That seems easy."

Erik snorted. "It's not." He withdrew a cigarette and lit one, blowing smoke over his head. "There's always some problem and I get sent to fix it."

"You sound like you regret it somehow."

Erik gave Francisca a wry smile. "Where are you going later?"

"Got my own shit to do. You know, laundry, get that stove fixed, stuff." She waved at Erik. "That's after I make sure you get to work! Hurry up."

"When I'm done with my coffee."

"Shoes are at the door."

"Thanks."

Erik frowned when Francisca pulled into a large lot full of cars. Ahead loomed a tall building with many windows, and a wide sign on the side with a beaker that had a stylized 'κ' in the center.

"This is the processing department," Francisca announced. "Please don't screw this up for me."

"I promise to do a good job," Erik replied.

"Call me when you're ready to go home."

"I don't have your number!"

"I put it in your phone."

"That's right."

Erik stepped out the truck and waved at Francisca before walking across the lot. Approaching the steps, he paused when he saw a tanned woman with long red hair exit the building, wearing a dark overcoat and sunglasses. She smiled at Erik and held open the door for him as he ascended the staircase.

"Thanks," Erik murmured.

"No problem," the woman said as he stepped past her. Erik felt her press against him and turned sharply as his cheeks burned.

The woman grinned and waved at Erik then left down the staircase. He shook his head and entered the lower level. The room was brightly lit, with florescent strips along the plain beige walls. Dotted around the lobby were large framed photographs of chemicals in beakers, tubes and dishes.

Erik stepped across the pale yellow waxed tiled floors, approaching a walnut desk in the room's center. A young blonde woman entered from the hall behind the desk in a pale reddish-brown suit and approached, smiling brightly, though she appeared slightly nervous.

"Good morning," Erik replied.

"Good morning," said the service operator. "Do you need anything?"

"I just got assigned here," Erik said. He dug through his pockets and frowned when he withdrew a wallet. Opening it, he found an employee identification card with the name 'F. Maxwell Hauser' listed with his facial picture and a clip holding two fifty-note bills. "They called me this morning and told me to come down right away." Erik withdrew the card and handed it to the woman.

"May I ask you something?" said the operator as she set his card aside and typed away at her laptop.

"Sure," Erik answered, "anything."

"Did you get into a fight?"

Erik smiled and leaned against the counter. "Yeah," he drawled, "my wife doesn't like it when I look at other cute ladies."

The woman paled and the computer chirped. "I'll have your packet sent up once it's finished printing," she said. "Also, the employee cards have been updated. You seem to have an old one."

"That's fine by me." Erik tapped the counter. "Please direct me to where I'm supposed to be."

"Two-eleven. Go down this hall on the right and take the second elevator."

"Thanks."

The operator handed Erik his identification card and he left the desk, heading to where she indicated.

Stepping off on the second floor, Erik entered a cube farm, where he spotted many workers at their desks behind tan cubicles. He noticed offices along the walls with number plates and followed them until he reached one room labeled eleven.

Trying the handle, Erik opened the door and gasped when he spotted a tall pale woman with long thick curly red hair sitting at a terminal, wearing a tight blue blouse and matching skirt. At the edge of her desk was a name plate labeled 'Clairese Avers'.

"Shit," Erik yelped and the woman looked up, startled.

"Ferdian?" Clairese yelped, stunned. Erik backed away and Clairese rose from her seat. "Wait, where are you going?"

Erik took off for the exit, pushing open the door leading to the stairwell. He reached the staircase and vomited, coughing and gasping for breath as he held one hand against the wall.

The door opened behind him moments later.

"What's the matter?" Clairese called.

"I'm sorry," Erik murmured.

"I'll call Maintenance. Come on."

"Give me a minute."

Erik sucked in a shallow breath as he recalled that Clairese was a Chemical Technician, working on secret government level contracts. He then touched his sore face, remembering his fight over components involving a project.

"Why are you here?" Clairese called, scattering his thoughts.

"I got assigned," Erik answered.

"I'm in trouble, aren't I?"

"Why would you be?" Erik turned around and gave a faint smile. "Show me around, will you?"

Clairese frowned. "You need to stop fighting so much," she reprimanded.

"Hey, I can't help it when they start stuff with me." Erik shrugged. "They should learn to take as much as they dish."

"Maybe you like it a little rough?"

Erik chortled and walked with Clairese back to the offices.

Clairese showed Erik where the break rooms were and the restrooms, then where his assigned terminal was located. Erik found his cubicle had an employee packet across the small desk, a large black binder full of paper with printed code, and his new employee identification tag set near it.

"Is that your full name?" Clairese asked as Erik came out of his coat and draped it on the back of his chair. "I thought it was Ferdian Smith."

Erik picked up the employee tag and clipped it on his shirt. "It's whatever they give me," he answered. Clairese sucked in a shallow breath and Erik glanced back at her, smiling gently. "Hey," he murmured and pet her shoulder. "You're okay. I just investigate things and fix problems, that's all."

"That doesn't assure me much," Clairese muttered and pushed away his hand. "All right Mister, your job is to input your snippet of code and run tests to make sure it's not buggy."

"That's it?"

Clairese nodded. "That's it. What did you expect in computational chemistry?"

"Wait, what?"

Clairese waved off Erik and left his side. Erik grunted and pulled out his seat, plopping into it. He leaned over, turning on the computer and the monitor flickered to life as the machine went through its boot sequence. Erik grabbed the employee manual and paged through the data.

After reading company policy and his duties, he set it aside and logged into the database with his given key written in his manual. Moments later, he heard a ping and a message appeared on the side of the screen.

O_Alameda: Hey, new guy. Don't tell me you're sleeping with the boss.

Erik snorted and typed a message in return.

FM_Hauser: Are you jealous?

Erik then stiffened when he realized the implications. He turned around in his cubicle, facing the blank beige wall cornering his side of the farm.

"*Damn it,*" Erik thought as he turned back around and typed to the employee on the other side.

FM_Hauser: Look, I didn't pull any strings to get here. We happen to be good friends.

Moments later, several pings sounded and Erik groaned at the messages across the screen.

O_Alameda: Sure and I'm the President.

Z_Zachary: I'd totally tap that.

A_Montergras: Stop giving him shit. Let's meet up for lunch.

C_Avers: Back to work boys. Or I might have to punish you all with punch cards. =^_^=

The messages dimmed and Erik pushed away from the keyboard. Moments later, another message, this time in a private window, appeared on the screen.

Emote_Cheer: Did you fix it yet?

Erik raised an eyebrow, confused. "*What are they looking for?*" he wondered and made his reply.

FM_Hauser: I didn't. How soon you need it?

When he received no other answer, Erik glimpsed at the overhead clock, noting the time.

"Back to work," he muttered and closed the messenger windows, then flipped open his binder, finding a large printout consisting of hexadecimal code. He grunted and searched his program menu, finding the debugging module then began his task of inputting lines.

THIRTEEN

Once noon struck, Erik heard other coworkers leaving their desks and making their way to the elevator.

"Hey, Hauser," a voice called to him.

Erik turned in his seat, facing a short thin young man with shaggy light brown hair and light green eyes. The young man wore a tan blazer over a white t-shirt and dark brown jeans. He noticed the young man's employee identification tag read 'Orpheus Alameda' clipped to the lapel.

"Is it your turn to mess with the new blood today?" Erik asked as he stood and grabbed his coat.

"Sure, I'm part of the welcoming committee," Orpheus jibed. "We always treat the new guy out to lunch."

"Don't let this pretty face fool you," Erik cracked. "I can get dangerous."

Erik walked with Orpheus toward the break room where he spotted a tall athletic young man with short wavy blond hair in a dark gray suit leaning against the counter, holding a mug of coffee. Erik noticed the man wore darkly tinted glasses as he approached.

"Hi," Erik said brightly and glanced at his nametag, reading 'Antonius Montergras'. "Nice to meet you." He held out a hand. "If you're going to poison me now, let's get that out the way."

Antonius frowned and dropped his mug of coffee, stunned. The mug shattered, splattering coffee on the floor. "Son of a bitch!" he cried and backed away. "The fuck!"

"What?" Erik murmured and lowered his hand. "Do I really look that bad?"

"Naw, man," Antonius answered. He grabbed Erik's tag and peered closely at it, then back at Erik. "Maxwell Hauser, right?"

"That's what it says."

"Shit..." Antonius let go and took another step rearwards. "I need a fucking smoke."

Erik grinned and withdrew his pack of cigarettes from his coat pocket. "Have one of mine," he offered.

"Let's get going anyway," Orpheus announced. "There's this nice sandwich shop I wanna stop at before it gets crowded."

"What about the mess?"

"I'll bug Maintenance."

"Lazy bums," Erik teased and Orpheus chortled.

Erik followed the two out and bumped into another young man with tanned skin, indigo eyes and curly red hair with bleached tips. Erik noticed the young man wore chinos and a loose-fitting green dress shirt with an open collar, revealing a silver chain necklace holding a single bullet. The young man grinned at Erik and Erik gave a nervous smile as he walked past, hurrying to keep up with Orpheus's strides toward the elevators.

"Alameda," Clariese's voice called.

"Shit," Orpheus grumbled.

"What you do now?" Antonius mocked gently.

"I know you're not out yet." Clairese stepped out her office and waved at Orpheus to come over. "We need to talk about the database."

"I already patched that security breach," Orpheus protested as he approached. "Tony tracked it from the library down the street." He held out his hands. "Look, I can only do so much with a Level Two Clearance. If SID's breathing down your neck, there isn't much I can do."

"I'm sure you can do something with that nice big brain of yours," Clairese cooed and draped her arms around Orpheus's shoulders. "Because of that incident, they're watching me very close and I can't afford to lose this job." Orpheus appeared uncomfortable as Clairese leaned forward. "Please try a little bit harder for me? There's a pay rise in it if you can make it disappear."

"Sure, whatever."

"Thanks so much!"

Clairese let Orpheus go and Erik smirked as she glanced up at him, smiling brightly. Orpheus pulled out of his blazer, annoyed and stalked toward the elevators.

"Someone seems to like you," Erik remarked.

"Can it," Orpheus growled, punching the button.

The elevator doors opened and Erik, Orpheus and Antonius boarded.

"I'm thinking of the cheese steak," Antonius announced. "Wanna split with me, Alameda?"

"Sure," Orpheus muttered as he struck the lower level signal.

"I'm getting all veggies," Erik said.

"You ain't gotta be cheap, Hauser," Antonius protested. "We're chipping in."

"I'm not much of a meat eater."

"Damn, no wonder you're skinny!"

Erik snorted and withdrew a cigarette, putting one to his lips. He handed the pack to Antonius who took one. Later the elevators opened, revealing a parking garage. Cold air blew in around them and Erik withdrew a matchbook, expertly lighting his cigarette as he stepped off.

"No smoking in my ride," Orpheus grumbled as Erik shook out the match and flicked it away.

"I'm sure you can wait a bit," Erik retorted.

Orpheus rolled his eyes and Erik followed him toward a large sport utility vehicle.

"Hey," Antonius murmured as he lit his cigarette with a lighter.

"Yeah?"

"You know somebody named Erik?"

Erik gave a wide smile. "What about him?" he innocently asked.

Antonius shook his head. "Never mind... It's just you look a lot like this dude."

Erik chortled. "Hey, I just got that look, you know?"

Antonius nodded. "I guess so."

Orpheus pulled into a lot of a sandwich shop and everyone exited his vehicle.

"You know," Erik piped as they entered the shop, "I've never seen anything like that."

"What do you mean?" Antonius asked.

"We're programming a system for solving chemical problems, right?"

Antonius nodded. "It's easier than wasting time and resources in a lab when shit might blow in your face."

"Did you get into some trouble with some illegal programs, Alameda?" Erik asked as they stood in line behind other customers.

"The boss had SID on her ass last week after someone broke into the database," Orpheus explained. "They were looking for something, but I'm not sure what. My only concern was patching the hole, not seeing where it led."

"What if that hacker tries it again?" Erik wondered aloud. "What is it in the database they could possibly want?"

"We develop for Gen-Tech. If they lose their contract with AMASTCOMS, then we'll get the axe down on us."

"I can't afford to lose this job," Antonius complained. "They got really good health coverage and I need every penny I pay into it."

"Are you quite sick?" Erik inquired.

"I need to pay for another round of eye surgery," Antonius murmured. "Complications from albinism."

"Two-tone Tony," Erik murmured.

"Yeah," Antonius replied and chortled. "It's like I'm this black guy stuck in a white guy's body and with devil eyes to boot! How's that for insanity?" Erik laughed and Antonius frowned. Suddenly Erik gained a fist across his chin, throwing him rearwards.

119

"Damn!" Erik yowled and staggered backwards, grasping his face. "What was that for?"

"You bastard!" Antonius thundered. "You–!" He stormed out the shop and Erik looked helplessly to Orpheus who approached the sandwich stylist, giving his order.

Erik grunted and made his way outside, watching Antonius pacing and smoking. "What's that all about?" Erik demanded.

"Get away from me, man," Antonius spat. "You're bad news."

"You act like I did something to you."

"The fuck you mean?" Antonius shouted. "It's your fault–!"

"Hey," Orpheus said as exited outdoors with a bag of food. "Let's hit up the park and enjoy lunch."

"I can't," Antonius complained. "I gotta go."

"Go where?" Orpheus snapped. "Someone's gotta get that bitch off my back. I can't do this myself you know!"

"I'll help," Erik offered.

"I don't trust that son of a bitch," Antonius growled. "He's a fucking–!"

"I don't care what he does outside the office," Orpheus cut in. "I just want to go home and sleep for a change."

"Whatever." Antonius pointed at Erik. "You - you stay the fuck away from me, got it?"

Erik shrugged. "Whatever floats for you," he said softly. "If it makes you feel any better, I won't even talk to you."

"Let's go," Orpheus directed.

Antonius took another drag from his cigarette then flicked the smoldering butt aside. Erik returned to the SUV with Antonius bringing the rear, tense and highly upset.

Returning to the offices, Erik frowned when he saw the terminals on the cube farm offline.

"The hell is this shit?" Orpheus growled.

"I'll figure it out," Erik replied and Orpheus handed him his sandwich. "You enjoy lunch or whatever."

"If you get me out of this, I owe you one."

"No problem."

Erik headed for the break room and opened the door, spotting the young man with frosted curly hair sitting at a table. He played a game on his phone, filling the air with tinny 8-bit music.

"Hey," Erik called as he sat across from him.

"Hauser, is it?" the young man said.

"Yeah." Erik unwrapped his sandwich and bit into it.

"Been doing this long?"

Erik chewed thoughtfully before swallowing. "I was in Data Processing," he murmured.

"Pay's no better than Clerk Four."

"Really now?" Erik looked to the young man who continued playing on his phone. "Where's your ID?"

"At my desk."

"Why don't you wear it?"

"They know me."

Erik blew a short sigh. "The system seems to be down, you know," he said instead.

"It is."

Erik grunted. "Don't you guys have an IT department to fix it?"

The young man smirked. "We *are* the IT department." He

glanced at Erik. "Where'd you think you was?"

Erik shrugged. "Then where's everyone else?" he questioned.

"Bailed." The coworker returned to his phone.

"What are they, junior programmers?"

"Yeah. The only ones who can fix it are the best heads left around."

Erik scoffed. "I doubt I can do anything complex."

"You're a smart guy, Ferdian." Erik gulped hard and set down his sandwich. The young man looked up, grinning maliciously. "Show me your skills."

"What makes you think I can do anything?" Erik murmured and looked down at the worn table.

The young man kicked the chair Erik sat in and Erik stiffened. "If you don't, I'll reveal who you really are, and you don't want that, do you?"

"*Damn it,*" Erik thought, narrowing his eyes at the young man who continued to smile darkly in return. "*Two people who seem to already know me and not for anything good either!*"

"So what say you, Ferdian? Are you up to the task?"

"I'll try my best."

"Good. Get to it."

Erik grunted and pushed away from the table. "Why are you giving me grief?" he spat.

"Because I very well can."

Erik left the table and the young man grabbed his sandwich, biting into it. He followed Erik into the office and stood behind him as he sat at his terminal.

"Aren't they connected to the network?" Erik asked as he rebooted the machine to recovery mode.

"No, the management system is kept offline for security."

"So what's with the break-ins then?" Once the system loaded, Erik rooted around the file system, searching for the last disk image backup.

"They're looking for a specific database."

"Could it be on this inaccessible drive?" Erik asked once a login screen appeared.

"Let's see how deep it is." The young man leaned over Erik's shoulder and typed in several keywords, only to get denied access.

Unexpectedly a ping resonated in the air and a message appeared on the side of the screen.

"Hey," Erik murmured, "he's back again."

"What's that?"

"He messaged me earlier wanting to fix something. He's still waiting for this fix."

"Deal with it."

Erik typed back a short missive.

FM_Hauser: I'm still working on it.

Another ping followed with an immediate response.

Emote_Cheer: The data's hidden in the budget. The numbers are fixed.

Erik clenched his teeth, recalling the purchase orders as he wrote back.

FM_Hauser: Irregular data's already been found. Destruction's impossible from the cloud.

After a moment of silence, another message appeared.

Emote_Cheer: No protection software's ever impenetrable.

The screen turned dark, then abruptly began flickering rapidly. Erik stiffened when he heard grinding coming off the hard drive.

"The hell's going on?" he muttered. The young man chortled behind him and Erik turned in his seat, glaring at him. "What's funny?"

"You'll see," the young man said gaily and took the final bite off the sandwich.

Erik pushed away from the desk and stood, pacing while he waited for the flickering and grinding to end. He observed the other terminals, noting they also had the same condition and mimicked the same noises.

"This can't be good," Erik mused and put his hands in his pockets. Cold sweat broke out over his forehead and neck while he continued pacing anxiously.

After twenty minutes, a loud beep pierced the air. Then again and again as the computer screens came to life with a blue tint. Erik looked to one computer and gasped when he saw it displayed a message asking for an operating system.

"The hell!" Erik screeched. He jammed at the keyboard, only to get another bip. Erik approached another terminal, finding the same screen. "They've all been wiped!"

At once, the telephone in Clairese's office began ringing. Erik whirled around, facing the young man who leaned against his desk with arms folded across his chest.

"Who the hell are you?" Erik demanded and the young man grinned.

"I'm the one who's got your back, Ferdian," he answered cryptically.

"I want a damn name!" Erik shrilled. "You set me up!"

"You can call me Z."

Erik raised an eyebrow. "Like Zeya?" he said warily.

The young man snorted. "No, Zachary, you dummy." He nodded toward Erik. "I'll also accept Mister Zachary, Lord Zachary, or Master Zachary... Your choice."

"When Hell freezes over!"

Zachary laughed and peeled away from the desk. "Fine then. See you later."

"Do you even work here?" Erik demanded as Zachary headed for the elevators.

"Do you?" Erik rushed over, grabbing Zachary's sleeve and the young man yanked out of Erik's grip then pushed him effortlessly against the wall. "Don't you trust me?" Zachary asked as he leaned in.

"Not one iota," Erik snarled.

"Don't think you can handle all this yourself." Zachary tapped Erik's chest with his phone. "You have friends." He let go and the elevators opened, revealing Orpheus.

"I decided to come help," Orpheus announced as he entered the room and pulled into his blazer. "I couldn't enjoy lunch worrying about it."

"Forget it," Erik moaned. "It's destroyed."

"What?" Orpheus yelped.

"Erased," Erik said helplessly. "Wiped out."

Zachary waved at Erik and got on the elevators before the doors hushed close. Erik grunted when Orpheus kicked him in the shin, forcing him staggered against the wall.

"You're going to get us fired!" Orpheus screamed.

"I wasn't trying to," Erik yelped. "Someone hacked in from the outside."

"How is it possible? We're on a closed system!"

"But that security breach…"

"That was regarding the database, not the damn simulator!"

"Don't you have backups?"

"Those binders are just a portion. Each week they get destroyed!"

Erik yowled when kicked again. "Cool it!" He pleaded. "Look, there's got to be a master program floating around somewhere. Who sends up the binders for us to test on anyway?"

"You'll have to ask the boss. That's her thing."

Erik left the elevators and tried the door, peering inside. He found Clairese gone, her computer running and her desk phone still ringing. Erik approached the desk and tapped at the keyboard, finding the system unaltered and a message box open on the screen.

Emote_Cheer: I'm still waiting.

Erik clenched his teeth as he wrote back.

C_Avers: Why did you do this?

When he had no response, Erik picked up the receiver, hearing shouting on the other end, followed by heavy static.

"What the hell is wrong with you?" a male voice thundered. "We got word from Cybercom the mainframes are destroyed!"

"You sure you have the right number?" Erik replied.

"Who is this?"

"It can't be my problem. On my end, the simulator's not connected to an outside network."

"I–!" The static worsened and Erik heard the caller growling expletives. "I don't believe it." The line cut off with a slam and Erik placed the receiver back in the cradle.

"What is it?" Orpheus asked as Erik exited the office.

"We have to wait until the higher-ups come up with something," Erik answered.

"What are your plans?"

Erik pulled out his phone from his pocket and turned it on. Opening his contacts list, he found Francisca's number. "I'm calling a friend who might be able to help." Pushing the button, he waited as the phone buzzed, waiting for her to pick up.

"Hello?" Francisca greeted moments later.

"Hey there," Erik chirped. "You know anything about data recovery?"

"Sure," Francisca answered. "It's a pain in the ass, but I can do it."

"How many we got here?" Erik directed to Orpheus.

"Er, about thirty?" Orpheus answered, slightly intrigued.

"Thirty drives?" Francisca squawked. "How big are they?"

"Size?" Erik inquired.

"Two teras," Orpheus said and frowned. "Where are you going with this?"

"Two T's each," Erik said into the line. "How soon can you get that done?"

"Shit!" Francisca growled. "How soon you need them?"

"What's today?"

"Today's Monday," Orpheus filled in. "We gotta get the portion filled in before Thursday and it has to work by Friday - then the binders are destroyed."

"You got until Thursday," Erik said cheerfully. "Can you handle that?"

"I will fucking murder you!" Francisca screamed. "I swear, your scrawny ass will be in the creek in pieces!"

"I love you too." Erik cut off the line and turned to Orpheus. "Hey, help me dismantle these things if I'm going to save your hide."

"Shit," Orpheus grumbled.

"We're knee-deep in it."

"I got the keys. Start shutting the damn things down."

"On it."

Erik approached one terminal, keying in its shutdown sequence, then went to another while Orpheus unlocked the cables.

FOURTEEN

Erik stacked the removed hard drives into a small box that formerly held reams of copy paper.

"Was this the biggest one you could find?" Erik complained. "I only got twenty-two to fit!"

"It's the best I could find! " Orpheus protested. "I'll take them down and you grab the rest."

"Don't you have another box?"

"No!"

"Damn it."

Orpheus closed the box and hurried for the elevators while Erik searched the offices for something else to use. Hearing a ping off Clairese's computer, Erik entered her office, finding several messages across the screen.

Emote_Cheer: Don't ask such silly questions. You already know.

Emote_Cheer: I warned you what would happen.

Emote_Cheer: If you thought SID is bad, then FSS is worse.

Emote_Cheer: If you want me to save you, just tell me. But you'll have to follow my instructions exactly.

Erik's hand hovered over the keyboard, contemplating a response.

"*Clairese is in some kind of trouble,*" he mused. "*Something bad enough to involve Federal Special Services...*" Erik dropped his hand to his side when a message appeared.

Emote_Cheer: I'll give you three days to think about it.

The screen flickered off and the shutdown sequence started. Erik blew a distressed sigh and left the office, returning to the supply closet. During his search, he heard the elevator bell ping and the doors slide open.

"Lost something?" Zachary's voice called.

Erik whirled around and clenched his teeth as the young man approached. "Why are you here?" he growled.

"Why are you still here?" Zachary questioned. "Everyone got sent home after the crash. You shouldn't be here."

"I was working on data recovery."

"Liar and you know it."

Erik snorted. "Whatever. If you're not helping, then beat it."

"After I brought you dinner and everything!" Zachary complained. "How rude!"

"Where is it then?" Erik snapped, glaring back at Zachary. Zachary reached into his slacks pocket and withdrew a folded cloth bag.

"Here you go!" Zachary said cheerfully and handed the bag to Erik.

"What happened to dinner?" Erik snarled.

"I ate it." Zachary laughed and Erik growled, clenching his hands.

"You're working my last nerve!"

"Then I'm doing my job." Erik snatched the bag from Zachary's hand and stormed over to the desk where the remaining hard disks remained. "Are you heading home?"

"I have to get this recovered and get that project done," Erik explained. "Otherwise, I'm dead."

"Want some help?"

"You've done enough, thanks." Erik set the drives into the bag and returned to the elevators with Zachary at his heels. "Besides, I thought you didn't work here."

"I'm in another department."

"Then why are you hassling me?"

"I don't know why you got assigned to this department when you can't program worth shit," Zachary spat as he pushed the button.

"They told me it was data processing," Erik muttered and stepped on once the doors opened. "Someone else pushed my paperwork through and had me come in today."

"Moron!" Zachary slapped Erik upside the head. Erik growled and glowered back at Zachary who smirked as the doors closed and the elevator started its descent. "Someone's using you obviously, despite how much of an incompetent shit you are."

"Then why don't you take care of it?"

"My hands are tied."

The elevators opened onto the belowground parking level and Erik spotted Orpheus idling near the bay, waiting. Erik hustled over and immediately entered the front passenger side.

"Have you ever dealt with that wingnut?" Erik asked as he set the bag next to the box in the rear seat.

"Zachary?" Orpheus murmured. "Yeah, he's a little screwy. He's smart, but batshit crazy."

"Why is he picking on me?" Erik complained and shut the

door.

"I don't know. We just avoid his ass." Orpheus pulled out of the parking garage and entered the lot. "He hammers out code faster than we can - his daily limit is a hundred thousand lines!"

"Really?" Erik said, astonished as he unclipped his ID tag then pocketed it. "He told me he didn't work in the same department!"

"And you believed him?" Orpheus snorted. "We usually average twenty thousand. It's easier if we don't have to say anything to him."

"What if you have to?"

Orpheus grimaced and shook his head. "As long as he's busy looking at the code and not hassling us, we're fine."

Erik blew a disgruntled sigh and picked up his phone, dialing for Francisca once more.

"Do you want me to come get you?" Francisca said after the first ring. "It's almost closing time."

"I'm with a co-worker," Erik answered.

"Meet me at the noodle house."

"What's up?" Orpheus asked once Erik placed his phone on the dashboard.

"She wants us to meet her at the noodle house," Erik replied.

"I know where that is." Orpheus pulled into the street.

Orpheus stopped in the lot of a small yellow diner with signs of various noodle dishes in the windows. Erik stepped out and pulled up his collar against the cold as he crossed the sector.

Entering the eatery, Erik found Francisca sitting at a rear table, surrounded by plates of various dishes. He approached and smiled brightly as he pulled out of his coat.

"Thank you so much," Erik said gratefully and slipped into the booth across from her.

Francisca picked up her glass of tea, scowling at Erik with deep hatred. "I'd never thought someone as kind as you would make such an unreasonable demand," she said icily behind her drink. "You're going to pay me back in full, Doofus!"

"I promise to do the best I can," Erik assured.

"If not, you're becoming an organ donor!"

Erik laughed nervously. "Surely you jest."

Francisca narrowed her eyes. "Do you want to try me?"

Erik swallowed hard and withered under her harsh gaze.

"Here you are," Orpheus called. "I wonder where you went." He handed Erik his phone. "You left it."

"Thanks," Erik murmured, taking it.

"You still have your name tag on," Francisca noted as Orpheus slipped into the booth beside Erik.

"Oh?" Orpheus smiled slightly and unclipped the ID, setting it face down on the table. "I was in a rush and I forgot."

"Order whatever you like," Francisca said. "Doofus is paying."

Erik frowned and Francisca gave a malicious smile. "Why are you doing this to me?" he whined.

"I just got started," Francisca cooed. "Don't worry. It'll only get worse from here."

Orpheus chortled in response and Erik glowered at him.

"What?" Orpheus said innocently. "It's funny!"

A waitress in a yellow apron approached their table moments later. "What would you like to order?" she asked.

"The most expensive thing you have," Orpheus answered.

"So you'd like the 'all the fixings' special?"

"Great! Let's try that!"

Erik ground his teeth and shook his head when the server asked if he wanted anything.

"At least have a drink," a voice called. Erik looked up, spotting an older man with frizzy white hair, thick sideburns and dark glasses wearing a loose-fitting green suit walk up to their table. He leaned against a black wooden cane as he stopped at their table. "It's on me," he said.

"Do they sell alcoholic drinks here?" Erik asked warily.

"Wine, beer, whatever you like."

"Vodka?"

"Nothing like that."

"Strongest wine you can get your hands on, then."

"Hey!" the man barked at the servers. "Bring some wine over and the strongest shit you got!"

"Who is he?" Francisca murmured.

Erik glanced toward her and shrugged his shoulders. "Search me," he muttered.

The man pulled up a nearby chair and sat on the end, smiling brightly. "What brings you to this lovely place, eh?" he chirped, leaning his cane against the table's edge.

"Dinner?" Erik responded.

"Don't tell me you're that poor, boyo!" The man roared in laughter.

"Programmers only make thirty-five an hour," Orpheus

134

filled in, "and that's on the bottom end of the totem pole."

"Really now?"

"Fuck," Zachary's voice snapped from behind. Erik turned, finding the young man appearing annoyed as he approached the table. "I hope the old man hasn't been pestering you all."

"I just got started!" the man snapped.

"Don't mind this noisy old monster," Zachary muttered and gestured toward Francisca. "May I sit here?"

Francisca nodded and scoot over for him. "Who is he?" she asked.

"He's a drunk I'm renting from," Zachary grumbled and slipped into the booth. "Don't bother learning his name."

"Mell's just fine," said the man.

"Fine," Erik murmured. "Why are you here?"

"I have to drive his drunk ass home," Zachary snapped. "He likes hanging out here for the cheap food and drinks."

"What's with the long face?" Mell asked.

"He screwed up some major shit today," Orpheus described. "First day on the job too."

"Right," Erik moaned, "and I want to erase the memory for right now."

Mell chortled. "Then you've come to the right place!"

The waitress returned with a large plate holding noodles of various kinds with many meats and vegetables while a waiter brought up two bottles of wine and a pair of glasses, setting them on the table.

"Please enjoy your time," the waiter said cheerfully.

"Of course I will," Mell responded and unscrewed the top. The servers left while he poured himself a serving then another for Erik.

"How are you going to recover the data in time?" Erik asked, taking his serving of wine.

"It takes me about fifteen hours to recover two-hundred gigs," Francisca grumbled.

"There's two thousand gigs in a two terabyte drive," Orpheus clarified. "We have thirty of them."

Erik's eyes widened and he gulped back his drink as he crunched the numbers in his head. *She won't have any time at all!* he realized. *She needs six and a half days and she's only got barely half that!*

"Got some computer trouble, eh?" Mell murmured and downed his wine. "You should take it to a specialist."

"I can't," Erik complained. "If I get caught with it, I'm in deep trouble."

"Oh, high-level stuff, eh?" Mell snorted. "Then why are you talking about it here? There's ears everywhere."

"You already involved me, Doofus," Francisca growled. "You better not get my ass arrested!"

"I'm sure you'll do fine, lady," Zachary replied, grinning. "You seem strong enough."

Orpheus laughed and jutted a thumb toward Erik. "You should see that dummy take a hit," he crowed. "Tony clocked him a good one earlier and he just kept going like it's nothing."

"So you like fighting, huh?" Zachary asked.

Erik raised an eyebrow. "Me? Not especially," he answered. "Somehow fights always find me."

"Don't tell me you're a pacifist!"

"I'll throw down if need be," Erik said and handed his glass to Mell who refilled it. "I can hold my own too. But if guns are involved, count me out."

Zachary snorted. "Oh, scared of getting shot?" he teased. "How'd you serve in the Defense Forces then?"

Erik shook his head and drank his wine before answering. "No, it's not that I'm afraid." He winced slightly when his left shoulder ached in response. "I can't tell you why I have a great hatred for them. They bother me and I just don't like them." He waved Zachary away. "Besides, these scars didn't show up out of nowhere."

"I hate guns too, but I collect them." Zachary turned to Francisca. "Don't you have any?"

"I have an old hunting rifle I keep at home," Francisca replied. "Handed down from my grandmother."

"She's scary accurate with it," Erik murmured and handed his empty glass to Mell again. "I knew a guy once who could shoot up to a mile away."

"Really?" Mell said impressed as he refilled Erik's glass.

"A mile away!" Zachary said and grinned. "That's one hell of a guy. It's a surprise he didn't hang in the Defense Forces with that kind of skill for a lifetime!"

"I don't remember a whole lot..." Erik drank his third serving of wine and set his glass on the table, holding his chin in his hand. "I'm pretty messed up, you know."

"You know what's really messed up?" Zachary asked. Erik raised an eyebrow and Zachary grinned. "Getting shot."

"What you'd you know about that?"

Zachary held his finger and thumb into a gun-like shape and reached across the table, poking Erik's forehead. "Bang."

Erik shut his eyes, growing disconnected from his body.

FIFTEEN

Erik moaned as he roused to consciousness and sat up, finding himself in an unfamiliar room. He looked around, noting the dark blue carpet and pale blue walls. Several posters of martial artists and sports stars adorned the walls.

Stepping out of bed, Erik grabbed the sheets and wrapped it around his nude body. He approached the dresser and opened it, finding baggy jeans and loose t-shirts stuffed inside. Erik pulled out a set of articles and opened the bedroom door then peered down the hall that had hardwood flooring.

Finding no one else out and about, he spotted the bathroom at the end and hurried over, immediately shutting the door behind him.

Dropping the clothing on the floor, Erik felt around in the dark and found the switch, turning on the light. He released the sheeting as he looked in the bathroom mirror, facing a young man with shaggy red hair, tired violet eyes, freckled bruised face and scarred body.

Erik quickly showered and dressed, then returned the sheeting to the bedroom. He padded down the hall, entering the parlor on his left. To his right led to a large kitchen and Erik found the coffee maker on, with the hot drink already brewed.

Searching the cabinets, he found a mug and poured himself

a cup. Erik tensed when he heard movement and turned around, spotting Mahjin staggering in, dressed in loose-fitting charcoal slacks and a black bandana holding down his frizzy blond hair. His upper body was heavily scarred, the old injuries crisscrossing across his pale chest, back, and arms.

"Mornin' laddy," Mahjin muttered as he shuffled in and opened the cabinets, searching for a mug. "Coffee stuff's on the table there."

Erik looked in the direction Mahjin indicated, spotting a small kitchen table in the corner that had whitener and sugar on the surface. Erik took a seat on the other side while Mahjin rinsed out a cup sitting in the sink. The older man poured in coffee then returned with a spoon, placing it on the table.

Erik said nothing as he spooned in the instant creamer into his mug and stirred it. Mahjin poured sugar in his cup and Erik handed him his spoon in silence. Mahjin nodded, stirring his coffee before sipping it.

Erik drank his coffee, staring at the flowered peeling wallpaper.

"The funeral's in a few hours," Mahjin murmured. "I told Jerry I'd drive ya."

"Where's Missus Zachary?" Erik said softly. "I don't want to see her either."

"She's with Jerry."

Erik put down his mug as tears suddenly streamed down his face. Mahjin set aside his cup on the nearby counter and sifted through his pockets, withdrawing a pack of cigarettes and a box of matches.

"That monster shot her," Erik said in a far away tone, "just like that... Right in front of us!" He put his head into his arms, struggling to breathe.

Mahjin withdrew an unfiltered cigarette from the pack and tossed the container aside on the counter. He thumbed open the matchbox and shook out a match. Dexterously swiping the match head across the striking strip, he lit the roll of tobacco and dropped the matchbox into his pocket, then left the room only to return moments later with a white bottle of medication.

"Here," Mahjin said and tossed the bottle onto the table with a clatter. "Take one of those. It'll make you forget."

Erik sniffled as he sat up, noticing the bottle on its side against the sugar. He picked it up, noting it had no label. Opening the container, Erik shook out the pills into his palm, finding a red capsule, yellow capsule, and green tablet.

"Which one will help me forget?" Erik asked.

"The green one, but it has drawbacks."

"Like what?"

"Nightmares."

"What about the yellow one?"

"You'll see pink elephants on that one."

"The red one?"

"That's too strong for ya. You'll wake up dead." Mahjin reached over and picked up the pair of capsules. "That pill ain't gonna harm ya none," he insisted. "Aside from having horrors that's hard to wake from..."

"Because the drug's suppressing what I want to remember," Erik protested.

"Right that." Mahjin broke the capsules he held in half and snorted the powder inside them. He dropped the capsules into the sink and withdrew his cigarette in his free hand as he moaned, gripping the counter once he lost feeling in his body.

"Are you all right?"

"I will be in a minute," Mahjin groaned. "I've been doing this a long time."

"What happened to you?"

"War happened. War you'll eventually see." Mahjin smirked. "If you don't die, then you'll become a drug-addled nobody barely getting by in life."

"You're not a drug-addled nobody," Erik suggested. "You're somebody important."

"Only because of what I can provide." Mahjin let out a short bitter laugh. "If you give up your soul, don't complain when others trash it."

"Sure." Erik took the green tablet he held, downing it with his cooling coffee. "Should I wear a suit?"

"You should be able to fit Kevin's clothes there," Mahjin slurred slightly. "Check the hall closet."

Erik set aside his coffee and left the table. Approaching the corridor cabinet, he opened the door, finding several suits and well-made coats inside. Erik thumbed through the clothing, finding a set consisting of dark navy blazer and slacks with sky blue dress shirt. Taking it, he returned to the bedroom and changed, then grabbed the jar of pomade off the nightstand, slicking a dollop into his hair.

Setting the pomade aside, Erik noticed a small picture frame holding a faded photograph of himself, Kevin and Raider posing before an unmarked building. Erik stood in the center between Kevin and Raider with his arms draped over their shoulders, wearing a tank shirt and high-cut basketball shorts. Kevin wore a sleeveless shirt and cutoff denim shorts with his arms folded across his chest while Raider wore ripped jeans and tight white T-shirt, flexing his muscular arms toward the camera.

"I don't remember this," Erik murmured.

"Ready to go?" Mahjin called outside the door. Erik glanced up, finding Mahjin had put on a black dress shirt with matching tie and sport coat. Mahjin leaned against a black hardwood cane as he placed a pair of dark aviator sunglasses propped atop his head.

"Yeah," Erik said and put the photograph away.

Erik said nothing while Mahjin drove to the mortuary. Once they arrived at a large brick building with wide glass panels, Erik stepped out the car and made his way inside.

Entering a black and silver marbled corridor, there were several large heavy doors with brass handles populating the hall, separated by small light plates ensconced in bronze shields.

Erik noticed near one door rest a small ivory cushioned bench with a narrow oak desk holding a signature book. He walked over and glimpsed at the book, finding signatures of people he didn't know filling the pages. Running his finger down the page, Erik found 'Gerald Schumacher' in the list. On the relationship entry, Erik frowned when he spotted 'Brother' written in the category.

"*That creepy orderly was right!*" Erik realized and backed away, horrified. He bumped into Mahjin who approached from behind.

"What's the matter?" Mahjin grumbled and took up the pen.

"Too much for ya?" Erik pushed past him and hurried back outdoors.

Walking around the building, Erik found John Greenfield dressed in a dark auburn suit with light tan dress shirt and tie, and his long brown hair hung as an oily mess on his shoulders. He sat on the back steps, drinking from a flask.

"I have to get going," John Greenfield said and hiccupped as he stood once Erik approached.

"Where are you going?" Erik asked.

John Greenfield capped the flask and set it inside his blazer pocket. He smirked drunkenly at Erik and grasped his shoulder with a heavy hand.

"Hey, Ace," he slurred.

"Yeah?" Erik questioned.

"Protect him with everything you have."

"You mean Kevin?"

"It's painful, isn't it? That feeling..." John Greenfield tapped at Erik's chest. "I entrust you... I need you to do this for me."

"I'll try my best," Erik said softly.

"This will be difficult."

"Why? Why did they hurt Kevin and Mom..." Erik yowled when his shoulder was tightly squeezed.

"I'm sorry," John Greenfield rasped. "Shana was never your mother."

"Are you saying I'm adopted?"

"No."

"Then, what?"

"Just know you have people who care about you, your well-being, and want to see you succeed." John Greenfield

144

grasped Erik's face and held it in his hands. "You're very special to me." John Greenfield let go and draped an arm around Erik's shoulders. "Soon, I'll have to start on that new project. It won't be long before they try to take you away from me."

"What should I do?" Erik asked softly. "Where can I go?"

"There are some people I know who can help you disappear," John Greenfield said. "I'll introduce you to them."

"Why do bad guys want you?"

"Good looks aside..." John Greenfield chortled. "I created a new Synthoid that is entirely self-aware."

Erik unlaced John Greenfield's arm from around his shoulders and looked at the older man in shock. "What do you mean?" he yelped. "The AI can't be that flawless!"

"I had Smiley work on the artificial intelligence. It learns by trial and error like we do, also it works on a reward system. If it gains positive reinforcement, it'll keep doing whatever it's doing. If it gains a negative reinforcement, it'll stop what it's doing." John Greenfield doubled over, laughing. "I have become a god and the destroyer of worlds."

"Why did you make something like that?" Erik cried, horrified. "How could you make something so dangerous?"

"See, this is my ultimate project for the Public Defense Works." John Greenfield straightened his stance and smiled brightly. "This way, I can save lives without causing more needless deaths. The Synthoids are highly trainable and can be applied to *any* application. They're quite low-maintenance, resilient, and have a long shelf life."

"How long is this shelf life?"

"Twenty years, hopefully."

"You've lost your mind!"

John Greenfield giggled and tousled Erik's hair. "If it's too hard for you, you can keep your identity hidden," he said in assurance. "They won't have to know."

Erik gaped after the man, too stunned to protest while watching him stagger his way up the steps. After John Greenfield stumbled indoors, Erik walked around the grounds, pacing outside the funeral parlor. He entered the parking lot and looked at all the various cars in their variety of colors.

Erik spotted the familiar blue coupe belonging to John Greenfield and approached, trying the door. It opened and he slipped into the driver's side. Shutting the door, Erik stared back at the funeral home across the way. When he couldn't bear to look anymore, he let back the seat and laid down, staring at the navy ceiling.

"My life is over," Erik murmured, focusing his gaze at the overhead light plate. "I don't know what my life is anymore..."

Hearing a tap at the window, Erik sat up startled when he saw an athletic young man with steel blue eyes and a blond mullet on the other side. He wore a dark gray suit and navy horn-rimmed glasses. The blond waved and Erik leaned over, opening the passenger door.

"What do you want, Stearne?" Erik muttered as Stearne stepped in and shut the door.

"I wanted to drink somewhere secluded," Stearne answered, grinning.

"So my dad's car was the best place you could think of?" Erik grumbled and laid back in the seat.

"I wanted to drink with you. I'm sure you really want one

right now."

"I'll be fine."

"Bullshit and you know it." Stearne reached into his blazer pocket and withdrew a half-pint bottle of vodka. "I heard from your dad you were catatonic for days after you hurt yourself in grief."

"I don't remember..."

"That's fine. I would want to forget too if I saw something that violent happen in front of me." Stearne passed the bottle to Erik. "Kill it if you want. I bought it for you."

"What if I get blasted?" Erik complained.

"I don't think your dad would care right now."

Erik took the bottle and sat up, unscrewing the top. He took a gulp and winced when the liquor burned his throat.

Stearne reached into his other pocket, withdrawing a silver cigarette case. He snapped it open, withdrawing an unfiltered cigarette.

"Mind if I smoke?" Stearne asked.

"Roll down the window," Erik murmured and took another drink.

Stearne did as told and put the cigarette to his lips, then searched his slacks pockets, withdrawing a lighter.

"What's going to happen to me?" Erik asked. "Those guys who killed her might come after me next."

"That's a little paranoid, you think?" Stearne lit his cigarette and set the lighter on the dashboard with his cigarette case. "However, that's why I'm going to keep an eye on you," he replied and blew smoke out the window.

"You have your own life."

"I told you, you're my brother and it's my job to protect you."

"Because Missus Zachary asked you to?"

"Because I want to."

"Right." Erik took another swallow of vodka and groaned when he grew warm. "I don't want to be a burden."

"You're not a burden."

Erik continued drinking in silence while Stearne smoked. When he broke out sweating, he held the bottle between his knees and peeled out of his blazer, tossing it in the rear passenger seat.

"I don't know why you drink such awful stuff," Erik muttered and hiccupped. "What are you trying to forget?"

"I lucked out and didn't have to fight in the War because I'm an only child," Stearne replied. "However, I drink for other reasons."

Erik unbuttoned his shirt with one hand while he leaned over and rolled down the window with the other. He felt overwhelmed by his feelings, cringing when he replayed the scene in his mind, watching the officer shoot Shana in the head.

"It happened so quickly," Erik said softly. "Then he pointed the gun at me... I thought I was going to die right there."

"You're still alive," Stearne said in assurance.

"Why?" Erik cried. "Why does Dad have to work for evil people like that? Kevin's in a coma, the woman I thought was my mother is dead..." Erik took another gulp of vodka and leaned forward, pressing his head against the steering wheel. "Why'd they have to do that? Why can't the public security bureau do anything about it?"

"It's not in their jurisdiction for one," Stearne said in a low tone. "Secondly, it's considered a Federal matter. The Feds will cover up anything to save their asses."

"But if it's Federal, why aren't they doing anything?"

"Because the Organization works outside of that."

"Then who polices them?"

Stearne snorted. "Seriously now, and you wonder why the corruption is so bad." He flicked his tapered stub out the window and took another cigarette to light. "After an internal review, all they'll do is reprimand the offenders and send them home with pay or have them jockey a desk."

"What do you do?" Erik inquired.

"I'm in Investigations."

Erik sat up, giving Stearne a wary glance. "Then what's with you dealing with chemicals then?"

"Photographs." Stearne chortled. "I'm not a scientist like Missus Zachary."

"Wait... Are you saying she hired you to investigate something?" Erik let up the seat and leaned against it, recalling his past conversation with Stearne. "When you picked me up from the hospital you said you needed the money and she was better to work for..."

"Right."

"But you said you used to work at Gen-Tech..."

"Right. I investigated problems for them as well."

"So why are you getting close to me?"

"You know the answer to that." Erik looked to Stearne who smiled brightly. "You can trust me."

"How can I if you're busy breaking the law?" Erik snapped and Stearne snorted. "I'm not eighteen yet."

"I have to break a few rules if I want answers."

Erik finished the remainder of the vodka and chucked the bottle out the window. "Let's go in," Erik slurred and opened the door. He staggered out and leaned against the car, giggling. "I need to pay my respects."

"You shouldn't go in like that," Stearne reprimanded.

"I don't care!" Erik shouted. "Let's go!"

"Wait for me!"

Stearne hurried out the car as Erik stormed across the lot.

SIXTEEN

Erik stumbled up the mortuary steps and yanked against the door, throwing it open. He swayed on unsteady footing down the hall, searching for the viewing room. Erik encountered the desk near the large oak panel with long brass handles and pulled them open.

"Hey," he called, tottering in. "I wanna see her. Where is she?"

Some people seated in the pews looked back toward Erik with disapproving looks while others spoke softly to one another. Erik scanned the aisles, searching for someone he recognized.

Approaching the front row, Erik spotted Raider sitting in a pew wearing a black suit with gray dress shirt and his long black hair pulled back into a loose braid down his back. Accompanying him sat an older man with shaggy nape-length reddish-brown hair, dressed in a dark brown suit and wearing gray-tinted glasses.

"Hey," Erik slurred and poked Raider's chest. "I've seen you somewhere."

"Ay," Raider murmured. "You drunk, man?"

"Yeah."

"Sorry 'bout yer loss."

"So, why are you here?"

"Aunt Gina asked me to come."

"Gina...?"

"Genovera," the man filled in.

"Hey, Sullivan," Erik said and held out a hand. Sullivan shook it in return. "So Missus Zachary's your aunt...?"

"My old man's married to her sister," Raider replied. "Moms couldn't make it and he couldn't either. Work stuff or whatever."

"So Kevin's your cousin by marriage." Erik giggled. "That's great."

Raider raised an eyebrow and folded his arms across his chest. "What's funny?" he spat.

"Hey, guess what?" Erik suddenly said.

"What?"

"He's my best friend. We even share the same birthday."

Raider gave a brief nod. "That's what's up."

"Did you see him?"

Raider's eyes cast down toward the floor. "Yeah," he muttered. "He's in real bad shape."

"I seeing him afterwards. Come with me?"

"Sure."

Erik poked Raider's chest with his finger again and the young man looked up. "Hey."

"What?"

"I found a picture of us together."

"Yeah?"

"I don't remember it getting done."

"Company picnic last year." Raider grinned and beckoned toward Erik to come closer. Erik leaned in and Raider whispered in his ear. "We got totally blazed. That's prolly why you can't remember."

Erik giggled and pushed him aside. "You're bad," he teased.

"Hey, wanna light up later? I'm sure you need it."

"Sure, I'll see you."

"Cool."

Erik turned away and neared the casket surrounded by white lilies, looking down at the polished hardwood. He ran a hand across the glossy surface, seeing his muted reflection. Looking up, Erik noticed an easel holding a large studio portrait of Shana with feathered sandy red hair, wearing a bright yellow dress and sitting in a wicker chair, surrounded by vases of lilies on a soft gray background. Around her neck, she wore a long silver chain holding a golden charm of the sun and moon.

"Why can't I see her?" Erik murmured and turned toward the casket. "It's closed, isn't it?"

"What are you doing?" Sullivan called when Erik pushed off the bouquet of flowers on the burial box. "Don't do that!"

"Open up!" Erik shouted as he pulled against the heavy split lid. "I wanna see her!"

"Justin, don't!" Sullivan jumped to his feet and hurried over, grasping Erik's arm. Erik yanked out of his grip and shoved him to the floor.

"Don't tell me what to do!" Erik yelled. Sullivan scrambled to his feet and Erik stepped out of another grab, then hurled a punch, slamming his fist straight into the man's side. Sullivan gasped, stunned and staggered back.

"Hey!" Raider yelped and stood as Erik returned to the casket, yanking on the lid. Finding it refusing to open, Erik inspected the sides, searching for the lock. "You need to quit, man!"

"You shut up!" Erik snapped as he found the bolts and slid them apart. Raider intercepted Erik and grabbed his arm before he could open the lid.

"Don't do this," Raider warned. "I know you upset and all - but, man, this ain't right."

"Let me go!" Erik yanked his arm free from Raider's firm grasp and shoved him aside. Raider converged again and Erik pulled away, immediately putting his hands up in guard. "I will fight you!"

"Fine, so fight me," Raider spat. "But show some respect, man. This shit ain't cool."

"Suck it!" Erik shoved Raider back by the chest and Raider stumbled rearwards over his steps then steadied himself. He narrowed his eyes and charged, only to get an uppercut to the jaw that launched him to the floor.

"Shit..." Raider moaned and immediately blacked out. Sullivan urgently neared Raider's downed form, kneeling at his side.

Erik glared back at the crowd in the room. "Anybody else?" he bellowed. "Stay away!" When no one made a move, Erik turned toward the casket and threw open the heavy lid.

The room grew silent and he gasped when he saw Shana's embalmed body lying in repose, wearing the same yellow dress, though her long hair simply graced her shoulders. Erik ran a hand over the cold stiff skin, smearing the foundation painted on.

Erik's heart thudded in his chest and his hands grew

clammy as he let the silver chain run through his fingers. He gulped the acrid burning in his throat as his guts churned, roiling at the sight.

"Hey," Erik whispered. "Why don't you wake up?" He pulled against the chain around Shana's neck. "If you stay in there, they'll take this away." Erik yanked the chain, snapping it. "Hey, I broke it... Aren't you going to yell at me?" Erik grabbed Shana's shoulders, shaking gently. "Why are you sleeping in there? You need to get up!"

Erik leaned forward, putting his ear to Shana's chest. Hearing nothing, he took the charmed necklace with its broken chain. "I'm going to get this fixed for you," Erik murmured, grasping the casket's edge. "Please say something to me, anything..." Erik took in a shallow breath and let it out as tears streamed down his face. "Is it really true you're not my mother? If you're not my mother, then who is?" Erik clenched his hands and struck the casket's side. "Answer me!" he screeched. "Who is she?"

Erik gently touched Shana's chin and moved her head, spotting the borehole on the side of her head underneath her hair. Erik dropped his hand to his side and backed away as searing pain cut through his left shoulder. He gripped his shoulder as he struggled to breathe and shut his eyes when he saw the event play again in his mind.

"Justin–!" Sullivan called and Erik let out a throat wrenching scream as he fell to his knees, hunching forward.

Erik screamed again, batting at his head to rid the image in his mind. "Why?" he wailed, holding his head in his hands. "Why... Why'd they have to kill you? Why?" Erik wheezed for breath as his tears ran full force. "You're a good person. This doesn't happen to nice, kind people!"

"Justin!" Sullivan approached and Erik glared back at him.

"Stay away from me," he thundered and shoved the man away when grabbed for. Erik scrambled to his feet and raced out the room, pushing open the large doors. Looking down the corridor, he spotted John Greenfield arguing with Mahjin at the end, while Genovera sat in a chair, crying into her hands.

"You!" Erik shouted and stormed down the hall.

John Greenfield and Mahjin paused when Erik ran up to them. Erik roared as he threw a heavy punch into John Greenfield's chest, hurling him back against the wall. John Greenfield's head struck the partition and he slid to the floor, dazed. Mahjin hurriedly grabbed for Erik and Erik slipped out of his grip, swiftly booting the man in the groin then shoved him to the floor.

"Justin!" Genovera shrilled when Erik picked up the fallen cane with his free hand and pointed it at her.

"This is your fault!" Erik bellowed. "If you never came over and gave him that damn job - life was just fine before!"

"What do you want me to do?" Genovera cried. "I'm trying the best I can... I already have enough sins to pay for."

"Just die!"

"Dying won't bring her back. Dying won't improve Kevin's condition."

Erik threw the necklace at Genovera and she caught it. She glanced at it in her hands, frightened and confused. "Do it for me then," Erik urged. "Please, just kill yourself."

Genovera looked up at Erik, appalled. "I can't," she said

softly. "I'm sorry."

Erik raised the staff and Genovera flinched. "Tell him the truth," he seethed. "You already ruined my life! Tell him!"

"W-what?" Genovera yelped.

"Tell Smiley the truth!" Erik shrieked. "Tell him!"

"Oh..."

"You're just as evil!"

Erik bashed the staff into the wall near Genovera's head and she let out a terrified scream. Suddenly a severe shock blasted through his back and Erik yowled when jolted with electricity. He slumped to his knees, heaving for breath.

"That's enough," Stearne's voice called.

Erik grasped the cane and set it to the floor, leaning against it as he struggled to stand. Stearne released another volt and Erik immediately fell forward, losing consciousness.

SEVENTEEN

Erik's eyes snapped open and he found himself staring at a bloodstained ceiling. Sitting up, he noticed he sat in a small enclosed space that had bright plate lights and no windows or doors. Surrounding Erik was blood, lots of it, marring the walls and the floor.

About time you woke up!

Erik gasped and turned toward the sound, facing the young man with his appearance who wore a navy uniform with silver buttons.

"You're not real!" Erik screamed and scrambled to his feet. "Stop haunting me! Stop talking to me! You can't be real!"

The counterpart smirked and folded his arms across his chest. *I didn't knock you over the head that hard, now!*

"Get out of my life!"

I can't leave that easily when I'm a part of you, dumb ass! Erik's double chortled and waved a dismissive hand at him. *You keep suppressing me and I might just have to get rid of you.*

"How are you going to get rid of me?" Erik demanded.

The duplicate grinned cruelly and tapped at his head. *In here.*

Erik put up his hands on the defensive. "I'll keep fighting

you," he snarled. "I'll fight you no matter how long it takes."

The young man with his looks also took on the same stance, smiling maliciously. *Unless you fight me back at full power, you don't stand a chance!*

"Whatever," Erik spat. "Bring it!"

Destroying you is going to be so much fun!

"Don't play games with me!" Erik thundered. "You're just a figment of my imagination!"

Keep thinking that!

The counterpart rushed forward and Erik dropped low for a tackle, shouldering the young man in the chest and hurled him forward on the floor. The double tumbled onto his feet and blocked a punch with his arm, shoving Erik rearwards.

The duplicate formed a silver saber in his hand and slashed back, hacking off Erik's arm. Erik screamed in agony, clutching his profusely bleeding shoulder with his free hand as he staggered back, stunned.

Draw your power and fight me! The counterpart roared and Erik quickly turned out of another swipe. *You can't go on like this forever!*

"Damn you piece of shit!" Erik screeched.

What are you going to do, punish me? The double laughed and pointed his saber in Erik's direction. *Disappear! I want you gone!*

"You're always here, tormenting me..."

I still have other tricks up my sleeve to make you listen. The silver saber transformed into a revolver and the mirror image palmed back the hammer. *You're a problem to be dealt with and don't deserve to live! So just relax and go quietly...*

it'll be swift.

Erik charged as his counterpart unloaded his rounds, jerking when pierced in the arm and chest. When the gun jammed, Erik grabbed his double's wrist and threw him to the floor on his back. Erik then let go and dropped down, grabbing the counterpart's throat with his hand, squeezing with all his remaining strength.

"Back off!" Erik snarled.

The duplicate laughed and grabbed Erik's throat with both hands, compressing tightly. Erik saw red as he struggled to breathe and let go when his vision dimmed. The counterpart pushed Erik away and he slumped forward on his side, gasping weakly for breath.

"You win," Erik moaned. "What are you going to do to me?"

The double smiled crookedly as he rose easily to his feet and approached Erik. *You are a tool of destruction! Act like it!*

Erik's vision flashed in grayscale and he heard other voices speaking to him.

Who are you?

Why do you look like me?

Why do you keep attacking me?

What is it you want with me?

Erik's duplicate kicked him aside and stormed away, exiting through a hidden side door. Erik shut his eyes as he struggled to breathe and opened them again, finding other broken bodies that has his looks scattered around him.

Get up!

Become one with the pain...

Remember!

160

The counterpart returned moments later and stood over Erik. Erik looked up at him and the mirror image smiled brightly.

Ready to concede?

"What are you trying to say?" Erik grumbled.

You're not Human anymore.

"How would you know this?"

Ask me again when you finally get it.

The young man withdrew a large bore pistol and jammed it into Erik's head. Erik shut his eyes and the blast followed, striking out his world.

Erik suddenly found breathing difficult and rocketed upright, gasping and gulping for air. Icy cold water beat on his skin and he abruptly vomited when raging pain clawed through his back and in his groin.

Erik looked around his surroundings, realizing he sat in a shower stall with cold water streaming down his back. Hearing thunderous footsteps, Erik looked up, facing down a trio of rifle barrels. On the other end holding them were officers in navy uniforms, caps, and polarized glasses.

"You're in no position to fight," one officer growled, "so don't even try."

"Then call Medical Assistance," Erik said weakly. "If I die, you lose your case."

"They really did a number on him," murmured one while the senior officer unhooked his radio and told the dispatch operator his intentions.

"Well, someone doesn't want him talking obviously,"

muttered his partner. "Who'd go through that much trouble torturing the poor bastard?"

"Shut up both of you," the senior warden snapped. "Keep an eye on him. They're coming." He stormed out the room.

"I know you're not Public Security," Erik croaked. "They'd kill me already."

"That's why they hired us to find you," replied the junior guardsman on Erik's left. "They're in on it too, you know."

"Hey, that was good thinking, duping us with them Synthoids," jeered the other. He poked Erik's head with his rifle. "We lost a few good ones because of your bullshit."

"Who called you in?" Erik grumbled.

"That nice gal at the front desk. Saw the article we sent in the papers."

"Move out the way," the senior officer bellowed. "The Med-Techs are here!"

The technicians in dark gray uniforms entered the bathroom as the officers stepped aside. Erik heard a small gasp and glanced up, noticing a muscular man with shaggy red hair and gray eyes gaping at him.

"Got anything for the pain?" Erik cracked. "Everything hurts..."

"Erik!" the medical technician yelped and grabbed for him as he slumped forward, passing out.

When Erik opened his eyes again, he found himself in a plain room slumped in an overstuffed recliner, facing a single small grayscale television set blaring a soap opera. Glancing around, Erik noticed pale green and gold flowered wallpaper lining the walls. He moaned and fell forward, dropping to the hunter green carpet.

"Oh, you're awake," Stearne's voice called. Erik looked up with bleary eyes, facing the young man who entered through the door in flared jeans and flannel overshirt. "How do you feel?"

"Sick," Erik murmured.

"Real men drink at funerals, right?" Stearne chortled. "I think you overdid it on that bottle there."

"You gave it to me!"

"Right, I did." Stearne crouched at Erik's side. "I'm sorry you had to get zapped like that. You were about to hit Missus Zachary and I like her a lot."

"I'm sorry..."

"Come on, I'll drag you to the showers and sober you up."

Stearne hooked his arms under Erik's and dragged his body across the carpet down the hall into a small bathroom of yellow and beige tiles. Erik groaned when dumped into the tub and Stearne sat on the nearby toilet. He leaned over, turning on the cold tap and a blast of frigid water poured on Erik. Erik stared vacantly back at the light yellow tiles in the shower stall.

Stearne appeared worried and rose to his feet. "What are you thinking about?" he asked.

"I want to die," Erik murmured.

"But if you did that, everyone would miss you."

"You wouldn't."

"I'm your brother; I would miss you." Erik gazed at Stearne standing over him then back at the wall. "I only want the best for you."

"You're assigned to protect me, aren't you?" Erik accused. "Somebody bad wants me for something..."

Stearne gave a faint smile. "You're a smart kid," he replied. "Can't keep anything from you."

"If I die, then they won't hurt Dad anymore, right?"

"No, that wouldn't be the case." Stearne shook his head. "Even if they killed everyone he knew, they need him alive. It's something he has they want."

"Why not just kill himself? I'd understand..."

"Your Dad isn't a big fan of Death, even his own."

Stearne stepped out the room and Erik sat up, getting drenched from the water streaming over his head. "*Is it really over those machines?*" he wondered. "*Why can't they just copy the damn things...*"

Stearne returned moments later with a change of clothing and towels. "I got you transferred into the Service Academy," he announced. "You already missed three weeks of Public School due to circumstances out of your control."

"I'm not sixteen," Erik complained. "I can't go."

"When's your birthday?"

"October twenty-second..."

"Then, you're fine." Stearne let down the toilet seat and dumped the towels and clothes on the lid. "If you're going to get angry, go after those beasts in their territory."

"You *want* me to join the Defense Forces?"

"You do your mandatory two years at twenty," Stearne explained. "So, might as well start early. If you move up in the ranks, you can find who's doing such nasty things to you."

164

"I only have twenty years to stick around that long," Erik protested. "If I don't find out by then..."

"I'm sure you will." Stearne smiled. "You have friends."

"What if Dad dies by then?"

"If for some reason that happens, keep fighting. Keep moving forward. It's not just you they're targeting... There are a lot of people who are threatened by them."

"Why me? Why nobody else?"

"Why not you? Why not anyone else?" Stearne left the room and Erik frowned, left cold and confused.

He later reluctantly peeled out of his waterlogged clothes and left them on the floor. Shutting off the water, Erik grabbed the towels and dried off, then wrapped the terry around his waist.

"Hey, Stearne," Erik called as he left the bathroom, padding down the corridor. "I need to find this guy's number." He paused in front of a room filled with computers, monitoring equipment, and telephones. Several corkboards lined the walls, pinned with photographs and notes.

Erik entered the room and approached one corkboard, finding photographs of several people he recognized.

"There's Sully, Mister Schneider, Mister Petra..." Erik paused at one photograph of a tanned middle-aged man with short sandy hair and narrow gray eyes. He wore a black suit with red tie against a pale blue background. Erik took out the pin and removed the picture, turning it over. He only saw a single name, 'Yagnersian Andrews'. "He's being investigated too," Erik muttered. "I wonder what that's about..."

Replacing the photograph on the board, Erik then stepped

out the room as Stearne entered the corridor. Stearne hurried over and shoved Erik aside, blocking the doorway.

"You didn't go in there, did you?" Stearne snapped. He immediately grabbed the door and slammed it shut.

"No, I-!" Erik flinched when Stearne poked his bare chest with a firm hand.

"Don't go in there, understand?" Stearne spat. "I don't want you even breathing on anything that's in there!"

"I'm sorry..."

"I told you to get dressed. Aren't you hungry at all?"

"Not really..."

"You should eat something."

Erik puffed a distressed sigh and returned to the bathroom, changing his clothes. He felt nervous when he heard Stearne pacing outside the door, then followed him into a small kitchen that had a small square table coupled by two chairs.

On the table were several plates, with one holding baked chicken fillets, another with rice, and the third grilled vegetables.

"What should I expect at the academy?" Erik asked as he took a seat at the table.

"A lot of drills and course work," Stearne described. "You'll learn a lot of stuff like tactics and strategy and every facet of the branches you want to eventually serve, such as Infantry, Mariner, or Aeronaut. By the time you age out, you're an officer and depending on your scores, you'll get assigned to a unit."

"I have to be right in the head to serve, right?" Erik

protested as Stearne handed him an empty plate. "The Defense Forces don't want crazy people..."

Stearne snorted while he spooned the food into his own plate. "You're wrong," he said pointedly. "That's where the Expendable Unit come in. It's only full of crazies and criminals."

"Even criminals?" Erik said, surprised.

"Why waste tax dollars giving bad people three hots and a cot, and free healthcare?" Stearne smirked. "So since they're so good at killing, make them kill the bad guys we want."

"So they just do their time and then after they serve they're let go?"

"It doesn't work exactly like that," Stearne clarified. "They serve the equivalent of their sentence and they must kill a certain number of targets in a particular order before release. If that kill number isn't met or done out of order by the time they're up for parole, it gets upped higher and they serve another two years."

"How..." Erik looked down at his empty plate, stunned. "But isn't that...?" He sighed, unable to formulate what he wanted to say.

"Sadistic? Maybe, but it lowers the crime rate," Stearne said in a positive tone. "Now as for the crazies, that's another touchy matter. The Keystone Reformation Center is one of the best sanatoriums around, with an eighty percent success rate. The patients there recover and return to civilian life either cured or stabilized and integrate back into society with little problems."

Erik shuddered at the implications. "How can that happen if they're forced to serve in the Defense Force?" he protested.

"It's through a program called 're-education through labor'. They dig ditches, work in the factories putting together parts and a whole lot of other odd jobs. It's the stability and constancy that resets the mind and gives them a sense of purpose."

Erik looked up at Stearne in disbelief. "What if someone is seriously mentally ill?" he demanded. "How can they work if they're that messed up in the head?"

"Keystone has the best doctors and specialists ever recruited. They believe mental illness is a result of intense trauma a person is unable to handle due to their environment. So they work with the person to help them heal their psyche and get them whole again or close to it."

"I see..."

"You only go there if you've failed your psychological exams," Stearne interjected. "You get evaluations when you first enter the academy, when you first sign up in whatever branch of your choice in the Defense Forces and again when you've served your contracted time and you're up for renewal or retirement."

"This is... Well..."

"I know, a lot to handle and process at once," Stearne said gently. "You have nothing to fear. It's just training at the academy, nothing heavy or serious. It's no different than regular school, but in this case, has a more military bent to it."

"If you say so."

"Your dinner's getting cold. Please eat."

"I'll try."

Erik put some food on his plate and picked at his meal,

overwhelmed and distressed. He sat at the table, impassive while Stearne ate. When Erik made no motions to continue his meal, Stearne put away the food and cleaned the kitchen.

"Do you want to play some cards?" Stearne asked after putting away Erik's share in the nearby microwave.

"No," Erik grumbled.

"Want to read any books? I have a lot of stuff on the shelf you can take a look at."

"No."

"You're more than welcome to see what's on the telly."

"Thanks, but no."

"It's not much since I'm a bachelor, but if you need anything, just let me know."

"Sure."

Stearne left the room and Erik put his head down on the table, breaking down into tears in his arms.

EIGHTEEN

"Hey, wake up," a voice called to Erik. Erik grunted and his eyes fluttered open, facing Zachary standing over him. "You fell asleep."

"What?" Erik groaned and stretched, then realized he was slumped in a booth.

"They're closing."

"Where...?" Erik glanced around, noticing Mell sitting across from him, pouring the last bit of wine into his glass. Next to him was another empty bottle. "Where did Franny and Orpheus go?"

"They went home," Mell answered. "Your old lady's got a lot of work to do and short stack promised to help her."

"What are you going to do with me?"

"I'm driving your drunk ass home, that's what," Zachary spat. "So, let's go."

Erik pushed him away when grabbed for. "Why are you picking on me?" he complained. "You like me or something?"

Zachary snorted. "I have no interest in tall skinny guys," he retorted. "Why do you care who I like anyway?"

"Not that I care who you see," Erik muttered and staggered to his feet. "It's none of my business."

"Oh, he's full of shit," Mell murmured behind his glass of

wine. "His head's full of nasty thoughts about this one guy in particular."

Zachary glared at Mell and the older man chortled. "What's that supposed to mean?" he squawked.

"Who do you like anyway?" Erik asked.

Zachary clenched his teeth and pointed toward the rear rooms. "Didn't you have to take a piss?" he said sourly. "Go and hurry so I can take your drunk ass home."

"Fine, then." Erik pushed past Zachary and made his way for the restrooms. Upon entry, he approached the sinks and ran the tap, then splashed his face, groaning. "I feel like shit," he grumbled and hiccupped.

Staggering for the door, the entrance swung open and Erik turned aside as Mell stalked in with a burning cigarette dangling from his lips.

"Hey, boy," Mell muttered. "What's taking you so long?"

"Don't tell me you were waiting," Erik quipped.

"He's my ride too."

Erik took the cigarette from Mell then stalked for the rear exit. He pushed open the doors and stepped out into the cold night air. "*What am I going to do now if I can't return to work this week?*" Erik wondered as he paced and smoked. "*I'm so screwed...*"

Moments later, a dark green micro van with tinted windows pulled up to where Erik stood and the horn cut the air with a short blast, startling him.

"Get in," Zachary called to him. "Or do you plan to walk home?"

"I'm walking," Erik retorted, flicking away his burned-down

stub.

"Bullshit."

Erik opened the front passenger door and stepped inside. "Don't act like you give a care about me," he groused.

"I don't." Zachary hit the accelerator and pulled around the restaurant, returning to the rear as Mell stumbled outdoors. "Get the door for me."

Erik turned in his seat and unlatched the handle, pushing the door open. Mell clamored inside and leaned over, pulling the door shut.

"I feel like shit," Mell grumbled.

"Don't we all," Erik drawled.

"Just crawl back there and pass out, please?" Zachary directed and turned his van around, entering the street. "I don't need your shit tonight, old man."

"I'll show ya old, boy." Zachary quickly lifted an arm to block when Mell rapped him upside the head with his cane. "I still got it!"

"Damn it," Zachary ranted, "go the fuck to sleep!"

Erik chortled in response. "Why do you put up with his antics?" he inquired.

"I just do," Zachary answered.

Mell grumbled curses as he reclined the seat back and held his cane crosswise across his body once he dropped back. Later snores escaped him.

Zachary pulled into an apartment complex lot surrounded by other cars and cut the engine.

"Hey, I didn't tell you where I lived," Erik protested. "Why are you having me sleep at your place?"

"This is where you live, dummy," Zachary said in annoyance and stepped out the van. Erik grunted then also made his way out, following him across the lot toward a towering complex. "You live at the old water tower district."

"I don't remember telling you that," Erik complained.

"You talk a lot when you're drunk, you know," Zachary noted. "Besides, it's listed on your VitaStat card, so why are you freaking out?" He pushed open the doors and made his way for the elevators with Erik at his heels. "You're in seven-forty-one."

"You're full of shit," Erik snapped. "You probably tried to roll me."

Zachary smirked. "You're right, I did. Thanks for dinner too."

"I..." Erik blew a dejected sigh, saying nothing as he pushed the button and the doors came open immediately. They boarded the elevator and Erik leaned against the wall, looking down at the floor while Zachary pulled out his phone from his pocket, playing a game on it.

The doors pinged and they stepped off. Erik made his way for the door marked '741' and searched his pockets for keys.

"You gave them to me to hold onto, remember?" Zachary called and withdrew a ring of keys from his slacks pocket with his free hand.

"You took my keys too?" Erik squawked and snatched the ring from him. Before he could put the key into the lock, the door swung open. "The hell...?" Erik felt cold air as he reached in and switched on the overhead light, revealing the apartment in disarray and his balcony windows open.

173

Stepping inside, his foot squished on wet carpet and Erik looked around in stunned silence, finding his furniture overturned, the couch cushions shredded, and shelves discarded of its belongings.

"You live alone?" Zachary called as he entered and paused when he saw the mess. "Wow, someone was looking for something."

"Yeah," Erik answered as he drifted into the kitchen. He dropped the keys on the counter, clenching his teeth at the sight of open cabinets and the contents rifled through. Erik picked up the receiver hanging from the phone buzzing its off-hook signal and replaced it in the cradle. Grabbing the percolator off the floor, he rinsed it out before filling with water then plugged it in. "Do you want coffee or anything?"

"Don't worry about it."

Erik left the kitchen and peeled out of his coat, watching Zachary upright the couch with ease. He dropped it on its arm along the way to his balcony and stepped outside, gazing into the cold night and the traffic on the street below.

"What were they looking for?" Erik wondered as he upright the overturned patio chair nearby. He turned away, closing the glass doors behind him and ignored Zachary sorting through his books off the shelf as he entered his bathroom, finding the medicine cabinet open. Turning around, Erik saw the bathroom closet open and all his towels tossed on the floor.

After removing his bandages and showering, Erik entered his bedroom and switched on the main light, finding the shredded mattresses on the floor and his closets open, with all his clothing discarded everywhere. The nightstand drawer lay overturned and its contents scattered. Erik grabbed a pair of flannel pants and stepped into them.

"Are you going to stay?" Zachary called.

Erik smelled coffee and returned to the parlor where he found Zachary sitting on his couch with a mug, staring at a framed photograph he held.

"What are you looking at?" Erik asked.

Zachary suddenly looked up and gave a tight smile. "Aren't you going to sleep?" he asked, placing the picture frame face down. "I'll be outta your hair soon."

"Do you want something from me?" Erik demanded.

"No, why?" Zachary stood, giving a devious grin. "Would you rather I skin you and hang it out to dry?"

Erik's face burned red and he frowned as Zachary let out a rolling laugh. Erik stomped back to his room and slammed shut the door. He moaned and held his head that throbbed in pain.

"Why is this happening?" Erik mewed. "What did I do?"

"You all right in there?" Zachary called from outside.

"Why are you still here?" The door opened and Erik turned, facing Zachary. "Please, just leave me alone."

"Grab some things and let's go somewhere else." Zachary gestured to the room. "If someone that nasty did this to your stuff, think of what they might do to you."

"I don't know what it could be that they want," Erik complained.

"Don't you have a suitcase or whatever?"

Erik ground his teeth, watching Zachary push past him and sift through the piles of clothes, searching for a suitcase. Leaving the room, Erik made his way back for the couch, sinking on the edge. He grabbed his coat and combed the pockets, finding his cigarettes and matchbook.

Erik smoked in silence, casually dropping ashes on the floor as he stared at the wall, overwhelmed. Zachary appeared moments later with a small suitcase and a hooded sweatshirt.

"Here, I got some stuff for ya," Zachary announced, tossing Erik the sweatshirt and he caught it. "Wanna crash at my place for a while?"

Erik narrowed his eyes at Zachary. "Why are you so nice to me?" he demanded. "I don't know you at all!"

"Because I want to be nice." Zachary approached and knelt toward Erik, grinning. "Would you rather I be mean to you then?" Erik pushed him away and Zachary chortled as he rose to his feet. "Come on. There's nothing left for you here."

"Yeah," Erik muttered and put out his burning stub into the couch arm. He stood and pulled into his sweatshirt then zipped it close. Erik lastly grabbed his coat and stomped out the room.

"What, no shoes?" Zachary called after him.

"Don't care," Erik called back.

Zachary set down the suitcase and returned to the bathroom, picking up the loafers left there. He hurried to the front door and launched one shoe at Erik standing at the elevators. Erik yowled when struck and turned as Zachary hurled the second shoe, hitting him square in the face.

"You bastard!" Erik screeched and Zachary laughed.

"Wait for me in the van," Zachary called. "I wanna take pictures for the cops."

"Whatever."

Zachary entered the apartment and withdrew his phone then went around, snapping photos. After he was done, he grabbed the keys off the kitchen counter then locked the balcony doors, grabbed the framed photograph left on the couch and took the suitcase with him downstairs.

Erik followed Zachary into a large two-bedroom apartment with a spacious parlor containing two couches and large-screened television on the wall. Many bookcases lined the walls, all holding videodiscs of various educational films and documentaries. Before the couch near the door rest a coffee table with several thick programming books.

"The bedroom's at the end," Zachary said as he placed the suitcase at the door. "The other room's an office."

"The couch is fine," Erik muttered and took a seat on the sofa's edge.

"I'll change the sheets in a minute if you're too tired," Zachary offered.

"You got a phonebook? I need to call Clairese."

"For what?" Zachary shut the door and headed for the kitchenette, rummaging through the cabinets.

"I can't clock in if there's no work to be done."

"I can't remember her number," Zachary replied. "It's Exeter eighty-five something..."

Erik picked up his cellular and dialed the number then paused, trying to recall the last two digits. "Sixty-two," he murmured as he thumbed the numbers and put the phone to his ear. After several rings, he heard Clairese's tired voice answer. "Hey, is everything okay?"

"Oh, hey," Clairese said sleepily. "Don't tell me you're drunk again."

"I'm drunk, but I'm not in too much trouble this time."

"This time?" Clairese snorted. "Are you in jail? I can't afford to bail you out of that."

"No. With a creepy co-worker."

"Ugh, don't tell me!" Clairese's voice suddenly became clearer. "Ew, seriously? You already had to take rounds for The Clap!"

"I'm not sleeping with him!" Erik yelped.

Zachary suddenly laughed. "Seriously?" he called back.

Erik glared at the young man leaning against the kitchenette counter, holding a mug of coffee. "I thought you were changing the sheets," he retorted.

"Stop it!" Clairese cried. "I don't want to hear gory details!"

"No, it's not...!" Erik blew a hard sigh and pinched his nose as he leaned forward while Zachary guffawed. "Look, he's letting me crash after my apartment's been broken into."

"What happened?" Clairese gasped. "Oh no, it can't be related to what happened today, you think?"

"I'm not so sure, but I'm working on fixing it right away," Erik promised. "You won't lose your job."

"If you need anything, let me know."

"I'll lock you in."

"What's your number? It's unlisted."

"I don't know it. It was given to me."

"Where can I find you?"

"I'll call you."

"Please be careful."

Erik shut off the phone and glared at Zachary who giggled behind his coffee. "What is it?" he snarled.

"She thinks you're into me?" Zachary teased. "How cute."

"I'm tired. I've had enough for one night and I've got a headache."

"You want anything for it?"

"Painkillers if you got any."

"I'll see what I can find."

Erik groaned and tossed his phone on the coffee table. Zachary returned moments later with a bottle of pills and a glass of water. Erik glanced up as Zachary handed them toward him.

"What do you want?" Erik asked, taking the items.

"Need anything else?" Zachary nodded toward the door. "I'm about to head back out. Gotta drag the old man back to his place."

"I don't need anything." Erik set down the glass and opened the bottle, shaking out two tablets.

"Food's in fridge, remote's on the shelf and bathroom's across from the office. You can do whatever you want."

"Thanks." Zachary left the room and Erik swallowed the pills he held.

Sitting in silence for some time, Erik began to nod off, only to sit up when he heard someone at the door. Erik immediately rose to his feet and clutched his hands when he saw the longhaired red-headed woman enter the apartment.

"The hell are you doing here?" Erik shouted.

"I live here!" The woman retorted, surprised. "What are you doing here?" Erik moaned and held his head as he staggered rearward against the couch. "Hey!" she called when Erik suddenly fainted.

NINETEEN

Erik felt a firm hand shake his shoulder. He slowly roused and sat up, squinting at Stearne dressed in a dark polo shirt, blazer, jeans and running shoes. Tucked under his arm he held a large manila envelope.

"What is it?" Erik mumbled and rubbed at his eyes.

"Eat breakfast and get ready for school," Stearne ordered. He grabbed a plate on the nearby counter with a slice of buttered toast, sausage patty, poached egg and fried hash, setting it with a dull clink before Erik. "You want oatmeal to go with?"

"I don't want to go," Erik grumbled and pushed the plate away, then put his head back on the table. "I'm planning to kill myself. I want to be left alone."

"Bullshit and you know it. Get up." Erik groaned and rose to his feet. "Here, this is your documentation." Stearne handed Erik the envelope. "Don't lose that."

Erik took it, then opened its seal and shook out its contents, finding a national identity number card, birth certificate, and VitaStat card. He noticed the ID had his face, but different data. Erik picked it up, studying closely.

"Erik Hart?" he muttered. "Wait…" Erik looked up at Stearne. "Does this mean I'm under protection?" Stearne nodded. "I'm not that hard to miss - there aren't many freckled gingers in town you know." Stearne grinned and withdrew portable electric clippers from his pocket.

"It's not going to matter once your hair comes off." Stearne thumbed the switch and the trimmers buzzed. "You're going into a military academy, remember? Off it goes." Erik growled under his breath and plopped in the chair. Stearne chortled as he approached and ran the shears through Erik's hair, cutting off the shaggy red locks. "Now you better be ready by Eight or I'm putting on the hurt."

"You really won't beat me, will you?" Erik asked warily.

"Do you really want to find out?" Stearne waved the trimmers at him. "I could clip your ear if you like. Then they really can't find you."

Erik paled and hurried away.

Once he showered and changed into the jeans and t-shirt left for him, Erik returned to the kitchen finding the plate put away, his hair cleared from the floor and the paperwork returned into the envelope. He collected the envelope left on the table, noticing it heavier than from before. Erik glanced inside, finding a packet. He withdrew it, noticing the packet contained the academy brochure and rules.

Erik slipped the papers back inside and hurried for the door. He ran into Stearne standing on the porch, smoking a cigarette. Erik nodded toward him then made his way for the orange and green-striped hatchback in the driveway.

"You can forget it," Stearne called after him. "You're taking the bus."

"What?" Erik cried and whirled around. "I don't even know where the academy is!"

"The bus stop is down the street and around the corner five blocks. Take the Uptown to City Limits." Stearne reached into his pocket and withdrew a black leather wallet. "Here's your allowance. I'll see you next month." Stearne tossed the wallet at Erik and he caught it.

"Next month?" Erik spat, flabbergasted. "I have to *live* there?"

"Don't get too many citations, because if you get kicked out, you're a dead man." Stearne waved at Erik. "Good luck."

Erik growled under his breath and stormed down the street.

While on the bus, Erik reviewed his paperwork and studied the new identification. It was a hack job, since he still had the same statistics, except for a different name. He wondered if anyone would notice if they looked hard enough.

Hearing the autodriver announce the next stop indicating the academy, Erik put away his papers and pulled the stop cord. Stepping off the bus, he frowned when he faced the campus surrounded by high gates with barbed wire across the top, two large lookout towers stationed on opposite ends of the complex and uniformed guards in tan patrolling with high-powered rifles. Several yards away was a single large white sign posted near the bus stop reading 'Welcome to Rockman Service Academy' in red block stencil letters.

Erik made his way down the gravel path toward the complex. He stopped at the guard's station near the front gate and the warden on duty left her post, approaching Erik.

"What are you doing here?" the guardswoman demanded as she held her rifle at ready. "No civilians."

"I'm a new cadet here," Erik explained, keeping an eye on her rifle. "I overslept and missed my ride."

"We'll see about that." The guard reached for her communicator and depressed the button. "We have a suspicious rat onboard."

"Did it give a name?" a voice responded amid static.

Erik withdrew his wallet that had his altered identity cards and handed it to the guard. She kept her rifle trained on him as she snatched the leather holder and thumbed through it. The woman read off his information and moments later the voice on other end of the line confirmed the results.

"He's going to be trouble," the guard said, giving Erik a critical look. "I can tell." She tossed back his wallet, landing it at his feet. "Good luck, buster. You're gonna need it."

Erik picked up his fallen wallet as the guardswoman returned to her post. The main gate slid open moments later and Erik made his way across the lot, glancing at the signs along the way.

Passing several parked cars before the building containing the administrative offices, Erik pushed open the glass doors and entered a long corridor with many doors and panels. He tensed when he noticed a guard armed with a rifle follow him several paces behind.

Reaching the end at a large dark wooden door with a small placard reading 'Major Calhoun, Chief Administrative Officer', Erik rapped on the panel and a voice called for him to enter.

"I suggest you show some respect to Major Calhoun," the

guard said to Erik as he opened the door. "I hope you have good manners, boy. The Major hates uncouth barbarians."

"Sure, thanks for the tip," Erik said sourly and entered the office.

Tall bookshelves lined along the room's walls, full of tomes about military history, tactics, psychology and torture methods. On the door's other side was the large walnut desk with a plush leather executive chair behind it before a large pane of glass facing the courtyards. Outside, Erik spotted cadets doing exercises while a drill sergeant barked orders at them.

Aside the desk rest a large stack of folders and papers, with the other side full of miscellaneous paperwork and an ultraportable laptop. At the edge was a nameplate, denoting the desk belonged to 'Elise Calhoun'.

The woman dressed in a tan uniform had short brown hair and narrow gray eyes. She stood, scowling at Erik's presence once he neared the desk. Erik swallowed hard when he noticed she was tall and muscular.

"Stand straight!" Calhoun snapped at him. Erik stood straighter, pulling his shoulders back. Calhoun approached and slapped him upside the head. Erik stumbled forward and glared back, rubbing at his head. "I said, 'stand straighter'!"

"I'm doing the best I can," Erik spat back. His head whipped to the side from a swift jab.

"Who told you to speak?" Calhoun bellowed. "Shut your face and stand straight!" Erik rubbed his jaw and received another punch that launched him to the floor on his side. "Stop fidgeting!"

Erik struggled to get up, only to get a swift kick in his guts.

He groaned and tried to get on his knees, gaining yet another kick in his ribs. With the air booted out of him, Erik gave up trying to stand and lay on the floor dazed.

"Get up!" Calhoun thundered and stomped on Erik's back. "Stand and salute me, you weak, incompetent, malingering punk!"

Erik staggered upright and gave a weak salute. He received a hard slap across the face, forcing him rearwards. Erik stumbled back and shook off his stun. He blew a hard sigh, squared his shoulders and raised his hand in salute.

"That's better," Calhoun muttered. "You might make it." She returned to her desk and leaned against the edge. "You're in the Litchfield Barracks. Check in, change, and report to Orientation after Second Mess."

"Second Mess?" Erik murmured.

"Lunch, moron." Calhoun narrowed her eyes at Erik. "Read your manual and memorize it. You *will* be quizzed." She returned to her chair. "Don't think I'll show you any favors since you've been referred by that bastard Gelnika. Your ass will be handed to you in equal measure." Erik paled, unsure whether to silently curse the man or be relieved. "At ease, Cadet. You may leave my presence."

Erik relaxed his stance slightly and immediately picked up his fallen envelope and wallet, then made haste for the exit.

Erik frowned when the guard followed his stride as he left the offices, even once he came outdoors. Erik tried to ignore the man shadowing him and walked about campus, looking at the tan brick buildings.

He noticed the buildings had a letter marking its sector, after passing one labeled 'Bradford' and another 'Coldwater'. Erik figured 'Litchfield' was 'L Sector' and continued his trek for the building. He tensed when the guard kept pace behind him and tried his best to ignore the armed man.

Entering the Litchfield building, Erik walked down a corridor with dark green walls and buzzing strip lights along the ceiling. Noticing several doors with name placards, Erik stopped at one labeled 'office' and knocked.

"You might as well go on to the barracks and grab a uniform," the guard said to Erik. "They'll straighten out your paperwork later."

Erik glared at the man who held his rifle at ready, noticing he wore a tan visor, wide brown sunglasses and his uniform had only a serial number across the left breast, while the right noted rank. "Why do you keep following me, Private First Class One-Ninety Sixty-Two C?" Erik groused. "Why do you keep pointing your gun at me?"

"I'm assigned to shadow you, Kid. That's all they told me."

"You wanna shoot me dead?" Erik turned, facing the man. "Come on then, shoot me. It's not like I really want to live anyway." The young man paled when Erik approached and grabbed the rifle's barrel. "It feels heavy. How many you got in there?"

"Back off, Kid," the guard said nervously. "Don't play around like that."

"Why not?" Erik pulled the rifle's sights at his head. "Pull the trigger, Mister. You really mean it, don't you? Come on, shoot me."

"Stop fucking with me, Kid," the warden snapped. "I'm not gonna shoot you."

"Why not? You keep pointing it at me."

"Rules and shit."

"So what does it take to get you to shoot me?" Erik shoved the young man away. "One hit? Two?" He dropped the envelope and clenched his hands at his sides. "Do I have to make the first move?"

"The fuck, Kid," the guard spat and took a step rearward. "You're nuts."

"I'm not," Erik growled. "I don't like guns."

"T-then you came to the wrong place."

"I'm asking you nicely to stop pointing that at me," Erik snarled. "Or I might have to hit you."

"Hitting me won't do anything but cause you to gain a demerit," the warden snapped. "Get three of them and you're scrubbing floors with a toothbrush."

"How many do I need to get kicked out of here?"

The young man raised an eyebrow. "The fuck you mean?" he griped. "You're *trying* to get put out?"

Erik smirked. "Maybe," he retorted. "How many do I need to get put out of here?"

"Twelve."

"Good to know."

Erik turned on his heel and stormed for the door at the end.

TWENTY

Entering a large room filled with bright plate lights along the walls and green cots dotting the floors, Erik noticed several cots had a pallet of sheets and a navy jumpsuit nearby. He grabbed one at random, finding it had 'Cadet' listed as the rank and a serial number '192-03A'. He stripped of his clothes and pulled into the jumpsuit, buttoning the loose uniform.

"Look here," a voice called, "fresh meat off the wagon."

Erik calmly folded his jeans and T-shirt as a pair of pale young men with gray eyes and cropped red hair entered the room, also in the navy uniform.

"Check it out, Goti," one said. "Skinny little thing too."

"Wonder what he got sent here for?" said the other. "He doesn't look tough at all."

"Who does he think he is? Still got his trainers on!"

The pair stomped over to Erik, their black combat boots thudding across the tiled floor. Erik grunted when pushed aside and he whirled around, glaring at them. He saw they appeared similar, except one had a small scar above his right eyebrow.

"What do you want?" Erik snapped and leaned forward, squinting at the serial tag on the young man's shirt. "Number One-Ninety-Two Fifteen?"

"Can't you say 'hi', dumb shit?" spat Fifteen.

"I got a name," Erik retorted and rolled his eyes at the other. "I don't feel like telling it, Number One-Ninety-Two Fourteen."

"Yeah," said Fourteen, "Number Three."

"I'm not here to make friends." Erik turned on his heel. "Get out of my way."

"What if we don't move out your way?"

Erik blew a hard sigh and ran his hands over his sheared head. *"I don't want to fight these clowns,"* he mused. *"They're just picking on the new guy."*

"Well?" pressed Fifteen.

"If I let you beat me up," Erik said, "will you go away?"

The pair appeared surprised and Fifteen suddenly screwed up his face. He doubled over, laughing.

"Are you serious?" the young man crowed. "You'll just let us hit you?"

"Get it out of your system," Erik snapped. "I won't hit you back. Just get in your licks and be done with it."

"Fine by me," said Fourteen and he abruptly smashed his fist into Erik's solar plexus. Erik held his sides as he fell to his knees, stunned. He gagged and dropped onto his side, wheezing for breath.

"Damn, he really let you hit him, Goti!" Fifteen said, astonished.

Fourteen crouched on his haunches before Erik, smiling. "You're crazy," he noted.

"Maybe," Erik seethed.

"I'm Gottfried, but you can call me Goti."

"Sure..."

Gottfried held out a hand and Erik reached up, giving a limp shake. Gottfried gestured with his chin toward the young man behind him. "That's my twin, Heinrich."

"Henri if you want," Heinrich clarified and he knelt forward, giving his hand. Erik shook his hand as well, then gave his name. "Erik, eh? Nice to meet you."

"If that's how you greet newbies who come in here," Erik rasped, "I seriously doubt your people skills."

Heinrich chortled and pulled Erik upright. "Be careful in making friends in this place," he warned.

"It's like high school," Gottfried interjected, "but with dangerous weapons and nasty attitudes."

"Do you guys go around punching people to read them out?"

"Maybe," Heinrich replied.

"It don't take that long to get a goddamn toothbrush!" a voice shouted at the door. "Double time, you varmints!"

Erik snorted when the pair saluted him then jogged off to another room. He headed for the exit and paused when he met the guardsman.

"What did they say about me?" Erik demanded.

"Why you wanna know?" the warden snapped.

"Because you keep pointing that gun at me."

"Like I said, it's rules and shit." He waved the gun at Erik. "I turned in your papers you dropped to the office. Don't be so careless."

Erik stormed toward the young man and the rifle pressed against his chest. "I'm thinking of a way to get you in a bad way," Erik threatened. "You won't like it very much."

"You're full of shit."

"So shoot me."

"Get the fuck outta my face."

Erik stomped on the man's groin, forcing him crumpling to his knees. "Now you have a reason to point that at me," Erik snapped over the guard and walked past him, exiting outdoors.

Erik crossed the courtyards and approached the mess hall, a large gray building with blacked-out windows and tall double green doors. He pushed against the doors and only one opened, swinging wide. Stepping through, the door suddenly slammed back into his face, knocking him down. Erik sprang to his feet and barreled through the entrance, entering a dimly lit hall with plank tables and chairs.

Many young women and men in navy uniforms sat assorted at the tables over dark brown trays with white square bowls. Erik noticed the newest cadets had freshly shaved bald heads, while older recruits had varying degrees of short hair. Erik kept his chin up and walked across the floor toward the food line where several men and women in white uniforms and black hairnets stood behind pots and ladles, waiting to serve food. One young woman smoked a cigarette, appearing bored.

Grabbing a tray and a bowl, Erik pushed his container toward one serving cook, gaining a spoonful of green sludge dumped in.

"Keep it movin'," muttered the cook and she dragged on her cigarette.

Erik looked around, finding no one behind him. "There's no line," he protested.

"Move it," she spat and dumped ashes in his tray.

Erik grunted and moved onward, gaining more sludge, one

lumpy and white and the other gloopy and brown. After getting a fork and spoon dropped onto his tray, he left the food line and searched for an empty seat. The only one he found was with a group of young men and women, who talked boisterously amongst themselves.

Erik approached and put down his tray on the table with a clang. The conversation suddenly stopped in response as Erik took a seat. He picked up his spoon then scooped up the lumpy white mass. When he felt eyes on him, Erik glanced up, raising an eyebrow. "What?" he said. "I'm starving and hadn't eaten this morning."

Before anyone said anything, Erik yowled when suddenly kicked in the back and shoved out of his seat.

"Thanks for warming it for me, man," said a familiar voice as Erik tumbled to the floor. "And you brought me lunch too? I can dig that."

Erik growled at the tanned young man with a large purple and black bruise on the left side of his face. He immediately sprang to his feet.

"I've had enough people pushing me around!" Erik screeched. "This isn't funny!" He threw a punch and the young man caught it.

"Ay, cut it out," he said and smirked at Erik. "You got me good the last time, but I seen yer shit before."

"You—!"

"She ain't even been in the ground a week and you're still trippin'." He released his hold and Erik stood there, flabbergasted.

"I've seen you before," Erik said once he recognized Raider

who grinned back at him. "Zeadeas, at the funeral... What are you doing here?"

"My old man caught me with the tea I was holdin' fer ya," Raider replied. "So he busted my ass over here the other day, to learn some discipline and shit." Erik yelped when grabbed by the sleeve and yanked down into the seat. "How the hell you get over here?"

"The bus," Erik replied and Raider guffawed.

"Stick with me, and you ain't got no problems."

"Good to know."

"Were you really gonna eat this shit?"

"Yeah."

"Take it." Raider pushed the tray over to Erik.

"Sorry about knocking you around," Erik murmured.

"Don't trip off it, man," Raider assured. "You wasn't with it that day."

A pale young man with tan freckles across his cheeks and dark green eyes started laughing at Erik. Erik glowered back and the young man outstretched his arm, offering his hand. Erik continued to scowl and the young man smiled, flashing straight white teeth.

"Hey," said the young man, "I'm Joe."

Erik reluctantly took Joe's rough hand and gave a firm squeeze. "Nice to meet you, John," Erik greeted in false cheer.

Joe increased his grip and his eyes hardened though he continued to smile. "You're trying to be a hard ass, aren't you?"

"Maybe."

Joe gave Erik a long critical look. "Don't worry, Brother. You'll have plenty of time to learn my name and you'll be screaming it later."

"Seriously?" Erik said through gritted teeth and tightened his grip. "It's like that?"

"Yeah, it's like that."

Erik jerked Joe's arm and pulled him across the table, forcing his face mere centimeters from his tray. Erik grabbed Joe's collar and leaned in toward his ear. "Let's get one thing straight - I got your name wrong on purpose because I don't want friends," Erik snarled. "I especially don't want to be friends with a jerk like you." Joe struggled to get up from his awkward position and Erik tightened his grip. "Are we clear?"

"We're clear." Erik shoved Joe back into his seat and resumed picking at his meal. Joe dusted off his shirt and folded his arms across his chest. "I hear you, Brother, loud and clear," he continued. "I know we're going to get along just fine." Erik stiffened when he felt Joe's foot press against his leg. "But that's after I get in your pants and get that stick out of your ass."

Erik slammed down his fork as his face grew red. "Shut up," he sneered. "Stop saying disgusting things."

"Maybe if something was in it," Joe went on, "I would."

Erik leapt to his feet and lunged across the table, throttling Joe around the throat.

"Hey!" Raider cried as Erik and Joe crashed to the floor and the other cadets started cheering, hoping a long drawn-out fight would ensue. "Break it up!"

Joe laughed at Erik who shook him furiously in rage. "Is that the best you have?" he crowed. "You really don't mean it!" Joe easily knocked Erik's hands away and grabbed his collar, hurling him over onto the floor. He quickly flipped over, straddling Erik's thighs instead. Erik's eyes widened as Joe leaned in, holding down his shoulders. "Now isn't that more comfortable?" he teased. Erik kneed Joe in the groin and let loose a swift jab in his eye. Joe let out a weak laugh as he crumpled forward. "You hit like a girl," he groaned.

"Let me go," Erik snapped, kicking at the young man who still refused to move. "*Damn it, he's strong,*" Erik realized and kicked harder, only to have the Joe grab his leg and twist firmly, flipping Erik over onto his face.

Erik yowled in agony and Joe leaned forward, panting hard for breath. "You really like that, yeah?" Joe hissed. "I've got plenty of positions for us to try."

The noisy chaos suddenly cut silent and Erik looked up from his place on the floor, spotting a tall bronzed muscular man wearing black sunglasses, olive uniform, and pith hat storming in, his long strides thudding across the floor.

"What the hell is going on here?" he thundered as the other cadets immediately stood at attention in response.

Joe let go and scrambled to his feet, immediately saluting the drill sergeant once he approached. Erik staggered upright and stood with his feet together, back straight and hands at his sides. The sergeant leaned in, glaring at Erik, then glared at Joe who failed to keep composure and had a goofy smile on his face.

"This behavior will not be accepted," the sergeant snapped. "Latrine Duty, both of you - now!" The large burly man turned on his heel and marched out the door.

Joe relaxed his stance and marched after the sergeant. Erik clenched his hands, growling under his breath.

"Better get goin', man," Raider urged. "You got twenty-eight buildings of that shit, man - with a baby toothbrush!"

"Right, dude," said a lanky young man with light gray eyes. "Might as well get it out the way as fast as possible. We gotta get up at Five."

Erik blew a hard sigh and made his way across the floor, throwing open the double doors. He glared at Joe who continued to smile brightly at him and received a bat upside the head from the drill instructor.

"Here are your brushes," the drill instructor said, handing them a small toothbrush ensconced in plastic. "Start at Alpha Sector and work your way to Zeta Sector. I want those tiles so clean I can eat off them." Erik reluctantly took a brush and winced when screamed at. "Now hustle!"

Joe scurried off for the administrative building and Erik jogged after him. He glowered at the young man's back, hating his very existence.

TWENTY-ONE

Erik entered the toilets in the administrative offices armed with a toothbrush and a paper cup of undiluted bleach. Joe entered moments later and picked a corner behind the door, immediately getting to work.

Erik turned to the sinks and dipped the brush into the cup, then scrubbed the stainless steel handle. "Give me a reason why you're pestering me," he snapped.

"No reason," Joe replied from his corner.

"Liar."

"Can you prove it?"

"Are you that forward?"

"Just with people I like."

"What is it about me you like?"

When Joe gave no answer, Erik ignored him, overwhelmed with worry.

Taking the majority of the evening and into the night, they were later met by Heinrich and Gottfried who entered the barracks, also armed with toothbrushes.

"Latrines?" Erik asked, nodding his head toward the toilets.

"No, showers," Heinrich answered, nodding toward the gang showers in the opposite direction. "Already in trouble on your first day! You really must be unruly."

Erik grinned. "I'm no badass," he admitted. "I just tried to straighten out that wingnut and here I am."

"Who?"

Erik turned, finding Joe gone. "Joe," he answered.

"Picking on *you* for a change, eh?" Heinrich said and chuckled. "Well, good luck! I hope he doesn't send you into the hospital."

"Hospital?" Erik raised an eyebrow. "What are you going on about?"

"The last new blood he targeted didn't even last *four days*. He broke both his legs clowning around."

"Clowning round, huh?" Erik murmured. "Four days...?"

Gottfried nodded. "We'll keep an eye out if you like," he offered. "We've been here as long as he has."

"Why won't anyone do anything about it?"

"His father owns this place."

Erik paled. "What."

Heinrich waved Gottfried ahead and grabbed Erik's arm, pulling him closer. "Listen, do as much as you can to avoid trouble with him," Heinrich murmured. "Rumors are his father has ties with some big military contracts and is trying to groom him to be the best so he can show off."

"That Joe is a little unhinged to be a soldier," Erik remarked. "How did he pass the psych exams?"

"He didn't. His father paid off the instructors."

"So why is he terrorizing the rest of us?"

"Because he very well can! Just stay out of his way."

"What if that's somehow impossible?"

"If you can last four years, then you can outlast anything."

"Thanks for the warning."

Erik pulled away and returned to the toilets, finding Joe on all fours in a stall, scrubbing at the tiles.

"Have a good talk about me?" Joe called.

"So what?" Erik spat.

"What did they tell you?"

"Why do you care?" Erik focused on the sinks, scrubbing away at the lime buildup on the faucet.

"I only want friends," Joe said sadly. "That's not too much to ask for."

"I don't want friends," Erik snapped. "What part of that don't you understand?"

A low chortle escaped Joe. "I'll *make* you my friend," he vowed. "I have many games in mind for us to play."

Erik rolled his eyes. "Right."

Joe began humming a song and Erik tried his best to ignore the unsettling sensation in his guts.

Pushing himself on through the night, Erik fought sleepiness as he continued scrubbing the restrooms throughout the other buildings. Rage kept him awake, as Joe would continue to talk at him, unnerving him with his unsettling sleaze.

When the final bathroom was complete in the Zurich Field building, Erik dragged his sore body across the commons toward Litchfield. A horn played a melody and the lights in Litchfield turned on.

Erik entered through the doors, made his way down the hall and entered the barracks where he spotted the other cadets straighten their cots and head for the gang showers. Moaning in distress, Erik shuffled to his sleeping area and dropped the toothbrush on the floor, then fell face-first into the cot.

"You gotta get up, sucker," a female voice called over to Erik. He opened one eye, facing an olive-skinned young woman with close-cropped curly light brown hair.

"I wanna sleep," Erik complained.

"Morning drills, baby. Up and at 'em!"

"Have one of those guards shoot me and put me out of my misery."

The young woman giggled. "I can swipe you some coffee if you want."

"Just kill me. I prefer that."

"But then who's gonna fill in for Antony at the basketball game later today?"

"What's up, Kaye?" another voice called. A pale young man wearing a blue cap, dark glasses, and gloves in addition to his uniform approached offside. "Hey, that's the big dummy from yesterday!"

"Hey, you want part of my policy?" Erik said sourly. "I'm only worth a few hundred."

Kaye giggled again and nudged the young man's chest. "Look at that clown, Tony."

"I'm looking," Tony replied and snorted when Erik limply raised his hand, giving them an obscene gesture.

"Well! Mister is really pissed with us cutting into his beauty sleep," Kaye drawled. "Let's get outta here anyway."

"Hey, you know how to play basketball?" Tony asked. "We're a man short. One-ninety-two's playing against One-forty-five today."

"I can learn," Erik muttered.

"Morning drills are at Five-Thirty," another young man said to Erik upon passing. "You skip and you're cleaning the toilets."

"Already did them," Erik grumbled as he hid his face in his arms.

"Either that fool's stupid or crazy."

"Both, prolly," said another and they laughed.

Erik immediately dozed off, snoring softly.

Coming to in a foggy haze, Erik recognized the familiar bips of monitoring machines and looked around, finding himself in a sterile white room with IV lines in his right arm. He frowned when he noticed a pair of armed guards outside his door.

Moments later, an older woman with short silver hair wearing a dark pantsuit under a white consulting jacket entered the room, followed by a female officer in a navy uniform wearing a messenger bag.

"What is it?" Erik grumbled as he sat up. "I got nothing to say to you two."

"After you've recovered from your serious injuries," explained the doctor, "you'll be immediately sent into the Sector Isolation Holding Unit."

"And you need two guys outside the door to keep me here?" Erik let out a weak laugh. "I'm too messed up to even move, let alone run."

"You've escaped capture countless times," the officer snapped. "I'm here to fingerprint you and get your details. The doctor will make sure you're compliant."

"I see, they sent in you two knowing I don't fight women," Erik spat. "Fine, I'll play nice."

The officer withdrew a small tablet from her bag and took out the attached stylus, pecking at the screen. "Give us your name to start," she stated.

"Ferdian Ucal," Erik responded.

The officer rolled her eyes. "We already have all your known aliases. We've found your stash of phony VitaStat cards."

"Even if you input my National Identification Number, all it'll show up is my latest identity," Erik quipped and grinned. "Whatever you'll ask me, I'll disprove it and shut it down."

"We don't have hours to trace who you really are. Just tell the truth."

"Get a warrant and maybe I'll try harder." Erik smirked as the officer growled. "Look, ladies, you're really wasting your time. I really don't know my own name. I'm lucky if I can remember what happened that landed me here."

"We found Contraband and an illegal Armament among your possessions. Tell us who you were running for and maybe we can reduce your sentence by four years."

"I'm just an addict. I run for nobody." Erik shrugged. "Just book me for that and get it over with."

"Are you now or ever have been a member of the terrorist organization INTERTEC?" the officer asked instead.

"Never heard of those guys," Erik replied. "Even if I did, would I ever admit it?"

"Are you now or ever have been a member of the United Federation Defense Forces?"

"What kind of stupid question is that? We all did our time - it's mandatory." Erik blew a raspberry and waved the woman away. "I did my two years like everyone else. Why would that matter?"

"Are you now or ever have been employed by Army Missile and Aviation Systems Troop Command Support?"

"Take a guess."

"Gateway Protective Services?"

"Same answer."

"Genetic Technologies?"

"Really?"

"Cybernetic Command?"

"Come on now."

"Kanbal Industries?"

"I'm not that smart."

"Mercado Corporation?"

"Next question."

"Midco/Sanato Limited Removal Company?"

"You're pushing your luck."

"Rayshine Incorporated?"

"Like I care."

The officer grumbled curses as she continued tapping at the screen. "Have you ever been a patient of Metro Sanitarium's Centerville Complex?"

"You'll have to get my records, lady," Erik retorted. "Try again."

"Keystone Rehabilitation Center?"

"Without a lawyer, you're sunk."

"Have you ever been a student at Rockman Service

Academy or its Military Institute?"

"Now you're really digging up corpses." Erik laughed. "Look, you can waste time and money keeping me rotting at that detention center while you do your dirty work. I can sit it out."

"It'll be easier if you just comply. We've got you on a seventy-two hour hold under Involuntary Commitment, so basically we can pretty much pry as much as we can in that time."

"Then you should know I have a virus that's going to kill me quite soon," Erik noted. "Have the doctors take a look at that."

The officer glanced to the doctor who paled.

"We haven't finished running the genetic tests yet to see if that's true," she said. "It takes forty-eight hours for the basic sequencing..."

Erik chortled and folded his arms across his chest. "By the time you get your results, I'm dead," he vaunted, "and then you still can't prove shit."

"I need to make sure our records are updated," the officer announced, setting aside her tablet on the nearby end table. From her pack she took out a databoard with a touchscreen and pecked at the interface, bringing up an application. "Your right hand, please." Erik gave her his right hand and she took his fingers, placing them on the screen. The device buzzed and she frowned.

"What's wrong with it?" asked the doctor.

"No fingerprints," the officer answered.

"Try the other one?"

The officer puffed an annoyed sigh and took Erik's other hand, gaining the same results.

"I'm not a Synthoid, if you're wondering," Erik replied when the officer became visibly irritated. "I'm sure my DNA proves who I am."

"We've input your DNA in the database already," the officer snapped. "We know you're not Kevin Zachary. You look nothing like him and he was in a coma for a decade."

"What are you saying, that he's my twin?" Erik let out a weak laugh. "Get out of here."

"You are technically a chimera," interjected the doctor, "but there are subtle genetic differences if we know where to look."

"What are you talking about?" Erik spat. "So you're wasting your time trying to connect me to anything. I'll be dead by then, remember?"

"So you mean to tell us you already knew you were under surveillance," the officer snarled, "and infected yourself to evade capture?"

Erik nodded. "Sure, let's say that."

The officer puffed a sigh and put away her devices. "Since you refuse to comply," she announced, "we're going to get a court-issued drug interrogation."

"I want a lawyer if you're going to stoop that low," Erik demanded. "I may be crazy, but far from stupid. I have rights, you know."

"Domestic terrorists have no rights."

The officer and the doctor stalked out the room and Erik groaned, running his hands through his hair. His options were steadily dwindling, as he had few choices in which to fight his charges.

He knew he had slightly better chances with a pre-paid auto-defense lawyer than a live one, since the ambulance chasers tended to be unscrupulous money-hungry cons working for the highest bidder. Even if he did fight the lesser drug charge, that would mean admitting various contacts that got him the Contraband in the first place.

However with the major charge of domestic terrorism hanging over his head, he had very little in the way to sway the courts in believing his innocence, as his rights were automatically stripped.

"Aetheric computer gods, I need a lucky break," Erik prayed. *"If I can get out of this jam, I might become religious soon..."*

TWENTY-TWO

The public security officer returned with an upright stand holding a large computer workstation and camera, followed by the doctor and two others, a young man in a tan suit with a black briefcase and a young woman in a beige dress holding a stack of folders.

"We have a pair of lawyers for you to choose from by the State," the officer announced. "Also, we have the pre-paid counsel. Which do you prefer?"

"I'm taking my chances with the computer," Erik spat back bitterly.

"The use of pre-paid counsel will be tacked onto your court fees. Before we begin proceedings, I must warn you pre-paid counsel has lie-detection equipment such as voice analysis and facial mapping. Do you wish to continue?"

"Hurry it up. The painkillers are wearing off."

"Very well then. The State has issued your drugged interrogation. We have the warrant here, already signed and notarized."

The woman in beige withdrew a sheet of paper from one of her folders and handed it to Erik. He crumpled the warrant and tossed it on the floor.

"Just explain how this digi-court in a box works and get

on with it," Erik growled.

"The pre-paid counsel will act on your behalf, given your testimony," the officer explained as she typed at the workstation's keyboard. "The Digital Court System will provide both prosecution and defense, given the evidence provided."

"I don't have any priors, so this should be quick." Erik snorted. "If anything, your case is weak and it'll be dropped. I'm going to walk out of here and die somewhere."

"Are you sure you wish to continue?" The officer typed in several commands and the computer pipped in response as it started its boot sequence.

"Bring it."

The doctor approached with a pen syringe filled with a clear serum and administered it into his intravenous line while the officer adjusted the camera's swiveling arm, directing it toward Erik.

"You have waived your right to silence and have agreed that any admission you hereby give will be used," said the officer as she quickly typed. "You have also waived the right of trial by jury by proceeding with DCS."

"I want an automatic appeal," Erik snapped. "You violated my right to silence by issuing a drugged interrogation. Whatever I tell you will be thrown out."

"Automatic appeal guaranteed," said a mechanical voice. "Proceed with charges."

"As of today's date, you Ferdian Ucal, possible alias, have been formerly charged with possession of Contraband, possession of military-grade Armaments without official issue and domestic terrorism," the officer announced. "Do you accept these charges?"

Erik frowned, mulling over his decision. He figured he could request evidence of the matter. They had the drugs and weapons easily, though the terrorist charges might be difficult to prove since they had no fingerprints to work with and only his DNA.

Given he had a DNA match to Kevin, they already ruled him out as suspect since he was comatose during the timeframe given. Erik thought about other ways they could have obtained his DNA and recalled Synthoids carried his DNA, since they were approved Federal Replicants meant to replace his real physical body in war.

"Whoever's carrying out crimes in my place want me hung for real," Erik realized. "No," he said. "You have to prove it was really me and not a Synthoid. Good luck with that, because they're government machines and you'll need an Information Notice to gain access to their databanks. They won't give it to you since technically they're Active Service and the information's classified for fifty years."

"Counch charges as follows," said the mechanical voice. "Declaration of unlawful detainment and detainment due to insufficient evidence and suspension of protection of freedom. Request of waiver of past charges with reasonable suspicion. Official State Agents must bear the burden of proof."

The public security officer ground her teeth in response and Erik smirked.

"I got you cornered," he thought. *"Good luck trying to access that data. Federal trumps State and they won't give*

up anything. As far as they're concerned, those people killed were terrorists and the use of Synthoids in public were due to a secret program."

The computer beeped and the digitized voice spoke again. "Charge Number Three of Domestic Terrorism dropped as unlawful use of force or violence committed by Defendant cannot be proven, due to no known Federal property or persons coerced or intimidated to advance political or social objectives."

"Is that it?" Erik asked.

The computer beeped again. "Charges One and Two of seizure and search of property accepted."

"All right!" Erik declared, pumping his hands. "I win. I can die in peace and you can get my fines after the funeral."

"Hold on," the officer said as data immediately scrolled across the screen. "There's something else."

Erik quirked an eyebrow. "What else could there be?"

"Due to the illegal usage of Federal property, charges of Defendant in violation of criminal laws appear to influence government policy affecting the conduct of mass destruction, assassination, or kidnapping primarily within the territorial Federal jurisdiction accepted," stated the computer. "Charges of conspiracy to murder, assault, kidnapping of Federal officials, stalking, arson, bombing, vandalism, destruction of Federal property and economic control by association with known urban revolutionary guerrilla warfare terrorist organization INTERTEC accepted. Defendant pleads guilty."

"The hell?" Erik screeched, appalled. "I don't know who INTERTEC is! I'm not with them!"

"Audio and video evidence obtained by Public Security available," stated the machine. "Does Defendant wish to continue?"

"Yes," Erik growled.

"Video and audio evidence from Grand Lobby of Ulvaeus Hostel, at Six-six-three-five Twenty-Eighth Street, Downtown Keeley, timestamp nineteen-hundred hours, thirty-two minutes and forty-nine seconds Central Time, date unknown due to no input required..."

Erik felt as if his blood froze in his veins when he heard his voice speaking to the hostel's secretary.

"Are you some secret special agent?" the clerk said.

"I work for INTERTEC..." his voice said.

Erik sucked in a shallow breath as his hearing abruptly cut out on him. His skin suddenly went numb and his heart thud hard in his chest as he broke out sweating.

The captured surveillance tape from the Hostel was all they needed. His admittance was the only evidence they needed. Even if he hadn't outright commit crimes in the organization's name, his saying he worked for INTERTEC by association made him complicit, even when they couldn't prove anything else.

His stomach lurched and Erik leaned over, retching on the floor. He hurled again, hacking up his soul and whatever else left inside his guts. There was no way he could appeal whatever judgement they sentenced after that serious charge, even if he vouched for cruel and unusual punishment. A guilty verdict on a terrorist charge automatically stripped him of his rights and gave the immediate death penalty.

"They're going to keep me drugged up and torture me to

get everything I know," Erik thought in horror and gagged. *"Since I'm dying, they'll use that time to pound out of me every snippet they can get their hands on!"*

Erik moaned and slumped back into the hospital bed as the room spun around him. The doctor grabbed his left wrist and slipped on a clear-bodied hard plastic brace that had circuitry inside, snapping it into place. She pulled the tamper-proof sealant tab, locking it firmly in.

Erik glanced up, noticing she spoke and he slowly shook his head. She then took his right wrist, placing on a bluish-green metallic brace. He blinked and the doctor pointed in the opposite direction toward the public security officer who held up a small controller. She too spoke and he had no idea what she said after the doctor locked the brace in place. The officer pressed a button on the receiver and a mild shock went through his arm, jerking his limb.

Then the doctor left his side and lifted the sheets at the foot of his bed, placing another monitoring tether on his right ankle. His leg jerked slightly when he felt the cold copper contacts against his skin.

Erik looked down at the collars he had in disbelief. One was an automatic drug injector that emanated a continuous release of truth serum while the other was a wireless tether transponder that continually pinged his location at all times. If he moved outside the coordinates set inside or broke the circuits, he automatically committed a destruction of State property offense. The last one was a secure continuous remote contraband monitoring device that detected if he had any illegal drugs in his system through his skin.

The male lawyer placed his briefcase on the foot of the bed and snapped it open, withdrawing a sheaf of paperwork. He handed them to Erik. When Erik refused to pick up the paperwork, the lawyer set them in his lap.

The officer wheeled away the computer and the lawyers packed up their belongings, following her while the doctor checked Erik's vitals on the monitoring machines.

Erik swallowed hard after watching her leave once the full extent of his fate dawned on him. *They were going to keep him alive even if by machine to carry out their sentence.* Only after they got their answers, then he would be allowed to die.

Erik pulled his hair and screamed.

A cool compress touched his face and Erik grunted. He looked up at the red-haired woman who appeared concerned over him and sat up, gripping the side of his fiercely throbbing head.

"What are you doing here?" Erik moaned and frowned when he realized he lay on the floor. "Who are you...?"

"Gina, remember?" the woman replied. "Ooh, I hope you didn't hit your head too hard."

Erik glanced over her, finding the coffee table split in half, the glass shattered, and the thick books scattered on the floor. "Damn," he grumbled and looked toward Gina. "Do you live with that weirdo Zachary or something?"

Gina snorted. "This is my place," she said. "He comes over sometimes if he has to work late."

"I don't know if I even have a job tomorrow..."

"Don't tell me you were already fired!" Gina said, stunned.

"I screwed up major," Erik explained and gave her details about the situation and his concerns.

"I see," she murmured, nodding. "So this mysterious guy set you up and is threatening your boss."

"Yet her computer is the only one that didn't get wiped," Erik protested. "He's giving her three days before he turns her over to somebody worse than FSS and SID. I'm thinking she's mixed up in something illegal."

"Just go in like normal and see if there's anything new," Gina suggested. "You said you had friends working on recovering the drives, right?"

"Right, but they might need more help. They don't have a lot of time."

"I'll see what I can do." Gina handed Erik the compress and left his side, heading for the rear rooms. Erik moaned and tucked an arm behind his head as he lay back on the floor, draping the compress over his eyes. "Do you have your friend's number?" Gina called.

"It's in my phone," Erik called after her. He listened to Gina return to the parlor and take his phone, then go into another room.

"No, it's a friend," Erik heard Gina say. "He told me you were having some problems..." The door shut, drowning out her voice.

Once the compress became warm, Erik groaned and sat up, tossing the towel on the broken table. He rose unsteadily to his feet and staggered toward the kitchen. Searching through her cabinets, he found nothing he wanted then opened the refrigerator, spotting foil-covered plates and a half bottle of sangria.

"Nice," Erik uttered and grabbed the bottle. He made his way for the entrance and opened the door, peering out into the corridor. Hearing a snore, he spotted Zachary sleeping against the wall at his feet. "Hey." Erik nudged Zachary with his foot and the young man snorted as he sat up, instantly alert. "I wanna smoke."

Zachary looked up, squinting at Erik. "There's this nice patio we can hang out at," he said and rose upright. "Come on."

Erik shut the door behind him and followed him down the hall. They went through a side door, leading to a courtyard.

"Why'd you lie and say it was your place?" Erik spat. He plopped into a wicker chair at one glass patio table and placed his wine nearby.

"I didn't lie," Zachary muttered and leaned against the wall behind him, hands in his pockets. "I just wasn't specific."

Erik dug through his pockets and withdrew the earring and business card with one hand and his cigarettes and matches with the other. "You lied to me. How do you know Gina?"

"We're good friends." Erik set the card and jewelry aside then struck a match, lighting a cigarette. Uncapping the wine bottle, he raised it toward Zachary with his free hand and Zachary shook his head. "I don't drink."

"Why not?" Zachary said nothing and Erik tapped his ashes with his free hand while taking a long gulp from the bottle with the other. "You don't smoke either, do you?"

"I have other vices," Zachary replied.

"Like what?"

"If I told you, I'd have to kill you."

Erik dropped his head back, looking at Zachary. "Seriously?" he drawled. "You have some illegal fetish or something?"

Zachary smirked and Erik sat forward, continuing his drink and smoking. He flicked aside his burned-out butt and picked up the business card, holding it between his fingers.

"You thinking of something?" Zachary asked once Erik finished the wine.

"Yeah, this number I got." Erik tapped the card against the table. "Somebody gave it to me but the number didn't work."

"Have you tried calling it again?"

Erik set aside the wine bottle. "Got a phone? Gina's on mine."

"Yeah." Zachary withdrew his phone and handed it over to Erik. Erik stiffened when Zachary put a hand on his shoulder and leaned toward his ear. "If you go through my phone," he hissed, "I will spoon out your eyes."

"I'm just calling the number!" Erik protested. "That's all!"

"Good." Zachary pet Erik on the head and returned to his place against the wall.

Erik struck a match and lit another cigarette then quickly thumbed the number. Putting the phone to his ear, he listened to the ringing on the other end, only to cut off suddenly. Erik glanced back at the cellular, finding the total call barely lasted ten seconds.

"Same thing like last time," he muttered.

"What is?" Zachary inquired.

"I called it before and nothing."

Zachary reached over, taking the phone from Erik's hand. "And somebody gave you this number?"

"Yeah, some old pilot named Thompson."

Zachary returned to his place against the wall and played a game. "You owe him money or something?"

"He wanted to know if I was still working."

"Oh?" Zachary sniggered and Erik glared back at him. "You keep fucking up that pretty face and they won't pay you a damn anymore."

"It's not that!" Erik squawked.

"It's kinda late, so try again in the morning, you think?"

"I'm staying out here to smoke a little more," Erik said instead and blew a hard sigh. "You don't have to keep me company."

"I'm not keeping you company."

"Whatever."

TWENTY-THREE

Erik let out a yelp when suddenly overturned and he hit the floor.

"Get up, you piece of shit," screeched the sergeant. "Up, one two! Move it, move it!" Erik sprang to his feet and endured the nonstop yelling in his ear as the sergeant ordered him to upright his cot and fold his sheets, then perform a hundred jumping jacks followed by a hundred push-ups until exhaustion. If he waited too long between sets, the sergeant kicked him in the side and barked louder to move. "Now run, maggot!" the sergeant thundered over Erik after he struggled with the last push up and fell on his face. "Run like the wind! Because if you don't run, I'll blow a cap in your ass a mile wide! Move it!"

Erik grunted when kicked in the leg and scrambled to his feet. "You're really not going to shoot me," he spat.

"Like hell I can, maggot!" The drill sergeant withdrew a canister gun from his holster and fired a solid pellet into Erik's leg. Erik cried out in stunned surprise, clutching his thigh. "Now, move it!"

Erik fought tears as he ran outdoors with the sergeant shouting orders at his back. After running the entire track around campus, when ordered another round, he clenched his teeth when he saw Joe jog up and keep pace as he ran beside him.

"Hey, Brother," Joe chirped. "You ready to work on those lady arms?" Erik narrowed his eyes and increased his speed. Joe easily caught up. "I wonder how your legs look like," Joe went on. "I bet they're pretty shapely."

Erik came to a sudden stop and hurled a side punch into Joe's stomach, crumpling him at his feet.

"That's it, Number Three!" screamed the sergeant. "You're hauling shit in the pit!" He approached Joe and kicked his rear. "Get up Number Seven! You're going to help this idiot."

"Damn it," Erik complained as Joe rose unsteadily to his feet, grinning.

"See, no matter how much you try to rid of me, I'm still here," he crowed. "Let me show you where the pits are."

Erik ground his teeth and jogged after Joe toward a large hole in the ground full of sand. Nearby were several shovels, a wheelbarrow, and pickaxe.

"What's the point of this?" Erik complained as Joe cuffed his sleeves and picked up a shovel.

"We're digging a hole," Joe explained and pointed toward a post a yard away. "We dump the dirt over there. Then after they tell us to stop digging, we retrieve the dirt and put it back in the hole."

"You bastard," Erik snapped. "I'm missing breakfast!"

"At this rate, you might miss lunch and the basketball game too." Joe tossed Erik a shovel and Erik caught it. "Let's dig!"

Erik ground his teeth as he chopped into the earth and released soil into the wheelbarrow. He then took the accumulated dirt and dumped it at the post before returning with it empty. Joe said nothing as he continued digging and dumping dirt. He would pause, watching Erik take the pile to the post and dump it, then return to digging.

When the second mess bell rang, Erik chucked his shovel into the ground and leaned against the tool, panting for breath. He noticed Joe slowed his shoveling and looked longingly in return.

"Stop staring," Erik growled as his ears burned red.

"I can't help it," Joe replied. "You've got a cute ass." Erik picked up his shovel and Joe leaned out the way of a swing, grabbing the shaft. "Hey, you almost put me out with that swing," he said lightheartedly. "Better be more careful." Erik growled and dropped the shovel then stormed for the mess hall. "Hey, where do you think you're going? They're not going to like that you know!"

Erik shoved open the large doors and stomped inside, making a direct line for the trays and bowls. He said nothing as he approached the line cooks and they filled his tray with food and utensils. Erik then returned to the corner plank tables where he spotted Raider, Kaye, and Tony with a group of others talking lively. Erik dumped his tray next to Raider and slumped in his seat.

"Here," Raider said, passing Erik a mug of black coffee. Erik murmured his thanks and swallowed the contents. He winced when he realized it was cold. "Second day here and they already got you doin' hard labor." Raider snorted. "I'm the badass 'round here but I know when to act like a robot. I hate working."

Erik set aside his mug. "How long does it take to do Labor Duty anyway?" he muttered.

"Some last a week, maybe two," said a stout dark-skinned woman with wide light brown eyes. She reached across the table. "Lucy Jackson," she greeted.

Erik nodded and gave his name. "I would shake your hand," he murmured, "but I'm a bit filthy. Sorry to be rude."

Lucy grinned. "It's fine." She withdrew her hand and pointed her thumb toward a lanky tanned young man with blue eyes on her right and an athletic coffee-colored young man with light green eyes on her left. "Hartlan and Sharif. They both come from a line of long-timers."

"Long timers?"

"Military families."

"You?"

Lucy nodded. "I'm a military brat too. Stick with us and you won't have to worry about a thing."

"So you gonna join us on the basketball team?" interjected Sharif.

"I don't see why not," Erik answered.

"It's all regulation," Tony informed. "No street moves."

"I think I can manage." Erik blew a sigh. "Besides, I'm nobody."

"Sure," murmured Sharif, "and about to be a dead somebody in a minute."

Erik looked up when the doors burst open and the drill sergeant stormed in. Erik did a lazy salute once approached and received a hard punch in the side, felling him.

"Outside, maggot," the sergeant bellowed. "You'll be

digging holes all night! Move it!"

Erik sighed and staggered upright, then jogged back outdoors.

After enduring a long day of digging that lasted until evening, Erik retreated to the barracks and gathered his towels, looking forward to a cold shower to wash away the grime. With his mind focused on soap and sleep, he bumped into another person and fell forward, hearing a yelp.

"Get off me, you perv!" a young woman snapped.

Erik sat up on his knees, looking at a short young woman with buzzed dark hair and hazel eyes. He noticed her nametag labeled '192-01E'.

"Sorry," Erik muttered. "I'm tired."

"So, you're the resident dummy of our unit," the young woman said as she stood and dusted herself off. "I heard you replaced one of our ballplayers. You better not make us look bad."

"What do you mean?"

"Don't you know how to read?"

"I hadn't gotten around to it." Erik grunted when kicked in the chest.

"Stupid!" the young woman huffed and stormed past him.

Erik groaned and picked up his fallen towels, then made his way for the gang showers. He stopped immediately when he spotted Joe naked and twisting a towel he held in his hands. Erik yowled when snapped in the side with the cloth.

"Why are you messing with me?" Erik spat and pushed past him for the benches. "Cover yourself please. I don't want to see your junk."

"I don't believe in towels," Joe said brightly and snapped at Erik again. Erik winced when struck across the shoulder. "I like hanging things out to dry."

Erik took off his sneakers and threw one at Joe. Joe giggled and ducked, then snapped the towel at him once more.

"Damn it," Erik shouted, "back off!"

"You better hurry up and get ready for night class," Joe reprimanded. "They have more torture than just running around and digging holes."

"Like what?"

"You'll find out."

Joe left the room and Erik blew a heavy sigh. He looked ahead at the gang showers and then back at the door where he knew Joe would be hiding. Erik toed off his socks and approached the showers, turning on the handle. He stood under the cold water, getting soaked.

Rinsing himself of dirt and grime, Erik dragged himself into the barracks where he spotted Joe fully dressed in a dark green jumpsuit sitting at a cot, shining a pair of boots with polish.

"You bastard," Erik growled.

"What is it now?" Joe asked nonchalantly, smirking at Erik. "Trying to get used to the hosing? Wait until Winter when they hose you down outside and make you run about campus."

"Don't act like you wasn't at the door."

"I'm not," Joe replied. "When I realized you were going to be a hard ass, I decided to jerk off in here." Erik clutched his hands, growing enraged. "Here you go." Joe threw a boot at

Erik, beaning it upside his head. "I polished your boots."

"Thanks," Erik said sourly and picked it up.

"We have classes on military history, tactics, codes, and other various skills, like swimming in armor for example," Joe went on as he buffed the other boot. "We also have martial arts training."

"What are you taking?"

"Aside from the standard hand to hand combat, we have martial art electives. I'm taking up wrestling."

"How nice."

"Here you go!" Joe threw the other boot at Erik and he caught it. "Try not to be late for class." Joe rose to his feet and Erik glared at Joe as he approached.

"What else do you want with me?" Erik snarled.

Joe grinned as he leaned toward Erik's ear. "You know what I want," he murmured then turned away, stalking out the room.

Erik moaned in distress, running a hand over his head. "*I don't know how I'm going to survive all this,*" he wondered. "*The best I can do is try...*"

Over the next several weeks, Erik endured hard labor and the occasional beatings. At one point he finally became too exhausted to fight back and started doing as told. Erik later started making efforts to attend drills and his classes, trying to absorb all he could.

Erik enjoyed his time at the mess hall and playing basketball with Raider and his small group of friends. They worked together to make the time pass easier and rearranged their schedules to maximize their time spent with one another. Erik noticed Raider was the *de facto* leader of their group, followed by Kaye.

The group would compare notes and Erik realized he could recall anything he read and easily passed the tests with Raider's help. Erik later discovered anything involving bodily skill - such as playing basketball, participating in drum and brass corps or combat training - came easily to him after he copied what he had to do and effortlessly repeated maneuvers without thought.

Erik's team started using him during basketball games as a fill-in, having him play any position. The other cadets grew aggravated with his behavior, since they found him difficult to read and his team started winning more games.

It later became a daily occurrence to spar with the group during their downtime to improve their performance. Lucy, Hartlan and Sharif decided to make it their duty to be extra harsh toward Erik during their matches when they realized he skillfully mimicked what others did.

Kaye and Raider then started betting on his matches, teasing the others and pointing out their errors when they lost to Erik again. His only source of difficulty consisted of defeating Gottfried and Heinrich who double-teamed him mercilessly.

"I swear, they're telegraphing each other or something," Erik moaned after another match landed him in the infirmary.

"Maybe it's a twin thing," Raider said and laughed. "Psychic and shit, ya know?"

"Whatever it is, it's scary."

"We should do this again," Heinrich said, smiling brightly. "I'm having fun."

"Give him a week to recover," Gottfried said, rolling his eyes. "I doubt he can deal another round with us."

"I can go another round!" Erik protested. "I was only knocked out for a second!"

Raider smirked. "Yer ass was out cold for a good twenty minutes," he drawled. "You done, man."

"We can't stay long, so we'll catch you later," Heinrich murmured.

"See you," Gottfried said in parting and waved at Erik.

"Don't be a hater!" Erik called after them as they left.

"Are you gonna avoid gunnery class again?" Raider asked, taking a seat on the edge of Erik's cot.

"I don't like guns," Erik grumbled.

"I can't keep covering you, man."

"What's your best time?"

"Two minutes." Raider snorted. "Only because I don't wanna draw attention to myself."

"I can probably beat your time, but I don't want to."

"I dig it." Raider rose to his feet. "Want anything from the canteen?"

"I'll live." Erik waved him away. "I'll catch you later." Raider nodded and left the room.

Erik said nothing when a guardsman later approached, warning him about his detention notice for his refusal in taking part in rifle handling instruction. Erik left his cot and made his trek to the administrative offices, readying himself for a lecture by Officer Calhoun.

"What is your issue?" Calhoun snapped when Erik stood at attention at her paper-strewn desk. "You've been here six weeks. This bullshit should be over already."

"I have plenty, ma'am," Erik replied. "They never gave me the psychological exam when I first entered here. Six weeks isn't long enough."

Calhoun appeared thoughtful and wrote a note on a sheet. "Do you sleep at all?"

"I'm too exhausted to even dream," Erik admitted. "They work me hard here."

"Are you saying that you cut up on purpose?"

"I believe so."

"I'll make a note of that." Calhoun's pen scratched across the page. "I hear you avoid the rifle training."

"I don't like guns."

"How can you be an effective soldier if you don't shoot?"

"I'm sure there's a place to put me that doesn't involve guns."

Calhoun raised an eyebrow at Erik. "Are you a pacifist?"

"I don't know. Depends on the Military Occupation Specialty."

Calhoun narrowed her eyes at Erik. "You're dismissed," she said sourly.

"What's my punishment for my infraction this time?"

"You're going to take apart a rifle and put it together again." Erik paled as Calhoun smirked. "You'll do it until you can part that rifle in your sleep. The best time we have is thirty seconds. I expect you to do it in less."

"Why are you picking on me?" Erik demanded. "I'm still

skipping that class."

"I'm not," Calhoun drawled. "But as long as that bastard Gelnika sponsors you, I have no reason to be nice." She smiled. "At this rate, you must want to go through the torture training program."

"Have I earned enough demerits?"

Calhoun snorted. "What demerits?" Erik turned on his heel and marched out the room. "Don't forget to pick up the line in the hall," Calhoun's voice called at his back.

Erik furrowed his brow and approached the payphone in the corridor. Taking the receiver, he heard jazz music playing in the background once he put it to his ear. "Hello?" Erik greeted.

"Happy birthday, Ace," John Greenfield's voice slurred. "Are you having a good time?"

"No," Erik said sourly. "I'm having a horrible time."

"I need you to do this for me, please," John Greenfield said softly, his voice cracking. "I know it's a big undertaking..."

"Don't cry," Erik murmured and leaned against the wall. "I'm trying to keep it together."

"Good. I'm really proud of you."

"Do you hate me?"

John Greenfield chortled. "No, why would you ask me something silly like that? I love you very much in fact. Very, very much..."

"I don't know..." Erik sighed and slid to the floor, tightening his grip on the receiver. "Making conversation I guess..."

"Listen to me, real close..."

"I'm listening." Erik twisted the cord around his finger, waiting for John Greenfield to speak.

"I don't want anything to happen to you," John Greenfield said softly. "I can't lose you. I don't think I'll make it if I did..."

"Nothing's going to happen to me," Erik murmured. "I'm tough."

"No, I mean it. If I lose you, I'll die. I will really die."

Erik ground his teeth as his nose burned and his eyes watered. "You're not being fair!" he protested. "You piece of shit, you're being unfair!" Erik clenched his hands and held them to his head as he heaved for breath. "The whole thing's unfair!" he wailed. "Why? Why did this have to happen? How could you? You bastard!"

John Greenfield said nothing as Erik broke down sobbing. Once Erik calmed, John Greenfield began speaking. "You're right, it's my fault," he said in a flat tone. "It's my fault that you're in pain and I accept that. I'm sorry I'm not strong enough to help you..."

"Please, just kill yourself," Erik said coldly and sniffled. "I'd feel better if you did. Just kill yourself and disappear."

"Now you don't really mean that. Don't say things like that."

"I mean it!" Erik cried. "Just die already!"

"Ace!" Erik ground his teeth, shaking in rage. "Ace, listen to me." When Erik said nothing else, John Greenfield sighed. "Look, I want you to do something for me." When he had no response, he started pleading. "Please, do this for me. Will you? Please?"

"What is it?" Erik snarled through gritted teeth.

"Keep fighting and prevail... Let your spirit prevail at any given cost…"

Erik shook his head, puzzled. "What a weird thing to say…" he muttered. "You're drunk."

"And please, keep yourself alive so that we'll meet again."

Erik breathed a heavy sigh. "I won't forget…"

"I have to go now."

"Yeah, whatever…"

"Ace…"

Erik hung up the line before John Greenfield could say any more. He drew up his knees, holding them to his chest and wrapped his arms around them. The payphone began ringing and Erik ignored it, burying his head in his arms as tears streamed down his face.

TWENTY-FOUR

Erik vowed to ignore his feelings, closing himself off to others and spoke very little unless spoken to, though he made an effort to interact with his friends. Erik pushed himself as hard as he could during his training and sometimes performed hard labor when he was caught fighting Joe who seemingly made it his personal mission to pester him.

Erik avoided the holiday phone calls and refused his allowance sent each month, preferring to spend time alone and not accumulate any personal effects. As time passed, he delved past his limits, studying until exhaustion to erase any responses he had until he became almost an emotionless robot.

One afternoon, Erik made his way toward the mess hall and filled his tray with the indescribable food, then took his seat next to Raider who sat across from Kaye and Lucy. He nodded at Hartlan and Sharif who sat with them. Heinrich and Gottfried approached moments later, sitting on the other side of Erik.

"Scoot over," Gottfried muttered, nudging Erik's side.

"Switch hands then," Erik retorted.

"I'm severely left-handed," Gottfried snapped.

"So switch with Henri."

"His right ear is bad." Gottfried bat Erik's ear and Erik grunted in response. "Now yours too."

"So what do you think your final scores will be?" Kaye asked as Erik picked at his food, fuming in silence.

"What are you going on about?" Erik murmured.

"We have a big test coming up," Lucy explained. "We're putting all those martial training skills to use by fighting each other."

"That fencin' shit is hella cool," Raider answered. "I wanna see who can keep up."

"They're talking about putting me through some torture training program because I keep skipping rifle class," Erik muttered. "They're making me take it whether I like it or not."

"Why not skip and take a demerit?" Hartlan interjected. "You're not made for this sort of thing, so just act up on purpose so you can go home."

"I've been here eight months," Erik said softly. "I can't go home. I don't have a place to go to…" He puffed a short sigh. "Even after acting out, they ignore it. I even asked Calhoun about my demerits and she acted like I was talking crazy. I'm sure I've racked up more than twelve."

"What do you plan to do then?"

"If they're going to torture me, I might as well suck it up."

"Can they really do that?" Heinrich asked, appalled.

Lucy nodded. "It's called the Enhanced Interrogation Methods Course for a reason," she explained. "If we get captured by the enemy, they'll try some really crazy stuff to get you to talk."

"I thought we didn't have to do that until our fourth year here," Gottfried protested. "That doesn't sound like it's good for the psyche."

"Some people have broken over the course," Sharif interjected. "They get sent away to Keystone to recover."

"Do they ever recover?" Erik murmured.

"Not all of them," Lucy said gravely. "Anyway, what's your specialization?"

"My specialization?" Erik raised an eyebrow. "What are you talking about?"

"You're gettin' pretty good with the rapier," Raider noted, nudging Erik in the ribs. "Though you ain't fast enough to keep up with me."

Erik snorted. "All I have going for me is speed," he grumbled. "I'm not strong enough... I doubt I'll ever be."

"You'll make it, believe it," Heinrich assured. "Just keep working hard."

"If you say so..."

"Some folks have their specializations," Lucy cut in. "Like Antony for example, he's a badass all-around fighter."

"Antony?" Erik piped. "You mean Tony?"

"No, Antony. You hadn't seen him lately because he's always out practicing."

"Dre said he might come over to hang with us for a change," Kaye said. "You've seen that tall skinny dummy. He's a lot like you."

Erik's face flushed scarlet. "Don't they get in trouble for skipping other classes?" he asked. "I don't see them when I get my rounds of hard labor put in."

"They've passed everything thrown at them," Lucy said and snorted. "I hate trying to top Antony."

"Don't tell me he's the one who can assemble a rifle in

234

thirty seconds."

Lucy nodded. "Dre's a close second in thirty-three, but don't let that idiot fool you."

"What do you mean?"

"Andre's a genius," Hartlan filled in.

"When it comes to anything military-related," Sharif piped.

Hartlan nodded. "Sure, but throw him on the street and he's a goner."

Erik moaned, holding his head in his hands. "Why do I bother?" he mewed. "I don't understand the point of all this."

"The point is that we're going to take down the Synthoids," Kaye said. "The last batch is screwy and it's too expensive to do a recall."

"Why can't the soldiers take care of it?"

"They have better things to do, like fight stupid wars," Lucy replied, smirking. "It's cheaper to send misfits."

"Ain't nothin' wrong with canon fodder," Raider noted. "The pay's real good."

"I'm still holding onto that fifty I came in with," Erik groused. "I hadn't even found a soda machine around here." He pushed away from his tray and rose to his feet. "I'm going to check out the class and see what it's like. I might even ask Antony a few pointers."

"You gonna be okay, though?" Raider asked. "That EIMC's gonna sweat ya out."

"I think I can handle it," Erik said and stalked out the mess hall.

Exiting outdoors, Erik passed Joe along the way and Joe

grabbed him by the arm.

"Wait up," Joe said.

Erik turned out of the young man's hold and twisted Joe's arm at his back. Joe let out a surprised yelp when forced to his knees.

"I told you to leave me alone," Erik snarled. "What part of that don't you understand?"

"I'm not leaving you alone," Joe retorted, grinning. "I told you I'll have you screaming my name."

"Disgusting bastard," Erik spat and shoved him away. He stepped over Joe and entered the Harris Field building, searching for the classroom near the indoor gun range.

"Major Vanoe?" Erik called as he knocked on the door. "Major, I'm here about the rifle assembly..." Knocking harder, the door swung open and he entered the room, finding the classroom empty.

Erik glanced around, noticing the shelves were full of books about weapons throughout the centuries and various gun types. He approached the teacher's desk, finding paperwork on weapons schematics.

"Wha'cha lookin' at?" Raider's voice called. Erik gasped and looked up, finding Raider standing at the door.

"Why are you following me?" Erik snapped.

"Hey, thought you might need a hand." Raider approached the desk and rifled through the papers left there. "That's some cool new toys there," he murmured. "If we get some scrap lyin' 'round, we might be able to play with it."

"Can you read it?"

"Yeah." Raider tapped at the paper. "That one there's for

a plasma sword here, and this one... It's some weird shit, but it might work."

"How weird is it?"

"I can't draw worth shit, though," Raider admitted, "but find me somebody who can, and we can fix them flaws there." He chortled. "Never knew the old dude liked designing new toys. Shoulda been payin' more attention in class."

The rear door opened and a young man with curly blond hair in black uniform and navy polarized glasses exited, holding a bloody saber. He paused at the sight of them, surprised.

Dull pain ripped through Erik's shoulder in response and he winced. "Who are you?" Erik demanded. "Why is your uniform different?"

"I'm part of the security team," the young man replied.

"Bullshit," Raider spat. "They're brown 'round here."

"Stand back," the young man growled and held his saber at ready. "Don't make me have to hurt you."

"Aw, shit," Raider complained as he backed away. "Look man, we ain't got shit and we don't know shit. You ice us and you're wastin' yer time."

"No witnesses," the young man snarled and pointed his saber at Erik. "You should've been dead a long time ago, Schumacher. I'm taking you down first."

The swordfighter lunged toward Erik and Raider quickly stepped in, yanking the man's arm and reversed him. Raider twist the man's wrist, forcing the saber from his hand.

"Beat it!" Raider shouted at Erik as he kicked up the saber and stomped on the man's chest, launching him to the floor.

Erik took off running, making his escape. *"They're back to kill me,"* he thought frantically as he burst outdoors. *"How did they find me? I never told anyone who I was here!"*

Erik ran into the Ignatius Station building nearby and ducked into the first office he found unlocked, hearing gunfire riddle the corridor outside. Erik held his breath as he crouched behind a desk, shuddering. Moments later, the door slammed open.

"I can torture you to get the information I need," said the assassin. "I can start with your toes, taking them off one by one." The hired killer kicked at a chair, sending it flying. "Then onto your fingers..."

"Why are you targeting me?" Erik called. "I told you I don't know anything. My dad kept me in the dark on purpose!"

"Stop lying!" Erik cried out when a rifle blast took out a light overhead near him, raining smashed glass and plaster. "We know about your skills. We know he gave you the data in the case he died in some unfortunate accident."

"I don't know anything!" Erik screamed. He rose to his feet and the assassin kicked the desk, pinning him against the wall. Erik cringed when the murderer jammed the rifle's muzzle against his head.

A muffled explosion resonated outside, causing the ground rumbling beneath them as the windows in the room shattered from the shockwave. A loud siren suddenly wailed in response.

"All active soldiers report to stations," called a voice over the announcement system. "Enemy troops invading from 'H' Sector. This is not a drill. Repeat - this is not a drill. All soldiers to your posts or staging areas. All soldiers prepare for immediate deployment."

The terminator took off running and Erik pushed the desk away, slipping to his knees.

"Hey!" Raider's voice called moments later. "You in here?"

"Yeah," Erik called back. Raider raced in and knelt at his side. Erik looked up, noticing he sustained a gash across his chest. "You all right?"

"This ain't nothin'," Raider said, smiling slightly. "Is you okay?"

Erik shook his head and held his arms tight about his body, shuddering. "They're still trying to kill me," he mewed. "All over schematics I know nothing about or understand."

"I know what they're talkin' 'bout, man, and the shit ain't good." Raider took Erik by the arm and pulled him to his feet. "Let's book and I'll explain it to ya later."

"I don't want to go," Erik protested, pulling away. "They're going to want me dead anyway, so let them have at it."

"At least try to understand what they're killin' ya fer!" Raider snapped. "They iced your moms over this shit and she ain't done a damn thing!"

"I don't have the stones to put up with it," Erik complained as Raider pulled him along.

"Remember the shit they trained ya fer if you wanna come back alive."

"I don't want to live anymore."

"Then I'm ridin' yer ass to keep you alive, you stupid fuck."

Erik gave a faint smile in response.

TWENTY-FIVE

Barreling outdoors, Erik and Raider came across strewn bricks, shattered glass and twisted metal as the nearby building belched heavy smoke in the air. The complex was a scene of chaos as soldiers and military security scrambled about to their stations, readying to combat the enemy.

Raider pulled Erik for the barracks where they met with their group who hurried into body armor. Erik cringed when he heard explosions outside and the ground rumbled beneath them. The lights flickered in response before going dim.

"Are we actually going out there?" Erik squawked as he pulled into a breastplate and greaves. "What do they expect us to fight with?"

"All right you maggots, listen up," shouted the drill instructor as he stomped inside. "Some of you punks have been here longer than the new bloods, so you'll be unit leaders. Now I'm separating you groups so listen close."

"You okay?" Kaye asked as Erik sat on the edge of his cot, holding his head in his hands while he tapped his foot nervously on the floor. "You look ready to hurl." She dropped a helmet on his head. "Strap in, baby, 'cause it's gonna be a crazy ride."

"What are they sending us out there for?" Erik moaned as

he adjusted the bucket helmet. "We're not armed and totally not prepared for this."

"Recon work," Lucy responded. "They want us to find out how spies got into the complex."

"B-but they're loaded to the hilt!" Erik shook his head. "They'll kill us."

"Ay, man, we ain't gonna die, ya dig?" Raider assured. "All we gotta do is put our heads together."

"Right," Kaye said sunnily.

"Check this - I'm like a ninja and shit. We ain't even gotta take nothin' like pirates." Raider pumped his hands. "Lemme see what we gotta steal and we can make up that shit as we go on from there."

"Are you serious?" Erik cried.

"You group of fleshpots are Galkan Unit, got it?" the sergeant called as he neared them. "Your job is to secure the perimeter. Now fall in, Number Three Alpha, Number Ten Delta, Number One Echo, Number Sixty Gamma, Number Fourteen Iota, Number Twenty-two Kappa, Number Fifteen Lambada..."

"We got some guys missing," Lucy said over the sergeant's calls. "Andre and Antony's not here."

"We came back from Harris," Erik murmured. "I didn't see them."

"Henri, Goti, you two find out where they are," Kaye directed. "Zeadeas, you're sticking with Lucy and Sharif. I'm going with Erik and Hartlan."

"What about Echo over there," Sharif asked, pointing toward the short young woman with cropped black hair and dark hazel eyes who glared at them. Joe approached, smiling brightly and put an arm around the girl.

"Hey guys," Joe said cheerfully. "We're assigned to your little crew. This is going to be fun, eh?"

"Get your nasty hands off me," the young woman snarled. "Or I will break them."

"Ooh, firecracker, I like that." Joe giggled and released his hold. "What else will you do to me?"

"You stick with her," Kaye said sourly. "We're good."

"Oh, so you're putting me with the resident creep, huh?" the young woman snapped.

"You always stuck to yourself," Kaye protested, "and hell, we don't even know your name!"

"My name shouldn't matter," the young woman spat. "But if you really must know, the name is Danae."

"Then Danae, help out Goti and Henri. Put your heads together and figure out something."

"Whatever."

"Move out you pieces of shit," the sergeant shouted and the groups of cadets swarmed for the exits. "If any one of you bums try to escape, you're up for immediate dismissal!"

"Okay, so tell me what happened," Kaye said to Erik. Erik explained to her what he and Raider found.

"They killed Vanoe?" Hartlan murmured. "Over schematics?"

"It seems to be that way," Erik said gravely.

"Antony's the one you want for technical drawing," Kaye said. "He's probably assigned to map duty."

"Where do you think he might be? Did you see Tony

anywhere?"

"Shit," Kaye grumbled. "Let's check out the communications tower."

"What do you want me to do?" Erik asked as he followed his group. "I'm no use... I might hold you back."

"If we can round up Antony and Zeadeas, you can help check if the paperwork's right," Kaye said. "I noticed you can spit back whatever you've read."

"But it's a drawing," Erik pressed. "I can't recall that."

"You can still help out." Kaye opened the door and Erik's jaw dropped when he saw the carnage outside.

Several buildings were ablaze and many soldiers ran about as small arms fire tattered back and forth. The ground rumbled from explosions and pained screams filled the air among the shouting of directives. Some bodies were down on the ground in pools of blood and guts, having been executed in the most gruesome way possible.

"I-it's a warzone!" Erik cried.

"No shit, genius!" Kaye shouted.

"I wouldn't be surprised if someone's trying to shut us down," Hartlan said calmly as Erik retched at his feet. "We are technically assigned to destroy military weapons. That's the whole point of our training."

"I can't do this," Erik moaned and sagged against the wall. "Just go on without me."

"Let's go," Kaye ordered. "Communications Tower 'A' is closest to our side."

Erik sprinted across the yard with Hartlan as Kaye took

the lead. Dodging gunfire, they made their way to the next building and crouched down behind the wall away from the main area.

"They're waiting on us to get out there," Erik wheezed. "We can't run forever."

"They're gonna send somebody," Kaye said, "and you're gonna greet them."

"What?" Erik cried. "No–!"

Kaye shoved him out into the open and a soldier raced up to him, armed with a bayonet. Erik dodged several swipes aimed at his face and neck then Hartlan yanked back on his arm, pulling him down toward the ground. Kaye sidestepped the next attack and reached forward, grabbing the rifle's muzzle. She gave a forward stomp as she twisted the rifle away out of the soldier's hand, then jammed the stock into her enemy's neck, crushing his windpipe.

"All right, we got weapons!" Kaye crowed as Hartlan let Erik go and knelt at the dead soldier's side, searching his pockets. He took the sidearm, extra magazines, and a trench knife.

"Here ya go," Hartlan said, tossing Erik the combat knife. Erik caught it and pulled the long blade out of its sheath. "Get stabbity, soldier!"

"I-I'll try," Erik murmured.

"Next one! Let's move!"

Erik and Hartlan followed Kaye as they kept cover behind the buildings, slowly making their way to the communications tower. Hartlan picked off soldiers with his handgun and Kaye took down soldiers who closed in on them with her bayonet.

Erik kept his distance, cringing as he watched the two kill enemy fighters with ease.

Gaining ground toward the administrative offices, Erik noticed a heavily armed soldier with a closed polarized helmet wielding a plasma pack taking aim at cars in the parking lot, destroying the vehicles in a blast of flame.

"The records are housed in there," Erik said as a wall of fire and wreckage blocked off the front gate. "After he gets what he's looking for, he's going to torch the place."

"Sneak around back and get in," Kaye commanded. "We'll take him out."

"What else do you want me to?"

"Barricade the joint and hold out until we can get back with Zeadeas and Antony."

"I'll try my best."

Kaye stepped out onto the lot and whistled at the solider. "Hey," she called. "Over here!"

"Are you nuts?" Erik yelped.

"C'mere, you!" Kaye grabbed Erik's collar and shoved him forward. "Here's the guy you wanna toast. He's got all the stuff you wanna destroy."

"Wait!" Erik cried as the soldier raised his nozzle. "I don't!"

A single shot fired from behind and the soldier staggered rearwards, stunned when his helmet cracked. Kaye kicked Erik down to the ground and hurled the bayonet forward, jamming the blade into the soldier's chest. He turned and Hartlan fired again, piercing the tank. The tank exploded and Erik scrambled to his feet, scurrying away from the resulting plasma wave.

While other soldiers converged onto the scene, Erik ducked into the side door in the offices, racing down the hall. Hearing a clatter, he whirled around, lashing out with his combat knife.

"Well, well, you found me," a familiar voice called.

"Please, Zeya," Erik pleaded, backing away from the assassin in black who twirled a long-barreled high-powered revolver in his hand. "There has to be another way."

"I'm here to kill you," Zeya stated and grinned maliciously. "I guess you understand that much."

"You didn't kill me the first time when your master told you so," Erik snapped. "Why do you keep targeting me? I don't know a damn thing!"

"Stop lying! I'm a soldier, just like you, so stop pretending you're innocent." Erik backed way as Zeya moved closer. "We've been keeping a close eye on you for a long time. We know you share the same skills as he does - inherited a gift, I guess you could call it. Hence the change of heart."

"He makes non-lethal applications for the Public Defense Works program!" Erik cried. "What makes you think I know anything about his work? That's all I know from what he told me!"

"You idiot, your father's so called non-lethal applications have killed thousands! It don't take much to militarize those mining robots!" The assassin pointed his revolver in Erik's direction. "I'm not letting you get away this time. You should've taken the money the first time."

"Forget it, you arrogant son of a bitch," Erik snarled. "You hurt me, I will hurt you back."

"Then it's over for you."

Zeya fired and Erik yelped in pain when blasted in the side. His ears rang and he clutched his bleeding side searing in fiery agony as he staggered rearwards.

"*I'm dying*," Erik thought, glaring back at Zeya marching toward him. "*They're getting rid of me, of Dad, and my friends...*" He clutched the combat knife with a shaking hand in a vain attempt to keep calm under pressure. "*Because of what I saw and didn't understand. Something changed. The orders were changed...*"

It's painful, that feeling... Isn't it?

Protect him with everything you have...

You'd do the same for him too...

Zeya glowered back at Erik when he raised his knife in his direction.

"Do you really think you can kill me?" Zeya challenged and jammed the revolver's muzzle into the side of Erik's head. "Go on, cut me, but know this bullet is faster than you." Erik gulped when Zeya thumbed back the hammer.

"Suck on this, asshole!" a voice called. Zeya turned and a shotgun blast threw back the assassin, throwing him off his feet. Erik whirled around as Joe sauntered in, holding a large bore rifle in his arms. "Well, well, lookie here!" Joe vaunted at Erik. "And to think you was about to let that dickhead get rid of you."

Erik swiped at Joe with the knife, enraged. "Get out of my way!" he screeched. "Stop coming on to me!"

Joe smirked as he easily sidestepped Erik's mad slashes. "You don't know who you're messing with, little boy," he

247

thundered and slammed the rifle into Erik's side, instantly felling him. "I did you a favor, saving your shitty little life! The least you could do is fucking thank me!"

Erik turned over, striking the blade into Joe's thigh. Joe roared in pain and kicked Erik away, sending him hurtling onto the floor. Limping up to Erik, Joe rammed the rifle stock into his face before he could get up, instantly knocking him out.

TWENTY-SIX

"Prisoner Number One-Three-One-Two-Zero, Report," a voice called loudly.

A firm whack on his leg jolted Erik awake and he sat upright, startled. Two armed female Public Security officials pointed their rifles at him and a woman with wavy brown hair in a red blazer over a tan blouse and pencil skirt faced the foot of Erik's bed.

"Who are you?" Erik groaned.

"I am Inquisitor Alisaundra," the woman answered. "Before we begin questioning, do you understand your sentence?"

"What?" Erik blinked slowly and looked around the room. He noticed a pile of paperwork on his nightstand and picked them up, scanning its contents. "*Order of Supranet Electronic Tagging and Tethering Monitoring Device installed, Order of Offense Monitoring and Mandatory Electronic Interrogation advised, Order of General Rehabilitation until cured - involuntary commitment required until sentence is complete...*" Erik crumpled the papers and threw them on the floor. "I understand it, all right," he growled, "but I'm not telling you shit."

Alisaundra narrowed her eyes and folded her arms across

her chest. "We will stop your pain medications if you still refuse to comply," she threatened.

"Go ahead and pull all the stops." Erik held up his left wrist adorned with the clear brace. "You're already pumping in a steady stream of truth serum," he spat. "You don't get more truthful than that."

"Why are you still belligerent?"

"I can still tell the truth and be a hardass." Erik grinned. "Any more questions?"

"Who sold you the Contraband found on your person at the Ulvaeus Hostel?"

Erik grinned. "Nobody," he answered. "*Which is true,*" he mused. "*Palmer gave it to me.*"

"Who sold you the illegal Armament?"

"Same."

"Why did you reserve room seventy-three at the Ulvaeus Hostel?"

"I don't know why."

"Did you reserve the room seventy-three at the Ulavaeus Hostel?"

"No."

"Is your name Ferdian Ucal?"

"Yes."

"Was it Ferdian Ucal who reserved the room?"

"Yes."

Alisaundra puffed a hard sigh and pinched the bridge of her nose. "When did you reserve the room?" she grumbled.

"I don't know," Erik responded.

"According to the Hostel's records, it was reserved on a

Thursday."

Erik shrugged. "Then there's your answer."

"What were you doing Thursday?"

Erik laughed. "Seriously, like I know." He jabbed a thumb to his chest. "Lady, I stay high as a damn kite. I never know what day it is."

Alisaundra began pacing the room, thinking. Erik watched her as she held her chin in her hand with her head bowed in deep thought as she crossed the room.

"Do you watch the news or read the newspaper?" she asked moments later.

"Sometimes," Erik admitted.

"Did you read the paper or watch a newscast recently?"

"Sure..."

"What was the headline?"

"Public Security was looking for a domestic terrorist," Erik replied and frowned. "What's this got to do with me?"

"Is that why you infected yourself with a blood disease? You knew we were coming so you had to take yourself out."

"No, it was that doctor–!" Erik immediately clamped a hand over his mouth. His eyes widened when Alisaundra stopped pacing and whirled around, facing him.

"So a *doctor* infected you, is that it?" she declared, placing her hands on her hips.

Erik shut his eyes, cursing himself in his head. "*That damn doctor told me his name!*" he thought. "*Why would he do a stupid idiotic thing like that?*"

"Who was the doctor?" Alisaundra commanded. "Tell me the name of the doctor who infected you."

"Albero Hansen," Erik muttered.

"What? Remove your hand. I can't hear you." Erik lowered his hand and blew a hard sigh. He repeated the name and the Inspector nodded. "I see. What kind of doctor is he? What does he do?"

"Transplants."

"This disease he gave you, how long did he say it will last?"

"Three days."

"How long ago did you receive the injection?"

"The day I saw the article."

Alisaundra had a fleeting look of concern on her face, then became hard and serious. "Did you receive any phone calls after the injection was made?"

"No."

"Before?"

"No."

"Any days prior before the injection?"

"How many days?"

"One, two, three, two weeks, four weeks, a month, a year... any day."

Erik shrugged his shoulders. "Sure I got a call, but I couldn't tell you what day it was. I was high."

"What was the call about?"

"Which one?"

"So you got two calls?"

"Three."

"Three." Alisaundra ran a hand through her hair. "Where is your phone then?"

"Your guess is as good as mine."

"Did you lose it?"

"Yes."

"Did you give it away?"

"Yes."

Alisaundra clenched her teeth and glared a Erik. "Which is it?" she said evenly. "Did you lose it or give it away?"

"Both."

"Who did you give it to?"

"Lynne... Palmer..."

"Lynne Palmer." Alisaundra smiled triumphantly. "Good, we have a name." She stormed out the room and the officers followed her. Erik groaned in response, slumping back in bed. A twinge of pain seared down his back and he winced, sitting up.

Moments later a digital ring cut the air. Erik jumped, surprised and looked around desperately for the sound. He sighed in relief when he spotted the bedside phone on the wall near the nightstand, a single tan and black receiver.

"H-hello?" Erik stammered once he picked up the line. "Look, I can't talk. I'm being monitored."

"Isn't this a lovely surprise," a digitally masked voice said over the line amid heavy static. "To think you'd get in a snarl like this. How inconvenient."

"I'd rather not talk now. I'm under a court-ordered drug interrogation."

"Oh, so you have company. How sad. What a troublesome thing to deal with. And to think you'd deny my invitation for my party this weekend.

"I might not make it. I'm dying."

"Living is just a slow death, isn't it?"

"I can't come."

"But it'll be happening at the Square! All the hip kids will be there. I'm sure you can sneak away, can't you?"

"I doubt that I can."

"But I'm so lonely without you. It's been two years since we've last seen each other. I had a lot of fun..."

"Don't cry. I'll try my best."

"That's great. See you soon."

Erik noticed the armed guards at the door immediately scurrying away and frowned at the phone call.

"*How weird,*" he mused. "*Who else would know I'm here...? Unless...?*" Erik glanced out the door and spotted the beefy red-headed technician peering through the observation panel. The technician winked at him and walked away. Erik moaned and drew the covers to his chin as he sank into the mattress. "*This is getting too weird...*"

Hearing a small tone, Erik felt the disconnectedness come on quickly when the automatic pump in his IV released a flush of painkilling medication. Instantly growing numb, Erik fell over into oblivion.

Sensing warmth on his skin, Erik opened his eyes and squinted when faced with early morning sunlight. He shuddered, realizing he sat on the patio and noticed he had a blanket draped over his body. Standing, Erik hung the covers around his shoulders and returned to Gina's apartment.

Upon entry, he found the broken coffee table cleared away and Zachary asleep on the couch. Erik dropped the blanket over the young man then took up his suitcase behind the door. Opening it, he withdrew a simple wash and wear suit and a wrinkle-free shirt then made his way for the bathroom. Switching on the light, Erik found a single toilet, mirror, and tub with showerhead behind a glass door.

"Are you all right in there?" Gina called outside the door.

"I'm fine," Erik answered. He stripped off his clothing and removed his bandages, checking his injuries. "I usually heal faster than this," he grumbled, noticing the cut across his thigh weeping slight blood.

"What is it?"

"Need to tape up," Erik said.

"I'll get some."

Erik turned on the water and stepped in, shutting the door. He stood under the hot water, clenching his hands as the stream poured down his back. The fear and unease he felt tightened in his chest, making it hard to breathe. Erik ground his teeth when he heard the voices whispering to him.

These dreams are real...

The pain, the nightmares, all of it, everything...

They're more than just memories...

Erik clamped his hands over his ears and screamed. "Shut up in there!" he howled. "Shut up!"

You swore to never forget...

You need to remember...

Before they destroy you...

You need to see the truth!

"No!" Erik wailed and crouched to the floor. "Stop it!"

Accept it, despite the pain!

Fall off the edge of madness!

Kill them - annihilate them all!

The door suddenly slid open and Erik gasped, looking up at Gina who had an unreadable expression on her face. Gina stepped away as Erik rose to his feet. She immediately turned around and stalked out the room, saying nothing. He glanced over, finding several boxes of gauze and tape on the counter.

After Erik finished washing, he quickly bandaged his remaining injuries and dressed. Scooping up his discarded clothing off the floor, Erik entered the parlor, finding Gina on the other couch with a mug of coffee.

"I just made some," she said to him. "And you could've left your clothes there. I'll take care of it."

"Any word about progress?" Erik asked as he dumped the clothes in the hall and entered the kitchenette. He grabbed a mug left for him on the counter.

"Nothing at all," Gina admitted. "Just go in and play it cool."

"I'm sorry to involve you," Erik murmured.

"You're fine."

Erik prepared his coffee then took a seat across from Gina on the couch, sitting in silence. Zachary later roused and yawned as he sat up.

"Ready to go?" he murmured.

"In a bit," Erik replied.

"Give me a minute."

"Sure."

Zachary folded the blanket and left it on the couch's end, then made his way into the bathroom.

"If you need help with anything," Gina said softly, "feel free to let me know."

"I don't want to further involve you," Erik complained.

"You already involved me when you asked me to call your friends."

"It'll only complicate things!"

"Don't tell me you're actually worried about me!"

Erik grunted and turned away, sipping his coffee. "I'm not," he grumbled. "I'm worried about Francisca. She said she was going to help me disappear."

"Why do you want to disappear?"

Erik shrugged his shoulders. "It's a promise we made years ago."

"If that's the case, then why involve me? You must trust me on some level."

"We're not friends. I don't even know who you really are." Erik rose to his feet. "I'm just nobody to you, so please be more careful in what you involve yourself in. I tend to attract bad people."

"Then don't be so dependant on others."

Erik crossed the room and set aside his mug on the kitchenette counter as Zachary entered the parlor dressed in tan slacks and open dark brown dress shirt. He held Erik's coat draped on one arm and ran a towel through his damp hair with his free hand.

"Ready to hit up the office?" Zachary asked and tossed the towel aside on the couch.

"Sure," Erik answered, taking his coat. "I need to talk to Clairese anyway."

"Come on. I wanna get some tater tots."

Erik snorted and left Gina's apartment, making his way toward the exit.

TWENTY-SEVEN

Zachary pulled up to the drive-through ordering machine on the side of a fast-food restaurant.

"What do you want?" he asked as he rolled down his window.

"Coffee," Erik responded.

"You can get that at the office."

"I don't know. Sandwich or something."

"Good morning!" the operator said on the intercom. "May I take your order?"

"A cup of tots and a super burger with all the stuff," Zachary answered.

"That'll be five-eighty."

"Why are you buying me lunch?" Erik asked as Zachary drove to the receiving window.

"Who said the super burger was for you?" Zachary retorted as he reached in his pocket and withdrew his wallet.

"Excuse me for assuming," Erik muttered and gazed out the window.

"Here you go!" said a worker as he leaned out the window and handed over a small sack. Zachary took the bag and passed it to Erik.

Erik opened the bag, glancing inside while Zachary handed six bills in return.

"Keep the change," Zachary said and pulled away.

"Hey, you got two cups of tots in here," Erik said as he took out the sandwich.

"They know I like them a lot," Zachary answered. "So I let them keep the change."

"Why don't you just buy them from the store?"

"They're not the same." Zachary held out a free hand. "Gimmie one."

"They're hot."

"Don't care."

Erik plucked a small shredded potato bite and put it in Zachary's outstretched palm. Zachary popped it in his mouth and suddenly chortled.

"What's funny?" Erik queried, raising an eyebrow.

"Nothing."

"Really?"

"Gimmie another one."

Erik did as told, handing over the food while Zachary drove.

"You're out of the first one," Erik announced once the cup became empty.

"That's fine," Zachary murmured.

When they arrived in front of Kanbal's building, Erik set the bag on the dash and Zachary waved a hand at him.

"Take it with you," Zachary said.

"Don't want it?" Erik asked.

"I changed my mind."

"Whatever." Erik took the bag and raised an eyebrow when Zachary stayed idle. "So you're not getting out?"

"I got another assignment at a different satellite office,"

Zachary explained. "Call me if you need anything."

"I don't have my phone."

"I put it in your coat pocket."

"Thanks." Erik opened the door and stepped out.

"Hey, don't call me for stupid shit, okay?" Zachary called after him. "I don't wanna hear how bored as fuck you are."

"Good to know." Erik shut the door and made his way up the stairs. He entered through the glass doors into Kanbal's lobby and approached the secretary at the front desk. "Good morning," he greeted and leaned against the counter. "How's two-eleven doing?"

The secretary gave a strained smile and pushed back her headset. "There was no problem reported," she answered. "Why, what's wrong?"

"*Damn it,*" Erik thought and let out a short laugh. "I thought for sure we called somebody about that copier," he lied. "Our current Office Technician was out sick."

"I'll let the Maintenance pool know."

"Thanks." Erik hurried for the elevators and struck the button. "*I'm really screwed,*" he mused. "*Now they're going to get suspicious.*"

The doors opened and Erik sucked in a shallow breath when he faced a short young woman with tanned skin, bright dark brown eyes and bobbed raven hair. He admired her quarter-length powder blue sweater jacket that had small white buttons and sleeveless blue dress with small white flowers as the running pattern. On her small feet she wore navy flat-heeled shoes.

"You're beautiful," Erik said breathlessly.

The young woman's cheeks flushed slightly and she giggled in response. "Thanks," she answered. "You're pretty tough looking yourself."

"Bruised face notwithstanding?" Erik quipped and grinned as he stepped on the elevator. "I don't always look this macho - I'm pretty geeky as it gets."

The young woman giggled again and Erik reached forward, pressing the floor button he wanted. "Weren't you going somewhere?"

"I think I found it."

The doors slid close and Erik cleared his throat, overwhelmed by her flowery perfume. "Hey, what's that scent?"

"Gardenia."

"It smells really nice."

"Do you like it?" Erik nodded. "You know, I'm surprised that you work here."

"Just started... And I'm not doing so hot."

"Oh?"

"Yeah, I'm in big trouble." The doors opened and Erik entered the brown cube farm. "I'm on my way to get my head chopped off."

"I might be able to help."

"Really now?"

"There you are!" Clairese called as she stepped out her office, dressed in tan. "I thought you might not come in today."

"I'm here," Erik said sullenly. "Just hurry up and serve my head on a platter, will you? Save me as much pain as possible."

"That's why I called in a specialist. She said she might be able to help us with our problem." Erik looked to the young woman who smiled shyly. "Mister Hauser, meet Miss Hanalei Kahananui."

"Hana…!" Erik said brightly as he stuck out his free hand. Hanalei appeared dismayed as she shook his hand in return. "Pleased to meet you again."

"I'm sorry, Mister Hauser…?" she said stiffly.

"I wanted to give this back to you." Erik reached into his coat pocket and withdrew the earring. "I can never forget that perfume of yours."

"Er, thanks?" Hanalei murmured as Erik placed it into her palm and covered her hand.

Erik leaned forward toward her ear. "So let's have dinner tonight on me, sounds good?" he said softly and Hanalei's face flushed bright red in response. "It won't be something as lame as Burger Shack, promise."

"Tell her what happened," Clairese said loudly to Erik, "and maybe she can figure a solution."

Erik stood upright as his ears burned and Clairese gave him a disapproving look. "Sure," he said, glancing to Hanalei. "I'm having some coworkers recovering the data now. It should be ready by tomorrow."

"Anything else?"

"All I know is that they were wiped out remotely. Only the main one - belonging to Miss Avers - was left intact."

"Let me check it out," Hanalei said.

"Sure, this way."

Hanalei followed Clairese back into her office and Erik hurried into the employee break room. He set aside the greasy sack on the nearby table and grabbed a chair, plopping down into it. Erik moaned and ran his hands through his hair, blowing a heavy sigh.

A sudden chirp cut into the air and Erik searched his pockets, finding a basic brick-shaped phone.

"This isn't mine," he muttered as he glanced at the screen, finding it indicated a text message from an unlisted number. He pushed the button, retrieving the mail.

Unknown: Please take care.

Erik shrugged his shoulders and set his phone aside.

"Now tell me what's that about," Clairese's voice called to Erik from behind.

Erik looked over his shoulder, finding the young woman standing at the door with her arms folded across her chest. "It's not what you're thinking!" he protested and turned in his seat, facing her. "I have feelings and desires, sure, but I never acted on them."

"So leading people on is what gets you off then?"

"I–!" Erik put his hands in his lap and blew an anxious sigh. "I'm not sure."

"You seem all over the board though."

Erik let out a nervous laugh. "I'm really not all here, obviously." He smirked and Clairese appeared disturbed. "What is it?"

"Did you ever call that person you wanted?" she asked. Erik continued to smile, saying nothing and Clairese blew a short sigh. "Well then..." She glimpsed at the overhead clock behind Erik on the wall. "Do you want my dad's number?"

"What for?"

"He might be able to help you better than I can."

"You don't seem happy about it."

Clairese shut her eyes and raised a hand. "Just... Ugh." She stalked out the room.

"Whatever," Erik muttered and stood, taking his bag of food. He approached the employee refrigerator and opened the door, finding several cans of soda inside near a white foam container labeled 'poison' and a sandwich inside cellophane with a sticky note attached marked 'free'. Erik snorted and tossed in the paper sack.

Shutting the door, he faced Clairese standing offside with a business card in her hand.

"Here," she said, handing it to Erik. "Just don't get him hurt, please?"

"I can't promise anything," Erik said, taking the card. "Thanks, though."

Clairese returned to her office and Erik looked down at the glossy beige card titled 'Mercado Corporation' in bold lettering with the first letter in a gothic style script.

"*Brodie Avers, Telecommunications Analyst*," Erik read as he approached the table. Sitting on the edge, he picked up his phone and dialed the printed number with his other hand, then listened as the call went through.

"Good morning," a friendly male voice answered after two rings.

"Is this Lyndhurst forty-eight seventy-three?" Erik asked.

"You got the right number, buddy."

"Is this a personal number?"

"I'm not at home."

Erik crossed his leg at the knee and tapped the card he held against the table. "Do you work on phones?"

"Nah, just the system they run on. Been doing this since the War for the past twenty years."

"Past twenty years now, really?" Erik snorted. "Aren't you nearing retirement?"

"Yeah, next quarter they're cutting me loose."

"I thought you had to work thirty-five years."

"For the Gov, yeah, but everyone else, is twenty, maybe twenty-five. Some of the older businesses are thirty."

"That's a long time to work for one company."

"Hey, some aspire to get to the top and run that bitch."

Erik chortled in response. "Are they going to throw a party?"

"Yeah, I'll get that engraved silver watch and everything."

"What will you do afterwards?"

"Hell, I'll be fifty-nine by then. I'll probably go out on the lake or fish or something."

"You fish?" Erik razzed him. "Liar."

"It's fun. You should try it sometime."

Hearing a low tone, Erik stiffened, suddenly growing tense. "What are you doing?" he asked faintly.

"Working. Shouldn't you be?"

"Slow day."

Hearing another tone, Erik gasped and sat up straighter. "You're tracing me," he accused, "aren't you?"

"I already locked you in after the second ring, buddy," Brodie admitted seriously. "I also already tapped the call."

"Why?"

"That's my job." Brodie scoffed. "That block you got on there only makes the data invisible from civilians, not guys like me.

Also, even if your location's turned off, it's not that hard to tell where you're pinging from. Triangulation can zero me in within fifty meters."

"And to think you did clerical work."

"Shit ton of stuff to process, buddy. You don't know how many calls I intercept everyday."

"Do you always trace your own calls?"

"Not all the time."

"So why me?"

"Maybe I like hearing your sexy voice." When Erik said nothing, Brodie laughed. "I kid with ya, buddy," he jibed. "Just so you know, you got some unusual activity on your ten."

Erik frowned, growing nervous. "How can you tell?" he muttered.

"All phones emit signals, whether they're on a network or off."

Erik sucked in a shallow breath when pain suddenly erupted behind his eyes. He shut them as abrupt searing ache burned through his hands.

"Shit," Erik hissed, rubbing at his eyelids with his fingers.

"Just remembered something?" Brodie's voice called from afar.

"Maybe," Erik mewed and frowned when his vision turned hazy.

"What do you want for lunch?"

"I already got mine."

"I'll see you in a bit."

The line cut off and Erik uncrossed his legs then slipped off the table's edge. He pocketed the phone and card as he made his way into Clairese's office, finding Hanalei sitting at the desk with a microcomputer and Clairese standing over her. The small computer's black screen showed data in green scrolling rapidly across as it processed data.

"What are you doing?" Erik asked.

"I'm testing the vulnerabilities of your so-called closed system," Hanalei explained as she typed. "Your boss told me there's been breaches in the security off and on for several months and her team can't find who's doing it."

"Do you think it's an inside job?" Erik suggested.

"That's impossible," Clairese said, shaking her head. "They'd leave themselves wide open doing something that dangerous! Masking their location only slows down amateurs."

"This looks like it might take some time." Erik jutted a thumb at the door. "Want me to order a pizza or anything?"

"I like pizza," Hanalei said brightly and looked up at Erik. "Give me one with every topping they have on there!"

"It might kill you," Erik teased, grinning.

"I have a fast metabolism."

"Right." Erik left the door and headed for the elevators. Once the bell pinged, he heard his phone chirp. Taking it out, Erik glanced at it, finding a message.

Unknown: Please check conversion factor.

"The hell...?" Erik murmured and stepped on the awaiting cable car. "Conversion factor of what?" The pain in his hands burned stronger in response and the unease he felt in his chest tightened.

TWENTY-EIGHT

Stepping off the elevator, Erik spotted the tall athletic middle-aged man with barrel chest and short graying dark brown hair leaning against the receptionist's counter, chatting candidly. He wore a bright goldenrod dress shirt, yellow tie, tan slacks and loafers while strapped over his shoulder he had a green insulated case.

"Don't tell me you're turning on the charm again, Mister Avers," Erik called.

Brodie looked up and smiled brightly. "Feddy!" he said cheerfully. "Let's get started."

"I'm upstairs."

Brodie waved the woman away and jogged over to where Erik stood. "She acted like she didn't know what I was talking about!" he groused and chuckled as he followed Erik toward the stairwell. "But she's blonde, so I guess she's none too bright."

"Of course she wouldn't know Ferdian Smith," Erik retorted and withdrew his wallet. "This is what I go by now, apparently."

Brodie paled when Erik took out his employee identification card, showing him. "Why change your name?" he asked.

"I'm crazy, remember?" Erik pocketed his wallet then opened the door. He clenched his teeth when cold air blew in and his pain worsened as he entered the stairwell.

"What do you do here?"

"I thought the same as I was doing at Mercado," Erik replied, making his way upstairs. "But there was an error and I'm in some deep shit."

"How deep are we talking?"

"Can you do the same stuff you did with the phones to computers?"

Brodie snorted. "Nah, that's a different animal. Joey would be the guy to ask." Erik paused at the railing, stunned. "Hey, you okay?"

"I'm not sure," Erik answered slowly. He shut his eyes and blew a hard sigh. "I'm not doing so well."

"Let's sit down and enjoy lunch," Brodie suggested. "I didn't pay that cabbie to break the speeding limit for nothing, ya know!"

Erik smirked at Brodie who smiled gently at him. "Really?" Erik pressed and Brodie nodded. Erik chortled, hurrying up the steps. "You're a strange man."

"I can't help it," Brodie objected, following Erik. "I like what I like. I'm allowed that, aren't I?"

Entering the second floor stairwell, Erik heard a high whine and grunted, clutching the railing before he lost his footing. "Damn it," he growled, shaking his head.

"Something the matter?" Brodie inquired.

"I'm not sure." Erik glanced down the short hall at the other door on the end. "I'm feeling off."

"Meds wearing off?"

"Probably, yeah."

"How long's your lunch break?"

"Order some pizza for me," Erik said instead and took the

door closest to him leading back to the brown cube farm. "Main line's near the water cooler."

"Sure," Brodie said after him. "What do you want on it?"

"One with everything. The other is Boss's choice."

Erik pointed in the opposite direction toward the water cooler then returned to the employee break room, taking out his sack from Burger Shack in the refrigerator. He felt as if he moved in a fog while reheating his food in the microwave, then took a seat at the table.

Brodie later entered the room and made a direct path toward the window on the end. "That's all you got there?" he asked as he opened the panel.

"Don't tell me you expected a full-course meal from me," Erik teased.

"Hell, at least take off your coat, Feddy!" Brodie ridiculed. "You act like you're in a hurry to get somewhere."

"I can't really relax."

"You can relax around me, unless you're hiding something?" Erik appeared disgusted as he stood while Brodie chortled in response when Erik said nothing in return. "Aren't you then?"

"No, you pervy old man," Erik grumbled and slipped off his coat, then draped it on the back of the chair. The microwave beeped and Brodie left the window, extracting the meal as Erik dropped into his chair, holding his chin in his hand.

"You're thinking about something," Brodie noted, returning to the table. He set the food before Erik.

"I'm afraid," Erik said softly.

"Of what?" Brodie took off the case and set it aside as he sat across from Erik. "That you'd get sacked in a week and move on to another job?"

"Not that."

Brodie opened the insulated case and withdrew two cans of soda, one cola and the other lemon lime. Erik grinned when Brodie withdrew a half-pint bottle of vodka and passed it to him. "You're not really working anyway," Brodie teased.

"I'm a professional seat warmer," Erik quipped, opening the vodka bottle.

"So what happened exactly?" Brodie turned the case around and opened another compartment, withdrawing a wrapped sandwich, a pack of cigarettes and a glass ashtray.

"Didn't Clairese tell you?" Erik questioned. "I'm sure you have a clue."

"I'm not sure if Joey can dig around and find anything."

Erik took a swallow of liquor then recapped the bottle. "You know we're not on very good terms."

Brodie snorted. "What makes you think we are?" he countered.

"So all that fooling around you do?" Erik waved a dismissive hand before Brodie could answer. "Never mind - I don't want to know; I regret bringing it up."

"Fine," Brodie muttered, "I won't mention it."

Erik opened his bag and withdrew his sandwich and cup of potatoes.

"No ketchup?" Brodie interpolated, opening his can of cola.

"They're seasoned," Erik replied.

"Good stuff, I heard."

"They're okay."

Brodie unwrapped his sandwich and took a bite. "I told you

my couch is free anytime you want," he murmured. "Sweetheart told me about your place getting trashed."

"Did you look into it?"

"No records left around," Brodie admitted. "Your line was off the hook, and there was no pings near the area around the assumed time I could figure they broke in."

"Illegal professionals, you think?"

Brodie nodded. "It's way too clean."

"Someone's bound to make a mistake somewhere."

Brodie appeared thoughtful as he resumed his meal. Erik picked up a potato puff and ate it, finding the lightly seasoned fried vegetable blander than he expected.

"Will you come over tonight?" Brodie suddenly queried.

"I don't know, why?" Erik answered warily.

Brodie sniggered. "I want to make sure I picked up before you stop by."

"Rather you get yourself together before I stopped by."

Brodie chortled and Erik grinned.

Erik found concentrating on lunch difficult, overwhelmed by his general unease. Brodie continued chatting at him, at times diverging to overt sexual topics to make sure Erik was paying attention.

"Ugh, stop being so pervy," Clairese called as she entered the room with a slice of pizza in her hand. "You can't bang him, so quit trying."

Brodie snorted as Erik sat back with his face bright red. "I can't help it," he said sheepishly. "Besides, there's no one else here to try my charms on."

"How's progress?" Erik asked, ignoring Brodie.

"Nothing yet," Clairese admitted. "No back doors, no security flaws... Everything's clean so far. It's weird..."

"If it was inside, something would've set it off, wouldn't it?"

"Right, and we'd have logs of that sort of thing." Clairese blew a short sigh. "You don't have to stick around. You can just go wherever you want."

"I have a date tonight."

"She might not clock out of here until after nine."

"Call me then?" Brodie piped. "I'll send a cab."

"You're so kind," Clairese cooed and approached, pinching Brodie's cheek.

Erik's eyes widened and he pushed away from the table. "No," he yelped. "Don't bother trying to entertain me for four hours! I know you, old man!"

Brodie burst out laughing. "What? You figured out my plans already?" He laughed harder and waved Erik away. "I'm not so bad!"

"You're so *obvious*," Clairese said, rolling her eyes. "You know he plans to feed you drinks and feel you up when you pass out," she directed at Erik.

"I know," Erik spat, "and I'll call instead."

"At least let me try out my new margarita maker!" Brodie whined. "Darling brought it for me for our anniversary!"

Erik shook his head. "I don't do tequila."

"Have you ever tried it?"

"Don't answer," Clairese warned. "I don't want to know!" Brodie fell into another fit of giggles as she hurried out the room. "I don't want to hear it!"

Brodie doubled over, holding his sides as he continued laughing and Erik gripped the edge of the table, embarrassed.

"Stop messing with me!" Erik complained.

"I can't help it!" Brodie protested and took in a breath. "It's fun."

"Don't you have to get back to work?"

"In a while." Brodie calmed and opened the pack of cigarettes. He withdrew one, then passed the pack to Erik. Erik took a cigarette and Brodie reached into his slacks, taking out a lighter. "Are you in a hurry to get somewhere?"

Erik looked sharply at Brodie who grinned as he lit his cigarette. "No," he snapped. "Just stop thinking!"

Brodie burst out laughing again. "Why are you giving me such a dirty look?" he asked as Erik continued glowering when passed the lighter.

"You could think of a million other things," Erik spat and lit his cigarette. "Just not that."

"Does my thinking of *that* bother you that much?" Brodie teased.

"I don't care what you think; I just don't want to be a part of it." Erik reached over into his coat pocket and withdrew the business cards. "Check this out for me sometime." He tossed the cards across the table. "Whenever I call it, it rings, but never picks up."

"Who gave you that number?" Brodie asked and picked up the Kanbal Industries card.

"Pilot named Thompson." Erik tapped the table. "He wanted to know if I was still working."

"Working on what?"

"Skycatcher, I guess..."

Brodie nodded thoughtfully. "I'll see what I can do with it," he promised. While Erik brooded and they smoked in silence for some time, Brodie eventually put out his stub and drained his remaining cola. "I'll call you if I can find anything."

"Thanks," Erik muttered and ground out his tapering cigarette. He pulled into his coat and pocketed the liquor, then picked up his soda. "Are there any bars open around here?"

"There's a nice one a few blocks from the job," Brodie admitted. "Want me to drop you off there?"

"Sure." Erik left the break room as Brodie cleared the table. He entered Clairese's office and watched Hanalei work on her computer. Nearby rest an open pizza box with several slices left. Clairese sat in another chair in the corner, reading a magazine. "How goes?" Erik inquired.

"Still nothing new to report," Hanalei responded, typing at her terminal. "Whoever broke in disguised their tracks well."

"Let's have dinner tomorrow night," Erik suggested. "I'd hate to rush you."

"I'm sorry, Mister Hauser," Hanalei said and looked toward Erik, smiling sadly. "I'm sure we can make it up another time."

"Your choice."

Hanalei grinned and returned to her work. "Even if it's expensive?" she teased.

"Well, some warning would be nice."

Clairese chortled, turning the page. Erik turned his gaze her way and Clairese's cheeks flushed slightly. "I didn't say anything," she piped. "Just ignore little old me."

"Right," Erik spat and wagged a finger in her direction. "You're jealous, aren't you?"

"Who said?" Clairese retorted and Hanalei giggled.

"Good afternoon, ladies," Erik called when he heard Brodie exit the break room. "I'll see you tomorrow."

"Where are you going?"

"I'm drowning my sorrows at the nearest bar." Erik waved at Clairese. "Your father promised to keep his hands to himself."

"Call me if he gets too grabby," Clairese said and Erik turned away, heading for the elevators.

"So you are taking up my offer," Brodie said brightly once Erik approached.

"Only because I know I'll be drunk by then," Erik countered.

"Do you drink this heavily to suppress your feelings?"

Erik looked at Brodie, appalled. "The hell?" he squawked and Brodie chuckled. "No!"

The elevators opened and they both stepped on.

"It seems you're willing to put up with a lot," Brodie went on as the doors closed and the cable car moved.

"I have my limits," Erik grumbled and downed his soda.

The bell donged and the doors opened, revealing the lobby. Erik paled when a short young woman with light brown wavy hair and hazel eyes stood outside the doors, holding a large case. Erik felt ill at ease in her presence, despite the woman's uniform consisting of white shirt, black slacks and black tie. She nodded toward Erik as he and Brodie stepped off.

"Afternoon," the young woman greeted.

"I know you're not part of the Maintenance crew," Erik

murmured, tossing his empty can into a nearby trash canister.

"I'm the copy machine repair person," the young woman said, smiling slightly. "They make us wear these dorky uniforms."

"Good luck."

The woman stepped on and Erik hurried to catch up with Brodie who headed for the front doors. He glanced over his shoulder and spotted the woman pointed at Erik with her hand shaped into a gun. She mouthed the word 'bang' and the doors closed after her.

"Can't ever stop, huh?" Brodie teased.

"Huh, what?" Erik snapped, turning around. "What are you going on about?" They stepped outside and Erik flipped up his collar against the cold winds. "Aren't you cold at all?"

"You can always warm me," Brodie quipped. Erik hurried down the steps and onto the sidewalk. "The cab should be here in a minute," he called after Erik.

"Don't tell me you were so excited to see me," Erik said and withdrew his bottle of vodka.

"Okay, I won't."

Erik uncapped the bottle and guzzled the liquor. He rapidly began to warm once he emptied the bottle and chucked it into the street with a crash.

A taxi pulled up to the curb and Erik opened the rear passenger door. He slipped inside as Brodie followed him.

"Lighthouse, Downtown," Brodie said once he entered and shut the door.

"I was told Mercado building, Downtown," the driver replied.

"I can change my mind, can't I?" Brodie said cheerfully.

Erik leaned against his window, looking at the passing scenery. "What's this Lighthouse anyway?" he murmured.

"Join me and see."

"Don't tell me you're skipping work."

"Fine, I won't."

Erik glanced to Brodie who gave a mischievous smile.

TWENTY-NINE

The cab parked before a small white building with tinted windows. An aging neon sign giving the building its name flickered dimly above the large red door. Brodie paid for his fare and stepped out with Erik.

"You'll love it," Brodie said cheerily.

"It doesn't look in use," Erik groused and followed the older man up the steps.

"That's because only people in the know really know when the club's open. To everyone else, it looks like an empty building."

"Oh, so you'd know?" Erik ragged.

Brodie grinned and gestured ahead. "After you."

Pushing through the entrance, Erik encountered a dark enclave of activity, where several people filled the brightly lit dance floor and droning electronic music thumped through the large speakers lined on the walls.

Erik made his way to the empty bar, approaching a bored-appearing tender who wiped down the counter, wearing dark jeans and a T-shirt with the name of the club glowing from the blacklight. The woman had short sandy hair, thin eyebrows, and sleepy green eyes.

"What'll be, Kid?" the barkeep asked.

"Vodka on the rocks," Erik replied.

"Keep it going for him," Brodie said as he approached and placed a twenty-note on the counter.

"You his ride?" the tender grumbled as she withdrew a lowball glass and filled it with ice.

"I'm calling a cab."

"Oh, don't worry," Erik said amiably once the tender filled the glass with vodka and handed it to him. "He knows I can kill him if he tries anything."

"None of my business," the tender muttered. "Just don't cause trouble. I like money and those crazy kids like dancing."

"Sure."

Erik waltzed over to an empty table and Brodie followed, taking a seat across from him.

"What's with that look?" Brodie protested when Erik glared at him.

"Seriously, though?" Erik complained and downed his drink.

"I mainly like watching them dance," Brodie said innocently. "I don't always pick up one to take home..."

"You disgust me."

"I don't see you actively objecting," Brodie teased.

Erik snorted and swirled the ice before finishing the remainder of his drink. "I can be nice," he said, setting aside the glass. "Nothing wrong with nice."

"Sure, nothing's wrong with that at all."

A broad shouldered man with a large dark beard approached with a tray of four drinks. "Twenty dollars worth," he announced and set the glasses on the table. "You'd like anything else?"

Brodie waved away the server. "Nothing for me," he said.

"Have fun."

The waiter left the table and Erik pulled out of his coat. "You're planning something, aren't you?" he accused, draping the coat on his chair.

"Why do I have to plan anything?" Brodie argued while Erik picked up a glass and gulped its contents. "What if I just want to sit here and watch you drink?"

"Have one."

"I have to work in the morning."

"What makes you think I don't?"

"Sweetheart told me." Brodie placed his hands atop the worn table and leaned in slightly. "She was pissed because they were pre-selected to jumpstart that code and needed it done early. Suits on high pushed it through without warning."

"What?" Erik set aside his glass and started on his third drink. "I thought she was... What was it - Computational Chemist or something?"

"That's what she does."

Erik swallowed the third then started his fourth. He used his free hand to unbutton his collar and scanned the dance floor, watching several men and women dancing with one another.

"Is it warm in here?" Erik complained.

"Just you," Brodie replied.

"Do you dance at all?"

"I'm known to have a few good moves."

"Care to show them to me?" Erik finished his drink and picked up the last one remaining. Brodie smirked when Erik looked his way and pointed in his direction. "Not in any intimate manner," Erik spat.

Brodie put up his hands in mock surrender. "I'll keep it clean, promise," he said, grinning.

"Shut up."

Brodie laughed in return and Erik finished his drink.

Once the song changed, Erik dropped his glass and stalked for the dance floor, unbuttoning his cuffs along the way. He rolled up his sleeves and got lost into the music, ignoring the pain thudding throughout his body while dancing.

Erik continued moving about on the floor, stepping in time to the music. He felt watched and turned, finding a group of young men in all black sitting at the far table facing the dance floor, with several highball glasses scattered on the surface.

Brodie later approached with his tie removed and his shirt unbuttoned from the collar down, exposing the upper part of his chest. He bumped into Erik when a moderately paced song blasted through the speakers then bopped alongside the young man.

"I'm not dancing with you," Erik snapped and Brodie chortled.

"Who said you were dancing with me?" Brodie shot back. "We can still dance together and not be together."

"Bullshit."

"You're not bad. I'd never thought you'd have any good moves."

"I can Hustle to anything," Erik replied nonchalantly. "Even Swing."

"At least dance one slow one with me, please?"

"If I humor you, will you stop pawing at me?"

"Good deal. I'll lead."

Once a slow song played through the speakers, the couples on the floor partnered together and Erik sighed as he stepped into Brodie's arms. He stiffened when Brodie put his hands on his hips.

"Put your hands on my shoulders," Brodie instructed, "and just move with me."

"I'm not good at this," Erik muttered as he did as told.

"Obviously you've never danced with another person."

"I'm not particularly good at it."

"Loosen up some!" Brodie complained when Erik continued to move unyieldingly. "Settle down and follow my lead."

Erik closed his eyes, concentrating on the music. He began to calm slightly and draped his arms around Brodie's neck as he leaned in. Brodie sucked in a shallow breath and shifted his gait, his hips swaying to the music as Erik leaned in.

"Someone's interested," Erik muttered in Brodie's ear. Brodie broke out in cold sweat as his cheeks flushed red. "I can feel you against my thigh."

"Sorry," Brodie murmured.

"You're not sorry." Erik laid his head against Brodie's shoulder, relaxing as he moved in perfect rhythm with the older man. "You thought this would be a perfect chance to cop a feel since I'm drunk, right?" Erik started slowly moving his hands up and down the older man's back and Brodie swallowed hard, sweating more profusely as his hip movements became more urgent. "You feel nice in my arms," Erik whispered in Brodie's ear.

Brodie mewed and held tighter around Erik's waist when

the young man ground against him. "Don't do that," Brodie moaned. "Please, don't..."

Erik licked Brodie's ear lobe and the older man trembled. "You really like that, right?" Erik traced Brodie's ear with his tongue and the older man moaned softly.

"Please stop that," Brodie begged.

Erik nuzzled Brodie's neck and Brodie rolled his head to the side when licked at the base of his throat. Erik reached around, grabbing Brodie's rear with his hands and squeezed firmly. He slowly licked the older man's neck and collarbone, working his way back to his ear. Brodie ground himself hard against Erik and groaned when Erik pressed against him and squeezed again.

"You like that?" Erik murmured.

"Yes," Brodie rasped, "I really do."

"That's all you're getting out of me."

"What?"

Brodie gasped when the song ended and Erik giggled as he pulled the older man's hands away from his hips.

"Ah ha," Erik jibed and grabbed Brodie's belt buckle. "I tease." He let go and returned to the table, leaving Brodie standing on the dance floor, confused and aroused.

Erik sat at the table, drinking a glass of water once Brodie returned after several songs played, his face flushed red. Erik kicked out the other chair. "Drinking one with me?" he asked. "It'll do wonders."

"I'm going home," Brodie grumbled and gathered his tie left draped on the chair.

"You were in the back a good while," Erik quipped.

"Couldn't wait to rub one out?"

Brodie clenched his hands as his flushed face burned brighter red. "Stop teasing me, you son of a bitch!" he growled.

Erik grinned, pointing at the older man behind his drink. "Stop coming on to me then," he drawled. "I'll have to hurt you for real if you keep doing that."

"You're a cruel bastard, Feddy."

Erik beckoned to Brodie. "Gimmie a smoke."

"I'm leaving."

"Fine."

Erik set aside his drink and picked up his coat. He noticed the group of men on the dance floor's other side also leaving toward the rear doors as he passed others in the way.

Reaching the outside, Erik pulled into his overcoat and shoved his hands in his pockets. He headed down the walkway and noticed a dark sedan pulling alongside the curb. Erik slowed and the window rolled down.

"Going somewhere?" a voice called.

"Yeah," Erik called as he continued walking. "Why do you care?"

"We have unfinished business."

Erik reached the end of the street blocked off by construction and clenched his teeth as his left shoulder flared in pain. He withdrew his phone and scanned his contacts list. Finding Zachary's number, he dialed it.

The dark sedan screeched to a stop before Erik and the doors opened. Two men in dark suits and sunglasses exited the rear passenger seats with guns drawn and Erik immediately put up his hands when they approached.

"You were watching me in that club!" Erik cried, backing away. "You got the wrong person."

"Is that so?" Erik frowned when Antonius exited the front passenger side, wearing a dark overcoat, leather gloves, fedora and wide smoky sunglasses covered his eyes. "I knew you had to be the same son of a bitch that caused all that trouble from before."

"What are you talking about?"

"Get in the car."

"First tell me what this is about." Erik tripped over his steps and looked down, finding a metal pipe.

"You should have died then. If I don't kill you now, you'll just cause more trouble."

"Tough shit!" Erik kicked up the pipe and held it in his free hand as a futile shield once the men closed in around him. "If you want to kill me openly, that's on you."

"Take him down!" Antonius ordered.

Erik swung the pipe at one gunman, whacking his leg, then struck the other, crashing the lead over his head, instantly dropping him. Erik then took off in a sprint down the street, dodging return fire.

"Hey!" a tinny voice called. "Hey, pick up!"

Realizing he still held his cellular, Erik put it to his ear. "What?" he cried. "I'm getting shot at right now!"

"Hold them off if you can," Zachary's voice said. "I'm on my way."

"Where are you?"

"I'm tracking you now. Stay on the line."

"I might not be able to!"

Erik screamed in terror when a shot narrowly missed him, chipping part of the sidewalk. He stumbled forward and fell against a fire hydrant, knocking the air out of him.

"I'm missing on purpose!" the gunman shouted after Erik.

"Damn it," Erik hissed and pushed away, crossing a busy street. Narrowly dodging cars, he made haste onto the other side and ducked into an alley, hiding behind a refuse bin. Erik leaned against the pipe, heaving for breath.

"Can you hear me?" Zachary yelled.

"Does this have a speaker function?" Erik asked.

"Button on the right." Erik pressed the button. "Can you hear me now?" Zachary's hollow voice said louder amid static.

"You're clear."

"Do you know why you're a target?"

"No idea." Erik cried out when more shots fired in his direction. He took off down the alley, reaching another intersection.

"You're a highly-trained soldier," Zachary said as Erik crossed the street and pushed past pedestrians, searching for a safe place to hide. "You had some important sensitive information that could throw the government into shutdown."

"How could some dork like me have something so incriminating? I know nothing about Skycatcher."

"I don't know how you obtained the info or eluded them this long, but as long as you're alive, they'll chase you down forever until they erase you."

"I can't remember anyway!"

"They think you still do."

"I don't remember ever being a soldier."

"We all do our mandatory two years. When you did your time, something happened, something bad enough that they want you dead... After they get their information first, of course."

"What did I do?"

Erik turned the corner and ran into Brodie, crashing into him.

"Hey, Feddy!" Brodie yelped, catching him in his arms. "Why'd you take off like that?"

"Why are you here?" Erik wheezed. "You need to get out of here."

Brodie smiled and helped Erik upright. "I told you I took off for the afternoon," he said cordially. "I just called a cab and everything."

Erik turned around and pointed his pipe ahead as the gunman calmly walked through the crowd. "Get out of here!" he shouted. "Mister Avers, get out of here!"

"What?"

Erik dropped the phone and dashed forward, pipe held high with both hands. The gunman raised his pistol and fired. Someone screamed and everyone else on the sidewalk scattered, running in a panic. Erik halted, stunned, then realized he didn't get struck.

As the gunman coolly stalked away, Erik lowered his weapon and took in a shallow breath. Turning around, he found Brodie slumped on the ground, his bright yellow shirt rapidly staining with crimson.

Erik rushed up to Brodie's side and dropped to his knees. "Mister Avers, wake up," he cried, shaking the man's shoulder.

Brodie's eyes fluttered open and he smiled faintly at Erik. "Hey," he murmured. "That really hurt..."

"How bad is it?"

"Oh..." Brodie reached up, touching his side, then looked at his bloodstained hand. "Damn, I hadn't been this bad since the War..."

"Hold on, I'll call for help."

"Don't worry about it."

Erik turned to search for the cellular he dropped and looked up at Antonius holding it in his gloved hand.

"If you want help," Antonius said darkly, "then you'll come with me."

Erik growled and rose to his feet, clutching the pipe in his hands. "Don't do this to me," he snarled.

"You have no choice."

"You bastard!" Erik rushed forward and Antonius swiftly sidestepped his wild swings. "He's got nothing to do with this!"

Antonius turned around as Erik came down with an overhead swing and grasped the pipe in his free hand. "I've had enough of you," Antonius said calmly. "I'm not telling you again." He smiled. "You don't want your lover bleeding out, do you?"

"He's not my lover," Erik spat. "He's just a pervy old man I put up with."

"Let him die. It's your choice." Antonius let go and Erik lowered the pipe. He cringed when the pain in his left shoulder seared.

Watch closely as I break you...

"All right," Erik said dejectedly and dropped the pipe to

the ground with a clatter. "I don't want him to die."

"Pick him up."

Erik grunted and approached Brodie's downed body. "Come on," he muttered, pulling Brodie sitting upright.

"I'm dying," Brodie grumbled as Erik helped him to his feet.

"I don't want you dying with regrets," Erik snapped, hoisting the older man's arm over his shoulders. "Besides, if you died without jumping my bones, then you'd haunt me as a pervy old ghost."

Brodie let out a weak laugh. "Do I haunt your dreams that much?"

"Shut up." Erik walked Brodie back toward the dark sedan that pulled up to the curb. Erik opened the door and set Brodie gingerly inside, then slipped in after him. "Where are we going?" he asked as Antonius entered the car.

"What does it matter where we're going?" Antonius answered once Erik shut the door. "We have a lot of work to catch up on."

Erik ground his teeth, looking out the window as the driver sped through traffic.

THIRTY

Arriving at an old run-down motel, the driver pulled onto a weed-choked parking lot in the rear and Antonius stepped out the car. Erik exited the vehicle and went around assisting Brodie as the driver and Antonius entered a room on the end.

Erik helped Brodie inside the large room, passing a small table with two chairs near the door and led to a single queen-sized bed across the way. Erik noticed a tall brass floor lamp in the corner behind the door, a chest of drawers across the room with an LCD television hanging above it. He frowned when he smelled a strong chemical odor upon entry and set the older man on the bed.

Erik pulled out of his coat and dropped it to the floor as Antonius returned from the rear bathroom with a first aid kit.

"Why'd you bring us here?" Erik demanded as Antonius tossed him the kit. He caught it and immediately opened it, withdrawing packs of gauze. "I need to get him to the hospital."

"First you tell us what we want to know and we'll help him," Antonius answered. "He might not have a lot of time."

"Why are you doing this to me?"

"Don't worry about me, Feddy," Brodie murmured as Erik removed his shirt and patched his wounds. "I had a pretty good run."

"I'm not letting you die," Erik growled. "I'll tell them whatever they want and get you out of here."

"So get to talking," Antonius snapped. "It'll be easy if you just tell us right away and save you suffering."

"Why do you care?" Erik gazed up to Antonius standing over him. "Aren't you suffering too?"

Antonius frowned. "What are you talking about?"

"Someone's holding something over your head and they want you to get me so you can get whatever it is they're keeping from you."

Antonius laughed. "You're crazy."

"I know."

"So you're not going to tell me?"

"Why should I?"

"Because I'm asking you nicely."

Erik clenched his teeth and grunted when thudding pain raged in his head. "You weren't nice when we first met," he muttered and finished taping Brodie's side. "You clocked me good."

"Well, I was still pissed off at you. Still am, to be truthful with you."

"Even if I apologize, it won't matter."

"No, it wouldn't."

"I can't because I don't remember."

Antonius struck his fist into his palm. "Think, man, and remember," he urged. "I know you couldn't have forgotten. We were all in that shit program together and you fucked up major."

Erik shrugged. "Not a clue."

"You're not trying hard enough." Antonius gestured toward the driver and the man withdrew a pistol from his holster under his blazer. "If I finish off your friend, you'd be upset and of no use to me. But if you keep stalling, he'd die and you'll still be of no use to me."

Erik clutched his hands, growing uneasy. "*I can't remember what it was I was told to forget,*" he mused. "*If I make up a bullshit answer, Mister Avers is a goner either way.*"

"Have you figured it out?" Antonius asked, breaking Erik's thoughts.

"For someone who's been told to kill me, you've been awfully kind," Erik derided. "You act like we were friends before."

"We were."

"But I fucked it up, as you claim."

Antonius nodded. "Right."

The pounding in Erik's head worsened and he groaned, clutching his head as he leaned forward. "Stop talking," he moaned. "Shut up!"

"I didn't say anything," Antonius murmured.

Don't say things like that.

"I can't tell you anything," Erik cried. "I don't remember!"

"You do know, so stop lying!"

Let's continue to be friends...

"Shut up!"

You lied to me! How could you betray me?

"Why are you freaking out?" Antonius yelped, growing alarmed.

294

Let me die... I don't deserve to live...

"I hear something," the driver murmured.

"What is it?" Antonius demanded. "Find it!"

That feeling, in your mind, your soul, your core, your bones... What a horrible feeling to have.

Kill them, destroy them all!

"I hear it too," Brodie said, intrigued. "What's that noise?"

The driver sheathed his handgun and searched the room, seeking its source. Antonius appeared uncomfortable as cold sweat beaded on his forehead.

"It's bothering you, isn't it?" Brodie asked as Antonius removed his fedora and ran a hand through his blond hair. "Both you and Feddy don't look all that great."

"Please, stop talking," Antonius grumbled.

Erik suddenly screamed and the others looked at him, stunned. Erik sat up as he dropped his hands to his lap, his eyes blank. Antonius backed away once Erik stiffly rose to his feet.

"W-what's going on?" the driver asked as Erik stalked over to the lamp stationed behind the door.

Antonius tensed when Erik ripped the cord from the wall and hoisted the brass lamp in his hands then turned around, holding the lamp at ready.

"Why are you looking at me like that?" Antonius demanded as Erik approached. "Don't take me lightly, man. You'll regret seeing me mad."

"Oh, shit," Brodie murmured. "I've seen soldiers like that... They're crazy dangerous."

"Tell me a new one," Antonius growled as he tossed aside

his hat and stood on guard. "Don't make me fight you. I'll hurt you for real!"

Erik swung the heavy lamp and Antonius swiftly turned away, returning with a kick against Erik's leg. Erik faltered as he staggered rearwards and Antonius charged, shouldering Erik in the chest. Erik grunted as he stumbled rearward and Antonius grabbed Erik's arm, reversing him once unbalanced. Throwing him aside, the force of the blow sent Erik crashing against the drawers.

"You think you got me?" Antonius snapped as Erik shook off the stun and rose upright. "I know all your moves, man. We used to rumble together, so don't tell me you learned some new shit when you cut out on us."

Erik roared and sprang after Antonius. Antonius backed away and ran to the table, shoving it over as Erik smashed the lamp into it. Antonius picked up a chair and hurled it at Erik who swung the lamp's base, cracking it in half on contact.

Sudden banging resonated on the door while Antonius and Erik continued fighting. The driver hurried over to the door when he heard shouts on the other side.

"Hey, what's going on in there?" a voice yelled from outside.

The driver opened the door slightly and smiled brightly at the visitor. "Sorry we're being too rowdy," he said gently.

Antonius grabbed the lamp from Erik and hurled him over the floor. Erik struck the ground on his back and Antonius yanked the lamp from his hands then stomped on Erik's chest. Raising the base high over his head, Brodie stood as the door crashed open with a forceful kick, bowling the driver over onto the bed.

"The fuck!" Antonius yelped when Zachary stormed the room, armed with a saber in a blue and gold sheath.

"Didn't mean to crash the party," Zachary said and grinned. "Can I join? It sure sounds like fun."

"Don't underestimate me, man," Antonius snarled. "I can kill you with anything up in here."

"You don't understand," Zachary said as he withdrew his sword. "I'm telling you bastards to get out of here while you still have a chance." He pointed his blade at the driver's head before he reached for his pistol. "I wouldn't try that if I were you."

"What will you do if I don't do as you say?"

Zachary smiled brightly as he instantaneously ran his saber through the driver, splitting his head down through the torso before withdrawing as he cut the body in half. Blood splashed everywhere and Brodie jumped on the bed, frightened as Antonius dropped the lamp with a clang.

"What's with that attitude?" Zachary continued. "I'm telling you nicely - if you don't do as I say, I'm cutting you into giblets." Zachary pointed the bloodied sword in Antonius's direction. "Now let's forget I'm even here, or that you're messing with my friends. I'm sure the message is clear."

"Yeah, I got it." Antonius pushed past Zachary, racing back outdoors.

Zachary smirked and wiped the blood off his blade against the bedsheets, then sheathed the sword. He approached Erik on the floor and kicked him in the side.

"Get the fuck up," Zachary growled, yanking Erik by his collar with his free hand. He hurled the young man across the room, sending Erik smashing against the wall. Erik staggered to his feet with his hands clenched at his sides and Zachary withdrew his sword, pointing the saber's tip at his chest. "You almost cost us big time," he sneered.

Erik looked blankly at Zachary, uncomprehending.

"I don't think he can hear you," Brodie said quietly. "He's still under some weird trance..."

"How did you get involved?" Zachary demanded.

"He asked me to look up a number regarding the Skycatcher program," Brodie explained. "That's all I'm telling you."

"You tell me or you're losing some fingers."

Brodie's pallor paled as he stared down Zachary in defiance. "I don't care if you chop off my hands," he declared. "I'm not letting you hurt Feddy."

"You can't help him," Zachary said. "He's dangerous and can't be trusted."

"What makes you think I can trust you?" Zachary narrowed his eyes at Brodie. "Why should I hand him over to you when it's obvious you mean to kill him?"

"He's very dangerous. You'll only end up dead if you get too close."

Zachary pointed his saber at Brodie and Erik advanced, immediately taking Zachary's arm and twisting it at his back. Zachary yowled when Erik threw him face-down to the worn carpet. Erik stepped on Zachary's head with his heel while he wrenched the young man's arm out of socket, forcing him wailing in agony.

"Let go of my arm!" Zachary screeched as he dropped the

blade. "Come on!"

"Feddy!" Brodie called. "What's your problem?" He jumped down off the bed and shoved Erik aside, sending him to the floor on his rear. "What are you doing?" Erik appeared confused when Brodie clutched his side and stumbled rearwards onto the bed, panting hard for breath.

"Shit, you're really hurt," Zachary muttered as he got up. He gripped his arm and jerked it, popping his shoulder back in place. "Come on, I'll take you to the hospital."

"I'm not leaving Feddy," Brodie murmured.

"He'll be fine. Come on." Zachary approached and grabbed the older man by the arm then helped lead him back to his van outside.

Erik blinked slowly and looked down at the discarded saber left on the dark carpet. He ground his teeth when the voices he heard turned louder as he picked up the sword and sheath.

What matters is that monsters like you are eliminated.
You shouldn't exist - you're nothing!
You are so far from normal, you monster, you beast...
You're not going to live long enough to stop it anyway...
Just hurry up and die...

A digital ring broke his concentration. Slipping the saber back into the scabbard, Erik stood and searched the room for the sound. Peering into the bathroom, he found his cellular phone on the bathroom counter. Picking it up, he pushed the call button.

"Are you all right?" Gina's voice said worriedly. "Did something happen?" When Erik stayed silent, Gina blew a distressed sigh. "Oh dear, not again..." Hearing a series of tones, Erik slowly blinked as he refocused. He leaned against the wall once his legs grew weak. "Are you all right?" Gina called again.

"I'm not hurt," Erik said softly, "and that nutcase... He...!" When the full realization hit him, Erik's guts churned and he turned on his side, retching painfully.

"I'm sorry that happened," Gina said. "It happens. But now, you need to get out of there before someone finds you."

"I don't know where to go," Erik rasped, dropping the saber. "Zachary took Mister Avers to the hospital."

"I'll send a cab. Tell me where you are."

"Some motel..." Erik set the phone aside as he grabbed his coat off the bed and pulled into it. Taking up the cellular and sword, he headed for the front door and stopped dead in his tracks when he faced Antonius armed with a golden-steeled long sword. "The hell?" Erik yelped.

"I'm giving you one last chance," Antonius declared. "You decided to bring Armaments into this, so I'm not taking any chances."

"Armaments?" Gina's voice squawked. "Get out of there!"

"I'll get back with you," Erik said and shut off the phone.

"I don't care who sees us fight," Antonius stated. "The Cleaners will make it disappear as usual."

"I don't want to kill," Erik protested, dropping his phone into his pocket. "I don't kill."

"You're out of luck - I do." Erik backed away as Antonius advanced and held out his free hand. "I'm asking you as an old friend here, not because they told me to get rid of you."

"I don't remember you," Erik complained. "I can tell by your voice you're still upset with me because I did something..."

Antonius lowered his hand and withdrew his sword, holding it at ready from his side. "I'll forgive you if you just tell me what my handlers want," he declared. "Tell me the information and I'll let you go."

Erik shook his head. "I can't," he pleaded. "Even if I could, I don't want anyone controlling me."

"But you're already being controlled."

Erik backed away inside the room and Antonius stepped forward. *"Someone's already controlling me,"* Erik thought, grasping tighter to the saber's sheath. *"Gina mentioned something... She controlled me too..."*

Antonius charged and Erik jumped on the bed, missing the massive swing splitting the mattress in half. Erik dodged another attack, jumping on the chest of drawers. He pushed against the television hanging on the wall, ripping away its supports as the massive appliance crashed over Antonius's head, causing him crying out.

Erik pounced on him, knocking the young man to the floor. Erik jammed the saber against Antonius's throat and Antonius worked a hand free, grasping Erik's face. Looking through his fingers, Erik spotted beyond the open door a figure inside a dark van, parked across the lot and facing their direction.

"If he doesn't kill me, they will!" Erik realized and wrenched his head out of Antonius's grasp then sprang to his feet. He raced into the bathroom and slammed shut the door.

Antonius shook off his stun and pushed away the television. Jumping to his feet, Antonius grabbed his long sword and charged the room, slamming the blade into the panel.

Erik climbed on the back of the toilet and unlatched the window high above it. Pushing the window open, he tossed the saber first then squeezed himself through, dropping onto the ground below. Rolling onto his feet, Erik picked up the sword and sprinted across the yard, racing back for the service road leading to the highway.

"You son of a bitch!" Antonius shouted after him.

"Come on, catch up," Erik prayed as he increased his speed. Spotting a gas station ahead, he jumped the railing and ran onto the street, dodging cars along the road. Erik hurried to the building's rear and slumped against the wall, gasping for breath.

Looking to his left, he saw the service road continuing downhill toward more hotels and small shops. To his right, Erik spotted a bridge over an intersection in the distance. Hearing harried footsteps approach, Erik made a break for the right, running for the bridge. Antonius continued after him and Erik quickly made his way around cars coming off the highway as he neared.

Hastily climbing the railing, Erik yowled when sudden force pulled him back and looked over his shoulder, finding Antonius standing behind him, heaving for breath. The long sword pinned his overcoat to the concrete and Antonius grasped his sleeve.

"I'm not letting you go," Antonius wheezed. "You're coming with me."

"I can't go with you," Erik said and pulled his free arm out of his coat. Grasping the sword with his unrestricted hand, he yanked his other arm loose from Antonius's grip. "Let me go."

Antonius tightened his grip and dug in his heels when Erik dangled from the edge. "If I let you go, you're dead!" he cried. "Don't do this to me!"

"That's how they want me, right?" Erik spat and bat Antonius's hand with the scabbard. "Let me go!"

"No!" Erik continued striking Antonius's hand and head with the sheath. "Stop hitting me!" he yowled.

"Then let me go!"

"You know I can't!"

"Why?"

"Because Kaye's dying!" Erik's eyes widened and he immediately grasped the railing with his arm. Antonius helped him up and Erik dropped onto the sidewalk, dumbfounded. "You remember her too, don't you?" Antonius called, releasing his grip. "She was in our unit."

"I..." Erik tensed when the pain ravaged his head. "I don't know why I feel bad when I think about her."

"You don't really remember?" Erik gave Antonius a blank look in return. "Maybe if you see her, it might jog your memory, you think?"

"Only if you promise not to try and kill me again."

"It's fine. I'll just tell them I'm trying to get on your good side."

"Are your handlers the ones letting Kaye die?"

"That's why I'm asking you to tell me, to help her."

"You're lying..."

Antonius shrugged then picked up the sword and hoisted

it over his shoulder with ease. Erik staggered to his feet and pulled back into his overcoat, then walked with Antonius back toward the motel. The unease churning in his guts intensified and Erik held his side in agony.

"Are you hurt?" Antonius inquired.

"Just sick," Erik answered.

"I got something for that. The painkillers they give me makes me sick sometimes."

"You get headaches too?"

Antonius said nothing and Erik blew a heavy sigh. Once they approached the parking lot, Erik noticed the dark van gone and the motel room closed.

"Get in, it's open," Antonius ordered. He lowered the sword and it glowed in silver light, reforming into a pen with a golden nib.

Erik cautiously entered the car and tucked the saber between the seats. His phone chirped and Erik withdrew his device, looking at the screen.

Unknown: Abandon your fear. Move forward.

Erik thumbed back a message, only to get it automatically rejected.

"What's the matter?" Antonius called to Erik as he got in and started the car.

"I'm getting weird texts from someone," Erik answered.

"Did you call it?"

"It's unlisted and when I send one back, it doesn't go through."

"You're not planning on calling for help, are you?"

"I trust you."

Antonius directed a wary look towards Erik. "You shouldn't."

"If my trusting you kills me, then it's my stupid fault."

Antonius blew a heavy sigh and pulled out the lot, returning to the road.

THIRTY-ONE

Erik's unease gradually worsened as Antonius entered General Hospital's parking lot.

"Hold on," Antonius said as Erik tried the door. He reached under the seat and withdrew a bottle of pills then tossed the container toward Erik. Catching them easily, Erik opened the bottle, finding a mix of medications inside. "Red ones are for pain," Antonius explained, "green ones are uppers, blue ones are downers, orange ones are for anxiety, and if you see a yellow one, don't take that."

"What are the yellow ones for?" Erik wondered aloud.

"To forget shit."

Erik shook the pills into his palm and picked a green tablet and red capsule while Antonius stepped out the car, lighting a cigarette. Pouring the rest back, Erik left the yellow one in his hand. He glanced to Antonius pacing outside and pocketed the yellow capsule, then popped the other pills in his mouth.

Placing the cap back on the bottle, Erik threw them under the seat and exited the car. Antonius nodded as Erik shut the door and Erik followed the young man's lead, leaving the saber behind.

They entered through the glass doors and Erik clenched his hands as his headache intensified.

"You okay?" Antonius asked, quirking an eyebrow.

"Not really," Erik murmured. "I'll hold up okay though."

"Take a seat in the waiting room, will you?" Antonius directed. "I'll see if Kaye can get visitors."

"Sure."

Antonius left Erik's side and approached the front desk, chatting to the charge nurse. Erik made his way for the water fountain and swallowed the pills he held in his mouth. He then walked around the waiting room, peering at magazines. Pausing at one scientific magazine with a major article concerning the many uses of Corite, he picked it up and thumbed through the pages.

"Hey, Erik," Antonius called. Erik looked up at the young man waving at him. "Come on."

"Sure," Erik answered and folded the magazine, slipping it into his back pocket. He neared Antonius and they walked together toward the elevators.

"You look like shit," Antonius noted as the doors opened and they got on.

"I feel like it too," Erik murmured. "I drank a lot today."

"I'll find something for your hangover." Antonius pressed the button and the car began moving upwards. "That's if you still feel bad..."

"Just so you know, Erik's not my name anymore."

"What is it?"

"Whatever my current VitaStat card says."

Antonius pressed his lips together, thoughtful. "I see," he murmured.

"What's that supposed to mean?"

Antonius shook his head and the cable car came to a pause as the bell donged. The doors opened and Erik stepped out onto a silent corridor, hearing many machines working.

"Is she seriously sick?" Erik inquired as Antonius walked ahead.

"She's out of intensive," Antonius responded. "She's been sick a very long time."

"Cancer, is it?"

"They're not quite sure what it is. But I know what it is, and I'm sure you do too."

"What do you mean?"

Erik followed Antonius to a room with a name card outside the door reading 'Kaye Edgars'. Beneath it, another sign posted that masks had to be worn. Antonius picked up a surgical mask from a box set on a small table near the entrance and put it on. Erik did the same as Antonius knocked on the door before entering.

Erik frowned once he entered, finding a large-framed olive-skinned woman lying in the hospital bed under the sheeting, surrounded by wires and tubing.

"Hey," Antonius murmured as he reached the foot of the bed. "You awake?"

Erik leaned against the door, shuddering in fear. He gasped weakly for breath, clutching his chest and shut his eyes as he struggled to breathe.

You'd do the same...

"I'm sorry," Erik moaned, overwhelmed by a heavy feeling of guilt washing over him. "I'm sorry..." He held his head and slid to haunches, breaking down in tears.

Antonius looked over to Erik sobbing at the door. "You remember what happened," he called, "don't you?"

Erik shook his head and sniffled. "I can't," he wailed. "I don't…"

"You remember, otherwise you wouldn't be freaking out like that." Antonius approached and nudged Erik's side with his toe. "Do you hear me?" Erik ceased his crying and looked up as Antonius reached into his pocket, withdrawing a small iridescent stone in his gloved hand. "Give me the money and I'll give you more of where I got this."

"Corite?" Erik murmured. "How'd you get your hands on that? It's illegal to own that stuff unless you're in the Public Defense Works."

"There's a reason for that." Antonius smiled cruelly. "Now we got a deal, don't we?"

"What makes you think I got money?"

"Don't play with me, man." Erik held out his hand and Antonius dropped the stone into his palm. "Give me my money or I'm taking your soul." Erik clutched the Corite and cringed when Antonius caressed a hand through his hair. He held in his breath when grabbed by the nape of his neck as Antonius leaned in. "So will you do that for me?" Antonius murmured in his ear. "All I'm asking for is the money. I don't want nothing else from you."

"Where the hell you think I have that hidden somewhere?" Erik murmured. "You're taking a big risk asking me like this."

"You already agreed to the plan after begging me to help you, remember? You know I hate begging."

"Sure," Erik mewed and Antonius let go, wiping his face

against his sleeve. "I'll get it for you."

"Don't disappoint me." Antonius grabbed Erik's hair and yanked his back his head. "I understand that compelling feeling you have being on the verge of losing your shit - but remember, don't forget your job." Erik grasped Antonius's wrist with his free hand as the young man tightened his grip. "If something gets in the way of that, destroy it. That includes your feelings, your beliefs, and dreams of that monster stirring inside you."

Erik narrowed his eyes. "What if I am that horrible monster," he snapped, "and that guy you knew - your friend, your comrade - didn't exist?"

"Isn't it obvious?" Antonius released his grip. "You're dead, we're all dead, and all that fighting would be for nothing."

Erik let go and Antonius left the room, shutting the door behind him. Erik grunted and rose to his feet, then approached Kaye's bedside. He looked down at her pallid face and ran a gentle hand through her curly bronzed hair.

"I'll try my best to remember," Erik said softly. "I'll try harder... If I have to turn evil to do it, then I will." He breathed a heavy sigh. "I'm sorry." Erik took Kaye's limp hand and squeezed gently. "Please, forgive me."

You can't be forgiven...

Erik released Kaye's hand and pocketed the Corite as he stalked out the room. Ripping off the mask, he dropped into the chair outside the door and held his head in his hands, breaking down into another round of tears.

Moments later, Erik's phone chirped. He swallowed hard as he quickly collected his bearings and withdrew the phone, finding another cryptic message from the unlisted number.

Unknown: Never stop fighting.

Erik grunted and returned to the elevators. Once released onto the ground level floor, he made his way for the waiting room. Erik paused when he spotted the middle-aged man who had bobbed dark brown hair peppered with silver and pale green eyes behind circular glasses. The man, wearing a navy suit, spoke to the charge nurse at the front desk while holding his black riding coat over his arm. Before Erik could turn away, the man glanced up, catching sight of Erik standing several feet offside.

Erik ground his teeth, growling under his breath as the man approached, giving a derisive smile.

"I'm here solely for work-related purposes, Mister Ferdian," he said. "You needn't worry about me."

"I have every right to be suspicious, Giuseppe," Erik snarled.

"Now you know that isn't my name, Mister Ferdian." Giuseppe grabbed Erik's arm and leaned in. "And to think of this as an unexpected outcome... I'd never thought you'd hunt me so openly."

Erik bared his teeth. "That's enough." He prodded Giuseppe in the chest with his phone. "I have my reasons."

"I won't trouble you as long as you stay out of my way."

Erik wrenched his arm free. "Then one last piece of advice." Giuseppe paled as Erik whispered in his ear. "If you do anything to hurt my friends - and you know I have many - I will kill you. You know I have the ability."

Giuseppe cleared his throat and left his side, walking

briskly for the elevators. Erik approached the front desk and tapped the nearby bell. The glass dividing screen opened.

"I wish to see Brodie Avers," Erik announced to the nursing assistant. "He was admitted earlier."

"You still have some time before visiting hours end," she replied. "He's on the second floor."

"Thanks." Erik ran for the elevators and growled when he found both door indicators lit and slowly cycling through the numbers. "Bastard!" Erik hissed and hurried for the nearby stairwell. Throwing open the door, he raced up the steps.

Erik entered the second floor and wheezed for breath, leaning against the wall. When an orderly gave him a concerned look upon passing, Erik held up a hand.

"I'm fine," he gasped. "Heavy smoker."

The orderly nodded and continued his rounds. Erik left his place at the wall and scanned the name cards outside the doors. Finding the room Brodie resided in, Erik stood outside the door, listening.

"Thanks for checking it out for me, Joey," Erik heard Brodie say. "I appreciate it."

"I was a system engineer before," Giuseppe's voice said. "So it shouldn't be that difficult to track."

"I thought your thing was software."

"It is. But the brains behind those machines... That bastard was the project leader on everything we created."

"Why would the hardware be so important? It's always outdated in three years."

"He developed a lot of powerful applications. When the

new ordinances came down, he took off with my rival and that conniving bitch... At the time, we didn't know how much of a threat those three really were to us."

"So what of what you're doing now?"

"We're only recreating what he left behind all those years ago. Without his superior knowledge, his skill, and creativity, all we'll have are imperfect copies."

"Then why are you so interested in Feddy?" Brodie complained. "I'm only keeping him happy since you told me he's a Cleaner." Brodie groaned. "I don't know where I screwed up down the line - there's forty years of that shit."

"I have a need to know because he's hiding something important, something dangerous, and if I try directly, he'll only get further from me."

"For Feddy to keep running and hide who he really is... the kid's got his reasons."

"He has evil intentions, obviously," Giuseppe persisted. "You got hurt dealing with him."

"You must've forgotten last week after the quarterlies were due," Brodie retorted. "I got hurt then too."

Giuseppe sighed. "Fine, but if you end up disappearing, I warned you."

"Don't worry about it, Joey. Please look into that for me."

"Why would you care who broke into his place?" Giuseppe protested. "He's a bad guy and bad things happen to them for a reason."

"I promised I would do this for him. At least try!"

"Fine."

Giuseppe stepped out the room and Erik grabbed the man

by the arm, whirling him around. Erik yanked his arm around Giuseppe's neck and covered his mouth with his hand, pulling the man against the wall. He jammed his elbow into Giuseppe's side and Giuseppe let out a muffled cry.

"Still hurts like a bitch, eh?" Erik sneered in Giuseppe's ear as the older man doubled over. He grabbed for Giuseppe's holster under his blazer with his other hand and Giuseppe grasped his wrist. "Listen, I know you're looking for something and I know you're spying on me." Erik snapped the holster and Giuseppe tightened his grip on Erik's wrist. "You ordered my place trashed and the office too. You even dug into Osphena and Gina, hoping to find something." Erik tightened his grip around Giuseppe's neck and the man whimpered as his face turned red. "Know this, if you eliminate me, I'm taking you with me. It wouldn't be hard to trace it back to you, the main Defector."

Erik let go and withdrew the revolver as Giuseppe staggered forward, gasping for breath. Erik opened the chamber and dumped the bullets onto the floor with a clatter.

"You're talking out your ass, Mister Ferdian," Giuseppe growled as he rubbed at his neck. "You try anything like that and you're finished! All it'll take is a few keystrokes and you're done!"

Erik smirked. "Finished?" he spat and pointed the revolver at Giuseppe once the man turned around, facing him. "You forget what I'm good at." Giuseppe charged and Erik sidestepped the attack, throwing a powerful punch into the man's jaw with the gun. Giuseppe's glasses flew off his face as he whirled around before striking the floor on his knees.

Giuseppe spat blood on the ground and held his face in agony as Erik stood over him, pressing the revolver into the back of his head.

"You forget how scary I can get, old man," Erik seethed. "Don't go there with me."

"Are you threatening me?" Giuseppe growled. "I thought you didn't kill."

"You do as Mister Avers asked you to and be truthful. If you lie, then it'll only tell me how complicit you are into this matter." Erik lowered the revolver and dropped it to the floor with a clang. "Now disappear before I change my mind and might actually kill you for real."

Erik stalked past Giuseppe, returning for the stairwell and made his way back into the waiting room. He spotted Antonius sitting near the door, reading a magazine.

"That took a while," Antonius said as Erik approached. "Want me to drop you off anywhere?"

"You don't have to do that," Erik answered. "I can get a ride."

"I'm starving and it's late. What do you feel like?"

"I don't care. I just want more booze."

Antonius set the magazine aside and glanced up at Erik. "Feeling that bad, huh?"

Erik blew a short sigh. "Sure," he muttered. "Real bad."

"There's a nice place I know of. Come on."

Stepping outdoors, Erik dug through his pockets and withdrew his cigarettes and matchbook. He lit a cigarette, walking across the lot toward Antonius's car.

"Say, Tony," Erik said. "You said we were good friends,

right?"

"Yeah," Antonius answered and leaned against the trunk, withdrawing his own pack of cigarettes and lighter. "Why are you asking me this?"

"You knew me by Erik, right?"

"Yeah, and?" Antonius withdrew a cigarette and lit it, gazing warily at Erik.

"Did you know me by any other names?"

Antonius frowned, saying nothing as he continued smoking in silence.

THIRTY-TWO

Erik kept silent as Antonius parked in front of the yellow eatery that had signs of various noodle dishes in the windows and immediately stepped out the car. Pulling his collar against the cold evening winds, he crossed the lot and came to a pause when he spotted Mell in a dark overcoat standing outside several paces from the door, smoking a cigar.

"You seem tired," Mell acknowledged once Erik neared.

"A very long day," Erik grumbled.

"What do you feel like tonight? I'm buying."

"Something light and lots of wine."

"Sure, in a minute."

"Are you waiting for somebody?"

"Yeah."

Erik noticed Mell grow tense as he leaned against his cane and turned, spotting Gina and Antonius approaching. Gina appeared agitated, clutching her hands at her sides. She passed Mell, then abruptly stopped and turned, hurling a punch across Mell's face.

Mell yowled as he staggered back and struck the ground on his rear, stunned. Gina said nothing as she stormed up the steps and flung open the door. Antonius smirked and followed her inside.

"I'm fine," Mell groaned from his place on the ground before Erik could ask.

"What did you do?" Erik responded.

"What *didn't* I do is the question." Mell coughed and spat blood on the ground. He held a hand to his mouth and spat into his palm, revealing a molar. "Damn, girl broke my tooth..."

Erik shrugged his shoulders and entered the eatery, finding Gina in the rear booth, clearly incensed. He approached and slipped into the seat across from her.

"I can only do so much without arousing suspicion," Gina said and dug through her coat pockets. Withdrawing a single business card, she flicked it across the table toward Erik. "Your friend worked for them, right? Well, I pulled some strings for you to check out her position."

"What about Kanbal?" Erik asked, taking the card. Studying it, he read the bold serif type in two words divided by a red line as the logotype, underneath Midco over Sanato. With only the main office number for Human Resources listed on the front, Erik turned the card over on the back, finding a single sequence written in heavy angular strokes: 'Tyson 78-64'.

"You're done there," said Gina. "There's no way your friend can recover the drives in time. All it'll take is a few keystrokes and you don't exist."

"You're afraid I'm going to end up like Derrick Andrews if I get any deeper, am I right?" Erik set the card on the table. "Remember, you're the one who asked me to look into this. So if anyone should shoulder the blame, then it's you." Gina paled in response and Erik chortled. "Look, I can handle myself fine - I've done all right so far." He grinned. "Though I have to thank that wingnut Zachary, however. He pulled me out of tight jam today."

"Don't entrust your life in his hands," Gina warned.

Erik raised an eyebrow as Gina pulled out of her coat and draped it on the back of the booth. "Why would you say that?" he complained. "So he's a bit weird and irritating, but he seems cooperative…"

"He's a childish, selfish coward who only worries about covering his ass," Gina grumbled. "He's a cruel monster and if you deal with him, you'll only hurt yourself."

Erik reached across the table and took Gina's clenched hand, opening her fingers. "Are you saying a good guy like me would corrupt under his influence?" He smiled brightly and Gina frowned in response. "If I get hurt, then it's my fault for being stupid, right?"

"I'm telling you, just avoid him when you can."

"Is he useful at all?"

"When he wants to be."

"But you know I'm a bad guy already…"

Gina paled and Erik squeezed her fingers.

"Did you tell him to go away?" Mell's voice called.

Erik released his hold around Gina's hand as Mell approached with a wine glass. A server followed behind him and placed a bottle of sherry on the table with another empty glass.

Gina appeared irritated as Mell set his cane against the table and sat next to her, pushing her slightly to scoot over. He handed her his glass and opened the wine bottle.

"I told him," Gina muttered.

Mell poured sherry into her glass, then filled his own. "Well?" he pressed.

"Are you referring to me?" Erik inquired as Mell set aside the bottle.

"In the end, everything is still messed up," the older man murmured and downed his drink.

"But aren't I the reason?" Erik suggested.

"It might get worse if they find out..." Mell noted.

"Find out about what?"

Gina poured Mell another serving and the older man nodded. "Cooperate with him, will ya, lad?" Mell pleaded. "As a favor?"

"Well...!"

"Oh, hey," Zachary's voice called.

"Speak of the devil," Mell muttered behind his drink as Zachary approached.

"How are my two best friends in the world?" Zachary said brightly. Erik let out a mild cry when grabbed around the neck by Zachary's arm and the young man ran his knuckles roughly over his head. "You owe me a big favor, Ferdian," Zachary growled in Erik's ear. "Just you wait."

Erik paled as Zachary let go and plopped in his seat next to him. "So," Erik said weakly and cleared his throat. "What are we having? We hadn't gotten our menus yet."

"Why not ask around, Miss Lady?" Zachary said cheerfully. "Don't worry; I'll keep the little troublemaker company." Zachary jabbed his elbow into Erik's ribs, making him cough. "Am I right?"

Erik nodded and Gina grunted as she pushed away from the

booth. "Please behave," she snapped. Mell stood aside as Zachary waved her away and Gina blew a hard sigh before stalking off.

"Now what's this?" Zachary asked, taking the business card left on the table. "Midco/Sanato, huh?"

"That's where you're going next, eh?" Mell piped as he returned to his seat.

"Gina wants me to sniff over there and tie up loose ends," Erik answered.

"And she didn't bother to invite me," Zachary grumbled. "Rude ass bitch..."

"Hey!" Mell barked and kicked Zachary under the table. Zachary winced in return.

"What do you mean by that?" Erik asked.

Zachary grinned and turned toward Erik, poking the wing of his nose with the card. "You'll see."

Erik frowned and pushed away his hand. "I don't want you involved in my problems."

Zachary chortled. "That's where you're wrong," he chided. "It's my job to get into other people's problems. You're supposed to fix them, but you're so goddamn inept, it's laughable."

"Then why keep me on if I can't do the job right?" Erik spat. "Then I'm nothing but a waste of time!"

"Because, you have something they want real bad." Erik pulled away as Zachary leaned in. "They won't stop until they get you alone..." Erik swallowed hard as Zachary ran the edge of the card down the side of his neck. "The only thing on their minds is their single-minded directive." Erik shut his eyes as cold sweat broke out on his forehead. "Prevail," Zachary whispered. "Fight. Destroy. Shoot. Kill. Annihilate every last one of those monsters."

"I can't..." Erik murmured.

"Stop thinking and just do it. What you already saw can't be unseen. The more you think about it, the more it'll only drive you berserk." Erik clenched his hands when Zachary lowered his voice. "Stop fighting and go, fall off the edge. Become that very thing you hate."

"I don't..."

"Yes, you do. You know who they are."

"Why are you trying to control me?"

"All we're doing is pushing you in a direction we want. And once we put you where we need you, it'll finally end. You can finally stop dreaming."

Stop dreaming...

Wake up...

Realize the truth...

You will kill and do as you're ordered to...

We may never meet again, but we'll never forget each other...

Erik took in a shallow breath and his eyes snapped open, facing his counterpart in the navy uniform sitting across from him, grinning darkly.

"The hell you're here for?" Erik snarled and rose to his feet.

"What's with that for?" Mell squawked.

You know why I'm here. The young man with his looks also stood. *So many questions of why everything's the way they are, of why you're like this.* Erik's double smirked and gestured with a hand to the room around them. *Look around you! Look at them! These mindless people, those foolish drones you're so*

322

intent on protecting - they know nothing of the danger in which they live!

"What about them?" Erik demanded.

They come and go as they please, without a care in the world! And you want to protect them? For what? Because you don't want to live in a world where these people would end up just like you: used, discarded, or worse... mindless fodder for the war machine.

"What are you going on about?" Mell protested.

"I don't care about them. I don't really want to live."

Until you get rid of me, I'm not letting that happen!

"What are you saying?" Mell demanded. "You can't just leave like that!"

Erik pushed past Zachary at the table and stormed for the rear exit, passing Antonius sitting in a booth behind them nursing a glass of beer along the way.

"Where are you going?" Antonius called after Erik, rising from his seat. "Hey, wait!"

Erik pushed open the doors and stalked across the lot to Antonius's sedan. He opened the door, reaching under the seat to extract the saber left there. The counterpart appeared behind Erik, smirking.

What are you going to do to me?

Erik grasped the blade and turned around, slamming shut the door. "I'm going to silence you forever," he snarled. "I want you to stop haunting me, tormenting me..."

How are you going to do that? The mirror image laughed at Erik and waved him away. *You're temporarily severed from the surrounding world in an area of isolation space, where your movements influence and cause an effect on everyone else, by accelerating what you're programmed to do.*

"You know you just made no sense," Erik spat and withdrew the saber from the scabbard.

I just told you: you're dreaming and you're sleepwalking. The young man with Erik's appearance unbuttoned his cuffs and rolled up his sleeves. *I'm going to help you wake up.*

"How are you going to do that?"

If I told you that, then I'd be irresponsible. Erik's counterpart took on his fighting stance and beckoned to Erik. *I'd be careless and you'd lose your life. Without you, I can't exist.*

"So are you saying only one of us can live?" Erik dropped the sword sheath onto the ground with a clatter. "You have a bad conscience after all!"

Don't get ahead of me! I will destroy you!

"Come on, then!" Erik screeched. "Bring it!"

The double lurched forward and Erik stepped out of his rushing attack, swiping back with the blade. Erik missed his target as the reflection stepped around him, easily dodging his attacks.

Forget it! The counterpart swiftly eluded Erik's wild swings, further enraging him. *I'm going to haunt your scrawny ass forever until you give up! Your life is mine, sucker!*

Erik screamed and launched at his mirror image. The duplicate with his looks hastily evaded the strike and Erik punched through the car door. Turning, Erik received a hard snapping punch to the face that knocked him down flat onto the ground and he instantly lost consciousness.

THIRTY-THREE

Lately I've been having weird dreams...

Erik gasped once his eyes opened and he sat up with a start, panting hard for breath. Pain thudded behind his eyes and he moaned, running his hands through his hair.

Noticing a loud hum, Erik took in his surroundings and found himself in a dimly lit gray room. Looking for the source of the sound, Erik saw a large wide fan rest on the room's far side, blowing air into a corner. Around him were other green cots filled with sleeping men and women in navy uniforms. Examining himself, he realized he wore the same uniform that had '245-G' stitched on the arm.

This feeling of displacement...

Erik pushed aside the thin gray blanket and stepped out of his cot. He walked down the pathways, glancing at the other sleeping persons in similar attire. Discovering a few empty cots as he walked around on the gray-tiled floor, Erik wondered if anyone else was awake as he sought the exit.

Approaching a single chipped blue door on the end, Erik pushed against it, revealing a dimly lit corridor that had flickering strip lights along the ashen walls.

Do you know what happens after the end...?

Passing the gang showers and toilets, Erik reached a set of

stairs and descended them, happening upon another set of double doors in the same blue paint. Pushing them open, Erik entered a concrete courtyard lit up by yellow spotlights. A single bench was in the center of the yard, with a water fountain near the wall behind the door, and a tall gate blocking off the other end surrounded by ivy.

Erik spotted Kaye wearing a sling around her right arm playing a game of Chess against Antonius at a table on the yard's other side. A tall lanky young man with platinum blond hair styled into a flattop and dull gray eyes stood nearby, watching the game.

"Hey," Erik called and the tall blond looked up, grinning.

"Dude," he called back, "what are you doing up?" Erik frowned when the young man left the wall and approached, giving a friendly hug. "You okay, bro?" He held Erik back by the shoulders, peering at him carefully. "You know where you are?" The young man let go and held up three fingers. "How many?"

"Four," Erik muttered.

"What's my name?" Erik squinted, searching for a name tag on the man's shirt, only finding a number instead: '194-10D'. "C'mon, dude, you know it. Say it with me: 'Andre'."

"Andre...?"

"Leave him alone," Kaye called to Andre. "He's not doing well, you know."

"Hang with us, will ya?" Andre offered and grabbed Erik's hand, dragging him over to the Chess table.

"We should play Goh next," Antonius murmured, crossing his leg at the knee. He rest his elbow against his thigh as he held his chin in his hand, studying the pieces on the board.

"It's only because I kick your ass in Chess," Kaye teased as Antonius moved a piece on the board with his free hand. Kaye then knocked over a pawn with her bishop. "Check, dumb ass."

"Fuck," Antonius muttered.

"Are you still overdoing that Neuralgine?" Andre inquired as he let Erik go and leaned against the nearby wall, folding his gangly thin arms across his narrow chest.

Erik stood at the table, watching Antonius struggle to come up with a counter maneuver. "What's that?" he responded.

"A tranquilizer that also acts like a super strong painkiller and muscle relaxer," Andre explained. "It makes you trip balls while you feel ten feet tall and bulletproof."

"I guess…"

"Don't feel bad," Antonius said as he moved another piece on the Chessboard. "You're not the only one popping pills before each mission."

"Checkmate, moron," Kaye jibed as she knocked off the king's piece with her knight. "You're not paying attention at all!"

"Shit, I'm worried," Antonius complained. "The last run was a disaster! We got ambushed when we were reorganized to attack the main computer controlling the 'droids."

"Totally heavy stuff, dude," Andre agreed. "I'm kinda glad the commander got iced. She underestimated those guys."

"Don't say stupid shit like that, Dre," Kaye spat as she collected the pieces. "I think it was a setup. I mean, come on, they crashed from the *inside*!" Antonius helped reset the table. "They're not going to try another frontal attack. They'd be stupid to do that again."

"Why not become commander then?" Antonius asked.

"You're pretty good when it comes to tactical surveillance."

"Right, you warned them about being outnumbered on the direct approach," Andre assented, "and how we didn't have enough for reinforcements."

"I have to serve a lot longer to work my way up that high." Kaye glanced up at Erik. "You okay, or are you coming down?"

"I thought you got crushed out there," Erik answered slowly.

Kaye grinned. "At least it was just my arm," she said breezily. "I'm pretty lucky."

"You sure you okay to be out and around, dude?" Andre asked. "The last three fights you got banged up pretty bad."

"He's tough," Antonius drawled as he readied the Chessboard. "Otherwise he's stupid to keep getting up and fighting like that."

"Or zonked," Andre said and giggled.

"At least he came back alive unlike our other comrades," Kaye said icily. "Zonked or not."

"I can't wait to retire from active service," Andre complained and left his place at the wall. Erik stiffened when Andre draped an arm around his shoulders. "I'm not a fan of killing people, like Big Red here."

"Wait, what?" Erik yelped.

"But it's not *people* we're killing, Dre," Kaye interjected. "It's those damn Synthoids."

"Too much for me, dude..."

"Why not send other Combat Androids to get rid of them?" Erik asked. "If they no longer need soldiers... Why risk *our* lives?"

"You really need to lay off the pills," Kaye said sternly. "The

Synthoids are programmed to destroy *everything.* They won't stop until they explode."

"Right," Antonius filled in. "If we send *our* 'droids after theirs, it's a quick battle as to who has the newer machines."

"So why are we here again?" Erik pressed.

"We're part of the 'education through labor' project," another voice called to them. Erik looked up, facing a slender young man with ear-length frizzy blond hair, high cheekbones, and narrow blue eyes who entered the courtyard. He was dressed in the same navy uniform with silver buttons and armed with a blue steel saber. "What's the best way to save money? By sending out criminals and crazies to fight your battles!"

"Arizeh would know," Kaye muttered. "He's both!"

"What crime did you commit?" Erik asked as Arizeh approached the table and looked down at the game underway.

"What a bad opening," Arizeh noted as Antonius moved his pawn. "I bet she'll clean your clock in twenty moves."

"Bullshit," Antonius snapped.

"Does this mean if our next performance improves, we might be let off early?" Andre questioned.

"Maybe," Arizeh murmured and unhooked his scabbard from his harness. He crouched on his haunches as he jabbed the sheath onto the ground, watching the game carefully. "They'll send us to a special school for deprogramming and we integrate back to society exhibiting as many traits of normalcy as possible."

"How do you know so much about this?" Erik wondered aloud.

"I hear things," Arizeh murmured. "You better get ready

soon, though. We got another battle planned."

"I don't feel up to going," Erik said softly. "Have them put me on sick leave."

"You're better at attacking than defending. You *have* to go."

"I can't..." Erik pulled away from Andre and held out his hands. "I'm sick... I'm like really, really sick."

"How so?"

Erik opened his mouth to explain, then shut it as his hands dropped to his sides. He shook his head, unable to come up with any meaningful excuse.

People have opposing forces and yet they hesitate...

Erik left the courtyard, heading back upstairs. He passed a short slender young woman with cropped black hair and narrow hazel eyes who wore a pair of daggers strapped to her thigh. On her uniform, she had a label across the left breast labeled '194–01E'. Erik paused, looking back at her as she ignored him and made her way outdoors.

"Hey," Erik called to her.

The young woman halted. "What do you want, you failure?" she snapped.

"They told me we failed again because everything was beyond their expectations," Erik responded.

"Don't be ridiculous," the young woman said. "You're useless."

"I must be worth something if I'm still here!" Erik retorted.

"Do you think it'll end faster if you just tell them what they want?"

"But I'll get in trouble if I do that..."

"It's your choice." She pointed above her head with her

thumb. "There's more stuff if you want it. Go to the third floor."

"What makes you think I'm fiending for more?" Erik grumbled and folded his arms across his chest. "I'm insulted."

"If you want to play around, do it in moderation," the woman said in annoyance. "One of these days you're going to fuck with the wrong person."

Erik clenched his teeth as she opened the doors, going out into the courtyard. He turned away and ascended the staircase.

Erik entered the stairwell and made his way to the third floor. Pushing open the doors, he entered a darkened cube farm and noticed a solitary office at the end with its door open and light on.

"Hello?" Erik called. "Is anyone here?"

Scoping the room, he found no other body nearby and approached the open office cautiously. Peering inside, Erik saw an amber bottle of capsules on the desk surrounded by several charts and other paperwork. Swiping the pill bottle, he pocketed it, then thumbed through the papers, finding battle logs and notes about other soldiers in his unit.

"The fuck you doing here, boy?" a voice growled at him.

Erik gasped and looked up, facing a tall imposing man in a navy uniform with silver buttons, armed with a pair of high-powered pistols. He wore a cap with a wide visor over his graying dark hair and orange-tinted glasses.

"What's it look like, Commander?" Erik snapped.

"Get the fuck outta my office," the commander spat.

"Number One Echo said you called for me," Erik responded.

"This late?"

"She told me our losses are my fault, Sir."

"It is, boy." The commander stepped in and poked Erik's chest with his fingers. "Your father created those machines that's wreaking havoc on the country now."

"Then what can I do about it?"

"You know very well what to do about it." The commander scoffed. "We just want the new schematics he's drawn up and you're out of here, simple as that. Otherwise, we're going to keep sending you on suicide missions."

"What if I told you he doesn't write down his schematics and keeps it all in his head?"

The commander growled under his breath and pointed toward the door. "Get the fuck out my face, smart ass," he snarled.

Erik shrugged and left the room. Exiting into the corridor, he approached the phone in the hall and picked up the receiver. Erik immediately dialed the first number that came to mind.

After several rings, the line picked up. "Hello?" a voice groggily answered. "You've reached Chesterfield fifty-one twenty-nine."

"John Greenfield, please?" Erik requested.

"Speaking." Erik stayed silent, unable to come up with anything else to say. "Why do you keep calling me?" John Greenfield said. "What are you looking for?"

Erik shut his eyes and leaned forward, pressing his forehead against the wall. "They're shipping me out again," he said softly. "They said they're going to keep me until you give them the new schematics."

"Have you lost sight of your original purpose?" John

Greenfield pressed.

"I forgot why I lost it..." Erik blew a distressed sigh. "I've been taking a lot of Neuralgine lately... My comrades are worried about my mental health."

"You need to be careful with that. I don't want you to overdose."

"I'll try not to... But I can't sleep."

"Those dreams are real, all of it, everything! Each pain and ache and nightmare... those dreams, those memories, they exist. You exist." Erik opened his eyes and turned around, leaning against the wall. He stared at the peeling gray paint on the walls, noting each fissure and crack in the flecked color. "You are here for a reason..."

"Aside from being cannon fodder?" Erik said sourly.

"People who lose their hearts to the darkness, lose their reasoning and their willpower," John Greenfield said seriously. "They become monsters, completely controlled by the corruption."

"How does this pertain to me?"

"When you wake up, you might not be the same."

Erik bristled. "They told me they won't let me go!" he snapped. "So you're just going to let them *use* me? Are you really that selfish?"

"What's sleeping deep inside your heart?"

"What?" Erik ran a hand through his hair. "What kind of question is that?"

"Just answer it."

"I'm no monster," Erik spat. "I hate killing."

"So are you a heartless puppet?"

"Not really." Erik snorted. "I have to be far gone just to get through the damn missions they send me on."

"It wasn't supposed to be like this."

"Really now?" Erik snarled in contempt.

"It's too complex to explain..."

"Whatever."

"Remember to keep yourself alive so that I may see you again." Erik clenched his free hand, shaking in rage as pain thudded in his temples. "Have a good night."

"Good night," Erik muttered and slammed the receiver back on the cradle. Leaving the corridor back to the stairwell, he paused when he spotted Antonius standing on the other side once he opened the door.

"What are you thinking about?" Antonius asked. "You look pissed."

"When did you get here?" Erik demanded, surprised. "Don't tell me you were waiting for me!"

"I wasn't."

Erik moaned and ran his hands through his hair as he sank to the step, holding his head in his hands. "I'm losing it," he cried when his headache worsened. "I can't take this... I can't keep doing this."

"Hey," Antonius said softly and stood next to Erik. "You'll get through this. The pain will eventually go away."

"But when does it stop? Does it ever stop?"

"I wish I knew the answer to that."

Erik leaned forward, covering his head in his arms. Antonius said nothing as he sat next to him, distressed. "Why can't they get their best to reverse engineer those damn

334

machines?" he griped.

"I heard there's a component missing that's never been documented," Antonius suggested. "Kaye and Danae were talking about it when we were trying to figure out other weaknesses those 'droids had."

"I doubt they have anything else planned for those machines, other than mere military power and cheap labor for the mines." Erik let out a strained laugh. "They already perfected the E-Sys chips and the Dyna-widgets. What more can they come up with?"

"Cloning perhaps?"

Erik looked up at Antonius who appeared thoughtful. "I don't think I can sleep tonight," he murmured.

"Take another pill. No one's going to hate you for it."

"I'm worried about overdoing it. Andre's already concerned, worried about me snapping and then we'll accrue more losses..."

"So take a half of one."

Erik sat up and withdrew the bottle of pills from his pocket. Unscrewing the top, he shook out a small yellow capsule.

"Do you want the other one?" Erik asked. "I'd hate to waste it."

"Sure," Antonius said and held out his hand as Erik passed it to him. Antonius broke the capsule in half while Erik screwed the top back on the bottle. "You know the harder you wear yourself down, the stronger their hold becomes. It's a basic brainwashing technique."

"What are you trying to say?"

Erik set aside the bottle and took the capsule Antonius handed him. He put it to his nose and pinched a nostril, snorting the powder. Erik shut his eyes when he felt a rush of chemical euphoria flooding throughout his body, numbing from his head down his back. He sat back as the sedative effect took over and the pain he felt ebbed away.

"Are you all right?" Antonius asked when Erik's skin immediately flushed. Antonius tapped the powder in the capsule he held under his tongue and grimaced as he swallowed the contents, then flicked aside the empty container.

"I'm fine," Erik mewed. "Just let me stew here a minute."

"Can you feel anything?" Antonius called when Erik groaned and slumped forward.

"Not at all," Erik slurred.

"At least you can finally get some sleep."

"Don't leave, please?"

"Yeah, I'll stay here."

Antonius grabbed Erik's arm and pulled the young man back against him before he fell forward down the steps. Erik slumped on his side, resting his head in Antonius's lap. Antonius draped an arm over Erik's torso and his free hand stroked his hair.

Erik slowly drifted, alternating between drugged wakefulness and induced sleep, before nodding off.

THIRTY-FOUR

Erik moaned when he awakened to throbbing pain swamping his body, focused in his side, shoulder, and in his head and face.

"Hey!" Erik cried when he realized he couldn't see, surrounded in darkness from a hood tied on his head. Restricted in movement because of shackles arresting his wrists and ankles to a chair, Erik shook his head, unable to release his blindfold. "Get me out of here!" he screamed.

Erik wondered where he was and listened to the sounds around him. He heard nothing - no buzzing florescent lights, no humming air-conditioning or heating units, no wind against windows - only his own labored frightened breathing.

Erik tried to push back the chair he sat in, instead finding it immobile - bolted to the floor. He broke out sweating as his panic rose and many scenarios swirled in his mind of possible torture methods someone might perform against him to get him to talk - about what, he had no idea his captors might have wanted.

It then dawned on him that no one could possibly know where he might be. Erik sniffled as tears streamed down his face.

"*No one's coming to save me,*" he thought. "*I know if I die right now, my death means nothing... I'll only disappear."*

Erik grew uncomfortable in the chair as gnawing pain in his hips and lower back bothered him. He shifted slightly, trying to relieve the pressure. Erik's arms and legs were numb from the shackles around his ankles and wrists. He could hardly move his hands and feet and feared the circulation was cut off.

Erik tried moving his fingers. They worked slightly, though numb. He tried moving his toes and realized he still wore shoes. After a while, the confining footwear pinched his toes, sending pain through his feet.

Erik had no idea how much time passed. The temperature in the room stayed the same, not too warm nor cold and he heard nothing that could tip him off about the time of day.

After a long while, his stomach rumbled from hunger and his mouth was dry. He swallowed hard, recalling the human body was capable of surviving without food for three weeks, though for water - three days. Erik hoped his captors would be kind and maybe offer water, though they easily could be cruel bastards and have him die of dehydration.

He sighed. It then dawned on him he was taking his capture way too well. Anyone else locked in a room with no food or water for three days, no human interaction but their thoughts, would have already broken down into a gibbering mess. But Erik felt nothing - he felt flat, devoid of anything inside.

His desire to die was still strong, wanting to escape a cruel world that took everything he knew from him. From the woman he considered his mother, his best friend who was like a brother to him, to his father who cared fiercely about him, Erik didn't want to live anymore since living meant suffering. Suffering by cruel monsters who took pride and joy in dismantling his world over projects he didn't understand that involved his father and his friends.

Erik mulled about the part they played in crafting the Synthoids. From what he understood, they were at first created for the mining projects in culling Corite. Somehow they were militarized and the government started utilizing them in their various wars, making the use of volunteer human soldiers almost useless.

He thought about how flawless the machines could be, with their system of artificial intelligence and ability to pass as a Human due to the synthetic skin and internal lubricant that appeared like blood. He knew as the processing speeds became faster, it was possible the machines could calculate outcomes much faster than a mere human being, since humans were more prone to mistakes.

Pilots were still needed for aircraft and ships, since tests for fully computerized planes and boats proved unreliable, as they were vulnerable to hacking. Erik then considered if it was possible to hack a Synthoid and give it different commands, even to the point of using the machines in assassinations.

His thoughts turned about the older Synthoids and how they were decommissioned and dismantled. He knew some older models, called Expedients, were regulated to mining projects until scrapped. It wasn't a far-fetched idea of someone simply stealing one and reprogram the machines to cause harm.

Erik understood little about the programming language used in coding the machines. He knew of no popular language used and at best figured assembly was used, or maybe an esoteric language to make hacking impossible.

Erik had some knowledge of computing and engineering from going over books in his father's library, but the subject never interested him. He owned no video game systems, let alone a computer, though his father had one for his job and he had access to one at school. Erik wasn't completely off the grid, since he played video games at his best friend's house and occasionally watched television. He preferred books, playing some outdoor sports and hanging with his friends.

Erik didn't know where he fit in concerning why he was used as bait to control his father so the organization's demands were satisfied. He was useless alive, dead, or any other way.

"I'm nothing at all," Erik murmured. "I'm nothing, nothing but an insignificant speck."

Moments later, a door creaked open. Erik raised his head, listening carefully. He smelled dampness and heard an object being screwed. Before Erik could inquire the sound, a sudden torrent of water blasted into Erik's chest, slamming him back against his confines. He screamed, sputtering and choking for air when forced against his binds. The water turned off and Erik coughed, heaving for breath.

"Feel any better?" Joe's voice called to Erik as his footfalls splashed into the room. "I figured you might be a little thirsty..." The hood suddenly yanked off his head and Erik winced when the bright lights seared his eyes. "Now, this is what's going to happen: if you don't talk to me, I'm going to do very bad things to you."

Erik vomited water at Joe's feet and Joe clenched his teeth when his face reddened in rage. He forcibly slapped Erik across the face with his free hand, whipping his head harshly to the side. Erik grunted when he bit his tongue and glared at the young man standing over him.

"So, you're not going to talk to me?" Joe pressed. "Don't look at me like that or your face will freeze that way." Erik spat at Joe in response, landing a globule of bloodied spittle on his uniform. "You're going to be a tough one, eh? I'll show you tough."

Joe dropped the hood he held and went around the chair's rear, unlocking Erik's right wrist. Joe pressed a pressure point, causing Erik crying out when pain radiated up his arm and chewed through his chest. Joe then twisted Erik's arm and grabbed his hand, yanking against his pinky finger. Erik thrashed his head when Joe pulled back.

"No?" Joe questioned. "Do you want me to stop?" Erik broke out in cold sweat and rapidly struggled to breathe as Joe pulled a bit more, bending his finger as far as it possibly could go. "Say so, and I'll stop." Before Erik could say anything, Joe snapped the finger from its joint and Erik screamed. "Do you want me to keep going?" Joe shouted. "There's four more here!"

Erik wailed louder when Joe pulled down on his thumb, jerking it from the socket. The vicious crack of bones snapping sent Erik over his threshold, the agony clouding his mind. His skin paled as his body trembled from the pain and Erik squeezed shut his eyes, wheezing for breath while trying to maintain control.

"I'll let you think about that for awhile," Joe said pleasantly as he released Erik's arm and locked his wrist back to the chair. "All you had to do was talk to me and this could've been avoided." He stood before Erik with a crooked smile and devious gleam in his eyes, watching him struggle for breath as tears streamed down his face. "So, are you still going to say nothing to me, tough guy?"

"Y-you... bastard..." Erik hissed.

"Now that's better!" Joe smiled, giving a slow clap. "Great! Now that we have that out the way, I have some things I want to know..."

"I don't know anything..."

"Yes you do. You know a lot. It's in your file."

"Like what?"

"Like how you're the son of a domestic terrorist."

Erik's eyes snapped open, glowering at Joe. "That's a lie," he snarled.

"Oh? So prove me wrong and tell me otherwise." Erik stiffened when the young man stroked his head. "Otherwise I'll have to do more nasty things to you."

"I have no reason to lie."

Joe grabbed Erik's jaw in his hand and leaned in close to Erik's ear. "Or rather you want to see how far I'll take this," he murmured. "I must warn you though, doing this turns me on quite a bit." Erik jerked away and Joe chortled as he released his grip. "I only kid with you," Joe teased. "Or maybe I'm not full of shit at all and I'm telling the truth." He poked Erik's stitched side and Erik winced from the bullet wound. "Either way, I'm going to have you screaming my name."

"I don't care if I die," Erik spat.

"Oh? Then I'm going to make sure I'm extra careful and keep you alive every waking moment."

Erik's eyes widened and Joe stalked out the room, laughing robustly.

The lights switched off once the door shut, leaving him in darkness. Erik hung his head, silently cursing himself.

"Pain and Death I can deal with," he mused, *"but being forced to live against my will... how dare that bastard take my only choice away from me!"*

Erik shuddered from fear and cold. Overwhelmed with dread dealing with the sick twisted machinations of the director's son and trapped with nowhere else to go, Erik started crying again, this time silent tears of frustration.

THIRTY-FIVE

Roused by the scent of food, Erik awakened in a soft bed, surrounded by navy sheets. He noticed the room had pale blue curtains filtering the sunlight, light moss green walls, and a simple white ceiling fan with frosted tulip bulbs.

Erik sat up, realizing he was missing his shirt and his slacks loosely on his waist. He rubbed at his face and glanced at the bedside nightstand, finding a small analogue clock with its hands stuck at ten after ten and several thick books about security systems stacked nearby.

Erik yawned and rose to his feet then headed for the door. He opened it and paused when he saw Hanalei on the other side, wearing a short-sleeved yellow dress with red flowers as the running pattern. Erik smiled and Hanalei stepped aside.

"I was about to wake you," Hanalei murmured. "I thought you might be hungry."

"Don't you have to work today?" Erik inquired.

"Miss Avers told me not to bother today," Hanalei answered. "Her father got hurt..."

"I see..."

Erik entered the short corridor and stepped into a side door entrance leading to the small bathroom. He shut the door behind him and leaned against the panel, facing the mirror on the wall's other side. Erik frowned at what he saw: a thin young man with scarred chest and face, sunken violet eyes and thinning shaggy red hair.

"Franny brought over your medicines," Hanalei called from the other side of the door. "Do you want them now or later?"

"Now's fine," Erik answered.

Erik crossed the short path, looking into at the mirror as he approached. The door opened behind him as Erik peered into the reflective glass.

"I'm really worried about you," Hanalei said softly as Erik continued staring into the mirror. "She told me what happened..."

"What happened?" Erik retorted. "Nothing happened, nothing at all..."

"Your friend Antonius is worried you're taking Neuralgine again."

"Oh?" Erik snorted. "Why would he care?" He looked past his reflection, catching sight of Hanalei standing at the door. "Where'd he get that silly idea from?"

"We found one in your pocket."

Erik held out his hand toward her. "I want it."

Hanalei shook her head. "I can't give it to you," she mewed.

"Why not?" Erik spat, irritated.

"You tend to get particularly violent..."

Erik lowered his hand at his side, focusing his sights on his reflection in the mirror. "How can that happen?" he muttered. "It's just a sedative..."

"But it causes hallucinations," Hanalei insisted. "Violent

ones..."

"How can my hallucinations be violent?" Erik laughed. "I'm as harmless as they come." He frowned when he saw Hanalei's expression unchanged and turned around. "At least give me the painkiller," Erik protested.

"Sure." Hanalei left the bathroom and Erik looked into the mirror, frowning at his reflection.

"You look like shit," he muttered as Hanalei returned moments later with an amber bottle. She paused at the door, appearing disturbed. "What's the matter?"

"I'm unsure..."

Erik turned away from the mirror and grinned at Hanalei. "What's the name of the perfume you wear?"

"What?" Hanalei said, puzzled. "W-why do you want to know?"

"I want to buy some, of course!" Erik smirked. "I like smelling it."

"I-it's called Jasmine Explosion Riot," Hanalei stammered. "B-but it's quite expensive..."

"I don't care." Erik folded his arms across his chest. "Now what are you doing wearing such expensive perfume?"

Hanalei's cheeks flushed slightly. "Well, I tried it on at the mall once," she murmured. "When I came to see you, you were all over my neck."

"Oh, is that so?" Erik crossed the floor and Hanalei stopped his advance by pressing the bottle of pills against his chest. He paused, slightly confused until she pressed harder against him with the bottle. "That's right..."

Erik grasped her hand, taking the bottle from her. With

his free hand, he linked his fingers through hers and leaned forward, sniffing her wrist. Hanalei's face burned bright red as Erik's nose traveled along her arm and up her shoulder, toward her neck.

"W-what are you doing?" Hanalei whimpered when Erik nuzzled her neck.

"So you admit you bought it because I liked it, huh?" he murmured in her ear. "You like it when I'm over you like this."

"I...!"

"You're not wearing anything today." Erik immediately pulled away, letting her go. Hanalei stepped rearwards, putting a hand to her chest. "What'd you cook? I'm starving."

"Sure," Hanalei said nervously and led Erik into the kitchen toward the small table set for two in the corner.

On the surface were a pair of large plates with a serving of scrambled eggs with cheese and diced tomatoes, grilled salmon patty, fried potatoes with mushrooms, and steamed rice. Near the plates of food were a kettle of tea and two cups filled with the steaming bitter beverage.

Erik took the chair nearest the wall and opened the pill bottle. He shook out two crimson capsules into the lid.

"I thought you had to take one at a time," Hanalei said as she sat across from Erik.

"I'm in a lot of pain," Erik replied.

"Wouldn't that make you sick?"

"No."

Hanalei reached across the table and Erik took her hand. "*E ka Makua Lani, Ho'onani'ia Kou Inoa,*" she sang softly. "*Ho'omaika'i mai'Oe I keia mau mea'ai...*"

"What are you saying?" Erik asked and squeezed her hand.

"Hawaiian blessing is all," Hanalei answered and gave a gentle squeeze back.

Erik smiled gently and reached forward, running his hands through her bobbed hair. "That's beautiful," he murmured.

Hanalei pulled away and picked up her fork. "Please enjoy the meal."

"I will."

Erik grabbed his cup of tea and sipped it, finding it strong and surprisingly bland.

"I didn't add sugar," Hanalei filled in when she noticed Erik's grimace. "I didn't know if you liked sugar in your tea, or honey or whatever you like."

"It's fine."

Erik ate his meal in silence, suddenly finding it difficult to come up with anything meaningful to say to Hanalei. Once they finished and Hanalei cleared the table, Erik broke the capsules in the lid and snorted the powder inside them into one nostril.

He sat back as his skin flushed and the numbing feeling spread throughout his body. Erik slowly reached for the bottle and shook out two more capsules onto the table.

"You shouldn't do that," Hanalei called to Erik when he picked up the pills and broke them.

"I'll be fine," Erik slurred. "I have a high tolerance." He snorted the contents with the other nostril then languished in the chair, saying nothing as his eyes rolled up and he stared blankly at the ceiling.

Hanalei spoke to Erik, getting no answer in response. She

approached and waved a hand before his face. He slowly blinked, staying silent. Hanalei picked up the bottle, glancing at the label. She frowned as she capped the bottle and took away the empty capsules.

Erik felt as if stepped outside his body, watching this other form with a pale slender scarred frame slumped in the hard burgundy diner chair, his pallid blemished freckled face staring into space. He found his thoughts hard to track, trying to make sense of the swirling nonsense in his head.

The telephone rang and Hanalei left his side. She spoke to the caller for several moments, then returned later with Erik's cell phone.

"I have to go," Hanalei said gently as she set the device on the table. "But I put my number in there. You can call me any time you want." She leaned forward, embracing him gently. When Erik made no motion to move, Hanalei sighed and pulled away, looking sadly back at him. "I don't want to leave you like this…"

Hanalei left Erik's side and entered the front parlor when she made another call, speaking softly out of earshot. She came back and ran a gentle hand through Erik's hair.

"Why do you do this?" Erik lazily looked down at Hanalei when she sat in his lap. "Are you hurting yourself because you still feel guilty?"

"*Yes, no, maybe,*" Erik thought once he felt himself return into his body. "*I don't know anymore…*" He noticed the young woman's soft form against his and sensed the unease chewing through his chest as he grew tense.

"It wasn't your fault, you see," Hanalei whispered. "You

were under those horrible drugs..."

"*Don't make excuses for me.*" Erik looked at her through foggy eyes, relishing her delicate touch when she stroked his head.

"I know I can't make you stop taking Neuralgine, but please, for your health..."

"*And for your sake...*"

"Do you want to see what the bottle looks like?" Hanalei suddenly asked.

Erik appeared confused and she left his side, hurrying into the bedroom. He broke out in cold sweat, worried and afraid.

The young woman reappeared at Erik's side holding a wide glass bottle no bigger than the palm of her hand. It had a pink jeweled cap and a small bulb on the end to spray the contents. The container held a small amount of pale yellow liquid inside.

"This is the largest size it comes in," Hanalei explained. "It's quite strong and I don't need a whole lot." She took off the cap and set it aside on the table, then spritzed some onto the inside of her wrist.

Erik's face flushed scarlet when the overwhelming scent filled the room. Hanalei set aside the atomizer and settled in his lap again. She took up his free hand and pressed her wrist to his, spreading the aroma.

Erik let out soft moan when Hanalei kissed his fingertips. "Now you'll have something to remember me by for today," she said cheerfully.

"Please don't leave," Erik begged and grasped her arms in a weak hold.

"I really need to go. I have a job to do."

"What do you do?"

"I'm a Security Analyst." Hanalei pulled away. "I'm on call as an independent contractor. If a business needs my service, I have to go."

"Stay with me, please?" Erik grabbed Hanalei by the waist and pulled her into his lap once more. "I've missed you."

Hanalei pet Erik on the head. "I'm sorry," she said softly, "I can't."

"Really?" Erik tightened his hold around Hanalei's waist. "Please?"

Hanalei gave a gentle smile. "Later tonight then; you owe me a nice dinner." Hanalei stroked Erik's cheek and he reluctantly released his hold.

Erik watched her leave and lifted his wrist to his nose, smelling the fragrance. He sighed, closing his eyes as he sank into the chair, ignoring his growing arousal stirring in his pants while he drifted.

Erik heard loud metal clanging and his eyes fluttered open. He groggily looked up, squinting when the lights flickered on as the metal door creaked open. Joe entered the room, carrying a large metal dog crate.

"What's that for?" Erik muttered as Joe set the crate in the room's corner.

"You'll see," Joe said brightly and left the room, then later returned with an empty coffee canister and a small handheld device. Joe shut the door and set the coffee canister inside the crate then approached Erik, smiling maliciously.

"What do you want?"

"Will you cooperate with me today?"

"No."

"You know I'll have to punish you."

"Whatever."

"Shall I break your other hand or start on your face?"

"Kick rocks."

Joe dug into his jumpsuit pockets and withdrew a pair of earplugs. He set them in his ears then calmly turned on the device he held. A high-pitched whine resonated in the room and Erik thrashed when piercing pain struck his head and severe nausea flooded his body. His chest constricted and Erik found breathing difficult.

"Shut it off!" he wailed.

"What?" Joe called, shrugging his shoulders. "I can't hear you. It's too loud!"

"Please!" Erik wailed and hunched forward, gagging with dry heaves.

Joe smirked and set the device on the floor then calmly withdrew a pair of black gloves. After pulling them onto his hands, Joe said nothing as he delivered a heavy backhanded slap across Erik's face. Erik grunted when he felt the weight from the gloves crashing across his jaw.

Joe viciously beat Erik, striking his face, punching his chest, and striking his groin and thighs. When Erik appeared ready to pass out, Joe picked up the device off the floor and turned it off. He pocketed the machine then went around Erik's rear, uncuffing his wrists and his legs from the chair's sides.

"Now be a good boy and go in the crate," Joe ordered. "Or you're getting worse than that."

"I'd rather die," Erik growled.

Joe booted Erik out the chair, sending him crashing onto the concrete floor. He kicked Erik again, turning him over onto his back.

"Tell me what you know," Joe demanded.

"Nothing," Erik moaned.

"In the crate now - or I'll destroy your hearing."

Erik struggled on his knees and put his weight on his left hand, then slowly sat back on his knees. "I'm not getting in there," Erik muttered and glowered at Joe. "This is taking it too far."

Joe's dark smile widened and he stalked out the room. He returned moments later with a large serving pot. Erik frowned when Joe said nothing, continuing to smile as he opened the lid.

Erik gasped when he felt heat emanating from the container and before he could say anything, he screamed when Joe poured boiling water over his head.

Joe kicked Erik in the back and slammed the pot over his scalded head. Erik immediately fainted from the overload.

THIRTY-SIX

When Erik returned to consciousness, he found himself on the floor of an unfamiliar kitchen, nose down in yellow flowered linoleum. He pushed himself up and fell over on his back, striking the floor. Erik groaned then shut his eyes when his world spun.

"Damn," he muttered.

Hearing a chirp, Erik struggled to sit up, holding his head once he rose upright. The vertigo worsened and Erik vomited on the floor between his knees. He spat on the tiles and reached up, grasping for the table.

Erik pulled upward and slipped forward on the hardwood. He squinted, noticing the cellular near his nose. The screen blinked, signaling a message. Erik grunted and reached over with a limp hand, mashing a button. He narrowed his eyes at the blurry screen, trying to read the message.

Unknown: You'll die if you hesitate.

"What...?" Erik grasped the phone and fell off the table, striking the tiles once more. He thumbed in the number he wanted and held the phone against his chest.

"Hello?" a tinny voice answered moments later. "Hey, you got Tyson seventy-eight sixty-four." After a short silence, the voice called again. "Ay, yo, I ain't got time for this prank call bullshit! Tell me the fuck you want or get off the fuckin' line!"

"I need some help," Erik slurred. "I think I overdid it..."

"Shit!" Erik heard an indistinct sound through the receiver. "Is that you, man?"

"Who am I?" Erik let out a weak laugh. "I'm not sure anymore..."

"Where you at?"

"I'm at Hana's place..."

"I'll be over. Hang on!"

Dial tone flooded the line and the cellular buzzed against his chest before growing silent. Erik stared up at the ceiling, noting the peeling yellow paint. He then cast his gaze to the overhead kitchen light, shutting his eyes when the bright incandescent bulb blinded him.

Erik's phone rang moments later and he groaned, picking it up. Opening his eyes, he noticed it had a withheld number. Erik pushed the green 'answer call' button and put the phone to his ear.

"Who is this?" he grumbled.

"How rude of you, Mister Ferdian," Giuseppe's voice answered.

Erik clenched his teeth. "How did you get this number?" he snarled.

"Your friend Miss Kahananui gave it to me."

Erik sat up immediately, breaking out in cold sweat. "What are you planning?" he screeched.

"What a dirty imagination you have!" Giuseppe chortled. "What makes you think I'm going to take her away from you?"

"If you do anything...!"

"What a small world we live in and the people we're connected with."

"Cut the crap, Giuseppe!" Erik growled. "Why are you doing this?"

"I'm only doing this as a favor for our mutual friend Mister Avers. She doesn't know we know each other, nor has any ties to your little meddling investigations." Giuseppe snorted. "Unless you're hiding something from me, of course and you're trying to trap me somehow."

Erik felt his breath catch in his throat. *"How much does he know?"* he thought. *"I can't have Hana hurt again...!"*

"I gather your silence is an admission of guilt," Giuseppe teased. "So she does have ties to your meddling."

"If you do anything to hurt her," Erik shouted, "I will seriously kill you! Where the hell are you?"

"You surely mean business, Mister Ferdian." Giuseppe blew a short sigh. "Calm that nasty temper of yours. If she's that important to you, hurry up and find her before I do anything to her. I won't leave any clues for you."

"How much time do I have?" Erik snarled.

"Let's make this fun. You have until noon."

The call cut off suddenly and Erik looked back at the phone, noting the time.

"It's only ten-thirty!" he realized. *"That barely gives me an hour and a half to find her!"*

Erik struggled to his feet and staggered about, crashing into the counter. He groaned and slid down to the floor, fighting the drugged grogginess overwhelming him.

Suddenly frantic banging resonated at the door.

"Hey!" a voice shouted on the other side. "Open up!" The door later banged open with a solid whack and hurried footsteps entered the house. "Fuck!" Erik seized when grasped by the collar and shaken firmly. He looked up at a dark olive-skinned young man with a mole near the right side of his nose, shaggy black hair and frightened dark brown eyes. "You with me, man? You with me?"

Erik blinked slowly and smiled drowsily in recognition. The young man let go and pressed his knee against Erik's chest to steady him against the counter. He reached into his slacks pocket, withdrawing a small brown case. Snapping it open, the young man withdrew a pen syringe holding a cartridge of light green liquid and tossed the case on the counter. He released his hold against Erik then grabbed his shoulder, kneeling down at his level. The young man jabbed Erik's chest, draining the serum.

Erik's eyes widened when he felt a surge of adrenaline coursing through his veins as he took in a shallow breath while his vision focused and the cloudy fog cleared. The young man removed the needle and Erik fell over on his side slackened, wheezing for air. Gazing up, Erik noticed his rescuer wore a cuffed pale yellow dress shirt that strained against his muscular upper body, pleated chinos and brown steel toed boots. He sat on the floor across from Erik, holding his knees as he looked down at the tiles.

"Hey," Erik rasped, "Raider..."

"Yeah?" Raider muttered.

"Thanks."

"Anytime."

"I gotta go..."

"Where?"

"Somebody's got Hana..."

Raider tensed and glared at Erik. "They did this to you?" he growled.

"I have until Noon to find her..."

"You got the address or whatever?" Raider scrambled to his feet. "I'll find her."

"No, no address... He used a withheld number." Erik handed Raider his phone. "Call that Lyndhurst number and tell him to find the record of my last call."

Raider set aside the pen syringe on the nearby counter and took the phone from Erik. He scrolled through the call list then pressed a button.

"Yeah," Raider said into the line. "He wants ya to trace the last number that called this phone. Can ya do that?" Raider stomped into the next room and Erik slowly rose to his feet once he regained feeling in his legs.

Erik made his way into the bedroom where he found Raider pacing and holding the cellular to his ear, while holding another messaging phone in his hand.

"Yeah, I got it," Raider said as he rapidly thumbed notes. "I'll call ya back if we need anything." Raider paused, looking at Erik. "Grab yer shirt and let's book," he commanded. "We ain't got a lotta time."

"Sure," Erik murmured.

Raider pocketed both phones and opened the closets, hurriedly sifting through them. "There ain't shit in here!" he muttered.

"I'll do without," Erik responded. "Let's just go already!"

358

Raider pushed past Erik and walked briskly outside. Erik followed him and paused near the door, finding his overcoat hanging on a hook against the wall and his loafers on the floor. He stepped into his shoes as he grabbed the coat then shut the door behind him and entered the corridor.

Finding the service elevator out of order, Erik ran for the steps and made haste down them, then exited outdoors. He found Raider waiting for him in a compact metallic golden-green sedan with oversized tires parked in front of the complex.

Erik pulled into his coat and hurried into the car.

"Hold on," Raider said as he shifted gears. Once Erik shut the door, Raider peeled out of the lot, burning rubber as he shot through the open gate and onto the street.

"How fast can this get?" Erik asked.

"One twenty-five in twelve seconds."

Erik snorted. "That's a little slow."

Raider shrugged. "It's fast enough."

"Where are we going?" Erik demanded.

"General Communications building," Raider answered as he shifted gears and sped along the road, occasionally weaving through traffic and cut through the alleyways.

"General Communications...?"

"Yeah, the Central Network. They control everything - internets, phones, satellites - all that shit. If a computer chip's in it, they run it."

Raider pulled into in the lot of a large looming building over five hundred feet tall and circled around, approaching close to the doors.

"The hell?" Erik squawked once Raider screeched to a stop. He clutched a hand to his chest when fierce throbbing pain shot through it. "That building's like fifty stories!" he cried.

"Forty-seven, but whatever," Raider snapped as he reached into his pocket and withdrew Erik's phone. "Git yer ass in there!"

"Call Hana's number and have Mister Avers track it," Erik ordered.

Raider nodded and Erik stepped out the car. He pulled the coat tight around his body against the cold then hurried across the lot.

Pushing open the front glass door, Erik stepped into a short hallway leading to a row of elevators. He spotted a glass case on the nearby sidewall that had a listing of the building numbers and its occupants. Erik scanned the names, searching for Giuseppe's name. His finger paused on the name 'Joseph Stone' in office 3826.

"I found you, you bastard," Erik muttered. "Thirty-eighth floor, room twenty-six." He raced for the elevators and jammed his finger into the button until the doors opened then stepped on. Erik pressed the floor button he wanted, forcing the cable car ignoring other floors as it steadily rose in its ascent to the desired location.

Once the bell pinged, the doors slid open and Erik stepped out, searching for room 26. Finding the numbers on the floor odd, he turned around, running in the opposite direction.

Counting the even numbered doors, once Erik reached the twenties, he zeroed in on his target. Trying the handle, Erik burst in, finding only an empty office with a desktop computer humming slightly on the ebony, steel and glass desk.

"Where are you?" Erik shouted. "Don't make me tear this place apart!" He approached the computer and pressed the spacebar, revealing a database. Erik leaned forward, scanning the data.

"The purchase orders," he realized when he recognized the chemicals. *"The last one's supposed to ship tomorrow..."*

Erik tried the desk drawers, only to find them locked. He then searched the cabinets, also gaining no access. Erik let out a scream of frustration and struck the desk. Storming away, Erik stepped out the office and paused when he heard a high whine.

Turning, Erik faced Giuseppe armed with a shock baton.

"You don't seem desperate enough," the older man snarled and lurched forward. Erik immediately sidestepped the attack, whirling around him.

Giuseppe charged and Erik dodged the man's furious swipes, barely missing the electric prod humming through the air.

"Don't pretend to be innocent with me!" Erik thundered. "You're just as evil!"

"You're such an addict... You can't function without another hit!"

Giuseppe followed Erik's counter dodge and jabbed the baton into Erik's chest. Erik let out a restrained cry when struck and the violent force of the blow rent him rearwards several feet, his back crashing against the partition. Erik groaned as he slumped to the ground, dazed.

"I'm counting on you to lead me to those missing parts I seek," Giuseppe growled over him. "You have that component you're hiding."

"What makes you think I'll easily give that up?" Erik rasped. "I don't care how much you want for it."

"I know you have a superb photographic memory. Just give me the schematics and I'll stop targeting you."

"I told you, my long term is shit!"

"Liar!" Giuseppe jabbed the prod into Erik's thigh and Erik screamed, hunching forward as he grasped his leg in great pain. "I know you have perfect recall regarding anything you've read and physical skill!"

"I can't draw worth shit, old man!" Erik screeched. "Lay off!"

Giuseppe smirked and switched off the shock baton. "That's all I needed to know."

Erik ground his teeth and shut his eyes as he rapped his head against the wall. "*Damn it!*" he chastised himself. "*I leaked some info...*"

Giuseppe turned away and paused when his cell phone rang in his blazer pocket. Pulling out the device with his free hand, he glanced at the screen and furrowed his eyebrows when he saw the number. "How unusual," he murmured and answered the call. "Good afternoon," he greeted.

"I got your punk ass now," a voice snapped over the other end and terminated immediately.

Erik shook off his stun and rose to his feet. Giuseppe turned toward him and Erik rushed forward, stepping out of another attack. He grasped Giuseppe's arm, twisting it around his neck once the prod whined when the older man switched it on.

"Tell me," Erik snarled in Giuseppe's ear. "Tell me what you're looking for or you might just hurt yourself."

"Listen carefully, Mister Ferdian," Giuseppe wheezed. "In order to keep alive, dirty deeds must be done."

"Shut up!" Erik tightened his grip and the older man winced. "You can't tell me what to do!"

"Are you a bad person because they sent you on dirty missions? Do you still feel guilt?" Giuseppe gagged when Erik increased his hold. "I didn't expect you to live this long..." he said thinly.

"You wrecked my life!" Erik sneered. "This isn't something you can simply apologize for."

"In this world, there are bad people..."

"I'd feel sorry for the Maintenance crew having to clean up your spattered brains!" Erik jerked Giuseppe's neck in a painful angle, forcing the man crying out. "It'll fall out with just one hit..."

"Yo, Erik!" Raider's voice called.

Erik released Giuseppe as a heap on the floor and delivered a swift kick into the man's side. Raider appeared at the corridor's end, armed with a saber in a black sheath that had a crimson-wrapped handle. Raider immediately withdrew the sword when Erik took on his defensive stance.

"You find her?" Erik called back.

"Naw, man. I was about to ask ya the same!"

Giuseppe chortled and Erik looked down, then gave another stomp into his chest. He then grabbed the man by the shirtfront and hurled him against the wall. "Where is she?" Erik screamed. "Tell me, or so help me, you're dead!"

Giuseppe raised the stun wand, jamming it into Erik's thigh. Erik yowled and released his hold when ferociously thrown back, striking the floor. Raider dashed forward, swiftly jabbing Giuseppe with fast strokes, cutting into his skin before he had a chance to answer.

Raider moved as if possessed by a whirlwind, stabbing and stepping aside as he moved around the man, making it difficult to discern where the next move came. Giuseppe dropped the shock baton with a clatter once Raider jammed the blade into the man's side. Giuseppe grunted and bent backwards as Raider leaned in.

"Your ass is lucky I missed the important bits," Raider snapped. "Don't you roll up on us again!" Raider released his sword and Giuseppe grasped his bleeding side as he stood against the wall for support.

"I'd never thought you'd come back for revenge, Mister Zeadeas," Giuseppe said weakly. "Please, don't do that again."

"Then back the fuck off or next time I'll seriously fucking lose it!"

"Fine, we're stalemated for now."

Raider turned away, watching Erik slowly sit up from his place on the floor.

"Damn it," Erik moaned, running a hand through his hair.

"I'm surprised by the amount of effort on your part to find that girl," Giuseppe said faintly. "You should be careful in whom you make friends... They're nothing more than useless pawns to be thrown away."

Raider approached, giving out his free hand to Erik. Erik gave a faint smile as he grasped his friend's hand and pulled to his feet.

An office door at the other end of the corridor opened,

revealing Hanalei carrying a microcomputer case.

"Hana!" Erik cried and immediately closed the gap between them. Hanalei let out a surprised squeak when embraced firmly. Erik buried his head in her neck, taking in her scent. "I missed you so much," he murmured. "I was afraid I lost you..."

"I was never in any danger," Hanalei said, puzzled. Erik withdrew his hold and pulled Hanalei back by the shoulders, looking deep into her eyes. "The client asked me to work in the employee break room until others came in for lunch. When I found it was five 'til, I shut it down."

"Did you find anything?"

"Nothing, nothing at all... It takes at least twelve hours for a traceroute."

Erik raised an eyebrow. "Why'd he ask you to do something like that?"

"Let's get back," Raider called before Hanalei could answer. "My lunch break's almost over and I can't be slackin' off the damn job."

"Right," Erik said softly. He released his hold around her shoulders and Hanalei looked beyond Erik, frowning at Giuseppe sitting on the floor, hand to his bloodied side.

"Does he need Medical Assistance?" Hanalei asked.

"I'm fine, Miss Kahananui," Giuseppe answered and grunted. "It was just an accident."

Hanalei frowned when she noticed Raider picking up his fallen scabbard on the floor. Erik took Hanalei's free hand and led her back to the elevators, with Raider bringing the rear.

THIRTY-SEVEN

Erik stayed silent on the ride back to Hanalei's apartment, gazing out the front passenger window of the passing city scene. Hanalei sat in the rear seat with the microcomputer next to her, while holding her hands in her lap and her eyes closed.

"Wanna hang out for drinks later?" Raider asked when he stopped at a red signal.

"I thought you had to get back to work right away," Erik murmured. "Why are you following traffic laws?"

"What, I can't spend time with my friends or somethin'?" Raider spat in irritation and resumed driving once the signal changed.

"Sure," Hanalei murmured. "Bring over Franny too if you can catch up with her."

"She might still be busy recovering those drives for me," Erik replied. "Tomorrow's Thursday and she has to turn in what she finds, or I'm in deep trouble."

Hanalei's eyes snapped open and she relaxed her stance. "Why didn't you tell me?" she demanded, leaning forward in her seat. She touched Erik's shoulder and he tensed. "The company I work for could have helped."

"It's top-secret stuff," Erik replied. "I'm in trouble for letting that hacker wipe out those drives remotely. He's holding something over Clairese's head, threatening to turn her in to someone worse than FSS."

"Who would be worse than Federal Special Services?" Hanalei scoffed. "There's nothing that can get past Cybercom. They're the proxy used by the whole network!"

Erik looked back to Hanalei, stunned. "You work for Cybercom?" he yelped.

Hanalei's cheeks warmed and she sat back, giving a slight smile. "I'm their hired Gray Hat," she murmured. "I broke into their system on a whim and pulled up a bunch of personal information. I threatened to sell what I found to other countries or tinker with their data, forging all sorts of fun stuff - passports, credit cards, bank accounts, tax returns - for a high price to anyone willing."

"You can do all that?" Erik said, astonished.

Hanalei snorted. "Since it was all Government employee data, they got scared," she continued, smiling. "They don't know how much I can retain and recall. My memory is flawless - I could screw them over any time I want."

"Are you serious?" Erik cried. "What about their mainframes? Can you hack into them as well?"

"A mainframe is just a huge computer with high-level processing power," she answered. "It might take me some time, but it's doable."

"Because you broke in, they hired you?"

"Pretty much." Hanalei nodded. "They want me to keep the Black Hats out. As long as they keep paying me, I don't care how many White Hats hate me. I like money."

Erik grunted and returned to his seat, folding his arms

across his chest. He leaned his head back against his seat, thinking. *"The same day those drives were wiped, someone called Clairese about Cybercom's mainframes being down,"* Erik mused. *"I wonder if that code her team creates each week is housed on that system..."*

"Wha'cha thinkin' 'bout?" Raider asked.

"I'm trying to connect some dots," Erik murmured. "Hey, Hana, do you work close with Cybercom and their computers?"

"No, they just send me on various retrieval assignments or security checks," Hanalei replied. "They also have me on call for any one of their satellite agencies in their network."

"Like Central Communications?"

"Right."

Erik grinned and started laughing.

Raider glanced at Erik, appearing disturbed. "You okay, man?" he asked worriedly.

"That bastard told me he wasn't leaving any clues, but he just left me another one." Erik turned toward Raider. "Let's stop by Francisca's place tonight when you get off work. Get some liquor and order some pizza. I might have some new ideas."

"Yeah, sure."

Raider later pulled in front of Hanalei's apartment and Erik stepped out then opened the door for her. She exited, taking the microcomputer with her.

"Come pick us up right after work," Hanalei said.

"Yeah," Raider responded. "What kinda drinks y'all want?"

"Vodka," Erik replied.

"Something to go with the vodka," Hanalei chimed and

Raider smirked. Erik shut the door and Raider peeled out the lot with tires screeching.

Once Raider left their line of sight, Erik walked with Hanalei into her complex. "I'm going to need that other medication," he said softly as they ascended the staircase.

"What does it do?" she questioned.

"It helps me remember more clearly. The downside is that I get nightmares."

"I'll give it to you."

"Sorry about your door," Erik murmured. "Raider had to kick it in when he found I overdosed..."

"It happens."

Once they reached Hanalei's floor, Erik walked with her toward her door. He paused when he found it open and the interior ransacked.

"Who would do this?" Erik murmured. "Is it because Skycatcher's canceled?"

"I'm not worried," Hanalei said cheerfully as she entered behind him and stopped near the door, toeing off her flat-heeled leather shoes. "Whoever did this couldn't find a thing, because I don't keep anything here."

"So you know about the program?" Erik turned to Hanalei as she set her computer case near the door. "What do you mean nothing at all?" he inquired, aghast. "No floppies? No CD's? No flash drives?"

"It's all in here." Hanalei tapped at her head. "I do write it down but then I destroy it. After that, I can recall to the letter and recreate anything. The same goes for books - ask me any book I may have read and I can tell you any passage down to the page number it's found on."

"Is it selective?"

"Sadly, no." Hanalei giggled. "So if I read a trashy pulpy adventure novel, I can recall it verbatim. So I'm quite conscious of what I read."

"I see." Erik slipped off his loafers and set them near the door, then entered the apartment, peeling out of his overcoat. "Can you tell me anything about it?"

"Not until I get a certain call."

"I'm sorry for causing such a mess. I need to clean the kitchen and everything."

"Don't worry about it." Hanalei shut the door and headed into the bedroom. Erik set his coat on the couch and made his way into the kitchen. He carefully picked up the used syringe left on the counter and placed it back inside the case. "Why don't you carry any Revialine with you?" Hanalei called.

Erik looked up as she entered the kitchen, dressed in a powder blue cardigan and pleated miniskirt with white tights. In her hands she held the white pill bottle.

"I never thought about it," he murmured.

"Do you have some kind of death wish?"

Erik shook his head. "Not especially." He held out his hand and Hanalei unscrewed the top then shook out two green tablets into his palm. "It never occurred to me."

"Do I distress you that much?"

Erik gave a gentle smile and reached forward with his free hand, brushing through Hanalei's bobbed hair. "Just the opposite," he cooed. "In fact, you turn me on quite a bit."

Hanalei's cheeks burned bright scarlet and Erik released

his hold. He approached the sink and turned on the tap while she closed the bottle then put it on the counter. After swallowing his pills with a handful of water, Erik looked back to Hanalei who left his side, rummaging through a small closet.

"Have a seat and relax," she said, taking out a mop and bucket. "I'll be with you in a few."

"All right."

Erik returned to the parlor and sat on the couch's edge. He noticed the cordless on the coffee table and grabbed it, pushing the call button then dialed Francisca's number.

"Hey," Francisca answered after several rings.

"How's it going?" Erik asked brightly.

"Oh, it's you," Francisca said sourly. "What do you want?"

Erik reclined on the couch, putting his feet on the arm and laid back. "We're coming over later after Raider gets off tonight. What kind of pizza you want?"

"You know Hana and I are lactose intolerant!" Francisca spat.

"They make those specialty diet pizzas, don't they?" Erik complained. "Come on, don't be a hater!"

"I'm coming up against some massive encrypted data," Francisca said instead. "The cypher's pretty tough. Your friend can't crack it."

"Hana might be able to do it. She's plenty smart."

"I didn't know she did that sort of thing."

"What did you think she did?"

"She was always vague with it. She told me if I had any problems, just call her and she'll fix it."

"Good deal. We might need to brainstorm and put our

371

heads together."

"Did something heavy happen?"

"Yeah, real heavy."

"Just turn up when you're ready. The last of the drives should be ready by early tomorrow morning."

"Thank you so much."

"You're going to pay for this with every little thing you have," Francisca threatened. "I mean it - *every little thing*."

"You can use my body for whatever you want."

"You bet I won't?"

Erik chortled and glanced up when he noticed Hanalei standing over him. "Hana wants to talk to you."

"Sure, put her on."

Hanalei took the phone Erik handed her, smiling gently in return. "How was your day?" she asked and headed into the bedroom, then shut the door behind her.

Erik put an arm behind his head and blew a heavy sigh. Shutting his eyes, he relaxed slightly into the cushions, then later dozed off.

Erik felt a presence near his bedside and opened his eyes, watching a large shadowy form walk away. Turning on his other side facing the wall, he tucked his arm under his pillow to support his head and felt a thin cold metallic item. Feeling with his fingers, Erik's eyes widened when he realized it was an Armament.

"*Someone wants me to break out of here,*" Erik realized. "*I'll be dead soon and it won't matter... Unless...*"

Someone would rather I take care of the problem instead

of you. Erik gasped and looked up, facing his counterpart in an olive Defense Forces uniform. *That's right, and that someone put something in your lines to have me show up, otherwise, there's no other way.*

"You can't be here," Erik hissed.

You're right, I shouldn't, since they've done it wrong. The right way is more controlled, safer, cleaner, right? The double pushed Erik back on the bed and Erik seized in pain as the mirror image climbed atop him. *This way is more wild, uncontrolled, and dirty isn't it. But it gets the job done, right?*

"What are you saying?" Erik whimpered. "If someone put Contraband in my lines, the ankle brace would've gone off by now!"

The duplicate grabbed Erik's face and leaned in, staring deeply into his eyes. *Maybe it's not just Contraband. Maybe it's something else. Or maybe it's the pain finally getting to you. Or maybe it's the virus eroding your remaining sanity...*

"How much time do I have then? How many days?"

You will die, surely, but it won't be a physical death. The counterpart pressed his lips against Erik's ear. *Your sense of self will be erased and I'll take over - permanently. You as who you thought you were will fade, never to return.*

"My memories, my friends..."

Dreams. Strangers....

Tears streamed down Erik's face. "*Those controlling bastards did this on purpose!*" he thought, heaving for breath. "*They knew this would happen. I can't just be a personality they can control at will!*"

Erik's double sat up, smiling cruelly as he caressed a gentle hand down Erik's cheek. *But you are,* he answered. *You'll just fall asleep and dream and when you awaken, the Inquisitors will return with follow-up questions that you'll have no memory of. The people and names you mentioned will mean nothing to you. The witnesses they'll bring in will mean nothing to you.*

"Stop lying to me!"

The mirror image thumped Erik's forehead with his knuckles. *The lie detector tests will prove you're telling the truth. They'll assume your memory loss is due severe drug use. They'll hold you until the DNA tests return and it'll show your damaged genes. They'll have to let you go. Because as far as they're concerned, it was just a Synthoid that admitted those crimes. And you'll be a free man.*

"How will I be free? They're erasing me! They'll just keep on using me and using me until there's nothing left!"

You agreed to this, remember? You wanted this.

"I don't want to be a nobody! I am somebody!"

Then tell me your name.

"My name...!"

Erik screamed and shoved away the copy, sending him tumbling head over heels on the floor. He sat up and ripped out the intravenous lines in his arm then snatched up the Armament under the pillow as he stepped out of bed.

The armed guardsmen dashed into the room as Erik formed a blue-steeled broadsword in his hands.

"The fuck?" one guard snapped. "How the hell you sneak that in?"

"What does it matter?" Erik retorted. "I'm going to kill all of you..."

"The fuck you're crying about it?" the other guard spat. "Check this out, a crying wannabe killer!"

"I'm crying because I might have to take your life if you stand in my way," Erik said through tears. "I want to choose when I die. But if today's the day, then so be it."

"Fire!"

Erik shielded his face and absorbed the stinging blows of the rubber bullets bruising his body. After the shelling, he dashed forward and lunged, stabbing one officer in the chest and kicked him off his blade. Erik blocked an attack with the gunstock with his sword and whirled around, slashing into the second guard's back, felling him. He then turned and hacked off the legs of the third, sending him crashing to the floor moaning in pain.

Erik pant hard for breath, surrounded by blood.

"That really hurt," he hissed and pointed the blade's edge at the remaining injured guard. "I bet you hurt too, don't you?" Erik grinned. "I'm going to let you suffer some. Then you'll see how much I hurt."

Stepping over the guard, Erik entered the corridor and frowned when he faced Inquisitor Alisaundra racing toward him.

"You really screwed up," she called to Erik as he pointed his blade in her direction and she stopped several paces away. "You're stacking on more charges than you can count!"

"What are you saying?" Erik spat. "That any more resistance is futile? I'm dying and nothing else matters. Your evidence won't mean shit to a dead man."

"We have orders to keep you alive by machines until we get all the information we want!"

"Forget it!" Erik screamed. "I control how I live and die, not you!" He held the broadsword at ready. "You're in no position to even talk me down. I've already decided."

"You're full of shit - you're not prepared to kill anyone. You really won't kill me." Inquisitor Alisaundra smirked. "I can tell in your eyes you're no killer."

"Then let me go. If you can tell I don't kill, then why keep me here?" When Alisaundra kept silent, Erik narrowed his eyes. "It's political, isn't it? You're keeping me here for some other reason, aren't you?" Erik lowered his sword and stormed past her. He paused when he suddenly heard a pistol cock.

"So what if it is?" Alisaundra snapped. "You're not leaving until this investigation is finished and then you meet your maker when I'm through, understand?"

"I'm gone."

"You useless coward!" Alisaundra screeched.

Erik stalked down the corridor and tensed when he heard the public announcement system crackle to life.

"Let him go," said a familiar male voice over the speaker. "He'll just lead us to the rest."

Erik abruptly stopped and turned on his heel, glaring back at the woman who aimed a semi-automatic pistol in his direction.

"Where is he?" he snarled. "Tell me where that bastard is!"

"The information is useless to you!" Alisaundra spat.

Erik dashed forward as she fired at him, quickly dodging her shots. Making a bounding leap under Alisaundra's guard,

Erik smashed his pommel hard into her chest, throwing her back onto the ground with a fierce thud. He landed atop her and grasped her throat with his left while raising his sword with his right. Erik forced back the woman's face as he jammed the blade into the floor near her head, slicing her ear.

"Tell me," Erik snarled as he leaned in, staring deep into her hating eyes glaring back as a manic grin spread on his face. "Do I have the eyes of a killer?"

Alisaundra paled though she continued to glower.

"*Póngase en marcha, mi amigo!*" Albero's voice called from the corridor.

Erik looked over his shoulder, stunned. Hearing the stairwell door clatter shut, he scrambled off the woman's body and snatched up the sword, racing down the hall. Erik rounded the corner and took off for the stairwell exit.

Hurrying down the steps, Erik burst through onto the bottom floor, happening upon a parking garage. Across the way idled a dark red compact sedan with tinted windows. Erik hustled over and tried the back door, popping it open. He jumped in as the car took off with a screech and slammed the door shut.

"You bastard," Erik snapped, setting the broadsword in the rear windshield dashboard. "You ruined my life. You used me like some kind of puppet for your bullshit cause I could care less about! Thanks to you, I'm a bloody mess!"

"It comes with part of the job," Albero answered as he calmly darted in and out of traffic, easily going over seventy miles per hour. "You get sent in, you erase things, you get out."

"I didn't agree to this!" Erik screamed and punched the

seat with fists. "Acid, you bastard! They beat me and poured acid down my back! I don't even know what for!"

"I'll fix you and keep you alive, but you'll have to obey my orders if you want me to cure you of that virus." Albero glanced at Erik from the rearview mirror, grinning. "To protect what's important, you have to become evil, understand?"

"What about the Supranet Tethers?" Erik demanded.

"They've been deactivated. We can't cut the circuits right now, but at least they've stopped pinging."

Erik stewed in the rear seat, shaking in rage. With no other options, he had no choice but to go along. Going along fed his rage, as it meant giving up his right to choose.

Soon his rage faded into dull pain and lightheadedness as the effect of the painkillers waned. Realizing how much blood he lost running from the wounds in his arm, Erik wavered and leaned forward, swallowing hard to keep down the acrid taste building in the back of his throat. Soon the dull ache became a raging overwhelming monster, twisting his insides from the tension.

Erik moaned and vomited at his feet. "Please," he mewed. "Don't let me die..."

"You'll live, *muchacho*," Albero answered gently.

Erik sagged on his side in the rear seat, succumbing to the agony.

THIRTY-EIGHT

Upon awakening, Erik found to his horror that he was stripped naked and stuffed inside the large dog crate.

He looked up, finding Joe sitting across from him in the straight-backed metal chair, tapping a shock baton in his hand.

"You finally wake up," Joe said. "Now, talk to me. Tell me what you know about the program."

"I don't know anything," Erik protested.

Joe narrowed his eyes. "Liar," he accused. "You know. You know it all. How else would you be so skilled as you are? You must have built one to practice against."

"I know nothing about the Synthoids. I don't know how to build one..."

"You keep lying... That's bad." Joe flipped the switch on the side and the wand hummed as electricity coursed through its coils. "I'm going to hurt you now. If you want me to stop, just tell the truth."

Joe reached forward, poking Erik through the cage. The electrified end struck Erik's naked skin and he wailed in pain when burned as his body spasmed from the shock.

"I want names, numbers, caches and storehouses of where your friends kept those nasty machines," Joe demanded. "Cough up the answers!"

"I don't know!" Erik wailed.

Joe huffed and turned off the prod, then rose to his feet. "You're a hard one to crack," he muttered. "I might have to come up with something special just for you." Joe reached into his pocket and withdrew a small bottle of water. He unscrewed the top and approached the cage, setting the bottle before Erik. "See, I'm not a cruel person," Joe said kindly. "I'm sure you want that real bad." Joe then stalked out the room and the room grew dark once the door shut after him.

Erik tried to grasp the bottle through the cage with his fingers, only to knock it over and poured the liquid over the floor. He broke down in tears.

Erik lost sense of time since Joe never timed his visits. He would randomly come in and demand answers, shocking him and threatening to dump water on his skin to increase his torture. When Erik still refused to give Joe the responses he wanted, Joe unleashed a pointed baton and jabbed Erik's skin with it, striking various pressure points.

Erik grew exhausted and steadily weaker from his lacking sleep, the chronic pain and hunger he experienced. He frequently cried and begged for release, only to get laughed at and tortured again.

"What's your name?" Joe asked one day as he entered the small concrete room.

"My name..." Erik mumbled.

"Yes, your name." Erik shook his head, unable to recall in his foggy haze. "Then tell me your number and rank."

"My number... One-nine-two Alpha..."

"Rank?"

"I'm unsure..."

"Birthday and blood type?"

"October twenty-second, O-negative..."

"Good, you're still here... For the most part." The door opened and in walked a tall thin young man with shaggy red hair, violet eyes and freckled face. "See that over there? That's you."

Erik squinted at the soldier with his face, wearing his old academy uniform and armed with a violet-sheathed saber. "I don't understand..."

"We got a whole lot of information, your range of emotions, and your skills and programmed it into that Synthoid," Joe said breezily. "Isn't it great?"

"Are you going to replace me?"

"You? No, you're not being replaced. But this one... He's going on a very special mission."

Erik's eyes widened and he thrashed in his cage. "No!" he screeched. "No, don't do this to me! Don't do this to me! I'll tell you whatever you want, but please, don't kill him."

"Oh?" Joe chortled. "So that's your weak point, huh? Family... How sad." Joe approached the cage and knelt before Erik. "You see, I don't have a family. My mother died when she gave birth to me and it was only my father. He wasn't any good. He hated me, despised me, said I got in the way of his work."

"I'm sorry... Please don't take my dad away from me."

"I should. He worked really hard to destroy my father. He stayed away in his lab, always working to defeat that monster, to come up with one better to top the last one your dad created!

But he was always behind - it was never good enough!"

"Why kill him?" Erik wailed. "I didn't do anything to cause their rivalry!"

"You *did* cause it," Joe snarled and stood, then kicked the cage. "You kept my father away from me. He neglected me, beat me when I got in the way, and eventually he grew sick of me." Joe waved to the room around them. "He kept me locked away, in a room like this. Then he needed the room to build another one of those infernal machines, so he put me in the doghouse! It doesn't feel good at all, does it?"

"I'm sorry," Erik sobbed. "I'm sorry, I'm so very sorry... You're right, it's my fault. It's all my fault..." He grasped the cage's bars. "But please, don't kill him. Punish me instead. Do whatever you want, but please, don't kill him."

Joe's countenance softened and he crouched before the cage. "You'd really do that for me?" he asked. "Will you really let me do whatever I want?"

"I don't want anyone else to get hurt or die. Please, don't kill anyone anymore..."

"It's impossible. These machines kill. The toymakers only destroy the ones that can't be controlled."

"Let me help," Erik begged. "I can find a way to stop them all and destroy them."

Joe raised an eyebrow. "How would you do that?" he asked.

"All I have to do is ask him. He created them, after all." Erik shook the cage's confines. "Please, just let me ask him. He has to be alive for me to ask him."

"All right." Joe unlocked the cage and withdrew a bottle of water from his pocket, setting it on the floor. He then rose to his feet. "You can get out now."

Erik looked at Joe in stunned silence as the young man exited the room. He struggled to crawl out the cage and collapsed on the floor.

The Synthoid continued standing there, its eyes unblinking. Erik weakly reached for the water and knocked it over, making it roll away to the opposite wall. He grunted and crawled forward on his knees and his good hand, reaching the wall. Finally grasping the bottle, Erik found difficulty in twisting the cap, then held the bottleneck between his teeth as he pressed against the partition. Staggering to his feet, Erik shuffled to the machine standing at the door. He held the bottle in his free hand and pressed it against the Snythoid's arm.

"Hey," Erik rasped. "Open this for me, will you?"

When he gained no response, Erik grabbed the machine's arm and collapsed against it, sliding to his knees. Too weak to stay up, Erik fell over on his side, immediately losing his grip on his world.

You have to destroy...
You have to kill...
Until there's nothing...
These urges I have...
Only one left alive...

Bright light seared Erik's vision as he roused. He squinted and put up a hand to shield his eyes as he wavered in a hazy cloud of pain.

"*Voy a llamar a que el éxito!*" Albero's voice said triumphantly. "*¡Buenas tardes, hombre!*"

"What?" Erik murmured and sat up, finding himself on a table atop a shower curtain. Nearby, a swivel crane-arm halogen lamp shone in his direction. Albero, who wore a white apron spattered with blood over his stained dress shirt and slacks, busied himself in cleaning instruments in a bucket of bleach on the kitchenette counter. "What happened to me?"

"I removed your appendix," Albero answered. "You were feverish and vomiting uncontrollably."

Erik touched his side near his navel, noticing a small scar there. "No stitches?" he asked.

"We have sealant these days, no need for stitching. It's too unclean."

Erik carefully removed himself from the table and tottered for the bedroom area where he spotted a pack of cigarettes and lighter next to a glass ashtray on the nightstand.

"I need something for the pain," Erik grumbled.

"Tequila?" Albero suggested.

"Vodka."

"I'll pick up some soon."

Erik shook out a cigarette from the pack and pulled it with his lips, then lit it, expelling harsh smoke in the air.

"Hungry for anything?" Albero called as he rummaged through the small cabinets, coming across a small skillet and bottle of cooking oil. "I've got bran flakes and sweet peppers and eggs. You need a better diet - more fresh fruits and vegetables."

"I want booze," Erik snapped and made his way for the heavy dark curtains at the window, peeling them aside. Outside he saw a large lot and in the distance a large castle-like complex with a large domed roof and barred windows. "Where are we?"

"In the outskirts of Menoka," Albero answered and placed the skillet on the small two-burner counter stove. "That there is called the Industrial Complex, also known as the Sector Isolation Holding Unit. It's where military criminals and anti-government agents are housed."

"Wouldn't this part of town make it company housing then?" Erik wondered aloud as Albero poured in oil then picked up a kettle set on the counter and filled it with water. "Usually they make housing not far from high-security Federal jobs like that. They don't want to risk leaks..."

"It's true." Putting the kettle on the stove, Albero turned the knobs then focused his attentions to the refrigerator. "We're in the transient hotel while I'm awaiting my paperwork to get certified. You are my assistant."

"What do I assist you with?"

Albero withdrew a bowl of sweet peppers from the cold storage and returned to the counter. "Executing criminals."

Erik turned toward the doctor in shock. "The hell?" he squawked.

"What's with that look, *mi amigo*?" Albero laughed and wagged a finger at Erik. "Their last licensed prison executioner died and they needed someone with a lot of skills. There aren't that many you know." Albero took up a butcher knife from the drain board and a handful of peppers, chopping them with expert precision. "Besides, we have some friends coming up that just need to sleep and not necessarily in dirt, eh?"

Erik ground his teeth and stormed away from the window.

"*I hate this*," he thought, grinding out his stub in the astray. Lighting another cigarette, Erik smoked and paced. "*Bit by bit, he feeds me some info and yanks the control a little bit tighter...*" Looking at his wrists and right ankle, his simmering anger burned stronger in response to the tethers. "*This can't be all part of a big plan...*"

"Better rest up. We have a busy day tomorrow."

Growling, Erik glared back at Albero who busied himself in frying the colored peppers. He stormed over, snatching up the butcher knife left on the counter and Albero calmly withdrew a revolver from at his back with his free hand, pointing it at Erik's head.

"Tsk, tsk, *muchacho*, what a bad thing you're doing," Albero said, not once looking at Erik as he continued frying the food. "Now really think about it. I'm an unlicensed doctor accused of nefarious things. You don't want to get on my bad side, eh?"

Erik paled and dropped the knife to the floor with a clatter. "*That monster could be telling the truth,*" he thought fearfully and gingerly touched his side. "*What if he poisoned me to mimic those symptoms? What if he implanted explosives in me claiming he was taking out my appendix?*"

Erik dashed for the small tan-tiled bathroom and dropped to his knees, gagging into the toilet.

Albero set his revolver on the counter and whistled as he turned over the food.

THIRTY-NINE

Erik staggered to his feet once the waves of nausea passed. He turned on the tap in the basin and splashed his face.

"How do you want your eggs?" Albero called.

"Whatever you want, don't care," Erik called back, staring into his reflection. Staring back was a thin young man with shaggy blond hair, a scarred crooked nose, watery violet eyes and scarred freckled face, with one prominent dark line crossing over his left eye and down his right cheek. "Who are you supposed to be?" he murmured and turned the knobs, shutting off the water.

Pulling against the mirror, he revealed a small medicine cabinet. Inside was a small cosmetic bag, a soft-bristled toothbrush, a tube of brightener, a contact lens case, and a single set of porcelain fronts floating in a cup of antiseptic. Erik shut the cabinet and started the tap in the shower.

"Do you want sugar in your coffee?" Albero said loudly.

"No."

Albero suddenly appeared at the bathroom doorway as Erik stepped into the stall and ran his hair under the steaming water. "Would you like for me to join?" the doctor asked. "I'll wash your back if you like."

"Pass me the soap there, will you?" Erik said instead,

holding out his hand.

Albero peeled out of his bloodied clothing and toed off his shoes. He grabbed the soap off the sink and joined Erik in the shower. "Ooh," he murmured when splashed by the scalding hot water. "You might not want it that hot on your back, *hombre*. It's still a little raw."

"I guess you could wash it for me," Erik murmured as he toed the handle, turning down the pressure. Albero handed Erik the soap and he ran it over his greasy hair, building up a lather.

"There's clean towels over the toilet there," Albero noted.

"Hand me one please?"

Albero grabbed the towels there and gave Erik one, watching him silently as he washed, running the soap over his skin, then followed by lathering the towel and wiping down once more, avoiding his injuries.

"Who did that to you?" Albero murmured.

Erik turned around, handing the older man his towel as he stood with his head under the water. Albero took in a shallow breath, staring at the deep raised red scars crisscrossing savagely across his pale skin.

"Please," Erik intoned, gesturing with his hand.

Albero took the towel and soap, gently running the bar over his back first. Erik cringed and leaned his arm against the wall, struggling to breathe through the pain as Albero gingerly rubbed at his skin.

The man then knelt down, rubbing the soap over Erik's buttocks and across his thighs. He traced the trail of chemical burns with his fingers and getting no response, he traveled down Erik's legs, soaping the skin, then followed with the towel, scrubbing. Working his way back up, Albero ran the towel up Erik's inner thighs, where the young man adjusted his stance.

"Why'd they hurt you like that?" Albero asked as he reached around Erik's frontside. Erik held his breath and tensed when the doctor soaped the front of his thighs and his injured member, carefully wiping the skin. Albero glanced up, watching Erik's reaction. Erik's breathing came in tight and his eyes remained closed. "You're out of commission for at least a month and then maybe it might not work right."

Giving a gentle yank, Erik grunted, but gave no other indicator of pain. The doctor then snaked a soaped hand between the cleft of his skin. Erik grunted again, saying nothing. Albero then followed with the towel and rose to his feet.

"You're clean," the doctor announced. "It looks like they've done a patch job and it might go bad, so I can pick up some medicines if you like."

Erik's eyes snapped open, looking down at the water swirling down the drain. "Thanks," he muttered, holding out his free hand. "I appreciate it."

"Don't mention it." Albero handed him the towel and Erik stepped out the shower, taking the towel with him. "Lotion's under the sink," he called over his shoulder.

Erik shuddered as he shut the door behind him. "What a kinky perv," he muttered.

Erik dropped his used towel on the floor at the foot of the bed where the discarded bloodied shower curtain lay and rummaged through the closets along the wall, finding suits of different sizes and shades inside. He frowned when he saw they were all larger than his frame and returned to the bed, yanking off the sheets and wrapped them about his waist.

Erik then entered the kitchen, finding his cup of coffee waiting for him and a saucer of grilled peppers and scrambled eggs on the counter. Taking a pepper slice, he munched on it and picked up the mug, taking with him to the small table in the space designated as the living room. Erik set the mug aside on the table and pushed up the pair of cushioned chairs that were pulled away toward the table. He then approached the small flatscreen television and pushed the button, turning it on.

"Anything interesting on the news?" Albero asked as he stepped out the bathroom, wrapped in a pair of towels - one about his waist and the other around his head. "It's almost like an obsession with me - I have to catch the morning, the afternoon, the evening, the night and the red eye!" He let out a robust laugh.

"Don't you ever get any sleep?" Erik responded.

"No." Albero approached the chest of drawers while Erik continued looking at the television screen, transfixed by the morning news reports droned by the beautiful almost mannequin-like reporters in their high-end suits and dresses staring vapidly back at the camera. "What size are you? Small?"

"Medium."

"I think I might have that. Any particular color? I got all kinds in here."

"None, really."

"Have you ever thought about cross dressing? You might be able to pass."

"Why would I want to do that?" Erik asked.

"You're an escaped convict, *hombre*. They might've let you go for awhile to drum up their campaign, but once they have enough money, it's *murete* for you."

When Erik said nothing, Albero withdrew a loose-fitting long-sleeved cream colored silk blouse and a knee-length black wrap skirt from the chest. He approached Erik from behind and draped the articles on the chair's arm.

"Why are you giving me this?" Erik growled, glaring up at the doctor.

"Softer fabrics go easier against a raw skin, *mi amigo*," Albero said brightly. "I don't have suits small enough for your frame, so I'll have to pick some up in town." Albero gestured toward the clothes, smiling. "At least try them on."

"I might ruin the shirt," Erik groused.

"I can buy more."

"Don't smile at me like that," Erik said sourly. "You're creeping me out."

"Don't make me wait all day."

Erik gingerly pulled into the blouse and found difficulty buttoning the shirt when he realized their reversal. When Albero approached to help, Erik shook his head.

"I got it," he muttered then rose to his feet, dropping the sheet to the floor. Erik tied on the skirt and Albero chortled when he noticed the skirt was shorter on Erik than he anticipated.

"At least it covers the important things," he chirped. Erik screwed up his face in response. "You don't see how really nice and cute you are!"

"Don't tell me you're turned on by this!" Erik snapped.

"Has your hair always been blond?" Albero asked instead.

"Stress and poor eating makes it that way," Erik replied and plopped back in his chair. "I'm actually a redhead."

"What color do you want to be?"

"Surprise me."

"Isn't it nice to have a good wash and fresh clothes and a nice meal before work?" Albero called as he returned to his closets.

"You're a real weirdo," Erik murmured and tensed when a knock later sounded at the door. "Were you expecting anyone?"

"Yes, a delivery. Please get it for me. I'd hate to answer the door undressed."

Erik growled under his breath and left his chair, storming over to the door. Throwing open the panel, he revealed a stocky young man in a white uniform holding a large black case in one hand and a large red serving tray with stainless covered plates in the other.

"Ma'am," the server murmured, nodding at him.

Erik growled under his breath. "Seriously?" he snarled, taking the tray.

"We get a lot of them who come out to see Doc Echevarria. He's very a skilled surgeon."

"So this is his place?"

The server nodded. "Hence me making a delivery." He set the case on the stoop. "I wish you the best of luck, Ma'am."

"Wait," Erik said, taking the young man's sleeve. "Doesn't he seem strange to you?" he asked softly.

The young man gave a strained smile. "Official or off the cuff?"

"Cuff."

The server waved Erik forward and he leaned over as the young man whispered in his ear. "Lady, he's a total loon," he said softly, "but he pays well and we don't question it." He stepped away and nodded to Erik once more, then returned to his service truck parked at the curb.

Erik paled and took up the case, bringing it inside then and shut the door.

"Doctor Hansen," he called and turned, finding Albero gone. Erik swallowed hard as he approached the table and placed the tray there. Scanning the room, Erik noticed the soiled articles were gone and fresh sheets replaced on the bed. He jumped, startled when Albero exited the bathroom, rubbing his hands on a towel. Erik frowned, noticing his bleached hair was now flaming red and his gray eyes now green.

"I've got everything soaking now," the doctor chirped and passing Erik, gave a firm whack on the bottom, waking him out of his daze. "Let's eat."

"The delivery guy called you Echevarria. You told me your name was Hansen," Erik accused as Albero approached the nightstand, taking up the pack of cigarettes there. "Which is it? What game are you playing?"

"I thought saving your life was more important," Albero said in a cold tone as he withdrew a cigarette and put it to his lips. "Why would it matter who I am?"

"You're the one that put a deadly virus in my system!" Erik snapped. "You're trying to erase who I am for some perverted reason!"

"You should be happy to spend time with me, you see. At least *pretend* you give a damn about me. That is your *job*, understand?"

"What's your damn issue?"

"My issue is none of your business, *mi amigo*."

"I'm gone," Erik growled.

Albero crossed the floor and as Erik stormed for the door. He opened it and Albero kicked it shut with a bang. Erik turned, drawing back with a swing and the doctor reached out, grasping Erik's wrist. Albero twisted with a vice-like grip the young man never knew he possessed. Erik whimpered as the doctor tightened his hold, bringing him down to bended knee.

"Ask me no questions and I'll tell you no lies," Albero said in a icy tone, glaring down at Erik with hard eyes. "Do you understand?" Erik sucked in a shallow breath as he stared unflinchingly into the cold seemingly soulless void while a hard hatcheted countenance masked his face. "Answer me."

"Yes," Erik breathed.

"What?" Albero cocked his head and raised his free hand holding his burning cigarette to his ear. "I can't hear you."

"I... I understand."

Albero released his hold and the vicious look shadowed his face passed quickly as he gave a pleasant smile. "Let's see what's for lunch," he chirped and approached the table.

Erik staggered to his feet, watching Albero obliquely ignore him as he removed the tray coverings. He entered the kitchenette and took the plate of eggs and peppers then returned, sitting across from the doctor.

Albero revealed the platter held a pair of sweet cream-filled croissants, a cup of orange juice, a boiled egg, a slice of hard salami with Muenster cheese, and a bowl of plain yogurt with sliced peaches spooned in. On the side was a mug of tea.

"Didn't you want any?" Albero asked as he picked up the cake. "Here, have the other one. Goes great with the tea."

"I-I drink coffee," Erik stammered.

"Tea's better for your skin. Have some."

"S-sure... T-thanks..."

Albero handed Erik the mug of tea and a teaspoon. "Want a sugar packet?" the doctor asked and Erik shook his head in response.

"I-it's fine..." Erik cracked and cleared his throat. "Really..."

He grew uncomfortable while eating his croissant with his eggs and peppers, sipping his tea while Albero made another cup of coffee. The doctor ignored him, giving his attention to the cable news channel that continued its chatter in the background.

Erik carefully watched the doctor as he finished his pastry then start on his boiled egg, sprinkling on the salt from the enclosed packet, then slicing it thinly with his butter knife.

"Say 'ahn'," Albero said and Erik's eyes opened wide as the doctor picked up the piece with his fork, offering it to him. He tentatively opened his mouth and Albero grinned while feeding it to him. Erik chewed slowly as the doctor resumed his meal, smirking to himself. "Want another piece?"

"No," Erik said hoarsely and cleared his throat, then sipped his tea. "The scrambled eggs were fine."

"Why do you look like that?"

"I didn't expect it..."

"I always wanted to try that."

"Oh..."

Albero said nothing else as he stirred his yogurt and scooped a serving with his spoon. He offered Erik a bite and the young man shook his head. "Lactose intolerant?" Albero asked. Erik nodded and Albero took a bite, smiling. "Tastes good."

Erik studied the doctor as he finished his breakfast, noticing the way he sat, with his left leg crossed at the knee and his foot bobbing slightly while he held the spoon with his right hand.

"Nervous about something?" Erik murmured.

"Got a job this evening, training another Synthoid to do as I do," Albero answered cheerfully. "It's a total pain teaching it procedure by inducing mistakes to get its error checking program buzzing."

"That's nice."

"Don't think you're simply staying lazing about all day," Albero said, smiling. "You'll have to work to eat here. You're going to keep me company." Erik paled when Albero gazed at him and his smile turned malicious. "You're going to make a beautiful scene in the most beautiful performance of your life."

Erik abruptly pushed back from his chair, shaking. "Is this how you intend to erase me? Tinker in my mind and hack at my body?"

"As long as I have a part of you, I can regrow anything," Albero said calmly. "I can clone any part of you as I wish."

"Who the hell made you a god and decide my fate?" Erik

screamed and bashed his fists on the table. "I decide my fate! I decide my life!"

"Is that so?" Albero rose to his feet and Erik took a cautious step away. "Why didn't you ask those people you killed that, eh? Why didn't you let them decide their fates, their lives?"

Erik gasped as his heart thud in his chest and his left shoulder seared in agony. "What are you talking about?" he asked weakly.

"Think about it," Albero said softly as he approached. "Who else would have a grudge so strong, as to use an innocent little boy like you, hm?" Erik backed away and Albero blocked his path, pushing against his chest. Erik fell rearwards, dropping on the bed. "No one gave a shit about your life and simply threw it away. You're just a useless pawn in another man's battle."

"What are you trying to say?" Erik mewed.

Albero sat next to Erik, caressing a hand through his hair.

"Do you honestly, really want to know the truth?" the doctor murmured. "Do you want to look, knowing you might find something that will destroy your world? Do you really want to risk that?"

"I-I do," Erik stammered. "I want to..."

"Do you want to pass up on another life, never having to know what evil things you've done out of your control?"

"W-what do you mean?"

"I can give you a new life," the doctor whispered in his ear. "You can live forever without fail, because I am God!"

"I-I'm not so sure about that..."

"Don't you want to know the sins you've committed?"

"I want to know my sins," Erik whispered back. "All of them. I want to remember... Even if it kills me."

Albero wrapped an arm around Erik's neck, quickly applying pressure with the crook of his elbow under Erik's chin, squeezing his throat using his shoulder and biceps while pushing the back of Erik's head. Erik gasped and choked for breath, grasping and clawing at the doctor's arm as his world quickly darkened before he went limp.

FORTY

Erik awakened with a start, drenched in cold sweat. He cried out when he faced Hanalei standing over him and scrambled away, only to fall off the couch and strike the floor.

"I didn't mean to spook you," Hanalei said gently. "Raider called and said he was on his way. So get showered and dressed."

"Don't do that," Erik moaned, holding his head. He sat up, frowning. "I don't have any clothes here to change into."

"I bought a smart outfit." Hanalei held up a shopping bag emblazoned with the local mall's logo. "I think you might fit it."

"How long was I asleep?"

"You were out like a box of rocks." Hanalei handed Erik the bag. "Go, hurry up!"

Erik took the bag, rising to his feet. He blew a reluctant sigh when Hanalei waved him away and he returned to the bathroom down the corridor.

Erik shut the door and gazed at the mirror across the room. IIe screwed up his face at his reflection, then looked down at the bag he held. Dumping its contents on the floor, Erik uncovered a bright violet button-down shirt with small black buttons, charcoal pleated slacks, dark gray short coat, black leather belt with silver buckle and muted gray trouser socks.

"Why?" Erik muttered, picking up the clothing. He set down the toilet seat and draped them across then peeled out of his overcoat and slacks.

Once Erik showered and changed clothing, he emerged from the bathroom and frowned when he found a violet and black striped silk tie hanging from the doorknob.

"Why are you making me do this?" Erik complained, grabbing the tie. He padded into the kitchen where he found Hanalei sitting at the table, drinking a cup of tea.

"If I have to make all this effort to look cute for you," Hanalei answered, gazing toward Erik, "you might as well look cute for me."

"You have a point," Erik grumbled and lifted his collar. "But you didn't have to go all out like this. How can you afford such brand names?"

"Like I said, they pay me well."

Erik grunted and rolled his eyes as he looped the tie around his neck. "I don't look good in suits."

"Please, for me?" Hanalei cooed. She turned to Erik and smiled brightly in response. "Do a little turn for me."

Erik blew an annoyed sigh once he finished knotting the necktie and turned down his collar. "We're just going drinking," he complained, turning full circle. "Why are you doing this to me?"

"Let me have this fantasy for awhile," Hanalei protested. "I don't know if I'll get this again."

Erik gave a faint smile. "All right," he conceded. "You win." He pointed at Hanalei. "But I want you to wear that perfume."

Hanalei smirked. "You won't be able to keep it together if I do."

"I can try!" Erik whined.

Hanalei wagged a finger at Erik. "Until we go to dinner like you promised."

Before Erik could respond, they heard tires screeching outside and a loud honk. Erik hurried into the parlor and approached the window facing the street below, finding Raider's metallic golden-green sedan in the lot idling near the front entrance.

"He's here," Erik said excitedly. "Let's go."

The telephone rang as Hanalei exited the kitchen. "Get that for me," she requested and Erik approached the parlor table, picking up the cordless receiver.

"Hey," Raider's voice said into the line. "Want me to grab anything else?"

"I want some cigarettes," Erik said.

"I got you."

"How was work?"

Hanalei returned to Erik's side with his coat and Erik nodded in acknowledgement before taking it from her then pulled into it.

"Man, I couldn't get shit done today," Raider griped. "The machines shut down and we couldn't get shit workin' and whatever."

"Are they connected to the network?"

"We'll talk 'bout that when we get to Franny's. I got stuff for her to look at."

"What's going on?" Hanalei asked as Erik turned off the

cordless and set it aside on the table.

"Take your computer," Erik requested. "Raider might need some help." He stepped into his loafers near the door then hurriedly made his way down the steps. Erik met Raider downstairs wearing an old leather jacket with multiple zippers and buckles, leaning against his car door and typing a message on his phone with its slide-out keyboard. "What's up?" Erik greeted.

"Yeah?" Raider muttered.

"What is it you do exactly?" Erik asked.

"I'm the doorkeeper at Midco/Sanato," Raider answered. "If you wanna job or whatever, you go through me."

"Is it because your family works for them?"

"It's easy and I ain't gotta work too hard." Raider smirked. "I can process apps all day in my sleep."

"Why not do anything that uses your brain?"

"I can do some computer stuff," Raider admitted, "but that shit's boring as hell."

"Right, with your photographic memory and all."

"It's a challenge tryin' to figure who gets in. I call around and see if the shit they wrote down's legit, ya know?"

"Let's get going," Hanalei said as she approached with her microcomputer.

"It's open," Raider muttered.

"Who are you texting?" Erik wondered aloud.

"Leanin' on somebody for some info. Check this shit out." Raider handed Erik his phone and Erik scrolled through the messages.

"They're threatening to send you a virus if you don't pay

them?" Erik squawked. "What are you into?"

"It's no big deal, man," Raider drawled. "He can't do shit to my car."

"Your car...?"

Raider chortled and took the phone from Erik. "Yeah," he went on. "They can crack into cars and shit through wireless now these days." Raider tapped his door. "This old beauty's dumb as shit. Ain't nothin' fancy under the hood."

Erik nodded and went around, taking his seat in the front passenger side. Raider got in moments later, tossing his phone on the dashboard.

"I wonder if those fancy cars give a signal since it's basically a moving computer," Erik murmured as Raider shifted gears and sped out the lot.

"They're always pinging," Hanalei piped. "They connect to GPS, emergency services, satellite radio and any other wireless networks you allow in."

"They're open, ya know?" Raider filled in. "They're all built the same and the security's shit, since whatever new parts they add in gotta talk to the brain."

"It's not that hard to get manufacturer's schematics," Hanalei interjected. "If I wanted to, I can take over any car I want and control it remotely."

"Oh, yeah, I almost forgot," Raider murmured and withdrew Erik's phone from his coat pocket. "I charged it for ya."

"Thanks," Erik mumbled as he took the phone and slipped it into his coat pocket.

"You're thinking about something," Hanalei noted.

"I can't call the guy I want to look into my problem since he's out of commission for a while," Erik explained. "I only have his work number."

"Maybe we can help."

Erik sighed and folded his arms across his chest. "I don't want to involve you guys," he complained. "It's already starting to get serious."

"Ay, man," Raider snapped, "it been got serious a long time ago." He stopped in front of a discount cigarettes and liquor shop.

"Whatever's cheap," Erik said as Raider put the car into park. "I don't have a real preference."

"Don't steal my ride," Raider joked.

Erik snorted as he left then leaned over, turning on the radio. Static crackled through the speakers.

"He can't get a signal on a radio that old," Hanalei indicated.

"Why keep the original in then?"

"I'm sure he has his reasons."

Raider returned moments later with a small black plastic bag. He frowned at Erik as he entered the car and tossed the bag at him. "The hell you doin'?" Raider spat and quickly switched off the radio. "You didn't change the station or nothin'?"

"I hadn't touched it," Erik said, appalled. "What's the big deal?"

"Just don't fuck with my shit, man." Raider put the car into drive and returned to the road.

"All right, fine," Erik grumbled. He sifted through the bag in his lap, withdrawing a pack of cigarettes and lighter.

"Don't be so uptight," Hanalei teased. "Both of you need to relax."

"I had a shit day at work," Raider growled.

"I brought some tea to relax you."

Raider suddenly grinned. "Nice," he said and raised his hand. Hanalei leaned over and tapped it.

"What's so great about tea?" Erik uttered, lighting his cigarette. Raider glanced to Erik and burst out laughing as Hanalei giggled. Erik raised an eyebrow. "What?"

"You'll see," Raider said cryptically.

Erik knocked on Francisca's door then leaned against the nearby wall as he lit another cigarette. The door opened, revealing the young woman in a yellow pullover shirt, tan slacks and beige loafers. She frowned at Erik and snatched his cigarette.

"No smoking in here, Doofus," she spat. "I got computers running!"

"Sorry," Erik said as Francisca put out the cigarette against the doorframe.

"What's with the fancy suit?"

"I made him wear it," Hanalei called as she came upstairs.

Francisca smirked and opened the door wider, revealing the parlor that had several servers stacked on tray tables against the wall. Orpheus sat at a table with a laptop, typing away.

Erik entered the room and pulled out of his coat then draped it on the couch's arm. "What are you working on?" he asked upon approach and looked over Orpheus's shoulder, noticing lines of code scrolling across the screen.

"Francisca cracked open that secured partition on the drive

and found something," Orpheus replied. "I'm running a decryption program to figure out what it is. They obfuscated it way too well."

"Set it over there, Hana," Francisca directed, pointing toward the coffee table before the couch.

"I brought booze," Raider called as he entered moments later, holding several shopping bags. "Two fifths of vodka should cover it, right?"

"Damn, you better not get rowdy," Francisca warned and shut the door after him. "I will plug your ass full of buckshot!"

"You ain't gonna do shit," Raider teased and set the bags near the couch.

"I could use a drink," Orpheus called back.

"Drink with us," Erik suggested. "You deserve a break."

"Right," chimed Francisca, "and that program is going to take a while to run through the parameters."

"Fine…" Orpheus left his seat and Erik gave a nervous smile as he stepped aside.

"You know anything about viruses?" Erik asked, heading for the couch.

"A little, why?" Orpheus answered. "I used to write some nasty programs back in the day."

Francisca took a swipe at Raider and he grabbed her hand, pulling her toward him. Raider grinned as he wrapped his free arm around her waist and blew in her ear. Francisca let out a surprised yelp and smacked Raider upside his head. Erik doubled over, laughing.

"Idiots," Francisca huffed and shoved Raider aside, then stormed into the kitchen.

Hanalei giggled as she sat on the couch's edge and pat the cushion next to her. Erik sat beside her, draping an arm around her shoulders. Raider took a seat in the recliner across the room and withdrew his phone from his pocket, pecking at the keys.

"I didn't know what y'all wanted," Raider piped. "I brought orange juice, cranberry juice, and lemon-lime soda."

"I want a ghetto Cosmopolitan," Hanalei replied.

"Ghetto Collins here," Orpheus said, taking a seat on Erik's other side.

"And I'll take a Madras," Erik answered.

"I thought you'd want a Screwdriver," Francisca said as she returned with several glasses and a bowl of ice. Setting it on the table, she withdrew the bottles and tapped them, then passed them to Raider who reached over with his free hand, tapping the outside edge. "With the way you smoke, you could use more Vitamin C."

"I decided to go easy tonight," Erik quipped and grinned, tapping the bottle's side when passed over to him. "You really don't want to see me drunk."

"Are you really that bad?" Orpheus asked as Hanalei tapped the tops and Raider guffawed.

"You'll see in a minute," Raider teased and Erik rolled his eyes.

"He's not that bad," Francisca assured, passing the bottles to Orpheus. He appeared confused and tentatively tapped the bottles then she opened them and began mixing drinks. "He might get a little grabby though."

Orpheus's ears suddenly burned red. "If you touch me," he warned, "I might have to crush you."

"Hey!" Erik complained and Hanalei and Raider laughed.

"Here," Francisca said and handed Erik his drink. "If you need to smoke, go in the kitchen and turn on the exhaust. The ashtray's in the cabinet. Shut the door too."

"Fine." Erik rose to his feet. "Join me?" he directed at Raider.

"I don't smoke cigarettes," Raider responded, grinning.

"Right, that..."

"I'll sit with you," Hanalei said and reached into Erik's overcoat, taking out the pack and lighter. Francisca handed Hanalei her drink and she left with Erik, heading into the kitchen. Hanalei shut the door while Erik approached the stove and pulled the chain near the exhaust fan, turning it on.

"You know anything about Skycatcher?" Erik murmured, setting aside his glass on the stove. "I've been told it's been delayed." He reached into the upper cabinets and found a ceramic ashtray inside.

"That was the last Operation you were in," Hanalei said, handing him his cigarettes. "You came back seriously messed up from it."

Erik set the tray on the stove and leaned against the nearby counter. Withdrawing one from the pack, he pointed the cigarette at her and she shook her head. Erik nodded and took the lighter, lighting his cigarette. "Why would he tell me it's back on?" he griped. "No one ever told me what happened..."

"Is it about what you found on your last mission?" Hanalei asked, setting the pack on the counter.

Erik narrowed his eyes. "Are you saying you knew all this time and purposely kept me in the dark?" He grasped Hanalei's collar and she took his wrist.

"Are you married?" Hanalei asked instead.

"No."

Hanalei unlaced his fingers and squeezed his hand. "So why are you wearing it?"

Erik blew smoke at her. "To keep away cute ladies who might want to jump my bones," he drawled.

"What about cute guys?" Erik razzed Hanalei and she chortled. "Then why hadn't you proposed to me yet?"

"I'm not worth it," Erik said softly and released his grip, running his free hand through her hair. "You don't want a guy like me."

"I told you it wasn't your fault. Stop holding it in."

"I can't help it."

"Yes, you told me, but you made me swear not to speak at all about it, even if you asked me again."

Erik scoffed. "Why would I do something stupid like that?"

"You told me you were afraid of being manipulated again."

"Are you saying I warned you and somehow forgot?"

"What kind of countermeasures are you thinking about?"

Erik snorted. "What?"

"You want me to hack into someone's car, right?"

"Maybe, but I'm not sure how skilled you are and if what I need is possible."

"Tell me what you're planning and I can tell you if I can do it."

"Can you find out if there were any pings from cars near my apartment on Sunday?"

Hanalei appeared thoughtful. "It might take a while, but it's possible." She smiled. "All I have to do is check the active directory when the last login was. I can look back as far as two months."

Erik grinned and picked up his mixed drink. "A toast to your awesomeness," he announced. Hanalei grinned and clinked her glass against his. "Let's order some take away. What do you feel like?"

"Whatever's fast and cheap."

"Chinese food then."

Erik finished his cigarette and ground out the stub into the tray, then exited the kitchen with Hanalei.

FORTY-ONE

Francisca sat across from Orpheus in a cushioned office chair, holding a glass pipe in her hand. "What kind of nasty programs did you write?" she asked. "Are you a hacker?"

"I'm not that keen on hacking," Orpheus admitted, "but I'm a pretty decent coder."

"You're a script writer?" Raider accused. "You suck, yo."

Orpheus's cheeks burned scarlet in response. "I work at Kanbal's tech department working their simulators," he said in a strained tone. "It's a challenge…"

"How'd you work for them anyway?" Erik inquired as he stumbled into the parlor with Hanalei and gulped his drink. "Isn't it difficult to get in?"

"Well, yeah," Orpheus answered.

"Don't you need high-level degrees and such?"

"They sent out a coded message. The first one to solve it got a job." Orpheus shrugged his shoulders. "I don't have a fancy degree. I learned on my own."

"I remember that call," Hanalei attested. "It was that Cherry Bomb incident, wasn't it?"

"Cherry Bomb?" Raider snapped. "Ain't it that virus that wrecks shit on a timer, right?"

"How'd you know about that?" Francisca demanded, facing

Raider. "I thought they shut that down."

"What are you guys going on about?" Erik protested. "Don't leave me in the dark!"

"We had a call from Cybercom today 'bout this virus nearly destroyed their mainframes and shit," Raider explained. "I checked out some part of it and I swear, I saw it before."

"Before?"

"A few years ago, a virus named Cherry Bomb disabled the infrastructure," Hanalei interposed. "The Feds offered big money to shut that person down, but nobody touched it, because they were afraid they'd get arrested."

"That's when Kanbal sent out a coded message to recruit the best brains to combat it," said Orpheus. "The Fed's hired crackers couldn't solve it."

"So you're saying there's a new version of it floating around?" Erik murmured. "I wonder if it's what got Clairese caught up in something major..."

"What's with that look?" Francisca probed, noticing Orpheus's discomfiture.

"It's nothing," Orpheus muttered and gulped his drink.

"I'm thinking of Chinese," Erik announced. "Who wants what?"

"I thought you wanted pizza," Francisca protested. "I can take some pink bismuth."

"There's a pizza joint 'round the corner," Raider pointed out. "Don't bother callin' it in."

"I need money," Erik stated.

"I got it." Raider withdrew his wallet from his jacket pocket and tossed it to Erik who caught it with his free hand. "Make it Supreme."

"I'll be back." Erik set down his glass on the table and picked up his overcoat. "Anything else?"

"Supreme's fine," Francisca said and Orpheus nodded.

"One with all meat on it," Hanalei said.

Erik raised an eyebrow at her as he pocketed the wallet. "You're just a heart attack waiting to happen," he teased and Hanalei chuckled.

Erik stepped out the apartment and made his way downstairs. Flipping his collar against the cold evening once he stepped outdoors, Erik hunched his shoulders, shoved his hands in his pockets then hurried across the lot.

Walking down the street, Erik turned the corner and spotted the pizza parlor on the other side of an alley. He entered the narrow space, passing a short young man in a black hooded sweatshirt, jeans, steel-toed boots and tinted glasses.

Erik grunted when bumped into and whirled around, freezing when he faced a pistol pointed in his direction.

"Cough up your money," the young man demanded.

"Are you serious?" Erik retorted. "I'm penniless, but I've got plenty of fists to give."

"You're ballsy, huh?"

"No, just crazy." Erik grinned and withdrew his hands from his pockets. "If you want my wallet, you'll have to get it yourself."

"You're fucking with me!" the young man spat, incredulous.

"Sure - reach in there and get it yourself. I'm not going to fight you."

"You're setting me up, aren't you?"

"Why would I want to do that?"

The young man raised his pistol, pointing it directly at Erik's chest. "Give it to me," he snarled.

"But what if I have a weapon in my pocket?" Erik teased. "Wouldn't that end badly for you?"

"You—!"

The young man pressed the trigger, only to grow pale when the gun clicked. Erik rushed forward and grabbed his aggressor's wrist, yanking him around.

"Who sent you?" Erik growled in the man's ear once he threw him against the wall. "Tell me, or I'm putting on the hurt!"

"You're full of shit!"

Erik yowled in pain when struck over the back by a heavy object. The young man shoved Erik rearward and turned, hurling a jumping punch. His fist cracked across Erik's jaw and Erik fell back, striking his head against the brick wall.

The secondary assailant, a stocky young man in black with a ski mask and dark glasses covering his face, hurled down his metal pipe for Erik's head. Erik caught it and threw him backward into the other fighter, knocking them both down into the ground.

"That really hurt," Erik growled as he rose to his feet. "You're really getting ahead of yourself..." He beckoned to the two as they scrambled to stand. "Come on, show me how bad you want me."

"*Usted está seriamente jodido!*" snapped the young man

414

with the pipe.

Erik stiffened when suddenly stabbed in the side by an unknown assailant. He turned and the pipe crashed into his head, taking him down. Erik slumped onto the ground on his side, dazed as he watched through a red-tinted hollow world the three figures in black running away. Erik squinted his eyes, noticing the third member in a black double-breasted wool jacket over a dark hooded sweatshirt and skirt with tights.

Faint recognition hit Erik hard in the guts. *"That girl..."* he mulled before meeting darkness.

The raging pain in his back roused Erik first before the cool breeze. Erik groaned and sat up, discovering he lay on a comfortable bed surrounded by a vast array of computing equipment. The gently humming monitors gave a soft glow of colored swirling patterns from their screen savers, dimly lighting the room. Erik noticed a window above him was open, letting in the cool night air.

"How much would the rent be?" Albero's voice said from afar.

"Two thousand," said a woman's voice.

"Ooh, just for that little old thing?"

"It's a real work of art, honey. A real work."

"Three then?"

"That should cover it."

"Buenas noches, querido!"

Erik heard a door noisily swing shut and footsteps clamoring up a stairwell. He tensed as the door opened, revealing a pudgy young woman with short orange hair and thick black cats-eye glasses, wearing jeans and a loose-fitting t-shirt.

"Oh, you're up," she said.

"You're not going to cut me up, are you?" Erik asked.

"I'm not licensed to practice medicine."

"Doctor Hansen isn't either."

"Oh, that crazy Mexican white boy is. Just ignore his delusions." She laughed and when she saw Erik appeared serious, cleared her throat. "You got a name, honey?"

"It's whatever they give me," Erik murmured. "The last one was Ferdian Ucal."

"Right, you're that terrorist guy that's been all over the stations!" The young woman put her hands on her hips. "You know, I'm really going to have a time fixing you up."

Erik cringed when he noticed a gleam in her eye. "H-how?" he sputtered. "It doesn't involve body parts, does it?"

"First it'll involve getting those tethers off. I was able to spoof the signals, but they're still active."

"You got a name?"

"Bunny."

"Bunny?"

"Right, it's Bunny."

"What kind of name is Bunny?"

"What kind of name is Ferdian?" Bunny retorted. Erik snorted and she left his side, switching on a nearby lamp, brightening the room. "You can explore the house if you want," Bunny called over her shoulder as she sifted through a stack of books. "I'll be doing very boring things for a while."

"I want to change clothes," Erik protested, rising to his

feet. "The mad doctor's got me in women's gear."

"But that's the game, honey." Bunny said. "They're looking for a *dude*, not a *chick*. You might as well get used to that getup for awhile."

"I doubt I can pass."

"My brother's a skilled makuep artist. He'll make you so pretty even the boys'll want you."

Erik blew a heavy sigh. "How long do I have to pose as a chick?"

"Until we get a Synthoid to die in your place, then you can take on a new identity in a nice little island and live a quiet peaceful life."

"A new identity? A nice little island...?"

"You can never return to your old stomping grounds, honey." Bunny returned to a terminal and moved her mouse, vanishing the screen saver. "Once you're pegged a terrorist, that's it. All your friends and family's suspect. They'll watch every move you make, every phone call, every book you check out from the library..."

"But–!"

"There's no but's, honey. It's all gone. Even your savings." She brought up a program and began typing. "They'll take every asset you own because any money you make they'll assume it'll go back to terrorism."

"I'm not a terrorist!" Erik snapped. "I'm... I..." He groaned and ran his hand through his hair. "I'm not sure who I am anymore."

"If you're hungry or anything, there's pizza, pot-pies and pack ramen downstairs in the kitchen."

"Thanks..."

Erik stormed out the bedroom, making his way down the steep staircase.

Erik noticed the apartment was split level as he met the front door and continued his descent into the lower level, where he entered a large room that had a kitchenette on one side and a living room in the other with a small water closet in the back.

Erik noticed a young man with close-cropped reddish-brown hair nursing a drink in one hand and smoking a cigarette in the other while slouching at the kitchen table. Draped on the back of his chair was a white blazer.

"Is that vodka you got there?" Erik called.

"No honey," the young man answered, "it's gin."

"Hard day at work?"

"Yeah. Damn Public Security raided the place and we all had to disappear."

"Got any vodka?"

"Shelf above the fridge there."

Erik approached the cabinet above the refrigerator and found a half pint bottle of vodka stashed inside among boxes of crackers and spices. He decided to liberate it instead of gaining a glass of ice as he unscrewed the top.

"You know Bunny?" Erik asked as the young man kicked out the adjacent chair for him at the table.

"Yeah, she's my sister. Cute little thing isn't she?" The young man giggled and downed his drink. "Nobody ever finds her cute. I wish someone did."

"What do you mean?" Erik took a big gulp and immediately

felt better when some of his pain dulled.

"She's always asking me to bring one home. 'Shanty, find me one, it's not fair you get all the cute ones!' Or 'Shanty, it's not fair you get all the action.' If only she knew the truth..."

"The truth about what?"

"I never get any action. Nobody likes a clubber. It's too much of a curse really."

"Do you find me cute?" Erik asked as he gingerly sat across from the young man and gulped the contents of the bottle.

The young man looked over at Erik with bleary eyes and gasped when he recognized him. "You're that—!" His chair knocked to the floor as he quickly stood.

"I didn't kill those people," Erik protested and downed what remained in the bottle. "I don't remember anyway... But I'm here to change my looks and disappear. Bunny said you could do it, Shanty."

"It's Shanter," he growled. "Nobody but my baby sister calls me Shanty!"

Erik raised his hands in mock surrender. "Sorry, *Shanter.* I just need your help in passing. Can you do that for me?"

"I think so, Mister...?"

"Ferdian for now."

"Hungry at all?"

"No. Would like more booze though."

"Check the cabinets for more if you like." Shanter waved away Erik. "I'll see you in the morning."

Erik grunted as Shanter wandered off, making his way drunkenly upstairs. Grunting when the stinging ache continued bothering him, Erik went on mission searching the cabinets for more vodka.

While looking, Erik came across old instant photographs of Shanter and Bunny when they were younger in plain frames scattered about the parlor. Curiously, Erik noticed the faces of the caretakers were marked out in black permanent ink.

Continuing his rummaging through whatever cabinets and drawers he found, his search was rewarded when he searched inside the water closet's septic tank, finding a locked waterproof box, a bottle of organic Kazakh vodka and a hundred proof Polish vodka.

Taking the Polish vodka, Erik entered the parlor and dropped in a plush blue and gold riveted armchair. He guzzled the alcohol until he no longer felt pain nor wakefulness.

FORTY-TWO

So tangled are the threads of Fate...

Erik opened his eyes, finding himself in a sterile white room. He lay in a hospital bed and noticed he had several intravenous lines in his arms and hands and his wrists confined by soft leather restraints. He frowned when he noticed a breathing tube down his throat. Surrounding the bed were several medical monitors, a ventilator and other machines.

The door opened and in stepped John Greenfield, wearing a dark brown suit with matching tie and his long hair pulled back by a black band.

"Can you hear me, Ace?" he called, approaching the bedside. Erik glanced up at him, puzzled. "They told me your heart gave out." Erik's eyes widened in shock. He then winced when his chest thudded in pain and the heart monitoring machines chirped from the activity. "Your old one couldn't take the stress anymore... Luckily you were able to get a transplant." John Greenfield ran a gentle hand through Erik's hair. "Your new heart is an artificial one, so you'll have to be careful with it until they make a new biosynthetic one. I'm just happy you have another chance to live." John Greenfield crouched near Erik's bedside. "I'm sorry those monsters hurt you like this," he said softly. "I'll do everything I can to save you. I promise you won't be taken from me..."

"Gerald?" Genovera's voice called outside the door. She entered moments later, wielding a dark briefcase. Erik looked in her direction, noticing the woman wearing a navy A-line dress and black flats. Around her neck she wore a gold chain holding a pendant depicting the sun and moon. "How is he?"

"He's holding up," John Greenfield answered as he stood. "They've informed me everything's in working order."

Genovera narrowed her eyes. "Don't tell me," she said in a low tone and shut the door behind her.

"Listen, Ace," John Greenfield said, ignoring Genovera as he reached into his blazer pocket and withdrew a pen syringe fixed with a brown liquid-filled cartridge. "I've been assigned to a highly sensitive job and I won't be home for a while..."

"What's that you have there?" Genovera demanded. "Don't be reckless!"

"The information isn't for public consumption and there are only a few select people who know of its existence. I'm afraid you will be considered a threat by association..."

"How could that be?" Genovera cried, alarmed.

"I realized the same one who caused Kevin's condition and killed Shana will soon target you," John Greenfield said calmly. "They can't get rid of me until my use runs out. I still have a little while before they get what they want, so what I'm planning probably won't agree with you."

"*Joe was right,*" Erik realized as tears streamed down his face. "*He said they will kill those who can't be controlled... They will kill him if I don't do something about it.*"

"Do you want to help me destroy them?" John Greenfield asked. "It'll be a difficult path... And I understand if you refuse."

"How dare you be so selfish, Gerald!" Genovera spat. "You're a cruel bastard!"

"You're just as cruel," John Greenfield answered. "You dragged us in to suffer with you. So you might as well ride it out."

"You–!"

Genovera dropped the briefcase she held and bat John Greenfield upside the head. John Greenfield dropped the syringe as he turned around, grasping her arms when she swung again, arresting her. He frowned when he noticed the necklace she wore around her neck.

"You have no reason to be upset with me," John Greenfield snarled. "I worked hard all year on this and for you to not support me... I'm disappointed."

"Gerald, think about what you're saying!" Genovera protested. "You're not making any sense anymore."

"*Please stop fighting,*" Erik prayed, looking at the two argue. "*I want to help. I want to stop them. They're after me too...*"

"Roland says this is the only chance we have to get out of this mess," John Greenfield assured. "Once they bypass us, we're Terminated anyway."

"He agrees to this?" Genovera wailed and broke free from John Greenfield's grasp. "You're both crazy!"

"The crazy ones are those monsters who kept using us and discarding us when our use ran out, or destroying those who rebelled against their tyranny." John Greenfield gestured toward Erik. "I gave my soul to that company and this is the thanks I get! One son in a coma and the other barely alive with a mechanical heart! How long do you think that'll last?"

"They only last twenty years," Genovera said softly, "but..."

"*Twenty years...*" Erik mused. "*That's how long I had if I joined the Defense Forces... Now that's hampered if I have a bad heart.*"

"But do they care? Not one iota!" John Greenfield faced Erik and gripped the railing. "Listen Ace, I know I'm asking a lot from you, but I need you to keep fighting for me when I do eventually pass on. You don't have to do this by yourself... We have friends who also are fighting for the good of this world."

"This is impossible," Genovera groused. "We're fighting an uphill battle." She turned away and picked up her case left on the floor. "I refuse to take away his choice."

"You don't think we're strong enough?" John Greenfield called after her. "Just think of what the world would be like if we let them run free with our creations."

"The worst scenario I can dream of is total annihilation," Genovera replied, "but there has to be another way to prove our technology won't be used that way and for you to get your revenge on the world that wants to erase you."

"Don't you want revenge as well?"

"I do, but not like this."

"Ace, here's what I want you to do for me." John Greenfield knelt at Erik's side. "Become a strong person this world can't break. Find something important to you and protect it. If I can't make you into that sort of man, then I've failed as a parent."

"Don't say stupid things like that," Genovera mewed as she approached. "I'll protect you too, Justin. I'm serious."

"Even if we die, we'll protect you," John Greenfield vowed.

"We'll even protect you even after we die if it comes to it." Genovera stroked Erik's head and brushed away his tears with her thumb. "We have our faith in you and you can trust us."

"I have only a warning for you," John Greenfield murmured as he stood. "They will hold you somewhere and will try to break you. They will endlessly torture you until you give in. Under no circumstances will you tell them what you know."

"Does he know anything?" Genovera asked as John Greenfield picked up the syringe and uncapped the needle.

"No, he doesn't," John Greenfield said, "and I prefer to keep it that way."

"What are you giving him?"

"Farolital, a sedative-hypnotic." John Greenfield injected the serum into Erik's intravenous line. "I'm sorry I'm forcing you to do this," he said sadly. "I'm only doing this as precaution."

Erik moaned when his body grew numb and his vision blurred as a low drone buzzed in his ears.

John Greenfield leaned forward toward Erik's ear. "Ace, can you hear me?" he whispered and took Erik's hand in a gentle hold. "Squeeze my hand if you can." Erik gave a weak grasp in return. "This isn't an order, but a request. Remember everything I tell you when you let your spirit prevail at any given cost." Erik squeezed his hand again. "Let your spirit prevail..."

"Gerald, we have to go," Genovera called. "They're waiting for us downstairs."

"In a minute," John Greenfield called back as he rose to his feet. "Go ahead. I have something else to tell him."

"I see."

Genovera stalked out the room and John Greenfield released his hold on Erik's hand. He reached into his blazer pocket and withdrew a black glasses case. Opening it, he took out a pair of olive oversized lenses and placed them on his face.

"Your job is to find those people and destroy them," John Greenfield said in a dead tone. "Find where they're hiding and make them disappear."

The monitoring machines chirped wildly as Erik became overwhelmed with the implications. *"He's asking me to kill people!"* he realized in horror. *"I can't..."*

"Ace, I know killing goes against your principles because of what happened to Shana and Kevin," John Greenfield said as he picked up the used syringe and put it in the glasses case. "I'm not going to force you to do something you don't want to do, but hold on to that hatred. Give in to that pain and suffer and show them how much you hurt."

"I don't want to kill... But they'll kill me first if I don't get them out the way." More tears streamed down Erik's face. *"Why does it have to be like this?"*

John Greenfield snapped shut the case and pocketed it, then walked around the bed and grabbed Erik's left shoulder, squeezing firmly. "Never forget who did this to you," he said sternly as Erik winced. "But if you go and die a needless death, I can never forgive you so please, keep yourself alive so that I

426

may see you again."

Erik looked up at John Greenfield, frightened when he saw no emotion in the man's face. His brown eyes appeared dead, almost lifeless.

"He's serious!" Erik considered. *"He really does want me to kill them since he won't be able to... Has the pain and stress finally broke him?"*

"Since you refuse to kill willingly, let that rage out when you hear these words: 'keep yourself alive and we'll meet again'. Hate them, degrade them, punish them, fight them, kill them, destroy them until nothing else remains."

"I don't want you to hate me..." Erik looked away when his world dimmed. *"But to ask me to do this... You've gone crazy! The whole world's gone crazy..."*

"Fight, prevail, destroy... Do that for me, will you, Ace?"

Erik lost the fight against the drug, closing his eyes when the fuzziness reached his brain and he felt himself drifting in the darkness.

FORTY-THREE

Erik awakened to the scent of food cooking and the sounds of jazz music playing.

He tumbled over to the floor falling out of the plush chair and staggered upright, making his way into the kitchen.

In his fog, he spotted Shana in a sweatshirt and jeans taking out a pan of hash patties from the oven. John Greenfield dressed in a t-shirt and sweatpants sat at the table reading the paper, with a mug of coffee in one hand and a burning cigarette in his nearby ashtray.

"Morning, Mom, Dad," Erik mumbled.

"Hi, Honey," Shana replied.

"Hey, Ace," John Greenfield answered and turned the page in his paper.

Erik approached the table and Shana handed Erik a mug of tea. "You look dreadful, Honey," she said. "This'll perk you right up."

"Thanks," Erik murmured, taking a seat.

"How do you want your eggs?" Shana inquired.

"What are we having with them?"

"Toast and tot patties."

"Fried. What kind of jelly we have?"

"Marmalade."

Erik blew on his tea and realizing it was warm, took a gulp. The shot of caffeine shook loose the fog of sleep and Erik blinked, realizing he sat facing Shanter on his right and Bunny tended to the stove, cracking open eggs on an aluminum skillet.

"Damn," Erik mewed and reached over, taking Shanter's cigarette.

"With us now, eh sonny?" Shanter jibed.

Bunny broke out laughing when Erik glared at them, puffing hard on his cigarette.

"Shut it you two," he growled. "I was having a really good dream."

"What a weirdo, huh Bunny?" Shanter teased. "Thinks of us as his surrogate parents, the poor little sod. Lost and can't get back home."

"The music," Erik grumbled. "My dad... Used to play a lot of jazz..."

"I like it," Shanter replied. "Black classical music, you know. Very hep stuff."

"Right, real gators," Bunny drawled and giggled again as she flipped her eggs over.

"Should I be afraid?" Erik asked.

"Of what?" Shanter asked. "All I'm doing is bringing out your natural beauty, honey."

"I think he's asking if he might like it too much and want to stay pretty," Bunny interjected.

"I'm just carting this image for awhile," Erik explained. "Until it's finally over."

"What if you have to cart it for the rest of your life, honey?" Erik looked up at Shanter who kept his head behind the paper, turning another page. "What if it never ends?"

"I'll be dead by then," Erik said seriously.

"Here you go everybody," Bunny announced as she finished preparing plates. "Enjoy." She passed one to Shanter and one to Erik, then lastly took the remainder for herself. "See, Shanty, this is how you cook," she teased. "That way you'll keep a man."

"Right, a man's heart is through his guts," Erik quipped and laughed with Bunny as he put out his cigarette.

"No, a man's heart is how good the sex is," Shanter countered, folding away his newspaper. "That way they won't stray looking for something better."

Erik snorted. "You're full of it," he said.

"Here, check this."

Erik stiffened when Shanter took his free hand and reached under the table, forcing his fingers along his thigh. Erik's eyes widened in response. "T-that's a long john you got going there," he sputtered.

"Nine and a half while it's down, honey," Shanter said pointedly. "Imagine how big it is while it's up." He released Erik's hand and Erik quickly snatched away from him, taking up his teacup.

"I don't want to know," Erik said softly and rose to his feet. "Where's the kettle? I'll take more tea."

"Stove," Bunny said, pointing behind her. She reached over and slapped Shanter aside the head. "Stop being so mean!" she squealed.

Erik poured himself another cup of tea and returned to the table, eating his breakfast in silence.

After the morning meal, Erik offered to do the dishes while Shanter headed upstairs.

"You want to talk to me about something?" Bunny asked as she helped dry and stack.

"Nothing in particular," Erik murmured, looking into the murky dishwater.

"Is that why you were crying in your sleep? You miss your family?"

Erik paused in scrubbing the pan he held. "You heard me?" he whispered.

"I was up late programming and I heard a weird noise," Bunny explained. "I came downstairs and you were curled up in the chair, crying. I pet your head a bit and you eventually stopped."

"I usually don't remember my dreams," Erik muttered as he dipped the pan in the rinse water and handed it to Bunny to dry.

"Are they still alive?"

"No. They're dead."

Erik turned away and stalked upstairs, entering the bedroom.

"In here," Shanter's voice called. Erik peered over, finding a walk-in closet and entered through the entrance, marveling at its spaciousness.

"I've never seen one this big," Erik said in astonishment. "You even fit a dressing table in here!"

"Fabulousness can't be contained, honey," Shanter said as he combed through racks of dresses. "Have a seat. I'm trying to figure out what to dress you in."

431

"I found the hair dye!" Bunny called outside the closet. "Have him come down."

"Go on," Shanter said, waving Erik away. "It shouldn't take long."

"What color are you putting in?" Erik called back.

"Brown."

"Hm," Shanter muttered, "I might be able to make it work."

"In the kitchen," Bunny's voice called from downstairs as Erik hurried down the steps. He saw she had a chair backed against the sink and a small extended hose attached to the faucet.

Erik took a seat in the chair and Bunny wrapped a plastic smock about his upper body. "Are you giving me a haircut too?" he quipped.

"Just the split ends," Bunny replied and picked up a pair of hair shears.

Erik closed his eyes, listening to Bunny hum along to the jazz music that continued filtering from the parlor while she clipped his hair. Erik then smelled the pungent scent of the hair dye as she worked it into his scalp and slathered it on his locks.

"Lean back for me," Bunny ordered and Erik pressed his back against the seat, wincing when the soreness grated into him. "Too hot?"

"No, you're fine," Erik said thinly. He focused on his breathing, trying to keep calm when the dullness began to fade, replacing with aching throbs.

Bunny rinsed out the dye and then applied a cool stinging cream to his face. "If we're going to put paint on you," she joked, "might as well prime the canvas."

"What about my eyebrows?" Erik asked.

"I'm bad at them," Bunny answered. "I usually let Shanty trim mine." After washing off his face, she fluffed his hair with a towel. "All done," she chirped. "Let's see how it looks."

Erik snapped open his eyes and sat forward, looking back at his reflection with smooth clear skin and chocolate brown hair cut into a shaggy bob. "How strange," he murmured, taking the mirror Bunny held up.

"It's your eyes, honey," Bunny said. "It's a rare combination, and your eye color alone is quite rare. You'll have to cover them with contacts."

"What's a good color?"

"Brown. Everyone has brown. Nobody notices brown."

Erik ran his fingers over his scar near his eye, then turned the mirror around, handing it back to Bunny. "Do you two do this often?" he asked, rising to his feet.

"What, make men into beautiful women?" Bunny asked and chortled. "It's become that way these days."

Erik took her face in his hands and peered close into her eyes. "What do you see when you look at me?" he demanded.

Bunny took in a shallow breath and stared back. "I see... I see someone who isn't happy."

Erik let go and stomped upstairs.

"What palette you think I should try?" Shanter called. "The neutrals to start?"

"Whatever goes with brown eyes, I suppose," Erik answered.

Shanter peered out the doorway and smiled at Erik. "You're really starting to look cute," he said. "Here, have a seat at the station. I'm going to show you what I can do, then we'll adjust for your contacts."

Erik approached the dressing table, finding several boxes and compacts of colored eyeshadows, lipsticks, and bottles of foundation along with various sized brushes.

Erik sat on the cushioned stool and Shanter tilted Erik's chin in his hand, turning his face in one direction and the other. He then picked up a small palette and began pouring in various creams into the shallow dishes.

"Ooh, honey, you're an odd shade," Shanter murmured when he brushed on the foundation on his chin. "I might have to make this special..."

Erik shut his eyes, listening to Shanter mutter to himself as he opened several pods of pigmented colors and mixed them, taking his brush to apply color and critique. Once he gained the right match, Shanter took out a set of tweezers from a drawer and plucked Erik's eyebrows into shape. Erik clenched his fists against his thighs, grinding his teeth against the pain, slightly relieved to focus on a different area of agony that wasn't his back.

Shanter began humming as his movements turned brisk and light with the brushes as he used Erik's face and neck as a canvas, dabbing on stains and other colors to his lips, across his nose, his cheeks and on his eyes.

"I think it's a great work of art," Shanter said proudly once he finished. "Take a look for yourself, honey."

Erik opened his eyes and glanced at the mirror, startled at what he saw. He touched the mirror and recoiled as he peered at his reflection. Staring back was a person he hardly recognized, as his scars and freckles were gone, replaced by smooth clear skin.

"You can hardly tell I'm wearing anything," Erik said in amazement.

"That's how neutrals are supposed to look," Shanter said, rolling his eyes. "You look like you're not wearing makeup when you really are."

"I doubt I can learn something like that."

"Practice, lots of it." Shanter waved a brush at Erik. "You want to pass, don't you?"

"I have to…"

"Then practice a lot. Get some cheap shit at the dollar store and practice until you get it right. Then go to the mall and get some really good shit that won't break out your skin." Shanter waved Erik away. "Now let's try on some clothes."

Erik backed away as Shanter sifted through a pile on the other end of the closet he left on the floor.

"I wanna see," Bunny called. Erik poked out his head, spotting Bunny sitting on the edge of the bed and she squealed. "Ooh, you're just too cute!" she cried, clapping her hands. "You did a great job with this one, Shanty!"

"Here, try this on," Shanter said. "I think this might be a good fit."

Erik took the turquoise maxi dress handed to him and draped it over his arm. He unbuttoned the blouse he wore and turned away, peeling the fabric off his back. Bunny let out a terrified scream, holding a hand to her mouth when she saw the grisly scars down his back.

Erik locked eyes with Shanter who looked up, startled.

"Holy shit," Bunny yelped. "Who did that to you?"

"Just a terrible accident," Erik replied stiffly and gave a tight smile. "It's nothing."

"Nothing my ass! It's gotten infected!"

"Don't worry about it."

"No way!" Bunny jumped from the bed and grabbed Erik's arm, yanking him out into the bedroom.

"What's going on?" Shanter asked, concerned.

"Some asshole tortured him," Bunny snapped and forced Erik sitting on the bed's edge. "Stay put. I'm fixing you up."

Shanter came out of the closet and watched Bunny hurry out the room, clamoring downstairs. "What is she going on about?" he protested. "She's always blowing things out of proportion. I'm sure there's nothing wrong with your back. Fancy a little welt or something, right?"

Shanter approached and paled once he saw the extent of Erik's injuries. He gagged and hurried toward a wastebasket near one of her workstations, retching in it.

"How long it's been like this?" Bunny demanded once she returned, carrying a tan flight bag in one hand and a large towel in the other.

"A few days, I guess," Erik murmured and shrugged his shoulders.

"Shit," Shanter moaned. "How the fuck you handle that after *a few days*?"

Erik waved an idle hand. "I just drift with the pain I suppose."

Bunny crawled on the bed behind Erik and dumped over her flight bag, unloading numerous tubes of antibiotic ointments, anti-itch lotions, burn salves, skin creams, and all manner of tapes, rolls of gauze and pads, and smaller medical tools. She touched his back and he cringed.

"I'm sorry I have to touch you," Bunny said softly, holding her towel to his back. "I'll have to squeeze out the gunk."

"Don't hurt me too much," Erik murmured.

"I'll try not to." Bunny gently touched her fingers to a spot in his upper back and pressed her thumbs against the skin, pushing upwards. Erik tensed as a flash of pain tore through him and he twisted the blouse he held in his hands, letting out an anguished cry. "Oh, I'm so sorry," Bunny mewed.

"We don't have any painkillers," Shanter said softly. "The best we have is whiskey."

"Please," Erik pleaded.

Shanter nodded and hurried downstairs.

Bunny squeezed again, drawing the pus out of his wound and Erik jammed the blouse into his mouth as he screamed.

Shanter bound up the steps with a bottle of whiskey in one hand and a bottle of brandy in the other. He set down the bottle of brandy and unscrewed the cap off the whiskey, then handed Erik the bottle. "Cheers," Shanter said, raising his bottle. Erik nodded and did the same, then guzzled the drink.

Bunny continued squeezing and wiping away the drainage, while Erik moaned in pain as he continued to drink. Shanter sat across from him in the desk chair he situated before Erik, ready to catch him if he ever fell forward from his overwhelming ordeal.

"Why are you looking at me like that?" Erik slurred, looking up at Shanter with unfocused eyes.

"Like what, honey?" Shanter murmured.

"Like I'm pitiful…"

"You are, honey. A pitiful injured creature trying too hard

to be tough."

"It's not the only thing those bastards did..."

Shanter raised an eyebrow. "What did they do?"

"They want to erase me for good for their own sick reasons."

"Oh?"

"Come here." Erik waved at Shanter. "I have to tell you something."

"What is it?" Shanter left his seat and sat next to Erik, appearing concerned.

"Aren't I pretty? Can I pass?" Shanter stiffened when Erik reached over, grabbing his crotch through his pants. "They broke this, snapped it in half. If it were up to them, they'd cut it off, then I'd really be like your sister, wouldn't I?"

"Oh, honey..."

A sob wracked through Erik as he leaned his forehead against Shanter's shoulder. "I don't want to die," he cried. "I really don't... I can't..."

"I–!" Shanter quickly grabbed for Erik as he fell forward, blacking out.

FORTY-FOUR

Erik awakened in obscurity, with thudding sharp pain radiating in his head and throughout his body. He struggled to get up, only to find he couldn't move.

"I'm at the warehouse district," Erik heard an unfamiliar male voice say. "As you see, I'm using his phone. He's suffered a serious wound and lost a lot of blood, so if you don't come within thirty minutes, he dies."

"He has a minor skull fracture," said another male voice Erik recognized, "and a severe concussion. I also stitched up his other injuries. Whoever attacked him nearly finished the job... He's lucky you found him in time."

"Thank you, Doctor Schnell."

"*What is Schnell doing here?*" Erik wondered, intrigued.

"After he regains consciousness, I'll run more examinations," Schnell said. "Right now he's in no immediate danger."

"That's good to know."

"So are you going through with the plan?" Erik heard Gina ask.

"I don't know if I can," the other man answered. "I think I've waited too late..."

"I've investigated as much as I could on my end. I don't

think I can do anymore without your help."

"I'll call up some old friends tomorrow then."

"Before you do that, do you want a copy of what I recovered?"

"It might prove useful…"

"Will this threaten us further though? You saw what happened…"

"There's a possibility he may have memory trouble due to his head injury," Schnell advised. "When he wakes up, please let me know."

"How long are you holding him here, Taeo?" Gina asked desperately.

"As long as I need to."

Moments later, Erik heard a door latch turning then felt a warm hand take his. "I can't take it," Gina's voice mewed. "I really can't…"

Erik slowly roused and opened his eyes, squinting from the bright lighting. Everything around him appeared blurred and unfocused. He closed his eyes, slowly opening them again and his vision focused when he spotted Gina kneeling at his side.

"My head hurts," Erik murmured and looked around, realizing he resided in a plain gray-tiled room with beige walls and tan carpeting while lying on a plain brown leather couch. Across from the couch rest a basic oak desk, with a plain red office chair and a black multi-line telephone.

Gina gave a sad smile and gently squeezed his hand. "You're awake!" she said brightly.

"Where am I?" Erik tried to sit up and Gina pushed against

his chest.

"Don't move yet. You were hurt quite badly."

"So..."

"Do you remember anything?"

Erik blinked slowly at Gina. "Like what?"

"Let's start with something easy. What's today's date?"

Erik looked away, gazing to the window across the room. The skies were cloudy and gray, with high winds blowing snow flurries about. "Sometime in winter," he murmured. "Could be spring... It still snows in April, I think."

"What's my name?" Erik turned his gaze back to Gina and gave a faint smile in return. "What's *your* name then?"

"I'm not really sure," Erik replied, shrugging. "Do you know it?"

Gina appeared disturbed, though she continued smiling. "Are you in any pain at all?" she asked instead.

"Either I'm still drunk or someone's numbed me up pretty good." Erik grinned. "Don't feel anything..."

Gina puffed a distressed sigh and let go of Erik's hand as she rose to her feet. "Please rest for now," she murmured. "I'll see you later."

"See you later."

Gina stalked out the room and Erik touched his sore head, feeling a bandage wrapped around it. He gently sat up, finding his shirt and coat removed, and a gauze bandage taped around his torso.

"Are you scared?" a voice called to Erik. "Are you afraid you'd be considered too weak if you admit that you were?"

Erik frowned when a middle-aged man with tired green

441

eyes and long shaggy dark red hair streaked with silver entered the room, wearing a black wool overcoat and cap.

"Hey..." Erik started.

"You need to be careful," said the man as he approached. "It's a dangerous place out there."

"How did I end up here?" Erik demanded.

"I was following the people who attacked you," the redhead explained. "I found you knocked out and brought you here."

"How long have I been here?"

"You seem better now, so you can leave if you want."

"At least give me a name!" Erik snapped.

"You'll only forget it anyway."

Erik growled and leaned over, grabbing the man's lapels. "Tell me your name!" he hollered, shaking him. "I swear, I will gut you if you lie to me!"

The redhead laughed and released Erik's grip. "You're cute," he remarked and shoved Erik back onto the couch. "Please rest some more."

"I need to go," Erik muttered and sat up, planting his feet to the floor.

"You're a definite target right now and most likely used to draw out our friends," said the man. "So I suggest you wait it out for a while until the dust settles."

"I can't just wait around while things go on out there!" Erik shouted, glaring back. "They already tried to kill me!"

"If it pains you that much, then fine, I won't stop you." The redheaded man pointed toward the door. "Don't wait another moment. Get going."

Erik stood and narrowed his eyes, giving the redhead a

critical look when the man blocked his path. "You're not making any sense," he growled. "Get out of my way."

"And you're just as useless." He slapped Erik with a forcible blow, immediately downing him. Erik struck the floor hard and the redhead stepped on his back before he could get up. "I'm telling you in your best interest - there's nothing else you can do, so it's better if you end it soon."

"If I do that," Erik grumbled, "then I can't..."

"It's not betrayal if you did and no one will get upset. So, stop going in circles." The man crouched at Erik's side. "However, if you run off now, the answer you so desperately seek will disappear."

"Why are you picking on me?"

"I'm already on dangerous ground as it is... They too want me dead." The redhead dug into his pocket and withdrew a slip of folded paper and his cellular phone. "Have your friends investigate this for me."

"What makes you think I'm willing to bother with you?" Erik snarled.

"Don't let this opportunity go to waste. I wouldn't entrust a man's job to some fool." The man dropped the phone with the folded paper near Erik.

"What's this?"

"You want your revenge, don't you?"

"Sure, I do."

"I'll check on you later. Don't double-cross me."

"Why would I?"

"Someone might offer you something you very well can't refuse."

"Do you have anything to offer me instead?"

The redhead stepped over him, exiting the room. Erik groaned and sat up, picking up the paper off the floor. Opening its folds, he found a series of numbers scribbled across the page.

"Is this decimal," Erik muttered, "or hex with spaces removed...?" He sat back, wondering who would best unscramble the code. Erik picked up his phone and turned it on, finding the last number dialed in his call list.

"Zachary?" he thought, stunned. *"Why did they call him?"* Erik went through his directory and dialed Hanalei's number.

"Where are you?" Hanalei demanded after the first ring. "Are you hurt?"

"Write this down for me," Erik said and read off the numbers from the sheet. "Figure out what this does."

"Tell me where you are," Hanalei pleaded. "We'll come get you."

"Something isn't right and I need to figure it out. I'll talk to you later."

Erik pocketed the phone as he rose unsteadily to his feet and made his way for the door. He opened it, revealing another small office. Erik spotted the redhead at a single terminal, typing furiously away, while Gina and a thin man with long white hair and pale gray eyes behind thick square wire-framed bifocals sat at nearby desks sorting through stacks of papers. He recognized the man to be Schnell from his three-piece suit that had a silver pocket watch hanging from the vest-pocket.

"What's the meaning of this?" Erik demanded. "What's going on and why are you here?"

"I'm rebuilding a particular program," the redhead stated. "If I can hack a particular server, then I can swap data and watch the fireworks begin."

"Were you the one who broke into Clairese's servers?" Erik accused.

"No, it was someone else."

"What about the virus that shut down Cybercom?"

"Again, somebody else."

"Then what is it you do?"

"I'm an engineer... I design kick-ass applications."

"So, what are you working on now?"

"A repair manual."

Erik's jaw dropped. "You can't be serious!" he squawked. "You mean to tell me I almost got *killed* over a damn repair manual?"

"Not just *any* repair manual."

"Doctor Schnell, is he crazy?" Erik pleaded. "Is that why you're here?"

Schnell shook his head. "I'm a medical doctor," he answered, "not a psychologist."

"Then what's the deal?"

"Taeo asked me to help him find mechanical drawings... A specific set."

"Taeo... I heard that name before." Erik approached the desk and grabbed a ream of paper, flipping through it. "Why did you refuse to tell me your name?"

"A dead man needn't worth remembering," Taeo replied cryptically.

"Don't get flippant with me," Erik grumbled. "What kind of

specific mechanical drawings are you looking for anyway?" He paused and glared at Taeo. "Giuseppe was leaning on me looking for schematics about something too."

Gina paused, tense. "You didn't tell him anything, did you?" she demanded.

"I don't trust my memory," Erik murmured. "You shouldn't either."

"I'll see what I can find," Gina promised and set aside her papers. "I can take care of the paperwork if you like." Erik shrugged and Gina left her desk, exiting the room.

Approaching the terminal, Erik looked over Taeo's shoulder. "What kind of repair manual are you creating?" he asked.

"It's for a new variant of Synthoid," Taeo answered. "They're hot commodities, you know. Everyone wants one."

"But I thought the Synthoids already came with manuals," Erik complained. He grabbed a discarded page and glanced through the code. "This doesn't make sense, unless..." Erik glared back at Taeo. "You're sabotaging the system!" he cried.

"We couldn't do it by direct force like we did the last time," Taeo said brightly, "so we had to find another set of means."

Suddenly a digital ring pierced the air. Erik reached into his coat pocket and fished out his phone, finding Zachary's number on the screen.

"Where are you?" Erik demanded once he answered the call.

"You better thank me for actually coming out this way," Zachary snapped. "What I have is confidential company information. If they find out I'm giving it to you, you're coming to Hell with me."

"It's a setup. Just drop it."

"Forget it, you can pay me back later. I'll be there in ten minutes."

As Erik ended the call, the phone in the adjacent office began ringing. He hurried to the desk and picked up the receiver from the multi-line phone. Pressing the flashing red button, it changed into green and Erik waited for the call to switch over.

"You have it ready for me?" a woman's voice said over the line.

"How bad you want it?" Erik egged.

"What are you doing over there?" the woman snarled.

"What does it look like I'm doing?" Erik snapped back. "I'm working."

"Then I should just send the whole building directly to Hell!"

"Oh, because I show up, you want to destroy the whole thing?" Erik scoffed. "Weak threats don't scare me."

"I've been following your investigation and I know what you're planning. So you have three minutes to come outside and give me your backups."

"Even if you blew this place to the other side of the world, it's not going to stop the inevitable from happening."

"I want that data."

"Persistent, huh?"

"Come to the window."

Erik puffed an annoyed sigh and approached the window, looking outdoors. He spotted a short young woman in black skirt, tights, boots, pea coat, wool cap and glasses standing in a phone booth across the street.

"I see you," Erik said, "but you're full of it."

"If I have to prove I'm serious, then will you do as I say?"

"This is a government building. You put a bomb in here and they'll be on you like flies to shit."

"There are other methods."

Erik watched Gina exit outdoors below, wearing a black wool overcoat and sunglasses. She walked briskly down the sidewalk, heading for the parking garage. Moments later, a short young man in black hooded sweatshirt, jeans and boots sprinted from the alley, going in the same direction. Erik dropped the receiver and ran out the office.

"Where do you think you're going?" Schnell shouted when Erik slammed open the door and raced down the corridor.

FORTY-FIVE

Erik shoved the emergency door open and clambered down the stairwell, jumping several steps at a time. Reaching the lower level, he pushed against the door, stumbling outside into the alley.

Erik ran onto the street, finding the woman at the payphone gone. Hearing tires screeching, he turned as a black plumber's van with tinted windows roared out of the parking garage, barreling onto the street.

The van slammed into Erik before he could react, hurling his body onto the hood with a crash. The van lurched to a stop and Erik's body slid off, crumpling onto the ground. The van's tires squealed as the driver threw the gears into reverse.

Schnell ran into the street moments later when the black van took off, peeling down the alley. He ran up to Erik's broken body, noticing the young man's eyes were wide and vacant in his bruised and cut face. The doctor crouched at Erik's side, touching the side of his neck. He felt a faint pulse.

"Please hang on," Schnell murmured as he withdrew his cellular phone and immediately dialed for emergency services. "We can't lose you yet..."

A dark green micro van careened around the corner and sped down the road, screaming to a halt once it approached

Schnell and Erik. Schnell turned away, speaking to the operator as Zachary clambered out his vehicle and bound to Erik's side, dropping to his knees.

"Don't you die on me," Zachary growled. "You warned me about this setup..."

Erik's phone rang and Zachary reached into his pockets, withdrawing the cellular. Glancing at the screen, he noticed the number was unlisted. Answering the call, Zachary paled when he heard a mysterious woman's voice over the line.

"It's painful knowing how they use you for their ends whenever they can."

"What are you going on about?" Zachary snarled.

"Let's have a trade. We got the old lady. You have that red-headed slacker. They have something we want. Give it to us."

"He might be dead and you did this shit for nothing."

"You know he won't really die, is that right Arizeh?" Zachary clenched his teeth, growing enraged. "Maybe you should listen to our demands if you still want her alive."

"How do I know she isn't really dead? Put her on the phone."

"I'm not worthy of protection," Gina's voice said faintly moments later. "There is a meaning behind my suffering."

"What are you trying to say?"

"Please don't blame yourself if I die instead."

"What?"

"That's all you get to hear," the other woman snapped. "Now you have twenty-four hours to deliver the goods. Wait too long and she'll be dead."

"What if I decide to blow you off?" Zachary spat. "If he ends

450

up dead, he's useless too."

"We know you won't do something stupid like that."

The line suddenly cut off and Zachary dropped the cellular.

"Does it hurt that much?" Schnell accused and Zachary glared up at the doctor standing offside with his arms folded across his chest. "Then stop being so selfish and actually *do* something about it."

"I'm trying!" Zachary protested.

"All you've done is run and to where, against another damn wall!" Schnell said over him.

Zachary rose to his feet and dug his nails into his clenched hands as the distant wailing sirens drew closer. "All right," he growled. "I've got an idea…"

Awakening to a cool breeze and faint jazz music, Erik groaned as he struggled to get up, feeling a slight weight on his back. Erik saw he rest on a large bed in a room surrounded by computer equipment. At the foot of the bed lay the turquoise maxi dress with matching camisole top.

A loud shrill ring startled Erik, sounding three times in quick succession.

"Coming, honey," Bunny called as she came to the door.

"*Buenos dias*," Albero's voice said brightly. "Here's the *dinero* you requested. Where's my beautiful star?"

"She's still resting," Bunny answered. "We had a very rough night."

"Did you take her old jewelry? It'll clash with all the outfits."

"She'll be ready on time, promise."

Bunny stomped upstairs and dumped a stack of bills on a

nearby desk as she entered the room. "Shit," Bunny growled as she boot up her computer.

"What's the matter?" Erik asked.

"It took so long cleaning the gunk out your back that I forgot to finish running the blockers on the Supranet Tethers."

"Why not just leave them alone? I can wear pants and a shirt."

"No, you have to be totally femme," Bunny insisted. "Hence me waxing you while you were out."

Erik looked at his arms and legs, stunned to find them free of hair. "What else did you do to me?" he demanded.

"That's all. Shanty packed you a bag. It's downstairs."

"Anything else I should know?"

"Wear the cami tops so your healing back won't ruin any more shirts," Bunny stated as she began typing. "Roll your hosiery, don't pull on it and the lines go in the back. That's about it."

"Thanks for your help."

Bunny waved a hand over her head. "It's what we do."

Erik pulled into the camisole and then slipped on the dress. Leaving the room, Erik made his way downstairs and the door opened, revealing Shanter holding several bags.

"Leaving already?" he asked. "I got a few things before you go, honey. If you want to pass, you need to do it right."

"But, he's–!" Erik protested.

"He's patient. Come on."

Erik blew a hard sigh and followed Shanter's lead.

Once upstairs, Shanter gave a thorough lesson on how to apply his makeup and styling his hair. Erik then tried on shoes

452

the other man brought and stomped about the room, breaking them in.

Lastly, while Shanter manicured and filed Erik's nails, Shanter explained how to apply nail lacquer.

"Don't roll your eyes, honey," Shanter spat in irritation. "This is for your life and safety." Erik gulped and Shanter nodded as he continued. "I know this is only temporary. You're not soft like I am."

"Why'd go through all the motions then?" Erik asked.

Shanter shrugged. "You could be just a junior cop going undercover to stop people like that," he answered. "You could be a health reporter. You could be anything... I don't know. I don't know the reasons behind why someone did what they did in hurting you, but if my skills can help somehow, then I'll give you my best."

"What a noble thing to think," Erik said softly. "Yeah, I'm looking for the people who did that, hoping they might lead me to more of them. But it's for purely selfish reasons."

"Be careful, please?" Shanter examined Erik's drying nails. "Looks perfect."

"How do I look?" Erik asked, standing.

"Let me see," Bunny called. Erik approached and Bunny looked up from her terminal, frowning. "It's the eyes, Shanty. He'll need contacts."

"I got them brown, like you said," Shanter answered and sifted through a bag he had nearby. "Now which one? Dark brown, light brown, hazel brown, golden brown..."

"Dark brown should do it," Bunny suggested. "He'll look so different."

"Here you go," Shanter announced, withdrawing a small white palm-sized capsule. "You know how to put them in, right?"

"Shouldn't be too hard," Erik answered.

"Don't forget the eye drops twice a day. These you can leave in for a month. That should be long enough for your assignment, right?"

"Right," Erik murmured and left Bunny's side, taking the capsule.

Returning downstairs, Erik passed the parlor for the water closet and opened the small capsule, revealing a contact lens case and a small bottle of saline. Erik opened the bottle and added drops to his eyes. He then washed his hands and opened the lens case, revealing two dark brown molded soft plastic lenses. Erik picked one up with the tip of his finger and dropped back his head, sliding in the contact onto his eye. After doing the other, he blinked, getting them settled in place.

Looking into the mirror, Erik faced a slender brown-haired, brown-eyed young woman with broad shoulders, narrow flat chest and thin scarred arms.

They're slowly destroying your world bit by bit...

Erik left the room and Albero whistled at him as he entered the parlor.

"Looking good," the doctor said brightly. "I'm getting hard just looking at you."

"Shut up," Erik snapped and grasped the suitcase resting in the stuffed armchair. "Let's go if we're going."

"You'll need your assignment first, *mi amigo*," Albero warned, halting Erik. "Listen carefully. In five days, our dear

454

comrades are up for execution."

"I thought we had a month," Erik growled, narrowing his eyes.

"Who ever said we had a month?" Albero chortled. "My paperwork finally cleared and we're going in to put some special people to sleep."

"How are I supposed to help with that?" Erik spat.

"You're my pretty assistant, *Señora* Abella Vasquez," Albero explained. "You'll cover the female prisoners and I'll cover the male ones. I have secured uniforms, so we should easily get onto the compound without detection."

"I can't jab anything with needles," Erik protested. "They'll see my incompetence a mile away."

Albero grinned. "That's why we're going to practice!"

Erik blanched. "Practice on what?" he yelped, dropping his suitcase. "Corpses?"

Albero let out a rolling laugh. "Jokester, aren't you?" he cried and laughed harder. "I have plenty of fruit handy."

"Don't tell me you're serious!" Erik's face burned red as Albero continued laughing. Growling under his breath, he picked up the suitcase and stormed for the stairs.

"Ferdian, wait," Bunny called as she clamored hurriedly down the steps armed with bolt cutters. "We need to cut those things off while we have a little time."

"What's a little time?" Erik asked.

"One minute."

"Shit."

Erik set down his suitcase as Bunny knelt at his ankle, snapping off the device. He then held out his wrists as Bunny cut the clear hard plastic one from his left, then the metallic one off his right. A sudden shock jarred through his arm and Erik yowled as he dropped to his knees. Suddenly a loud pip sounded in the room once the metallic brace clattered to the floor.

"What's that noise?" Erik moaned, rubbing his wrist.

"The anti-tamper bomb," Bunny squealed. "It's going to blow up!"

"You can't be serious!" Erik screeched and scooped it up. "How much time we got?"

"Thirty seconds!"

"Shit!"

Erik sprang to his feet and raced for the bathroom. He chucked the tether down the toilet then jammed the handle. As the water flushed, Erik slammed shut the lid and raced out the room as a muted explosion blast apart of the septic tank, sending it smashing against the wall into shattered pieces as water gushed from the burst pipe.

"What a close one, honey," Bunny said in relief.

"Why the hell they put an explosive *on my arm*?" Erik screeched, horrified.

"Security," Albero said simply and waved at Erik to follow. "Come now, *vamos*." Erik huffed as Albero walked briskly for the stairs.

"Sorry," Erik murmured as water quickly pooled into the parlor.

"We got more than enough money to fix it," Bunny said simply.

"Thanks."

Erik picked up his suitcase and made his way for the door.

"Ferdian," Bunny called after him. Erik turned and she tossed him a key.

"What's this?" Erik asked as he caught it.

"When you get safe."

"Let's hope so."

Erik hurried outdoors for Albero's red compact sedan parked at the curb. Inside Albero smoked a cigarette, listening to pop music.

"She gave me something," Erik said as he opened the door and put his case in the rear seat while Albero started the car.

"What is it?" Albero inquired.

"Some kind of key. But I don't know where it goes." He shut the door and entered the front passenger side. "It's too small to be a house key."

"A lock key, perhaps?" Albero suggested.

"Not sure what kind it is... Locks come in all sizes you know."

Once Erik shut the door, the doctor took off down the road.

"Don't lose it then, eh?" Albero said cheerfully.

"I don't know where to put it."

"Maybe on a chain?"

"It's too obvious."

"How about at the bank?"

"How am I going to remember that?" Erik groused. "With my shitty memory, I'd never recall it."

"What did she give you the key for?"

"She said for when I got safe."

"Then you'd better keep careful track of it."

Erik blew a sigh and looked out the window.

Arriving back at the motel, Erik took his suitcase and entered the room after Albero opened the door for him.

"Now there's one last thing you should know," Albero announced once he shut the front door.

"What's that?" Erik muttered and approached the bed, plopping on the end.

"The entire castle is run by computer, from the doors to the heating units, to the sprinklers. If one part shuts down, that part is ignored and continues running. The aim is to shut it all down at once. If you time it a millisecond too late, you'll miss your chance."

"What makes you think I can shut down a computer I know nothing about?" Erik complained. "Why not send Bunny to hack the system?"

"The system was created with a closed esoteric language," Albero clarified. "The only clue we have is that it has a physical weak point somewhere. Bunny couldn't understand the mechanical drawings, so maybe you can study them?"

"I'll try..." Erik tensed as Albero approached and sat next to him, smiling.

"You're so cute," Albero said brightly and pet Erik's knee. "So, so cute."

"If you kiss me," Erik growled, "I'll stab you."

Albero chortled and wagged a finger at Erik. "Such a fiery personality. I guess what they say about redheads are true, eh?" The doctor then reached into his slacks pocket and withdrew a set of prints. "Here, study these things," he said.

"You only have a small amount of time once the prisoners are transported down to the funeral car."

Erik gave him a wary look. "Why do I have to destroy the computer?" he demanded. "I thought I was just putting select prisoners to sleep."

"Ah, but phase one of our plan. Phase two is shunting the crematory. It needs electricity to spark the furnace, you know."

"Without it, there'll be a gas leak," Erik murmured. "You're going to blow the place apart while you make your escape with the bodies..."

"Ah, now you're catching on, *Señora*." Albero pat Erik's knee again and handed him the paperwork. "Please study these things carefully."

Erik took the papers and the doctor left his side, taking the large black case situated near the door and brought it to the small table.

The first paper Erik noticed was an aerial photograph of the building itself, showcasing its glass dome in the center and five long buildings sprawling from it, branching into smaller towers. A note in black marker indicated the computer was housed in the domed area and the holding cells were in the four other arms.

While Erik committed the diagrams and prisoner numbers to memory, the doctor assembled various serums from vials of different colored liquids, using droppers and beakers. After Erik finished reading the papers, the doctor spent the remainder of the afternoon coaching him in his practicing needle insertion on citrus fruits.

Once evening came, Erik found sleep difficult and sat up

in the cushioned chair, fretting as the doctor slept in bed. He
turned the small key over between his fingers, counting softly
in the darkness.

FORTY-SIX

Erik spent the next several days practicing needlework on fruit while Albero went to town on various job assignments. In the mornings, Erik wore the dresses from inside the suitcase and applied makeup to his face, trying to get used to seeing himself as another person. He ignored his uncomfortable feelings while spending time watching the newscasts about events in town on television and listening for information about his escape.

In the evenings, Albero returned with groceries and additional creams and bandages, cooking small meals and helped Erik manage his injuries. After showing the doctor his increasing skills in using syringes properly, the doctor then gave instruction how to properly draw the right amount of serums and using intravenous lines.

Once Albero retired for the night, Erik spent his uncomfortable hours sleeping in the chair, refusing to share the bed.

On the morning they had to report to the complex, Albero cooked a light breakfast and served coffee.

"There's nothing to be worried about," Albero assured after Erik carefully showered and helped him dress and replace the bandages on his back. "We'll do just fine."

"I hope so," Erik muttered while sorting through the suitcase full of various dresses, camisole tops and hosiery.

"I have your uniform here, *Señora*," Albero called and withdrew a tan skirt and blouse from his closet. "I'll leave it on the bed."

"Thanks," Erik grumbled, setting aside the cosmetic bag containing his custom makeup kit.

"You'll have to wear stockings," Albero reminded as he set the uniform aside while Erik withdrew a tan camisole. "It's part of the uniform."

Erik pulled into the undershirt then the blouse, fastening the small black buttons. "These things?" he asked, picking up a roll of sheer taupe-colored pantyhose from the case. "How do I put them on without ripping them?"

"That's easy to do," Albero grinned. "Here, sit in the chair." Erik puffed a sigh and took a seat in the cushioned chair. "Now put out a leg and point your toes," Albero directed as he approached with a bottle of lotion. "I'll take those."

Erik tensed when he did as told and the doctor took away the hosiery from his hand, setting it aside on the table.

"What are you planning?" Erik asked as Albero pumped a dollop of cream in his hand and rubbed his hands together.

"You can't put on pantyhose on dry skin," the doctor reprimanded, crouching at his side. "They'll tear." He grabbed Erik's foot and slathered the cream on his skin.

Erik clenched his teeth as the doctor appeared expressionless while he methodically rubbed firmly into Erik's skin, thumbing his tendons and manipulating the bones in his foot. Erik whimpered as Albero massaged his foot, popping the joints in his toes. The doctor then worked his way up Erik's leg, pausing when he pumped more cream into his hands and continued to slather on the scented balm, working deeply into Erik's calves and up his thighs.

Erik shifted nervously in his chair when Albero set down his leg and picked up the other, starting with his opposite foot. Once finished, Albero took up the pantyhose, gently rolling them down. He slipped one end over Erik's foot, adjusting the material as he slid it down Erik's leg. Taking Erik's other foot he did the same, then let go once he pulled up the band to his thighs.

"Please stand," Albero ordered. Erik rose to his feet and ground his teeth as the doctor carefully reached around, pulling the pantyhose up to his waist, then snapped it in place. "There you go. Everything's set."

Erik's face burned bright red as the doctor returned to the bathroom and shut the door behind him. He left the table and gabbed the skirt, hurriedly stepping into it and hiked it up over his narrow waist. Once he zipped it into place, Erik smoothed out his clothing and took up the makeup bag, then approached the bathroom door. "Can I come in?" he called, knocking. "I have to paint my face."

"You can," Albero answered.

Erik opened the door slightly and peered inside, watching the man brush on light brown mascara on his eyebrows. "For a minute there I thought you were jacking off in here," he quipped.

"Just putting on war paint," Albero replied. He set aside the wand and opened the cabinet, taking out the jar of porcelain fronts. "It's a part of my performance as well. We have to put on a very good show. We have to do it with flourish."

Erik entered and set his bag atop the septic tank then opened it, taking the small bottle of liquid foundation and a makeup sponge. He opened the bottle and dabbed the colored concealer on the pad and looked into the mirror, applying a bit on his face.

Albero rinsed the false teeth and set them in, smiling into the mirror. "Smile when you rub that in," the doctor instructed. "Sweep up."

"Like this?" Erik said and grinned, wiping upwards with the sponge.

"Yes, like that."

Albero said nothing else as he withdrew his own cosmetic bag from the cabinet and applied foundation to his face, then lined his eyes with liquid eyeliner. The doctor then watched Erik as he finished covering his freckles and scars, then used the brown pencil to line his eyes before putting on pale eyeshadow on the lids of his eyes. Albero smiled when Erik lastly dabbed on pale lipstick to his lips.

"*Transformación completa!*" Albero said triumphantly. "I'll go polish our shoes. You curl your hair."

"With what?"

"Irons of course!"

Erik puffed a sigh and stormed out the bathroom, rooting through his bag. Finding a set of curling irons and a bottle of hairspray, Erik returned to the bathroom and plugged the irons into the wall, then turned on the appliance, waiting for it to warm.

"How do you think I should wear my hair?" Erik asked.

"Keep it simple," Albero answered.

Erik leaned against the wall, folding his arms across his chest and watched the doctor take out a pair of black leather shoes from the closet. Returning to the bed's edge, he opened his nightstand drawer and withdrew a jar of polish with a small rag, then began the task of carefully cleaning the shoes.

Arriving at the complex, Erik stepped out the car and swallowed hard as he walked across the lot toward a pair of guards armed with rifles at the front entrance. One guard gazed at him and smiled as Erik approached.

"Good morning," the guard greeted, tipping his cap.

"Morning," Erik said softly.

"Identification?"

"W-what?"

"Identification, Ma'am. This is Federal property. We can't let anyone in without proper identification."

"I–!"

Erik clenched his hands at his sides when the guard raised his rifle.

"Ah, *Señora*, please wait for me," Albero called as he jogged toward them with a small clutch purse. "So excited to begin work, you forget your purse again!"

"That's right," Erik murmured, taking the handbag.

"*Buenos dias caballero,*" Albero greeted as he reached inside his tan blazer pocket and withdrew his wallet. "My paperwork, eh? I'm the new executioner and this is my assistant."

Erik opened the clutch purse, finding a small wallet inside.

He opened it, revealing a single yellow identification card without a photograph, typed in Spanish and his small key. Erik handed the card to the pair of guards who examined Albero's open wallet and Erik's card.

"That's not valid identification, Ma'am," the warden said, handing back the card. "You'll need an official Federal VitaStat card."

"I lost my temporary one," Erik said quickly. "I know it takes two weeks to process. I pick up my real one later today at the DMV."

"Very well." The guard gestured with his rifle. "You may go on ahead."

Erik dropped the card into the purse and stalked ahead with Albero at his heels.

"That lady looks like a dude," the other warden murmured.

"Totally legit," said his partner. "It's normal these days."

Reaching another set of guards in the interior garden complex, Erik ground his teeth when the wardens gave him closer scrutiny.

"Go on ahead, Doctor," said the guard on Erik's left. "We need to ask your assistant a few more questions."

"Like what?" Erik spat. "I have criminals to put to sleep. So why are you holding me up?"

"You just remind me of someone," the guard responded, peering closely at Erik. "I know I've seen your face somewhere before."

"I just have that look," Erik replied sheepishly. "What more do you want from me?"

"I just don't like the way you look, lady. You seem *off* somehow..."

Erik shrugged. "Nothing off about me."

"Are you that one model?" the other guard asked.

"No," answered Erik. "I'm Arbella Vasquez, anesthesiologist."

"It's something..." The guard walked around Erik, checking him closely.

"Oh, maybe that soap opera actress?" the guard's partner suggested.

"I think it's something *else*..." Erik tensed when the guard pointed his rifle's sights at his thigh and traced up his leg.

"You think so?" questioned his partner. "I think I saw her in that one commercial..."

"No, I'm thinking Miss Vasquez ain't telling us the full story."

"Like what?"

"Like she's that terrorist criminal in disguise."

The guard's partner guffawed. "Yeah, right!" he hooted. "Like he'd come back here trying break *in*! I'd be more concerned if we *did* have him and he was trying to break *out*!"

"You're right, what a silly idea." The officer lowered his rifle. "You may pass."

Erik narrowed his eyes and approached closely, deftly touching the guard's neck as he leaned in. The young man held his breath and shut his eyes as Erik whispered in his ear.

"You're right." Erik sharply thrust his knee into the guard's groin, bringing him down onto the ground. The young man moaned and vomited at Erik's feet.

"I'm sorry," the other guard said, holding up a hand. "I didn't think he was going to harass you like that."

"You're fine," Erik grumbled and stepped over the bully guardsman's downed form, storming the inner compound's lobby.

Entering a row of offices that had sturdy steel doors contrasting against the pale white walls and tiled floors, Erik winced from the harsh blue-white plate and strip lights that artificially brightened the room. He squinted when his vision wavered, resisting the urge to rub at his eyes.

Erik passed guardsmen in navy uniforms armed with shotguns as he made his way down the stark corridor. Eventually he met up with Albero chatting with an armed guard at the end before a desk and body scanner near a barricaded door.

The doctor smiled at Erik's approach. "You finally arrive, *Señora*," he said brightly. "This is the last step."

"Last step of what?" Erik asked warily.

"We'll have to pat you down," the guard explained from behind his desk. "No one can come through without being thoroughly scanned. I'm waiting on a female guard to see to you."

"Y-you don't have to do that," Erik said, alarmed. "I'm willing to step through the body scanner, for real."

"Part of the procedure is the frisk, Ma'am," the guard insisted, "then the wand, then the scanner. We can't just skip rules."

"Can't you do it?"

The guard shook his head. "I'm not allowed to, Ma'am."

A loud buzzer resonated in the air and the locks automatically clicked. The heavy door ground open and Erik swallowed hard when the painted steel revealed Inquisitor Alisaundra on the other side. She wore the same outfit as he did, with the exception of a tan blazer over her blouse.

The woman stepped through and greeted the guard and Albero as he offered his hand to shake. "Good Morning, Doctor," she said amicably. "Thanks for working with us on such short notice."

"With me is my assistant *Señora* Vasquez," announced Albero. "She'll be watching the procedure today from the control room."

Alisaundra narrowed her eyes at Erik as she approached and Erik smiled, holding out a hand. "Why did you bring your assistant?" she demanded.

"At the last prison I worked for, they used an anesthesiologist before administering the poisons," Albero explained. "Your *compañero* here tells me you have no need for that here."

"You're right," Alisaundra said, giving Erik a long critical look.

"I-inspector...?" Erik murmured, lowering his hand.

"No, Inquisitor," Alisaundra corrected. She walked around Erik, studying him. "How many surgeries have you participated in, Miss Vasquez?"

"Er, over two-hundred," Erik responded.

"That is a lot of surgeries in your short life span..."

"Namely criminals and crazies." Erik let out a strained

laugh. "There's a lot of them."

"Are you married, Miss Vasquez?"

"Took a vow of celibacy. I plan to go into a nunnery once I retire, you know, to atone for my sins and such."

"You have an answer for everything, don't you?"

"You're the one asking questions, not me."

Alisaundra pointed toward the desk. "Please remove the contents of your purse."

Erik approached the desk and opened the small handbag, dumping over its cargo. Alisaundra came over as the guard sifted through the items, revealing the wallet, a pack of cigarettes, a small notebook, and translucent blue pen. He then sifted through the leather holder, taking out the yellow identification card and the small key.

"Is that it?" Alisaundra snapped.

"I didn't want my spare change setting off alarms," Erik replied. "Also, my cosmetics wouldn't fit in a bag that tiny."

"What's the key for?"

"A locked box at the Menoka Community Bank."

Alisaundra frowned and faced Erik. "I'll have to search your person for Contraband and the like," she stated.

"Right here?" Erik murmured.

Alisaundra gave a malicious smile. "Right here." She withdrew a pair of blue examination gloves from her suit jacket pockets.

"I'm allergic to latex," Erik stated.

"These have no vinyl, rubber or donning powder," Alisaundra said as she snapped them on her hands. "These are made specifically for sensitive skin and maintain tactile ability." She gestured toward Erik. "Please hold out your arms and stand shoulder-width apart."

Erik did as told and she lightly slid her hands over his arms, up his shoulders and neck, then went down his sides, from his armpit and to his waist. Erik swallowed a lump forming in his throat as she lifted his blouse slightly and tapped around his skirt's waistband then pulled on it.

"I'm not carrying anything," Erik murmured as Alisaundra let down his blouse and groped his chest. "*Please don't feel my back*," he prayed as she ran her hands down his sides.

"Criminals are known to tape weapons to their body," Alisaundra answered as she walked around and pat his rear, then went down his legs, working her way up his thighs.

"I'm not a criminal," Erik protested weakly. "Why would a criminal pose as anesthesiologist and go into the very detention center meant to hold him until he dies?"

"What an interesting question."

Erik held his breath as she groped his crotch and grunted when his vision flashed red from pain.

"Something the matter?" Alisaundra needled.

"No," Erik said weakly. "This is just very uncomfortable."

"I see," the inquisitor said and rose upright. "Thank you for participating."

Erik exhaled a shaky breath and returned to the desk, gathering his belongings.

"You're almost done," the male guard said as he withdrew a metal detecting wand from his desk and passed it to Alisaundra. Erik winced when the inspector tapped his shoulder with the wand.

"People have been known to hide weapons in interesting places," she said. "Now please, reassume the position." Erik puffed an annoyed sigh and stood as Alisaundra waved the wand over his body. "Despite my not feeling anything, you could still try to sneak something nefarious past me."

"You may pass through the scanner now," the male guard announced when the wand made no sound after Alisaundra finished scanning. Erik stepped through the large device and the guard nodded when the machine stayed silent. "All clear. You're free to go."

"Good to know," Erik mewed and stood before the door, waiting impatiently while the guard flipped switches at his desk.

Albero picked up Erik's purse off the counter and joined his side, taking him gently by the arm. "A man is never completely free of his urges," he murmured in his ear as the electronic locks unlocked and the steel door slowly ground open. "We are weak beings, always leaning toward doing evil, destructive things."

"What are you saying?" Erik whispered.

"Let your spirit prevail at any cost, *mi amigo*. Keep yourself alive until we meet again."

Erik took in a shallow breath as his head dulled in pain once handed the bag. He took it numbly and they stepped through the entranceway.

FORTY-SEVEN

Erik and Albero entered a large control room surrounded by computing equipment and many monitors. Several soldiers in navy and black uniforms manned the stations while a tall broad-shouldered man with short graying dark brown hair wearing a tan suit and orange tinted glasses stood in the center, looking at a panel of flickering video monitors. Attached to his waist, he wore a radio communicator.

"*Señor* Corbin?" Albero called as he entered the room. The man turned toward them and paled when he spotted Erik. Albero quickly crossed the floor and shook Corbin's hand. "They never told me you'll be overseeing the execution today. What a nice surprise."

"Yes, they called me to see if the prisoners were worth reforming," Corbin answered. "It's rumored they're former INTERTEC agents."

"Is that so? Have they confessed at all?"

"They have kept silent, even after the threat of death."

"How hardy they are! Well, let's see how they hold up, eh?" Albero laughed. "With these four special poisons, there's no way they can return from the dead!"

Corbin chortled and walked with Albero toward the exit across the room. "They are waiting for your arrival, Doctor."

"It's a shame you don't want to put them under first," Albero said as he headed for the door. "Do you enjoy watching them suffer?"

"I want to see them in their final moments," Corbin said darkly. "Watching the light leave their eyes, robbed of their power of existence... It's the ultimate form of control." Erik dropped the bag he held and its contents spilled over onto the floor. Corbin looked over at him, smiling. "Was that a little too morbid?" he asked.

Erik said nothing as he crouched down, picking up the fallen items to place them back in the purse. He noticed the pen came apart, showing a silver nib and picked it up, sensing warmth in his hand as it spread up his arm.

While the control technicians operated a series of buttons on their consoles and a loud buzzer sounded as the steel door slowly opened, the biggest monitor in the room brightened and cleared, showing a single white room with a gurney that had leather straps on the side.

"Sir, the execution is about to begin," called a technician once Albero passed through the door.

Corbin walked over the panel of monitors, watching the scene unfold.

In the white room, a door opened offside and a pair of guards dragged in a young woman dressed in an orange jumpsuit with a black hood over her head. She struggled as the guards beat her with their batons then dumped her roughly on the table.

Erik rose to his feet, watching in silence as the soldiers strapped down her limbs and Albero later entered with a cart that held four colored vials, one red, one yellow, one blue and the last one orange. Around his neck, he wore a stethoscope.

The soldiers stood offside as Albero picked up a syringe from the cart and drew from the red vial first, followed by the yellow, then the blue and orange. The liquids inside turned murky brown and he injected the drugs into the woman's arm. Erik cringed as the woman went through a series of convulsions before falling limp. Albero plugged in the stethoscope's earpieces and placed the sound device to the woman's chest, listening for a heartbeat. When he nodded, the soldiers untied the woman and hauled her body out the room.

"How many are supposed to die today?" Erik murmured.

"Nine," Corbin answered, smiling.

Erik watched the same event unfold with several more male and female prisoners. When the last one, an older man, was brought in, he fought intensely against his captors, eventually yanking out of their grips and snatched off the hood from his head.

Erik gasped when he recognized the man on the screen who had shoulder length brown hair and a dark scruffy face.

Corbin chortled, folding his arms across his chest. "I've waited a long time to see you die, Schumacher," he said triumphantly at the screen. "Finally your incessant meddling can end."

Erik clenched his hands as tears streaked down his face, watching the guards strike their rifle stocks into John Greenfield until he could no longer stand.

Suddenly, a high-pitched warning signal alarmed.

"What's going on?" Corbin snapped, glaring at the

technicians at their monitoring screens.

"Not sure, Sir!" a technician called from his terminal. "There are no faults in the system found."

"Do you think it's that hacker?" one joked.

"That one who took over the local stations last week," said another. "That was a riot. The Fed's best coder monkeys couldn't trace who did it."

"Well, they can't hack us," chimed a third. "We're on a different non-broadcasting network!"

"I'd like to see them try!"

You are a tool of destruction!

Draw your power and fight!

Static appeared on the viewing screens, taking out their various feeds. In its place, colored bars manifest and a robotic voice came through the speakers, citing 'calling all stations.' The technicians panicked and the control room became a frantic scene as they tried to trace the overriding signal.

"Don't do anything unnecessary," Corbin ordered. "Find the source and jam it!"

"We're trying, Sir!"

Corbin withdrew his personal handset radio and pressed the call button, only to hear the same robotic voice. "The hell!" he growled. "There's no way...!"

The robotic voice stopped and a cryptic message appeared in white LCD letters across the screens.

```
THE WORLDS OF DESTROYER

ENDS FOR ALL WITH YOU

ENTERS LIFE TO SEE
```

476

"What does this mean?" a technician cried.

"Turn on the emergency override," Corbin spat. "Do it now!"

A melodic tone blared through the speakers and Erik shut his eyes, grinding his teeth as the pain flared through his head. He took in a deep breath, shuddering when his skin grew cold and clammy.

"*I have to kill these people,*" Erik thought as he gripped the pen firmly in his hand. "*Will it end when I'm done? Will I finally wake up? Will I finally die?*" Hearing no answer, Erik felt the burning warmth radiate up his arm as the weapon glimmered dimly, forming into the blue steel broadsword.

Erik's eyes snapped open and he dashed for the soldier near the door before he could reach for his rifle, striking him directly in the heart cavity with a swift thrust. He then hurried onto his next target, hacking into the remaining technicians and sliced off limbs, goring them with the blade until no more remained.

Hearing a slow clap, Erik turned, pointing his sword toward Corbin who grinned.

"What power and combat strength," the man said. "So swift and deadly... You truly are a monster - I can see it in your eyes." Erik held his sword at ready, heaving for breath as Corbin approached, holding out his hands. "Are you saving me for last? Or is it that you can't strike me?"

Erik growled and took a step forward.

"Come on now, strike me," Corbin egged. "I know you can do it." He reached into his blazer's underside, withdrawing a high-powered pistol. "Or do I have to threaten you to do so?"

He released the safety and pointed it at Erik's forehead. "There, would that suffice?"

Erik dashed around him and Corbin turned out of a fast whirling slash attack. He quickly dodged and stepped out of Erik's thrusts and lunging stabs, before firing his gun once he found an opening, shooting the sword out of Erik's hand.

Erik charged and ducked low for a rushing tackle, grasping Corbin's leg and flipped him over onto the floor. He dropped down as he grabbed Corbin's wrist holding the gun and forced it away, smashing his finger into the trigger. The weapon unleashed its volley until it emptied, striking the console, causing an electrical charge that blew the machine. The overhead lights shut off as the machinery wound down and the monitors flickered into its digital death, killing the tone and leaving everything in darkness.

Erik snatched the empty gun out Corbin's hand and bashed the handle into the man's face, breaking his jaw. He continued striking until the pistol slipped out of his hand, dropping to the floor. Erik grasped Corbin's bloodied face and leaned forward, listening to the shallow breath gurgling in his throat.

"How dare you call me a monster?" he hissed in Corbin's ear. "You fiends created me."

A familiar high pip screeched in the room and Erik scrambled to his feet. He hustled for the fallen wallet on the floor and a sudden explosion tore through the mainframe, creating a blast wave that hurled Erik onto the floor and knocked him out.

Go on, pull the trigger. You know you want to...

Erik's eyes snapped open when he heard a door creak open and a wash of cold air filled the room.

"Your front door's open," called a familiar female voice. "It's crazy out there... My umbrella's ruined!"

Erik sat up and shuddered from the chilled sweat on his skin, finding himself in an unfamiliar bed covered by tan sheets in a plain beige room. Pushing the bedding away, he planted his feet on the floor, groaning and ran his hands through his hair. He paused, noticing the gold ring on his left hand.

"I brought you dinner," said the female voice in the other room. "I got the orange and almond chicken. Almonds are supposed to be good for you..."

"*Am I married?*" Erik wondered, holding his dully aching head in his hand. "Wifey?" he called.

"Yes, Husband?" the woman called back and giggled.

"Got anything for my headache?"

"I might have some powder aspirin somewhere."

Erik opened the nearby nightstand drawer, finding several amber bottles inside, with some containing various powders and others capsules. He recoiled when he saw a cockroach wriggle in the drawer among his belongings. Trying to swat it, the bug scurried off and Erik grunted, disgusted and worried.

Can she really save you?

Erik glanced up, facing his mirror image hanging over the closets facing his bed. He faced a haggard thin young man with a scarred freckled face, tired violet eyes and blond-streaked sandy red hair. Around his waist he wore loose gray pajama pants.

"Look at you," Erik grumbled and rose to his feet. He padded over to his mirror, examining his thin scarred frame. "You're just a living skeleton... Shouldn't even dare be alive in the first place."

Is that what you really want?

Erik shut his eyes and ran his hands though his hair, letting out a desperate moan in agony as he stretched.

Every pain and ache and scar is a painful, constant reminder...

"Why do they torture me?" Erik mewed and opened his eyes, peering at his reflection as he held his hands clasped on his head. "I just want to dull everything, forget everything... Why won't they understand?"

They never understand... They never listen...

"But *you* always listen, don't you?" Erik grinned and wagged a finger at his reflection. "You crazy, sick, sad animal. They should've put you down a long time ago."

You monster, you beast... You have no right to be here.

"You're right. I don't. We all don't, do we?" Erik left the mirror and rummaged through the open drawer. "Which one will make me forget? Is it the orange one or the yellow?"

"No!" the woman's voice screeched and Erik yelped in shock when tackled from behind. He struck the bed face-first and she took his wrist, locking her arms around his as she pulled away. "Please, don't do that," she cried. "Don't ever do that!"

Erik tentatively pat her wet head buried into his neck with his free hand, overwhelmed by the damp musk and faint flowery perfume emanating from her. "Fine, I won't," he murmured, releasing his hold on the pill bottle. It bounced on the mattress. "Why don't you just flush them all if it gets so bad?"

"It's not bad all the time."

Erik tensed when he noticed his arousal stirring slightly once he realized her soft form against his. "What are you doing here?"

The woman sat up and crawled over, staring intently at Erik from her position on his back. Erik grinned when she looked at him upside down, taking in her ruddy tanned skin and bobbed black hair. She wore a damp orange dress that had yellow and red paisleys as the running pattern. Her dark eyes appeared worried when she picked up the fallen pill bottle.

"Why are you looking at me like you don't know me?" she replied, frowning. "Don't tell me you took Neuralgine again..."

"I won't." Erik smirked. "You're more than welcome to take some dry clothes of mine if you want. They're clean."

"I'm Hanalei, remember?" When Erik said nothing, she puffed a frustrated sigh and clambered off him. "I'm sorry the pain is so bad," she murmured, smiling sadly at Erik as he flipped over onto his back and sat up, drawing his knees to his chest. "I wish I could take it away for you."

"Let me know when you do," Erik quipped.

Hanalei chortled in response and he beamed. She left his side, dropping the pill bottle along the way in his nightstand then returned to the bedroom closets. "Did that last bug squashing mission you mentioned stress you out?" Hanalei called as she opened the door. "Is that why you took it?"

"What mission?"

Hanalei rummaged through Erik's articles, searching for a suitable replacement. "Do you remember where the office you had to check in is?"

"What office?"

"Your complex doesn't even have Wi-Fi. My cell has bad

service when it rains." Hanalei withdrew a powder blue dress shirt and hung the shirt on the nearby knob. Erik rose to his feet and grinned deviously upon approach, swatting her rear.

"Ooh," Hanalei yelped and giggled. "What brought this on?"

"I just can't keep my hands off you."

Hanalei peeled out of her dress, revealing she wore a matching orange lace brassiere and panty set. Erik stepped in from behind and looped a finger into the bra strap, snapping it against her skin. "How many did you take already?"

Erik shrugged and gently grasped her fabric-covered breasts in his hands from behind. "The usual, I suppose?"

"Have coffee with me. Maybe you'll sober up and remember where you have to go."

Erik nodded and gave a gentle squeeze before letting go, making his way into the kitchenette. Hanalei later entered the kitchen dressed in the blue shirt and prepared coffee in the maker.

"Hey, what are you doing?" Hanalei mewed as Erik leaned in and smelled her neck.

"Doing what feels nice," Erik cooed in her ear, wrapping his arms about her waist. "Come on, play with me."

"Not now!" Hanalei giggled when Erik unbuttoned the shirt's bottom button. "Did you eat yet?"

"Maybe I want to taste you instead. Are you wearing underwear?"

Hanalei swat his hand. "Come on, stop!" She pulled away and Erik tightened his hold.

"Let me see, please?"

"You can always feel for yourself."

"I like looking." Hanalei continued to squirm as Erik methodically undid the buttons. Moments later, a knock resonated on the door.

"Go answer the door," Hanalei reprimanded when the knock sounded again. "Let me fix you something in peace."

"Fine," Erik grumbled and left her side. He crossed the parlor, noticing Hanalei's coat hanging on the rack nearby and her leather flats beneath them. Erik opened the door, facing an older man dressed in a long tan raincoat, boots, fedora, and dark glasses.

"I came to get you since it's raining," the man said. "Please gather your things."

"I'm having breakfast," Erik responded.

"What do you want on your toast?" Hanalei called from the kitchen.

The man frowned and gazed at Erik's left hand then back toward the kitchen. "You never told me you were married," he said. "You never told me anything at all, really…"

Erik smirked. "You thought it was for fashion?" he charged. "Why would that matter to you?"

The man grunted. "Please, hurry this along," he grumbled. "There's a lot to inform you for this particular mission."

"It can wait after coffee," Erik spat. "You can come in if you like or sit in the car. It's your choice." When the man said nothing else, Erik moved to shut the door and the man grabbed the edge.

"I can wait," he said sourly. "Go on and eat something."

Erik opened the door wider and held out a hand. "Couch over there. I won't be long."

The man entered and Erik shut the door behind him. Erik returned to the parlor where he spotted Hanalei frying eggs at the stove. On the table behind her were a saucer holding two slices of toast spread with cherry jelly.

"Put it on the toast," Erik said as Hanalei reached for a bowl in the drain board. "I like jelly on my eggs."

"What a strange combination," Hanalei noted and Erik handed her the plate. She scooped the yellow mass onto the toast and gave a brief smile in return.

"Thanks for cooking," Erik said softly and pulled out the chair at the kitchen table. "Sit with me?"

"The coffee's almost ready."

"I'm good." Erik plopped into his chair and held out a hand when Hanalei neared. "Come on, sit in my lap."

"What has you so on today?" Hanalei teased and settled in Erik's lap. "Don't tell me you want me to feed you too."

"You don't have to do that." Erik's free hand stroked Hanalei's thigh as he reached around with the other and picked up his toast. "Have the other one if you like."

"What about your guest?"

"He can wait a bit."

"Something's on your mind, isn't it? You're normally never this hands-on."

"You act as if I'm never this randy."

"You're not."

"Tell me if I'm dreaming."

"You are, everyday," Hanalei replied. "Life is nothing more than an illusion for souls already long dead..."

"So this dream is too good to be true then or are you being

facetious?"

"It is... It's whatever you want it to be." Hanalei stroked Erik's hair and put her forehead against his. "They're looking for something and are trying all your defenses."

Erik dropped the toast he held, growing tense. "Then that means they already know..."

"Or maybe not and you're just worried. Or maybe they know everything already."

Erik swallowed hard when the room seemed to inch closer around him. "Hana," he said faintly, "why are you talking to me like this?"

"Every symbol and construct you make, they've analyzed and deconstructed and filed away."

"What are you trying to say?" Erik held Hanalei by the shoulders and looked deeply into her eyes. "What are you warning me about?" he demanded. "Why are you saying these weird things?"

"I guess you can call me another layer of self-defense." The young woman smiled brightly, her eyes becoming crescent lines on her weathered face. "How literal you take it is open to interpretation."

Erik quirked an eyebrow. "All right, I'll play along," he said warily. "Though I'm not sure if I'm on a bad trip or awake..."

"Your deep-settled fears have made you aware of the digging and you've further closed yourself off to keep them from finding the truth."

Erik frowned. "So, I'm not safe from their prying no matter what they do."

Hanalei nodded. "All they have to do is order a chemical

confession and you really won't have any more defenses."

Erik embraced Hanalei firmly, squeezing tightly. "Please don't say anymore," he pleaded. "If this is a dream, I want it to be nice."

Hanalei embraced Erik in return, stroking his head. "But you can't dream anymore if you're dead. You have to find the key."

"They can't if I completely trash my psyche, right?"

"I wouldn't recommend it."

Erik nuzzled her cheek. "What should I do then?"

"There are three things I'm allowed to tell you..." Hanalei pulled away and held Erik's face in her hands. "First, anything you say will be used against you. Second, you have to tell the truth. Third, you have to do what is right."

"Do what's right, huh?" Erik grinned and pulled against Hanalei's cheeks. "What if I believe the lie I tell myself and the mindwarpers have no other recourse but to roll with it?"

"If the lie is the only truthful option," Hanalei said seriously, "then we have no choice but to admit it to the courts, as long as it's the only viable option."

"How much time do I have?"

"They can only hold you for seventy-two hours. If they can't gather evidence in that time, then you're released."

Erik grasped Hanalei's hands into his own. "How long are you going to keep me dreaming?" When Hanalei said nothing, Erik released his hold and pushed her away. "You got me boxed in, you think?" he murmured.

She stayed silent, peeling away as Erik slumped in his chair, drained. Hanalei left him there, staring out into the middle distance into nothing at all.

FORTY-EIGHT

"*Señor*..." a faint voice called. "*Señora*... Please be alive..."

The pain hit him secondly, spreading throughout his body. Erik cowered when bright light shone in his face. He squinted, looking into a hazy tan figure standing over him once the light passed.

"What...?" Erik grumbled and held a hand to his throbbing head. He recoiled and looked down at his hands, finding blood staining his hands and clothing.

"Good, you're awake." Erik's vision focused and he looked up, facing the doctor Albero crouching before him. "I've stabilized you the best I could, but you'll have to come with me if you don't want to die."

"What happened?"

"The furnace exploded, just like we wanted." Albero grinned. "You did a great job."

"No, something else..." Erik reached forward, grasping the doctor's shirtfront. "Those words, the song, those urges... Controlling me... You−!"

Albero chortled and unlaced Erik's fingers. "Are you all right to stand?" he asked. "I can't carry you. I'm exhausted from hauling all those bodies, *mi amigo* - I'm sorely getting out of shape."

"Why?" Erik growled. "Why are you controlling me?"

"If you want to know, I suggest you get up before those Agents capture us."

Albero rose upright and held out a hand to Erik. Erik grasped his wrist and the doctor pulled him to his feet. Erik staggered forward and looked down at the ground, blinking slowly.

"Nothing's broken," Erik mumbled and held out a hand, looking at the smooth bloodied skin before him.

"I think you've a bit concussed," Albero murmured.

"This body isn't mine..."

"I've got you."

Albero laced Erik's arm around his shoulders and led him toward an idled tan transport truck with a covered rear cab. The doctor opened the door on the front passenger side and helped Erik in, then shut the door. He went around, getting into the driver's side and switched gears before speeding down the road.

Happening upon a blockade guarded by a pair of soldiers armed with high-powered rifles, Albero slowed down and came to a stop as they signaled at him. He rolled down the window and leaned out as the pair approached and split up, with one going around the driver's side and the other on the passenger.

"Is this some kind of inspection?" Albero called. "I must hurry. My assistant got injured in the accident at Headquarters."

"We know about the accident," said the soldier as his partner tapped at Erik's window. "We've been told some prisoners have escaped and are posing as wardens."

"I'm a doctor," Albero said and chortled. "Do I really look

like a soldier to you?"

"We have to check."

"Go ahead. All you're going to find is a bunch of body bags." Albero reached for his revolver underneath his blazer at his side as the soldier left Erik's window and approached the rear cab.

"Find anything?" the solider near Albero called. Erik heard the doors swing open and a muffled crumpling sound. "Hey?"

Albero unleashed his gun and fired at the soldier, striking him in the back of the head. Erik jerked from the loud explosion of sound and spotted John Greenfield and a young man jump from the rear cab dressed in soldier's uniforms, racing over to the driver's side. They picked up the slain body and quickly returned to the cab.

"I thought you really killed them," Erik said softly as Albero set back his revolver. Hearing a knock at the panel behind them, Albero resumed his drive on the road, reaching the exit gate.

"I told you I was just putting them to sleep," Albero replied. "I'm not that ruthless of a man."

"I can't trust you," Erik grumbled.

"You don't have to. But if you leave my side, you'll surely be executed."

"I want my life."

"Then you'll have to stay with me, *mi amigo*. If you get too far away from me, you'll no longer exist."

Erik sat forward and clenched his hands, pressing them against his thighs as he struggled to breathe. "*You put something inside me to control me*," Erik thought, glaring back at the doctor. *"I'm going to find why you're so intent on controlling me and I will crush it. I'm not withstanding this for one more minute..."*

Albero noticed Erik's simmering gaze and smiled. "Ah, what a horrific expression you have on your face," he said brightly. "That's the first time you ever looked at me like you want to kill me."

"I do," Erik snarled. "I might not remember my name, but I'll never ever forget who you are or what you're doing to me."

"Good, hold on to that hate because you really shouldn't direct it at me, *muchacho*." Albero motioned with his head to the rear cab behind him. "It's him back there you should really unleash your hate on. It's his idea."

Erik gaped at the panel behind them as his heart thud hard in his chest. *"What is he saying?"* he wondered. *"Why would he do this to me...?"*

"Do you really want to confront that road?" Albero asked, breaking into Erik's thoughts. "It'll hurt you, more in any way you can imagine. More than the physical pains could ever provide."

"I'll take my chances," Erik muttered.

"Rest for now. It'll be awhile until we get to the emergency clinic."

Erik curled in his seat as the general unease he felt slowly turned into overwhelming fear. The fear then faded into pain that radiated everywhere throughout his body, taking him down into its crushing waves.

It's a wonder you're still alive.

Erik's eyes snapped open and he sat up with a start, overwhelmed in pain. He groaned and held his aching head, cringing as raging agony throbbed down his back. Looking around, he noticed his body covered in bandages while he rest in a simple bed in a small barely-furnished room. A small window overhead cast shadows from the shady pines while afternoon sunlight filtered in, illuminating dust particles in the air.

Erik grew uneasy when he heard the murmur of voices from another room and spotted near the door stood a slender tanned young man with freckled skin, shaggy brassy red hair and dull violet eyes, wearing a black Defense Forces Special Operations uniform.

"What are you doing here?" Erik grumbled and the counterpart grinned.

What else? I'm waiting for you to disappear.

"That's not going to work. I still exist."

Of course you exist - as a puppet to be jerked this way and that. Through genetic enhancements and tortuous training, you learned superior fighting skills and were molded into a force to be reckoned with.

"I'm not a fighting force!" Erik snapped. "I'm...!"

You're nobody, nothing at all. You're just a body used for dirty work, for dirty things and nothing else. You're trash, to be used and thrown away when your use runs out. They'll just manufacture more of you over and over again, to continue their destructive reign to bring some false sense of peace.

"I'm more than a serial number!" Erik shoved the bedspreads away and rose unsteadily to his feet. "I'm

492

somebody! Somebody's beloved son even..."

The duplicate crossed the room and Erik threw a punch, only to miss and fall over, striking the floor on his knees. The double stomped on Erik's back, holding him down and formed a violet saber in his free hand.

You are some body - just a serial number. One of many. Just accept it. The young man bat Erik upside the head and crouched before him, grinning. *You're nobody, not even anyone's beloved son. They used you, changing your personality and enhancing your senses and abilities to suit their demented needs.*

"It can't be just me," Erik mewed. "The fighting has to end sometime..."

Do you honestly think by destroying the machines the war will end? Erik struggled to get up and the double jammed his sheathed blade into his back, knocking him down. *All you have to concern yourself with is continuing the fight.*

"Fight and die, that's all they tell me! Forever and ever..."

As long as you breathe, you will have to keep fighting. Because it will never end.

"I don't want to do this anymore."

Then let me take care of it. That's all I'm asking you. Just for a little while? Erik looked up at the smiling young man standing over him. *Because as long as you're still here, they'll keep punishing you until you give in.* The counterpart unsheathed the blade and rammed it into Erik's back, forcing him doubled over, gagging. *Let go of this life. They've taken everything from you - friends, family, your identity... Your only concern should be survival.*

"What makes you think he'll willingly help us with our

work?" a female voice said outside the door.

"We'll ask him once he wakes up," said John Greenfield's voice.

"How much longer do you think this will go on?" Erik murmured.

As long as it takes. How can you not be angry at them for doing this to you? You didn't ask for this! The duplicate withdrew his sword and booted Erik in the chest, knocking him over onto his side. *Being beaten down and humiliated to transform you into some mindless mechanical thrall... These people are evil and sick! Don't you care about your life?*

"No..." Erik wheezed.

You better start caring because they sure as hell don't!

"I need more time to think... This is too much..."

You don't have a lot of time! Make a decision now!

"I don't think he'll like knowing you're using him as a sacrifice," said the woman's voice outside the door.

"I'm more worried about his health," John Greenfield's voice said. "Here's the doctor now."

See? Don't you hear them planning to use you again? If they really cared, they'd long release you, am I right?

"I think so," Erik muttered.

Next they'll send that kinky doctor in here to fully erase you and I can't save you. Don't let them take the only choice you have left!

"I want to die when I'm ready... Don't let them kill me."

You're still too attached to this sad life...

"So what... I don't have enough hate yet, not right now."

They're going to drive you cold and numb until you fall off the edge of madness and despair. Once they destroy you, you'll never be able to return to that life ever again.

"I know," Erik moaned. Tears pooled in his eyes and streamed down his face. "Don't remind me..."

Are you going to give in now? Just let me take care of it and you won't have to suffer anymore.

"I can't forget, not right now. I can't..."

You'll never forget. You'll never, ever forget. You'll always remember and you'll remind them of their mistakes over and over again. I promise to make them suffer as much as you have. We'll hurt them, punish them, destroy them until there's nothing left...

"I'll check on him if you like," Albero's voice said outside the door. "It's been quite some time..."

Prevail, fight, destroy... We'll kill them all so they won't hurt us anymore. When the fighting ends, then you can end your suffering. Just let me do that! Let's punish them!

"When the fighting ends," Erik said weakly, "I can finally end my suffering..."

First they weaken you physically, then they tear down your rational restraints, unleashing a cold unfeeling beast. The only way to feel alive is by controlling and stealing another's life. Only another monster can kill you. Only Death can set you free.

"I want to be free."

Then die!

FORTY-NINE

The door opened moments later, revealing the doctor Albero dressed in a black uniform and cap and a young woman wearing a light brown tank shirt and black cargo shorts.

"What are you doing on the floor, *mi amigo*?" Albero asked as he approached Erik's side. "Feeling any better?"

"No," Erik grumbled and wiped his eyes with the palm of his hands.

Albero withdrew a penlight from his pocket and slid a switch on its side, shining a blue beam of light. "How's your head?" he murmured as he crouched at Erik's side. Taking Erik's chin in his hand, he peered into his eyes.

"What do you think?"

"I have some painkillers if you like."

Erik narrowed his eyes. "I just don't want to feel."

"Are you afraid?"

Erik glared at the doctor as he shut off the light and pocketed it. "What would I be afraid of?" he snapped.

"Don't underestimate him," Albero said softly. "He's not ordinary and much more skilled than any normal soldier."

"Are you telling me or warning me?" Erik shoved the doctor away. "Please leave," he growled. "I don't want to be bothered."

"You hurt your head in the accident. I have to mind over

you."

"Why would that matter?" Erik drew up his knees, staring at the wall beyond the doctor, gazing at his counterpart standing behind the young woman who tapped his sword into his palm. "What if I told you I have these horrible urges?" Erik muttered. "What if there's this dangerous monster inside me who wants to kill everyone here?"

Albero chortled as he rose to his feet. "We all have monsters inside us," he replied. "Control is the key, *muchacho*."

"What if I want to just give up control and let that monster run free?"

"As long as we control those *impulsos demoniacos* inside us, we can live pleasantly."

Erik glanced at the young woman who appeared nervous. "Hey," he called. "What's your name?"

"Why do you want to know my name?" the young woman answered.

"I read somewhere if you know someone's name, you can control them. Do they control you?"

"We'll have to keep moving," the young woman said worriedly. "We can't stay in one place for too long. The Agents will track us down soon enough."

"If you're worried about them capturing me, then let me go. I won't talk." Erik let out a bitter laugh. "Look what they did to me already. What much worse can they do to me?"

"They'll open you up and go boom," Albero said brightly.

Erik's eyes widened as he stiffened, startled. "What did you say?" he snarled.

"You heard what I said."

Erik scrambled upright and the doctor continued to smile when grabbed by the lapels. "What are you saying?" Erik shouted. "You put a bomb inside me?"

"Of course I did - that's what I'm good at." Albero laughed. "My lovely creation, such a beautiful sight. You should see it - completely flawless. It is truly a work of art."

"Why are you using me like this?" Erik thundered. "Why are you controlling me?"

"I'm not the one you should be asking," Albero answered. "The one you want to find and destroy... He can answer those questions."

"If I don't do what you say, you'll just push the button, right?"

"It's really no different than those Supranet Tethers."

Erik shoved the doctor away and stormed for the door, throwing it open wide. *"What a horrible dream,"* he thought as he stomped across the floor, ignoring the small group working on various mechanical or computer projects. *"I just want to wake up..."*

Approaching John Greenfield who sat on the floor in the corner working on a Synthoid with his looks, Erik kicked the machine over and the older man looked up, stunned.

"Replacing me with another one of your stupid creations?" Erik spat. "Don't thank me for saving your life."

"Ace...!" John Greenfield cried.

Erik grabbed the older man by the arm and yanked him to his feet. "How could you let that monster do that to me?" he shrilled. "You selfish coward! You worthless piece of shit!" Erik violently shook him. "Thought you could just keep me as your caged beast until I died? Thought you could use me and throw me away when you're done with the mission? Because you can just build a new one, right?"

"It's not what you think," John Greenfield pleaded. "Please, be reasonable."

"Then explain it to me, because I'm apparently too stupid to understand."

"I don't have anything really to tell you. You already know."

"Why?"

"There's no need to explain."

"Then how long do you plan to continue? Until your body gave out?"

"It's necessary that you continue the fight," John Greenfield said softly. "Yes, it's a one-sided war, but if we can slow them down, it'll damper their ability to continue."

Erik narrowed his eyes. "Stop lying to me," he sneered. "This is more than revenge, isn't it? Tell me the truth - why are you pulling my strings so much?"

"I could say it's simply regret, but then again whatever my answer may be will never be enough to satisfy you." John Greenfield shrugged. "I could tell you how much I hated the direction the Public Defense Works were taking, especially involved in the Cybernetically Enhanced Neurotechnological Replicant Application project... But then it took everything from me, leaving me with little recourse."

"How is this little recourse?" Erik screamed. "How is using me like your bastard mechanical puppets recourse?"

"I've gone to a lot of trouble to plan this!" John Greenfield protested. "You don't understand the risks involved!"

"I understand the risks all right." Erik released his hold on John Greenfield's arm. "So win back your freedom by destroying them yourself. Don't involve me!"

"They'll eventually come for you too. I have to use every tool at my disposal to destroy the strongest links in the chain..."

Erik's skin grew prickly warm and the ambience of the room around him - the clatter of keys and clanging of tools - cut into a wash of static as the walls seemed to close in. He heaved for breath as he trembled in rage and swallowed hard, fighting the roiling in his guts. The burning searing agony returned in his hands and he launched a staggering punch into John Greenfield's side, knocking him to the floor.

The older man vomited at his feet and Erik ground his teeth, growling. When condemning words failed him and unable to come up with a million lines of curses to hurl at the man, Erik stormed over John Greenfield and flung open the door, stomping outdoors.

With burning stinging eyes and tightening throat, he stumbled down the redwood planks and took off running. Tearing through limbs and overgrown shrubbery, he met an unexpected drop-off at the edge of a cliff and tumbled down a rocky slope. His world capsized end over end as his body quickly picked up speed with every foot he descent, smashing into stones and greenery until he hit with a splash into a watercourse.

Panicking as he gulped in water, Erik tried to will his sore limbs to move toward the surface when he continued sinking. Below, Erik spotted glittering gems struck by the sun shining in from above. Over his head, Erik saw a hazy figure at the edge and fought to get closer to the dark cloud blotting the sky before his lungs gave out.

Cresting, Erik coughed up water and gulped in fresh air, finding instead his counterpart standing at the lake's edge. Erik cut through the water with heavy arms until he could no longer move and floated on, letting the current dump him onto the sandy banks. He shivered from the cold, unable to move. Overwhelmed in pain, agony, and distress, Erik broke down sobbing as the tears flowed freely.

"I give up," he wailed. "I can't do this anymore..."

Then stop holding a grudge against me, the duplicate answered. *Let me save you and I can set you free.*

Erik strained to move his head, only to find his body refused his mental commands. Looking up with his limited vision, he saw no one else out on the shore. "I know you're over there," Erik called, "so just hurry up and get rid of me. That's what you want, right?"

No one else can be trusted. I'm the only one you have.

"You're dangerous..."

And so are you... They made you that way.

Hearing footsteps crunch across the rocky shore, Erik clenched his teeth against the overwhelming pain swamping his being. John Greenfield approached, armed with a lightweight machine rifle.

Don't trust anything else he says. He's lied to you too many times...

"You're still alive," John Greenfield said, smiling. "I'm glad Agents didn't find you... I'd really hate having to kill again."

Erik shut his eyes and blew a hard sigh, ignoring the

radiating ache throughout his body. "Shut up," he hissed. "You're so full of it."

"Ace, please, just let me help you."

"What are you planning?"

"I can't tell you."

"Or rather you don't want to. Your plan requires me not knowing anything, right? Because you'll just erase me and switch on someone else more receptive to do your dirty work, right?"

John Greenfield let out a nervous laugh. "Ace, stop saying strange things. I think your injuries are getting to you."

"Then help me up."

John Greenfield crouched at Erik's side and took his arm, lacing it over his shoulders. Erik opened his eyes as the older man helped him to his feet and leaned against him. He stiffened when the duplicate blocked his path, pointing his unsheathed saber at Erik's throat.

Don't move, not even an inch, or you're dead!

"What's the matter, Ace?"John Greenfield asked. "Did you hurt your ankle?"

"You're not real!" Erik spat, narrowing his eyes at the mirror image.

This man is only going to use you again! How dare you forgive him letting those beasts operate on you like that?

"You bastard! What are you after then?"

Your soul, you idiot!

Erik turned out of a lunging stab and reached under John Greenfield's guard, snatching the rifle out of his hands then shoved him to the ground. John Greenfield rolled with the fall and Erik steadied his aim, pointing his sights at John Greenfield's head as he landed on his back.

"Ace," John Greenfield begged, "please, put down the gun."

"Don't move," Erik snarled.

"I won't fight you."

"Just answer my questions. All of them. Every last one of them."

"I'll answer whatever question you have, Ace. Just please, calm down."

Forget it! You're not denying my revenge!

Erik glanced over his shoulder and leaned out of another slash, then pulled away, turning the rifle around. The counterpart paused when Erik put his finger on the trigger as he pointed the muzzle at his head.

"Stop tormenting me," Erik thundered, "or there won't be anything left to save."

"Ace, please," John Greenfield pleaded, "don't do it!"

"I'll keep my hand where it is if you promise me not to flip the switch."

You're pointing the gun at the wrong person, the mirror image argued. *He's the one you should destroy, not yourself!*

"If I killed myself like I planned to all those years ago," Erik lamented, "I wouldn't be here now!"

John Greenfield's eyes widened. "Is that what you really want?" he pressed. "What made you feel like this? Why do you want to die?"

"How could you forget!" Erik raged, glowering at John Greenfield. "You were there!"

John Greenfield put up his hands. "I know, I know," he

said quickly, "but please, Justin, don't do something so foolish. They hurt me too, badly. The Agency fooled me, telling me my family would be safe if I took on that project. I had no idea they would keep me as their personal pet until they had no more use for me."

"What about me? Why throw me to the curb? You only cared about yourself!"

"I know I did a bad thing by using you as a catalyst for my revenge... But don't you understand? Those people using me are using you too! They'll continue destroying everything around them to get what they want and that's why we're working hard to stop them."

"Shut up!" Erik screeched and turned the gun toward John Greenfield. "That's all you do is talk! You pretend to care and you just use me too, just like the rest of those monsters!"

"I'm sorry for doing this to you, Son," John Greenfield said softly.

"The hell you are! Why do you do this to me?"

"I really don't like what I've become. I feel awfully terrible."

"You're so full of it! I don't believe you at all - everything that leaves your face is another lie! How could you do this to me? You let them control you and you acted on you baser instincts!"

"I don't know what else to tell you then..."

"Then don't!" Erik raised the rifle as he steadied his aim. "Don't near me," he huffed. "Don't talk to me anymore. Just leave."

John Greenfield reached forward and Erik jammed the rifle against his chest. "Please, Ace," John Greenfield bleated in a strained tone, lowering his hands.

"Don't you know how it feels being detained from the only family you knew, to be cut on and experimented on like some lab rat? Hell, those rats were treated better than I was!"

John Greenfield's face paled. "I know how it is," he murmured. "I really do understand!"

"Prove it to me. Or my finger might just slip."

John Greenfield narrowed his eyes, growing tense as he watched Erik's fingers on the rifle. "Then if you're serious, shoot me!" he spat bitterly. "If I'm the source of your pain, then go ahead, get rid of me!"

"Stop telling me what to do! I'll act on my own free will."

"Then do it!"

Erik's hand shook as tried steadying his aim.

You're really not going to kill him, teased Erik's duplicate as he appeared behind John Greenfield, aiming his sword under the man's throat. *You don't really hate him enough to do that.*

"*Everyone's telling me how to think and feel,*" Erik thought as he swallowed hard the searing lump forming in his throat. "*Why should I spare him anything? He knew the risks getting into that evil business. He let her talk him into it and he blindly followed, the weak bastard!*" Erik shut his eyes as the tears returned full force. "*She still died fighting and no good came out of it! Then he can suffer watching me die. I get what I want and he can finally realize how his mistakes hurt me. Maybe that'll get him to act...*"

Hesitate and die by my hand, moron!

"No!" John Greenfield shrieked when Erik quickly aimed

toward himself and fired.

A loud crack of pain drove deep into his skull as blood splattered across his face and his ears rang. Erik's body seized from the overload while his world spun when he dropped as a heap on the ground and the rifle clattered beside him.

Vaguely aware of strong hands grasping his shoulders, Erik opened his eyes, seeing everything through red mist. He felt the hands prop him up and arms embrace around his shoulders as he leaned against a warm solid mass.

Through the loud ringing, Erik heard a faint voice calling for him.

"I'm so sorry," the voice wept in his ear. "I'm so sorry, so very sorry. Please, please don't die. Not now..."

"You're not sorry at all," Erik mused as his red-washed world became mottled with spots. *"You're sorry your plans failed... I'm finally free of your influence..."*

Darkness, cold and complete, enveloped him and soon the pain followed with it, descending into nothingness.

FIFTY

Erik felt the fierce pounding in his head grow stronger as he gradually came to. He groaned once his eyes seared from bright light and quickly shut them, waiting for them to adjust.

The banging in his head seemingly beat in time to the ticking clock behind him, clicking with every second. Erik slowly opened his eyes and looked around, finding himself in the white-walled room once more. He faced the low table with the recording machine and plush leather chair that had a notepad resting in the seat.

Trying to move, Erik noted his body in a blue scrub shirt and slacks, bound in place with leather restraints around his ankles and wrists in a stiff-backed chair with heavy armrests. He grunted when he saw two intravenous solutions hanging behind him - one bag seeping a clear serum and another containing dark violet.

"Do you wish to talk?" the familiar voice of the doctor called as he entered the room, holding a chart. Erik ground his teeth, glaring at the slender olive-skinned middle-aged man in white consulting jacket over a tailored navy suit. The doctor threw back his long braid hanging over his shoulder.

"Why is it that I'm here again?" Erik snarled. The doctor paled as he picked up the notepad in the chair and loosened the blazer's front fastener. Taking the seat, the doctor struck the button on the recording device. Its gears turned, hissing softly in response. "Let's hear your best excuse!"

"I was told that you've had a relapse," the doctor answered timidly as he set the notepad aside. "It's terrible that you didn't finish your sessions..."

"Relapse my eye!" Erik screamed. "What's the real reason or are you just going to keep lying?"

"I've told you why..."

"Shut up!" Erik jerked against the restraints. "I'm not going to help you destroy me!"

"Is it a question of trust, then?" The doctor placed his hands atop the table's surface. "We can't help you if you don't help yourself."

"You know that's it!"

"So why is there so much distrust on your part?"

"Why?" Erik let out a short bitter laugh. "I'll tell you why, old man! I don't know a damn thing, but you assume I do. You keep beating me and injecting me and you're looking for something." Erik bared his teeth. "Keep trying, because I'm not giving you shit!"

"What has convinced you that?"

"I doubt you're here to help me figure why my memory is so bad, or why I have these nightmares..." Erik looked away, gazing at the pale blank wall behind the doctor. "You want information..."

"That's right. We're here to help you sort out your issues. They cause you pain and we want you well."

"There's another reason." Erik narrowed his eyes at the

doctor. "Why is it so important to you? What about me? Why aren't I important?"

"If we get to the details, we will eventually find the information you need to heal."

Erik shook his head. "It's incomplete... all of it, it's incomplete."

"What do you mean?"

"What if I'm really nothing, that I really don't exist, that I'm created from a lab and my memories are nothing but data?"

The doctor chortled. "What are you saying, that you're some alien or robot or something?"

Erik moaned in distress and shut his eyes. "I'm tired," he whined. "I'm tired of not knowing, of not understanding..."

"What is it you don't understand?" Erik stayed silent and the doctor blew an annoyed sigh. "What do you mean?" he pressed.

Erik shook his head again. "I'm tired. My head hurts..."

"Then let's talk about something that doesn't distress you, how about that?" The doctor said brightly. "Let's talk about pleasant things, happy things..."

"What's so pleasant about my life?" Erik grumbled. "I don't have pleasant memories."

"What about Hanalei Kahananui?"

Erik's head snapped upright and he glowered at the doctor. "What do you know about her?" he sneered. "Why are you asking me about her?"

"You told me quite a bit about her," the doctor said gently, smiling. "She's very dear to you, am I right?"

"I...!"

"Aren't the thoughts you have about Hanalei happy thoughts?"

"Well...!"

"Care to share some of your memories about her to me?"

Erik stared blankly at the doctor, unable to respond. *"Why is he asking me this?"* he wondered. *"I don't remember ever telling him this."*

"Didn't you say her favorite color was blue?" the doctor insisted. "What about her favorite food - isn't it fried eel?"

"Shut up," Erik spat and looked away.

"Didn't she enjoy tennis? You mentioned you enjoyed watching her play in the tennis club. You admitted you had a thing for mini-skirts, am I right?"

Erik clenched his scarred hands, growing annoyed. "Shut up!" he growled.

"She smelled like flowers, didn't she? You always liked the way she smelled. You said she reminded you of someone else you were close to."

Erik shuddered in rage as he ground his teeth, glowering at the doctor.

You're getting too close...

"You also asked her to keep her hair cut short because she's cuter that way, right?" the doctor continued. "Didn't you buy expensive barrettes for her with your pay and enjoyed that she'd put them in her hair?"

"Why are you telling me these things?" Erik snarled. "What are you trying to say to me? You're making up weird stuff, old man."

"I can play back the tapes if you like. You told us a lot of

510

things that bother you, especially the guilt that's driving you."
Tears suddenly streamed down Erik's face as he continued to
glare at the doctor. "It was unfortunate, that accident." The
doctor leaned against his desk. "That's what you called it, right?
You said it was an accident. But you knew it wasn't. You *wanted*
it to happen."

Erik struggled to breathe when the tightness in his chest
returned. "I'm through with this," he murmured as he shut his
eyes. "Please, stop talking about it."

"Don't you see why these sessions are important?" The
doctor pressed. "The more you speak freely, the more we can
uncover. Then you can stop hurting yourself with Contraband
and get better."

"You're hunting for something," Erik accused. "You want
something that you think I know, is that right?"

The doctor straightened his stance and adjusted his tie. "We
have these sessions to find who you truly are," he said calmly.
"This way we can heal your psyche and bring you back to a
peaceful state of mind."

"Maybe I'm fine not knowing who I am," Erik said faintly.
"Maybe I like staying in the dark about it. It might keep my
friends safe."

The doctor let out a short laugh and hastily put a hand to
his mouth to compose himself. "I don't think you have any
choice in the matter," he snapped. "You're a major threat and
you will be held here until you no longer pose as such. You can't
escape being a ward of the state."

Erik gripped the arms of the chair. "What are you getting
at?" he spat.

"We have reached a point where you can't sit it out and wait any longer," the doctor said evenly. "You have this need to remember and it has to come out in the open sometime, otherwise your mind will continue to deteriorate and you'll never get any restful sleep, always plagued by nightmares..."

"Maybe he's right," Erik mused. *"The more I keep running and trying to suppress it, will only make it worse..."*

"This isn't the matter of trust anymore," the doctor continued. "It's a matter of you getting well. You wish to be well, do you not?"

"I do..." Erik muttered.

"Then why hold back?"

"I don't know..."

"Yes, you do know."

Erik shook his head. *"He's right, I do know,"* he realized. *"But they asked me not to... They'll never forgive me if I broke down and confessed..."*

"You have to remember," the doctor went on, "for your sake..."

"If I finally told them what they want, I can die already. I can stop running and fighting and finally find peace..."

"What is the matter?" the doctor inquired. "Why do you keep holding back?"

"In my dreams, Hana warned me... In my dreams, I told her something important. Is that what I forgot? Are they using me to get to her?"

"Why can't you go through with it?" the doctor pressed. "What are you waiting for?"

"I can't," said Erik faintly.

"We're beyond that now."

The clock's ticking and the tape's hissing slowly hollowed out, echoing behind him. Erik felt the headache worsening, followed by many faint voices speaking to him at once.

Don't tell him...

He's going to kill them if you talk!

You can't do it alone...

Don't betray her...

"Don't retreat," the doctor called over the voices. "Don't withdraw again. We're finally getting so far."

Erik moaned when the voices grew louder, drowning out the doctor's voice.

They're only going to destroy you...

Don't tell him anything...

"Stay with me; open your eyes!" the doctor called. "We have to get to the end..." His voice faded into white noise.

CONTINUED IN BOOK FOUR:

LINE OF FIRE

Erik Hart's continued search for answers about the mysterious Divinity Project only leads to more trouble. What should have been a routine investigation reveals a newfound threat that may have dire consequences for all involved...

When an unforeseen tragedy strikes, the madness Erik tries to keep in check transforms him into something far beyond normal, pushing him over the edge! Will his blind rage turn him back into the monster he thought he'd left behind?